We humans have always classified things we couldn't understand or couldn't explain as dangerous and hostile. People who are different have been persecuted, tortured, and killed throughout human history. In fact, this is still going on today in many places. That's one of the reasons the Arverni – who are different from us – conceal their origins and their existence.

Get ready to immerse yourself in their world.

I hope you enjoy reading their story.

IGAN MICH

The Mark
of the Arverni

Fantasy
By

Igan Mich

IMPRINT

IGAN MICH

PUBLISHING

COVER DESIGN:
Igan Mich Publishing LLC

COVER IMAGE:
istockphotos/Valua Studio
Igan Mich Publishing LLC

EDITING:
Laura Peter

PROOF READING:
Stacey Peper, Nina Neumann, Laura Peter

TRANSLATION:
Nancy Twilley

PREPARATION FOR PRINTING:
Igan Mich Publishing LLC

PRINTING AND DISTRIBUTION:
CreateSpace An Amazon.com Company

ISBN:
978-0-9962802-0-4

Version 1.1
Saturday, October 10, 2015
© 2015 Igan Mich Publishing LLC
email: IGAN@IGANMICH.ME

MY JOURNEY

We have been traveling together on this journey for several years now. Our path was sometimes rocky and steep, but I never traveled alone. Things were often difficult and challenging, but there was always someone there to motivate and keep me going.

When I became tired, someone walked beside me; when I struggled to carry on, you all pushed me onward. I never felt alone!

I always held onto hope, and a clear intention to follow this path all the way to the end. As far as it went I wrote this for myself, and for those of you who have traveled alongside with me, as well as for everyone who loves to read fantasy stories.

Thank you for supporting me; let's keep moving forward together – ever onward, until we arrive.

February 2015 UN (Igan Mich)

PROLOGUE

The burning in my arms grows stronger, bringing me back from the brink of unconsciousness – back to a painful reality. I cautiously open my eyes, expecting to see something, but there's nothing there. Dried tears feel like glue.

Where am I? What's happening to me?
Thoughts flash through my mind faster than I can grasp them, battering my weakened awareness. With effort, I open my eyes and feel a throbbing pain. To my despair, I can only see darkness. A pulsing in my arms grows quicker and quicker until it feels as though it's on fire.

Someone is trying to control my body and mind. I resist, convulsing.

Stay strong, Sophie – you have to stay strong – I try to motivate myself.
Dad's words of wisdom were the only things that kept me going – no matter how annoying they once were – thanks, Dad. An intense burning in my arm distracted me from trying to take in what was happening. I slowly turned in the direction the pain was coming from. Something was holding me down – my attempts to twist away only increased the pain. It felt as though boiling water was running through my veins and exiting from my right arm. I closed my eyes and clenched my jaw. My groans drowned out a grinding sound trying to escape from my pursed lips. For a moment, I believed the burning was subsiding. I concentrated on the pain radiating from my arm, tears collecting in the corners of my eyes.
Dammit, what the hell is going on?

Very slowly, I turned my head a little farther to the right. My eyes had gotten used to the darkness by now, but I could only see shadows. The muscles in my arm contracted in an attempt to lift it up. This only intensified the burning sensation – without success I tried pushing my arm against the bed until I realized something was holding it back. In a panic I tried moving my limbs to no avail – I was paralyzed. A feeling of helplessness cocooned in endless terror.

Someone tied me to this, and something was causing a hellish burning pain in my right elbow.

Why am I so helpless? So tired … where am I?
I could hear it clearly. I didn't imagine it – someone was calling my name, again and again, louder and louder.

I have to answer. Somehow – I have to answer.
All attempts to cry out were fruitless. Fear is choking my voice; I envisioned manly hands clutching my throat. Squeezing without mercy. The harder I tried to scream, the harder it was to breathe. I heard nothing – everything was still. All I felt were tears streaming down my face.

You have to overcome your fear, Sophie. Now is the time to be strong!
How often had I heard that from Dad – how often had I thought…
That's it! Dad had taught me a little trick on how to act in dangerous situations - and so I took a deep breath, held it and started to count. He used to say it was a sign of strength. Essentially it was a silly game, designed to help me overcome my fears.
Sixty-one, sixty-two. My lungs screamed, begging for air.

Don't give up. This is just the beginning.

Ninety-three, ninety-four.
My thoughts slowed, the pain subsided, and I stopped crying. My surroundings became blurry.

Keep going Sophie, I told myself, *you can do it – you'll set a new record!*
One hundred twenty–two, one hundred twenty–three, one hundred thirty–three, one hundred thirty–four…
Against my will a reflex I could no longer control tore open my lips and forced me to take a deep breath. My lungs filled with air as though it were the last breath I would ever take. I had outwitted my fear through my own will to survive. My breathing and

heartbeat racing along at the same speed. The burning sensation was back and my arm was pulsing. I screamed as loud as I could, giving voice to the pain gripping my body. A piercing cry filled the room, allowing some of the fear to escape with it. As the cry fell silent, I heard someone open the door and call my name out loud

"Xama!"

The voice sounded familiar – there was something warm and protective about it, and it came at just the right time.

I've heard this voice before– hope began to return.

Vertigo overcame my senses, as though the bed was spinning – or perhaps it really was? I heard my name again, nearby right in front of me. A hand began moving next to my head removing something. I cried again, but this time they were tears of joy. A piercing, gleaming light struck my eyes, driving away the all-consuming darkness. Engulfed by a brilliant light I was blinded once more. I couldn't swallow, and my throat began to restrict – fear returned. When my eyes had adjusted to the light, I saw a face and heard someone call my name. I knew the face and the voice.

I tried to recall who that face belonged to – who was it?

In a flash, everything turned blurry as if someone had snapped the lens on a camera all the way till it couldn't go any further. The voices, still calling my name, faded away and seemed to recede. I wanted to say something, but my body wasn't responding. My eyelids became so heavy I could hardly keep them open.

Tired, I'm so tired! Everyone just go away, leave me alone. When I wake up, everything will be over. It will all be over.

Darkness spread, and I could feel the last bit of strength slowly abandoning my body. It seemed as though all my strength – everything I had left – was spilling over the bed, spreading across the room. Even my thoughts were fading, and a feeling of inner peace came over me. No more pain, nothing to hold me back from simply falling asleep and resting, forever.

Is this what it's like to die?
But there were still people there … I could hear faint, faraway voices. They came closer, then receded again. With every breath I took – each one could be my last – the voices sounded clearer. They were speaking in unison, chanting. Three words I had never heard before… words that will forever be engraved in my mind:

"Communitati – vis – nostrum
communitati – vis – nostrum
communitati – vis – nostrum"

The voices faded into the background but left something behind – the will to live. My breathing deepened and life returned to my body. I can't explain what happened. Next. It's as though a life force had collected in one corner of the room, then made its way towards me until it seeped into my body shaking off the suffocating exhaustion that enveloped me like a heavy blanket.

"Xama, wake up, you can't fall asleep!"

Someone was talking to me – I could still hear the monotone chanting in the background. The voice was clear and vibrant, and it breathed new energy into every cell of my body. I recognized the voice.

"Wake up, Xama."
*I cannot go to sleep now, **do not** go to sleep, Xama!*
My fingers clutching at the sheet, slowly balling into a fist – desperate to stay awake.

No pain?
Again, I strained to pick up my arm. All of a sudden, it began to lift with ease. A warm, soothing feeling was radiating through my entire body – an unstoppable force of life.
This thought kept me from being still, so I moved my left arm. Then both legs – I smiled – I was free!

The voices became clearer and more distinct. I opened my eyes to a startling scene. A group of men looking down at me, singing: »Communitati – vis – nostrum«

As they sang, they moved in a circle around me. They covered part of their faces with their hand, each resting his left arm on the man standing beside him making a chain - there was something else ... something very odd – inexplicable. They were all pressing their right thumbs onto the forehead of the man next to them.

Once again, a deep male voice interrupted my racing thoughts.

"Xama, close your eyes."

It sounded like a command, but it felt more like a protective reflex – so as not to witness what was coming next. Memories from my childhood surfaced. Back then, when I was afraid, I used to keep my eyes closed, believing that if I couldn't see anyone, then nobody else could see me either. Why couldn't things be that easy now?
Seconds felt like an eternity. Suddenly my arm felt as it had fallen asleep – like it didn't belong to me anymore. Hadn't I just moved it a couple of seconds ago clenching it into a fist?

Silence. Where have the voices gone?
Feeling both curious and anxious, I carefully opened my eyes What I saw next took me by complete surprise. I was somewhere else. The bed, the chanting, and the faces had all disappeared. My arm was perfectly fine. Only my heart was racing, pulsing all the way down to my fingertips. I saw a figure in front of me – one I recognized immediately.

Channing Tatum, from Magic Mike was gazing down on me, from a poster at the end of my bed. His sexy yet tender smile was totally gorgeous and somehow protective. He wasn't real, just a poster at the end of my bed. But that didn't matter. He reassured me that I was back in my room, in my own bed, safe and sound. It was all just a ...
Kay-Ky – Kay-Ky – Kay-Ky, what was it, anyway?

FIRST DREAM

My eyes were still locked on Magic Mike. Everything else faded away, as though a misty veil was blocking my view. A slight tickling on my cheek broke my transfixed gaze. A tear, freed from my eye, slowly trickling down.

What's wrong with me? Everything feels so weird, so surreal.
Was it that terrible nightmare?
Eventually my pulse began to slow down. It was a pleasant feeling, and I was sure Magic Mike had a lot to do with it.

Thanks, Magic Mike!
Engrossed in my thoughts, I asked myself what that strange dream meant.

It was more than I could process.
Did it mean anything at all, or was it all just nonsense? Whatever it was, it was Kay-Ky and totally insane.

My thoughts circled around and around and I couldn't stop thinking about it – it scared me.
I tried to calm myself down and kept telling myself it was just a dream. Jittery, searching for proof, I rolled my sleeve up –looking to see if anything was amiss, but there was nothing out of the ordinary. No pain, it looked fine. I took a deep breath and felt assured it was indeed a dream, my mind playing tricks on me. But what I didn't know yet was that my life was about to change forever.

My breathing matched the rhythm of my still racing heart. All of a sudden, I noticed that things started to go hazy even Magic Mike – otherwise clearly a good-looking man – looked like enveloped in a fog. An unpleasant feeling swept like a wave through my whole body, goosebumps appeared on my skin. I broke into a sweat, my thighs burned, and my legs started shaking.

Kay-Ky! What's happening now, what on earth is wrong with me?

From nowhere I felt my stomach cramp, crippled with pain. I closed my eyes, hoping it would go away, but it had the opposite effect. Everything began to spin. Anguished tears welled up in my eyes. They tickled my nose as they ran down my face. I opened my eyes and blinked the tears away. My senses hadn't lied; everything was truly spinning around my bed, like a mini tornado.

Kay-Ky, what's the matter with me?
Fear was choking me, just like in my dream. My attempts to scream for help resulted in nothing more than a whimpering sound. With difficulty, I gasped for air like a fish on dry land, hyperventilating. Instinctively I pulled my knees up against my stomach waiting for the next cramp to hit – not a good idea. The pressure pushed bile up into my gullet. It burned horribly. Aware that I was about to throw up; I ignored the cramps and left off the bed, lurching towards the bathroom. Every step burned as if I was walking on scorching hot coals. Despite the bathroom being only a few feet away, the effort took every last bit of energy I had.

You're almost there, I told myself.
If there's one thing I know how, it's how to achieve my goals. As I finally reached the door, I struggled to desperately keep the contents of my stomach from spewing all over the bathroom floor. I did this by strategically placing my hand over my mouth and holding it there as if my life depended on it.

Shit, this is bad!

In order to contain the mess I was about to make, I kneeled next to the toilet bowl and hugged it. I puked my guts out and emptied everything I had eaten in the last few hours. Feeling as though my stomach took an eternity to recover, I looked down at my artwork, a brownish lumpy collage of soggy muesli. The stench of vomit engulfing the bathroom. Just as I started to feel better, I heard someone pound on the door.

Claire, it's Claire at the door, it can only be Claire!
I kicked the bathroom door with my heel, but before it closed shut, I heard Claire's voice calling out for me.

"Sophie, Sophie are you in there?"
Why now? I forced myself up on my feet and tried to lock the door. But I couldn't – I didn't have enough strength to turn the key. Pushing my weight against the door to keep it shut, Claire became suspicious.

"Sophie, is something wrong? Do you need help?"
If she only knew, I thought to myself and cleared my throat trying to alleviate the burning caused by stomach acid. Coughing and wheezing, I forced my voice to sound normal.
"Everything's ok, Claire, I just got really sick, that's all – otherwise I'm fine. Just give me ten minutes and I'll come find you."
"Okay – but this isn't the first time, Sophie – is there anything I should know about? You're not…?"

This can't be happening! First I have a nightmare I don't understand, then I puke my guts out, and then my BFF comes up with a completely apocalyptic explanation for the whole situation. What's going on today? Has the whole world gone crazy?

There hasn't been an immaculate conception since the Virgin Mary. And bees don't have anything to do with human procreation either. I can absolutely and definitively rule out pregnancy – ridiculous, typical Claire. Preoccupied with my chaotic thoughts, I collected copious amounts of toilet paper and proceeded to clear the path of destruction I created. Feeling unstable and weak, I struggled to turn on the tap. I watched the water move towards the drain as if drawn in by magic, disappearing into a black hole. I interrupted the flow by holding my hands under the stream of frigid water. I bent down and took a long drink. I never imagined water could taste this good, my coarse throat feeling smooth once again. The shock of cold water splashing on my face jolted me back to reality

Minutes later I brushed my teeth, and rinsed my mouth out, feeling like a normal human being again. But could I show myself to Claire in this state? Claire, was thy type of girl who looked as if she had been born with perfect hair and make-up. She never left the house without at least a 30-minute three-step Claire beautification process. Her usual line was: "Man, you look pale," or "Why don't you get out and get a little sun?" This obviously meant that more work needed to be done on my appearance.

I straightened up and peered into the three-piece mirror on our simple bathroom cabinet. It was standard equipment here in the dorm; all the rooms had the same furniture and the same bathroom cabinets. "Bargain basement chic," as we called it. When I looked at my face, I immediately noticed a dark shadow in the middle of my forehead. Squinting, I tried to sharpen my blurry vision, but it didn't change what I saw.

I picked up a facecloth and placed it under the dispenser, squeezing out about a week's worth of soap. I scrubbed my forehead until a mass of white foam materialized. Once I rinsed my face, however, I was totally floored – the spot was still there, and even more obvious than it had been before. I looked closer, and I couldn't believe what I saw.

What I saw resembled a cross. It stood out smack bang in the middle of my forehead as though someone had painted it in various shades of grey. I spat on my finger and rubbed the cross like a maniac hurting myself in the process. One thing was clear: this wasn't dirt, and it wasn't paint I could simply wipe off. It was something else, similar to a tattoo. Shocked I lost all strength in my legs; I staggered backwards gradually, slipping against the bathroom wall, overcome by fits of tears. I huddled on the floor and wept uncontrollably.

THE MARK

With time, my cries fell silent. Hugging myself in the fetal position, I tried to master the situation and my emotions. I couldn't remember a time when everything had been this crappy.

What's wrong with me? First this sick dream, then out of the blue I throw up, and now there's this thing on my forehead.
I traced my fingers over it looking for proof of what I had seen earlier. For some reason, I thought I would be able to feel it. But everything felt completely normal – there wasn't a raised patch or any part of my skin that felt different. Once more I ran my fingers over the symbol, when suddenly a force stopped them midway. My thumb was moving towards my forehead as though drawn there by a magnet. As it made contact, I felt an electric shock. It wasn't painful, but it radiated through my fingers, my hand, my arm, then finally spread over my entire body.

Kay-Ky – what on earth was that?
Then, all of a sudden, the shock reversed course, and it seemed as if it was collecting energy into my body and concentrating it all in one spot, in the middle of my forehead.

What's happening to me? What's going on here?
I tried to lift my thumb, but I couldn't do it, it was positively glued to my forehead.
Helpless and scared, I felt something interfere with my thoughts. I saw images flashing by like a movie. Some of them seemed familiar, but others I saw the first time. The images moved quicker and quicker. I closed my eyes hoping to make them stop but I only made it worse. I strained to pull my hand way from my forehead. The second my thumb left my face the flow of energy stopped and the strange images disappeared. I wanted to cry, instead tried to control myself by taking a deep breath. Sometimes breathing helped me collect my thoughts and sometimes it didn't. Next thing a warm, comforting feeling began to blossom from the spot the energy had collected in my body.

Whewwww – wooowwww – Kaaayyyy-Kkkyyyyyy
Indescribably electrifying, pleasant, and warm – everything in my body felt so light – almost weightless.

Please don't stop – not now, when it feels so good!
A higher power read my thoughts, and the heavenly feeling spread even further. I had never experienced anything like it before, and the further it spread, the less fear and uncertainty I felt – I felt incredible; amazing in fact.

Kay-Ky – it feels so wild. The feeling of being in love and being loved all at the same time, like vanilla ice cream and hot chocolate all at once. I can't describe it – just Kay-Ky.
Relishing the feeling of pure bliss, I realized everything around went completely silent. No noise. No ticking.

What just happened – was I dreaming?

Something inexplicable happened when my thumb made contact with my forehead. A feeling of pure vitality surged through me – both physically, and emotionally.

Suddenly, Claire stormed into the bathroom breaking the peaceful atmosphere. She started right in, frantically spluttering words from her mouth like some lunatic. Typical Claire.
"Holy shit Sophie, what's up with you? What happened? What are you doing on the floor?"
From where I sat Claire looked taller than she was, yet somehow less superior than usual. The thought made me smile, and for some reason the sight of her, standing there red–faced and, scolding me like some irate teacher, resulted in fits of LOLs.
 Claire stood there, baffled shaking her head.
"You didn't take drugs or something, did you? Tell me you didn't, Sophie. We promised each other – no drugs!

Claire looked at me, shocked and disappointed. I wanted to explain to her … but laughter took hold of me and made me laugh some more.
"What is there to laugh about, when you're in here puking your guts out? What did you take, Sophie – tell me!

"Claire, I don't know what's wrong with me, but I definitely didn't take any drugs. To tell you the truth, I think its Kay-Ky that you would accuse me of such a thing."

"Be honest, Sophie!"

"Girl scout's honor!"

Claire kneeled down and looked directly into my eyes,

"Sophie, what's up with you?" Claire said, in a forceful yet unsettled way. "Should I call a doctor? What's wrong?

"Yes, Claire, you're right about that – only I don't know what happened. Do you notice anything odd on my face?"

I held my forehead right up to her; there was no way she could miss it, despite it being a light gray. It was certainly visible; Claire would notice it straight away. She was the type of person who waged war on every minute.

"There's nothing there! In a situation like this, you're trying to get me to look at a new pimple on your forehead? What are you doing? Stop it! You're lying on the floor as white as a corpse. Ten minutes before that you were puking your guts out, and now you're talking nonsense, laughing at things that aren't funny, can't explain to me what happened to you, unable to give me any kind of explanation for your condition and you keep trying to get me to look at something that's not existing?

Honestly, you're freaking me out."

"Sorry, Claire, but it's really important. Do you notice anything on my forehead – A symbol, a tattoo …"?

Claire looked at me with concern, frowning.

"No, there's nothing there! Your skin is almost too perfect, except for …"

She saw it. I knew she would.

"What?"

Anxiously I waited for an answer from her.

"There's a tiny – really tiny – mark on your skin, hardly worth mentioning, just a blemish. You should put a little foundation on it, no one will see it.

"I wish I had your skin."

How is it possible that she can't see it?

I needed to check once again but the fear that the cross might still be there held me back – still I had to look.

With apprehension, I pushed myself up from the tub. It wasn't as hard as I thought it might be. I had made a full recovery. With a worried look on her face, Claire helped me up.

I didn't need her help; my vertigo had completely gone.
About six feet away from the mirror, I stared at my reflection. I met my own gaze in a flash, all my interest directed at one spot. All my hopes were dashed! The symbol was clearly visible, right in the middle of my forehead, and it even seemed to stand out more clearly than before.

No – I don't believe it – please disappear?
A load came crashing down on me, and my knees buckled. My whole body floundered for a fraction of a second. I grasped at the sink, trying to keep my legs from giving in, upon seeing the cross any positive feelings I had had vanished into an emotional void which exploded in front of me. Claire noticed my unsteadiness and immediately grabbed me by my arm.
"Looks like I am still a little weak after all."
It was a clumsy attempt to downplay the situation. In reality, I felt like crap. Even my expression "Kay-Ky," which I often referred to describe extreme situations seemed inadequate!

What's happening to me? Where did this thing come from, and why does Claire not see it? Is this a sick joke?
.
I made my way towards the mirror – ever closer – so close I could almost touch it with my nose. My face looking back at me, unsettling I didn't let fear take over. Yes, it definitely looked like a cross, but at closer inspection I immediately realized that it wasn't symmetrical.
It is a cross – like the one they nailed Jesus Christ.
"Who did this to me?"
Claire looked at me, dumbfounded.
"Who did what to you?"

"This thing here!" Pointing at my forehead. "This cross, right here!"

Claire looked at my forehead again, and then stared at me, wide-eyed.

"There's nothing there, Sophie – there's no cross. Not even a little one – I don't see anything."

I could clearly see it, but it was invisible to Claire.

"So you don't see anything on my forehead – no cross – nothing at all."

Claire nodded – yes, nothing there, everything's fine.

"Could it be, Sophie, that you imagine it? Sophie, I think you're imagining things?" Maybe you've got a little too much on your plate right now. The stress of preparing for getting ready for our big birthday party, your diet, and all of that."

A few minutes ago, Claire's answer would have made me sob – like pouring oil on a fire. But strangely enough, it had the opposite effect, my emotions were settling – I felt better – safer and stronger.

Since she didn't see the cross, there was no point in mentioning it. It would only reassure her that I might actually be loosing my mind. "You're probably right. I did have a nightmare a little while ago – maybe all this is just a side effect." "What did you eat today?" "Well, just a small breakfast – nothing else – and what I had eaten all went down the toilet."

"I'll make some tea, then I'll go downstairs and grab us something sweet from the cafeteria. In any case, you're in no condition to go anywhere later. We can come up with some ideas on what we should do for our birthday party.

"You're right, Claire! Thank you for being here for me."

"Hey, what kind of a statement is that? Of course I'm here for you. Did you forget we were BFFs?"

Claire smiled at me.

"Now you need to lie down for a bit."

Claire helped me to my feet.

"I just need to go to the bathroom – you go ahead and make the tea. I promise I'll lay down."

"Promise me?"

"I promise, Claire. Tea and cake sound like a great idea."

"Do you want anything in particular?"

"If they have something with poppy seeds that would be great; otherwise just get something sweet."

I heard Claire fill up the kettle before she finally set off. I returned to the task at hand and went back and studied the cross with more intensity.

I discovered that it consisted of two vertical stripes, each about a centimeter thick. I pressed my finger on it ever so slightly tracing the edge of the ink. It felt normal to the touch. I pushed and pulled at my skin a little, and felt no pain. It seemed normal. Looking at it, I began to feel ok about it –good, actually. The nausea and vertigo were both gone. A minute ago, I was convulsing on the floor trying to come to terms with the condition I was in, and now things were looking up. It was a complete turn around, and all because I took another look at it.

I wondered if it affected me in any way.

I was already mulling over the best possible ways to remove it. It was a foreign object in the middle of my face, and it was scaring me. One thing was clear: it had to go. But how?

PLEASE DISAPPEAR

I had a clear mission to accomplish and that was the removal of the unsightly cross!!!

Rummaging through a myriad of ideas I came up with a couple of concoctions that might actually do the trick.

My trusted make up remover was one possible solution. It did get rid of multiple layers of waterproof mascara, so I didn't see why it wouldn't work. I proceeded to dig through my messy and sticky makeup bag in search for a scrap of cotton wool. Once found I soaked it with a hefty amount of remover, the fumes from it wafting up into my nostrils and making my eyes water. With bated breath, I placed the cool little pad on my skin and began the process of elimination. Rubbing on it with vengeance, the result was devastating - it didn't make a difference. The other option which was bound to be fool proof, would certainly have been nail polish remover, I mean… that was the equivalent of paint thinner. I repeated the procedure arduously. The only thing it did, was to leave an angry ruby red welt the size of a golf ball.

I decided to hide it with concealer – no luck!

At least the dizziness had vanished.

I tidied up the bathroom, which by now reeked like some sort of meth lab. I made my way into the kitchen and prepared the tea, removing the plates and mugs from the beige kitchen cabinet and placed the chinaware on the Formica table. I perched my bottom on the hard chair and eagerly waited for Claire to bring me something sweet.

"You were in luck, Sophie. I got the last piece of poppy seed crumble. Pretty cool, huh?"

Before she placed our treats on the table, she gave me one look and gasped.

"For God's sake, what did you do to your face?"

Embarrassed, I looked away for a brief moment.

Did something happen to you when you came back from the bus stop to pick up your sunglasses? Did you fall and bang your head somewhere?

I looked at Claire, surprised and confused.
"I did what?"
"Don't you remember? We were both waiting for the bus to take us downtown. You suddenly remembered you had left your sunglasses behind. Since the bus was going to take another few minutes you decided to go back for them.

Astonished, I looked at her. "Are you serious? When did that happen?"
Claire looked at her watch. "Hum… about half an hour ago."

"I'm confused Claire!" The last thing I remember was waking up from what must only have been a nightmare. In it I had been tied down to a bed against my will!

Sophie looked at me with perfectly shaped eyebrows she'd just recently plucked.
"Sophie, I'm your best friend. We share a depressing little dorm room in this shitty orphanage, and we've always been there for each other. Even if it's hard, or if you think it sounds crazy, just let it out. If you can't tell your BFF about it, then who can you tell?"
I looked at Claire with tears in my eyes and grabbed hold of her hand.
"You have to promise you won't tell anyone – promise me!"
"Have I ever not kept my promises?"
As a sign of oath, Claire picked up her phone and pressed it to her chest. Her phone was her lifeline; it was an extension of her. She never let it out of her sight.

I began to recount the nightmare.
"I was tied to the bed, had IVs and tubes coming out from both arms. My right arm burned as if on fire; I couldn't move!!!
"It doesn't make sense Sophie." I know that once you had run off to get your glasses I suddenly remembered that I too had left my charger in the room. So I sent you a text, but you didn't reply to

it, so I called you, but it went straight to voicemail. I had no choice but to follow you. I must have taken five minutes max to get here.

"See? I told you it was weird. The dream felt like I was under for hours. When I woke up, I was as sick as a dog."
"Tell me more about it. Sometimes dreams have hidden meanings".
I nodded and looked at Claire, wide-eyed.
"For a dream it was very realistic. I can remember every single detail, especially the physical pain – God it hurt.

"That's nothing new. I've had those before. I usually have them when I'm under stress."

Maybe she was right? I continued recounting the dream, but I could see from the way she was tilting and shaking her head, that she was finding it very difficult to believe me.
It was cringe worthy.

Describing the dream, was taking its toll on me.
On more than one occasion, I had to stop and pull myself together.

"Wow! Sophie! That's incredible. And you're sure you dreamt all that in the five minutes you were up here?"

Claire looked dumbfounded, as was I. – "It didn't make any sense. The timing didn't match up."

Claire wanted to change the subject in order to put me off thinking about it and asked me how I felt. I told her that despite having woken up in a terrible shock and running to the toilette vomiting, I was surprisingly feeling really good.

"It's as if a huge weight has been lifted off my shoulders", I said.
"When did you start feeling better?"

I retraced my steps back to when I started to regain my strength and realized it was when I saw the cross for the first time. But I couldn't quite say that to Claire, especially when she couldn't see it.

"Maybe you just needed to throw up?"

"Yes Claire, come to think of it, that must have been it. Once my stomach emptied itself out, I definitely felt much better."

"Well, there you go then. You obviously ate something that didn't agree with you. Maybe it was really bad indigestion or you ate something that was off.

I hesitated for a moment but realized Claire would never believe my version of events.

"Yes, that makes sense."

What Claire didn't know, however, was that it was clearly the cross that had healed me. I was certain of that.

"Very well. What you need now is something to take your mind off things. Let's get out of here."

"I don't know, Claire."

"Oh come on. If you feel unwell, we can always come back."
"Ok you win, let's go shopping."

"Great. That's the Sophie I know. You freshen up, and I'll get my things together, and don't forget to put some powder on that blotchy forehead of yours." I did as she suggested and covered the cross under a blanket of powder.

Seek and Ye Shall Find

I found myself fascinated by the symbol, the more I looked at it, the more captivated I was by it – As if under a spell.
If Claire couldn't see it, it was obvious no one else could either.

My mind was running away with me and all sorts of scenarios started popping up. One was Facebook, how embarrassing would it be if I were to be tagged with this thing cropping up on every photo? It's not like I could slap my hand on it ever time I heard someone say ... cheese?

Where's my phone? I need to see this for myself. I don't want to think about my friends seeing me like this. Definitely not about a picture of me with this cross on my head making the rounds on Facebook – that would be a whole new nightmare. That's it! Why didn't I think of it? Photographic proof. I'll just take a picture of the cross. If no one can see the cross, then a camera can't take a picture of it. That means that if I photograph the cross, you won't be able to see it on the photo. But then why do I see it in the mirror? I started digging in my bag, taking longer than usual to locate it - reminder to self, must buy smaller handbag.

My hands were trembling, managing not to drop the phone. I took a selfie and to my greatest relief, saw that my forehead was cross free!!! I was deliriously happy.

Claire sat, dusting a hint of shimmering powder to her perfect cheekbones. Once she was satisfied with the touch up we set off for a session of retail therapy, just like we'd planned.

When we met two years ago we discovered we shared our birthdays a week apart. We agreed then, that we would always try to celebrate them together.
In a couple of weeks, we'll both be turning sixteen. We've planned a massive "Sweet 16" birthday party. Lucky for us we have permission to use the recreation room here at Heaven Youth Home. Claire has come up with a wicked party theme,

which to be honest at the time I wasn't too keen on. Eventually, the idea grew on me and so we've now started to think of ways to decorate the hall – the plan is to make the room look like a gigantic crypt. The challenge is to find the right materials.

After a few hours, I was back in my room. Our outing turned out to be a bit of a disappointment. Claire had made her excuses and left, said something about needing to see Mike, perfect timing, which gave me time to research what happened to me and what I was bearing on my forehead. I made the decision that the moment I got hold of my laptop, I would go on Google, and type what I needed to find out - except that it suddenly dawned on me I wasn't even sure how to phrase what I was looking for.

I sat on the bed, grabbed for my laptop and placed it on my crossed legs. It was a gift from my father. Well, let's call it a going-away present – a heirloom, like lots of other things. Some of the items are still packed in a trunk in an allocated area in the basement. I haven't looked in the trunk since Dad died. It breaks my heart just looking at it. I can't bring myself to go through what's inside. When Dad died three years ago after a long, and unexplained illness, I came to live at the orphanage. The fact that my mother died due complications when she gave birth to me was the other reason that brought me here. Dad blamed it on fate, it was his answer to almost every aspect of life, except that on this occasion we both knew what had really caused mums death. It was pure negligence; someone had made a colossal mistake. I never got to meet her.

Five years ago Dad began to feel unwell. He visited many hospitals and endured endless examinations. Nobody could tell us what he was suffering from. The illness took hold, and he rapidly deteriorated and stopped searching for help. A year later he could no longer work and walking because too strenuous. The doctors said his immune system had turned against his body. They tried every new medicine, experimental drug and therapy that was available at the time – still nothing helped.

I can clearly remember the night Dad told me I was in great danger. He made me swear to a secret. I crossed my heart and promised I would do anything he asked. We left Michigan for Germany in a mad rush. I didn't even have time to say goodbye to my friends. Once we arrived, Dad brought me to Heaven and then checked himself into a hospital nearby. I visited him as often as I could, but he died a few weeks after we had moved there. I still don't understand why he decided to leave Michigan and why he did this to me. He did say that there would come a time when I would understand.

I was left completely on my own. Since I spoke only a little German as a result of having had private lessons – I made it my life's mission to learn the language as fast as I possibly could. Getting used to Heaven was something I thought would never be possible - Kids were always picking on me and I was more hell than heaven. I called the home Heaven, because I had a plan that would bring dad, mom and me together again. B,e the family we were meant to be - reunited forever.

I was desperate to leave this meaningless life behind – How hard could it be – perhaps as easy as getting off a bus?

But the promise I made to Dad held me back.

Why does everything I love get taken away? Why?
I still don't understand why Dad had to go. I'll never forget his last words as long as I live.
"You're something very special, Sophie, something unique, and you're going to discover it when the time is right. It's such a shame I can't be there by your side. Be strong, Sophie! Be strong! Promise me you'll fight, and you won't give up, no matter what happens. In a few years, you'll understand everything. Everything will make sense – that's why you have to stay strong, Sophie!"
First my Mom, then my Dad. Why is the world so unfair? Why did they both have to go?

Those were dark days, I cried a lot.

Back to the present, I unfolded my laptop and stared at the search bar trying to come up with how to best put in writing. I so desperately needed to find out.

What exactly should I search for?
I started with "Cross on your forehead." Google had 57,600 results. Crazy – I didn't expect that. I started to skim over the summaries. Most were about Catholicism and Jesus Christ. After reading an hour, I decided to be more precise.

"Invisible cross on your forehead."
At first glance, the results resembled each other. Again, Google gave me lots of hits on Catholicism, but just as I was about to give up, I noticed a blog. It was a few years old – from 2002 – I couldn't believe what I was seeing.

 A guy by the name of Anin had discovered a cross on his forehead. I felt the hair on the back of my neck rise. I read the article numerous times. A flood of joy hit me when I came to the realization that I wasn't alone and that someone else had or is still living with the same affliction.

Anin had written a very detailed article. He too had been plagued by nightmares, right before his sixteenth birthday, occurring several times a day. The cross appeared on his forehead and like me no one other than him could see it. I was starved for more information but as I scrolled down it became clear that Anin had stopped posting several years back.

Fingers shaking from excitement, I made sure to bookmark the page. To learn more about Anin I have to contact him directly. The only chance I have is to send him a PM, a kind of message within the blog system, and hopefully he will receive it via his registered email. The last article he posted ten years ago so that would make him 26. Come hell or high water I was going to hunt this man down. I needed an explanation from him – he was my only hope.

FIRST CONTACT

Full of excitement, my fingers flew across the keyboard, trying to register as quickly as possible to be able to send a message to Anin. A minute later, I had an email in my inbox with my login information.

Can he help me?
Fascinated by the possibility of getting some answers, I started a personal message to Anin. Hope springs eternal, and there was, after all, some chance Anin was still active. Or at least that he still had the email address and would answer me.

"Hello Anin, my name is Sophie. I did a search entitled "Invisible cross on your forehead" and your post showed up. The reason why I'm writing to you, is to tell you that I 'm experiencing the exact same disorder you've described, word for word.
I have a cross on my forehead too, and nightmares, and I don't know what's going on with me. Please, please help me!!!"

I started reading some of the entries from other members and was disgusted by the level of nastiness in some of the comments. The poor guy was only looking for help; instead he received a barrage of insults. It's no wonder he hadn't posted anything since then. Only I could relate to him.

My heart skipped a beat when I came upon the next blog post.

Anin, please send me a PM – I can help you! Don't post any more information on here. We're not alone. You're in great danger!!! Dreamer89.

"We're not alone," puzzled me – but what worried me most was the "you're in great danger" comment.

Only one way to get to the bottom of this, I have to sent another message to dreamer89.

"Hello dreamer89: can you help me get in touch with Anin?

*I have an important question to ask him. It's extremely urgent.
Thanks, Sincerely Sophie"*

The unmistakable sound of Claire's pumps hitting the linoleum floor snapped me out of a trance like state.

"Oh hi there. How was your date with Mike?"

"Funny you should ask it all started the minute we sat at our table. After having placed my order for a Skinny Latte, Alex walked in".

"You know Alex, the tall, dark and handsome one? – Has that Italian exotic look about him"

Well, anyway, he walked right past us then sat behind Mike - before I knew it we were making eye contact – giggling like star-crossed lovers.

I nodded again, wondering which Alex Claire meant. My nod was all Claire needed to keep going. "Well, while Mike and I were talking, Alex kept looking over at me. First he looked self-conscious, but then it was more and more often, and finally he smiled too."
"Are you serious? Mike takes you out for coffee and as soon as his back is turned you start flirting with the hot guy?"

"Oh, well, Alex started it – I just played along!"

"I've heard that one before. What do people say? It's all fun and games…"

"Oh don't be such a bore. You need to get out there – start socializing, invest in some cute outfits, show those killer curves off and some blush wouldn't hurt either. You're drop dead gorgeous, you should be flaunting your assets, not hide them under layers of dreary tops. If you continue this way, you'll become a bitter old spinster!"

Thanks for the advice, Claire, but I don't need to show my killer curves off in order to catch me a man.

"Anyway, what does Alex have that Mike doesn't?"

Claire looked at me, speechless, mouth hanging open.
"Halllooo? Isn't it obvious?
Alex is more attractive – more masculine – has an amazing body and oozes sex appeal."

Claire definitely had a type, and it wasn't the academic one.

"Maybe Mike would be someone you'd be interested in?"

"No thanks, I'm not interested in your sloppy seconds."

Claire knew she didn't stand a chance, so she tactfully changed the subject.

"Let's not talk about boys anymore." We're clearly not on the same page when it comes to them. Our opinions are just too different, and your day was too stressful to start a debate on principles. "Claire was completely right on that point. Today was too much – much too much.

"Should we watch a movie then?" Said Claire.
"Something relaxing – after what you've been through today, I definitely think movie night is the best medicine."

"Sure, why don't you pop down to the library and see what's on offer" – take you time."

"I still have some work to do on a presentation, just a few minor touches – I 'll be done once you're back"

Claire loves chick flicks, and I'm embarrassed to admit that as of late I've enjoyed cuddling up to her on our battered old sofa - making comments like... "Jennifer Aniston is starting to show her age".

A favorite part of mine was scoffing handfuls of greasy popcorn – still warm from the microwave, and the happy ending of course.

MESSAGE ME

L ost in my research, I hadn't noticed Claire standing before me waving a couple of DVDs.
"I found two movies and – hold on tight – one we haven't seen yet.

"Great, then we'll watch that one."

"I also brought *Vampire Diaries.*"

"Gosh Claire, you're so predictable, how many times have you seen that silly movie?"

"Not often enough – anyway, isn't it your turn to make popcorn and by the way… stop getting on my case about my addiction to Vampire Diaries". It's really not that bad."

As I was about to reply to Claire on the subject of her addiction, I spotted movement coming from the bottom of the screen, my heart missed a beat!!! A little envelope was bouncing up and down trying to catch my attention.

A reply from Anin??? That was fast!!!

I couldn't open the mail fast enough. Unfortunately, all the excitement was dashed when I read who the sender was – none other than dreamer89?

"Hello, Sophie – unfortunately I'm unable to get you in touch with Anin, simply because there's been no activity from him for quite some time. If you have further questions, don't hesitate to contact me at the following address:
dreamer@markofthearverni.com.
Please avoid using the blog for future correspondence – it is not safe! I believe we are being watched. There are unsavory characters lurking around with bad intentions – please be careful!"

That didn't sound good. What did he mean by "being watched?"

One positive thing that came from the unsettling message was the fact that someone had made contact. I'm sure there was more where that came from.

Unfortunatly I did not know whether he was someone I could trust. I replied immediately.

"Hello dreamer89,
I have many questions, but first and foremost I would appreciate you giving me a reason why I should trust you?
Sophie"

I read the draft through one more time, sent the mail and kept my eyes glued to the screen, hoping to see the little envelope excitedly bounce up and down sooner rather than later.

I was desperate for answers, and I knew I was going to get to the bottom of this. All my life I had been persistent in everything. I'd set out to achieve, and this was no different, I was more determined to get to the root cause of the predicament. I continued googling, trying different combinations to do with crosses mysteriously appearing on body parts. As predicted, most of them were related to Religious contents.

I started questioning that very fact, perhaps it did have something to do with faith. I couldn't be a hundred percent sure. I did know I wasn't baptized and allegedly neither Catholic nor Protestant. Did my background perhaps, have something to do with the cross? By routine, I refreshed my inbox. Lost in thought, my eyes wandered to my mailbox. There was a new message.

My fingers tapped on the touch pad at lighting speed.

From: dreamer89
Subject: What you should know …
1 Minute ago

I felt a tingling sensation. Goose pimples and hot flashes broke out all over me as if having an allergic reaction to something.

"Craaaazy" I said out loud!!! Claire replied with gusto.

"You're right, it's absolutely insane, he's about to kiss her on the neck and then…"

Trembling, I caressed the touchpad with my finger so that I could reach the icon that would open the message from dreamer89. Click, click, expecting to see paragraph after paragraph of information, a compilation of links, references to books, articles – the truth what happened to me.

I was taken back by a bright, vacant screen.

There had to be a technical fault – or maybe the file was too big and it would take some time before it would download.
Hurry up, what the hell is taking so long! That's it – there was nothing more coming.

However, the mail did have a title on the subject line, along with a link.

Kayky… I can't believe I missed it!

Dreamer89 had copied a link into the subject line and decreased the font to such an extent that it was hardly visible

What you need to know, http://bit.ly/1z58PHG

With butterflies in my stomach, I copied the link into my browser.

Claire had been chatting away into the background. I was obviously not paying much attention to her. I was making the right noises though – a ploy to keep her from asking me simple-minded questions and what my thoughts on vampires were.

"How do you like the movie, Sophie?"

Grinning, I looked at Claire and was able to squeeze out an authentic-sounding "suuppperr," which satisfied her.

Eventually, the site appeared. Actually it wasn't a site, it looked more like a login window. This was obviously created as a safety precaution. Except that no login details had been provided - that was stupid. I ran through possible combinations of usernames and passwords. I tried Sophie, and the password dreamer89 – it didn't work. This was mission impossible. Dreamer89 had to be informed about his slip up - and just as I was about to convey that to him – there it was.

From: dreamer89
Subject: Sorry – you need this…
1 Minute ago

User: Sophie
PW: Arverni
Sorry
- dreamer89 -

Not wasting anytime I proceeded to fill in the information to enter into the account. It accepted the passwords and began to come to life.

'Loading…'

The nail on my ring finger was chewed almost to the bone. Nail biting was a bad habit I had adopted under stressful situations.

A video??? That's unusual???

More butterflies began to swirl inside my knotted stomach.

GUINEA PIG

S uddenly, the video started. A boy appeared on the screen, filming himself with a flip cam. The picture was anything but high resolution, and very wobbly. The boy had black, shoulder-length hair that covered his whole face. I could hear hard rock music in the background, and I thought I recognized *Hells Bells* from AC/DC. I stopped the film, grabbed my laptop with the headphones and disappeared, into the bathroom for some privacy, away from Claire.

Was the boy dreamer89?
With the laptop on my knees and the headphones in my ears, I started watching the movie again and turned up the volume. I was right! Hells Bells hammered in my eardrums, and the boy appeared on the screen once more. His face was completely covered, and I wondered why he didn't want to be seen. He started to talk in a raw, cracking voice.

"Today is the 24th of May, 2002, experiment number 2."
The camera swung away from his face, turning 180 degrees. I saw a mirror.
The camera tilted, briefly revealing a glimpse of a bathroom. In the reflection, I saw a boy trying to mount the camera on a tripod. The picture wobbled. It was like I could feel his tension as he concentrated on setting the camera position. Again and again, he adjusted the picture, zooming in and out until the screen showed the whole reflection. When he was satisfied with his adjustments, he swung the camera back to himself and disappeared. I heard the music got much louder like he had turned up the volume. When he reappeared in front of the camera, he reached into the mane with his hands, parted the hair into two even sections, and pulled it back. I could see his slim, striking face for the first time. He looked very serious. But there was something else there – something that was difficult to put into words – something warm, sincere, and honest, but visibly layered with worry.

Wonder how old he is? He must be around my age – so he's 16, or maybe 17, but surely not much older.

I noticed how he pulled his hair back into a ponytail with a rubber band. He was practiced, and every movement of his hands was just right. It looked as though it was important to him to make sure everyone saw his whole face, and that he wasn't hiding anything. He looked at himself in the camera.

What is he planning?
He suddenly looked attractive instead of uncanny. He was handsome.

With a movement of his hand, he turned the camera towards his reflection. What I saw there hit me like a punch in the chest. I was not ready for it. Shocked, I slipped backward against the sink. My right arm hit something hard and started to hurt. When I heard the toilet start to flush, I knew what it was. Suddenly I lost my balance, and my laptop slipped from my knees falling to the floor. To keep the worst from happening, I tried to grab the laptop with my left hand, but I was too slow. It tipped, fell, and tore the headphones out of my ears.
Kay-Ky !!!

It hit the bathroom floor with a loud crack. Plastic pieces sprayed out onto the tiles, and I feared the worst. The picture of the boy pulling his hair away from his face displaying a cross on his forehead identical to mine was frozen in my retina.

He has the same mark! The same thing happened to him.
Elbows resting on my upper thighs and head in my hands, I breathed deeply and tried to calm myself down. Now I understood all his preparation with the camera and the mirror.

He wanted to document the cross and show that it's only visible in the mirror.

Kay-Ky, hopefully it's not broken! What happens next in the video?

The screen was still on, but the video player had stopped.

Good, the computer was still working

I put the headphones back in my ears and was ready to start the movie again when I heard Claire's voice in the background and a muffled knocking on the bathroom door.

"What's going on, Sophie, did you fall?"

"Everything's alright, Claire, I just dropped my laptop."

"You did what?"

"Yes, but everything's alright. Watch your movie."

I knew Claire wouldn't be able to resist this suggestion, so " Give yourself all the time you need, Sophie, I just wanted to know if anything happened to you." After I'd calmed Claire down again, I restarted the player. I sat on the toilet with my mouth open, my eyes absorbing all the information.

Dreamer, is that you?
Finally, someone can give me answers to all my questions.
Whoever this unknown boy was, both of us shared the same problem – His distinctive voice interrupted my thoughts...

"Today, it's been a week since I saw the cross on my forehead for the first time. It looks like it's changing a little. The outlines are getting a little darker, and the skin around it is changing color a little bit too. As I documented in the two previous experiments, the cross is drawn on with a very resistant ink. Attempts to remove it with soap, lye, or any other cleaner have failed. I almost think the cross is a type of tattoo, a change in the pigment of my skin."

Just like mine.
"As proof, I will now burn a part of it to see whether the tattooed skin heals like a normal wound."

Is he insane?
I hardly had time to think before I saw a long lighter with a big blue flame.

I could see something. It was the tip of a nail file, glowing bright red. He slowly pressed the glowing nail file onto his forehead. I felt pain in the same spot as I watched, and a quiet "Ow" escaped my lips as I averted my eyes. Rock music just hammered on in the background. The image was clouded by smoke. Smoke coming from his burning skin.

I can smell the scent of burning flesh in my nose – as a vegetarian, I'm disgusted. He is completely loopy! How can someone stand something like that without screaming? How can he do that to himself?
Once he removed the nail file from the skin, I could see he had burned the tip of a triangle into his forehead about a centimeter long. He had done it – he had burned the tip of the cross with the glowing nail file.

The camera turned off suddenly, and the video looked like it was over. But a glance at the display told me there were still five minutes left.

That means the video is still running.
There was one thing I was sure of: whatever the cross does to me, I'll never do something like that to myself, not in this life.
Appalled, I wondered what to do next. If that was dreamer89, then he was completely nuts. Did the cross drive him to do that? Did it influence him in some way, or was it just helplessness? Why did he hurt himself? Lots of questions – and no answers. One thing was certain: the boy in the video could help me and answer lots of my questions, whether he was dreamer89 or not. Then the boy appeared again in front of the camera.

"Today is May 25th, 2002. Reflection on experiment number 3."
I listened straining.
"Yesterday I burned a portion of the cross in experiment number 3." I stared at the screen, enthralled. "The burn destroyed all skin layers. The wound is draining a lot of fluid, but I didn't clean it. Everything looks normal for an injury of this extent. The triangle is surrounded by a reddish edge, which also signals that healing has already begun. Up to now, it seems like a normal injury; everything in this experiment has been normal, except for the fact that burning my skin yesterday caused no pain at all. This sounds strange."

Did I understand him correctly? He's claiming that the burn didn't hurt? That would explain why he didn't cry out or twitch.

"Today is May 28th, 2002.
Reflection on experiment number 3.

Four days ago, I burned part of my forehead in experiment number 3. The goal was to determine how the skin around the cross would react, and whether it had an influence on how the burned area healed.

When he looked in the mirror, I couldn't see any wound at all. Unbelievable! The area was covered with rosy skin, but the wound was gone – disappeared!
Hard Rock music was still playing, and so he began to describe his findings. "As you can see the wound has fully healed. The whole process took four days. "

A normal healing for a wound of this extent would surely have lasted two to three weeks, even if it were healing well. The cross definitely had a positive influence and shortened the healing period.

"The regrown skin is tattooed in exactly the same spot where the cross is, just as it was before. This means there is no way to remove the cross."
Of course, … he wanted to know whether the cross was like a tattoo now he knew it wasn't. But what was it? And where did it come from?

What is it that's on my forehead? And it's not just that – I can feel myself changing. My thoughts are different – what's happening to me?

FOLLOW THE INSTRUCTIONS

I had lots of questions for dreamer89, and the only way to get answers was to ask him directly.

Sender: dreamer89
Yes – that's me – what did you see?
1 Minute ago

I wrote the first thing that came into my mind.
"I saw your cross! You burned yourself! I need help – can you help me?"
It felt like time was standing still. The tea was finished steeping, and I tried and failed to take a drink without burning my lips. Suddenly, I was relieved to hear the signal for an incoming message.

Sender: dreamer89
I will help you!!!
1 Minute ago
Sacudere Sophie,
Of course I'll help you, and I know exactly what kind of a situation you're in. I went through all of it myself years ago. We need to talk, urgently, and I will find a way we can do so soon – safely. Email is not secure; it's dangerous, so please don't send me any details about yourself.
As soon as I've found a way to contact you, we can talk. Please promise me you won't do anything stupid in the next few days, nothing like what you saw in the video. There's an explanation for everything.
One last question, Sophie.
Where are your parents?
- Dreamer89 -

Why does he want to know where my parents are?

From: Sophie
To: dreamer89,

Both of them are dead; I'm an orphan.
Sophie

I didn't understand why it was so important. This time, the answer was quicker than I'd expected.

Sender: dreamer89
That explains everything. I will contact you – be STRONG.
1 Minute ago

His answer irritated me. Even more: it vexed me. Does this kind of thing only happen to orphans? Questions, and more questions, and then this crappy final sentence. How could he end his message with "Be strong?"
How could he use the phrase my Dad always said?

I grabbed my laptop went back to the room and laid on the bed. Everything I'd experienced during the day had left its mark, and despite feeling tense, I wasn't able to stay awake anymore.

The next morning Claire woke me up since I had slept through my alarm. I felt totally beat and physically exhausted. The only thing keeping me motivated was my hope that I might have only dreamed everything. The cross, dreamer89, the emails. I went to the bathroom to prove it to myself. Looking in the mirror was like being punched in the face. My wishful thinking burst like a soap bubble. There it was, the cross. Reality took hold of me once again. Practically hypnotized by my reflection, I had to look at the cross closer. It drew me in like a magnet. Bent forward to see the contours, the color, and everything else more closely, I stood in front of the mirror and gazed at my forehead. I could clearly feel it giving me strength and energy. It was a totally new, unknown feeling. Very pleasant and warm – it just felt completely Kay-Ky. Energy radiated from the center of my forehead, from the cross, and spread out over my whole body. It was like my fear had been transformed.

The cross reacting to me! But how could the cross know that I was looking at it?

A few experiments seemed to confirm my assumption: The cross had a positive influence on my psyche and my well-being, and all I had to do was look at its reflection

It felt as if my feet were falling asleep, from bottom to top and from inside to outside. The tingling feeling increased, slinking further up my legs. It kept moving until it was radiating through my whole body.

What is it? First it electrified me from top to bottom, and now from bottom to top.
Everything flowed together in the cross in the middle of my forehead. It was an unbelievable feeling, and difficult to put into words. I felt warm inside and comforted. Even the tingling transformed into a pleasant caress, which changed how I was feeling.

When I had come into the bathroom ten minutes ago, I felt miserable. I was tired and had no energy – almost a little depressed – now all that had been turned upside down.

Claire was already gone, since she had an appointment at the gynecologist this morning. If I understood her correctly, she had convinced them to prescribe her the pill. So, we both had our own things going on. Claire was taking the pill, and I had a cross on my forehead.

*I could no longer wait for dreamer89 to contact me; my only op-*tion was to write another email.

From: Sophie
To: dreamer89,
Hello dreamer89,
I need your help. How soon can we talk? I can't stand it anymore!
Sophie

I sent the message, grabbed my purse, stuck my laptop in my backpack, and set off. It took about fifteen minutes to get to school on the bus, and I kept an eye on my phone the whole way.

Had dreamer89 already read my email?

He was probably driving or working, just like every other normal person at this time of day. While I was still looking for an explanation, a new email from him appeared. There it was – a message from dreamer89.

dreamer89
Follow the instructions.
1 Minute ago

Sophie, You don't need to be afraid. Follow the instructions, even if it sounds strange! At the beginning, we'll need to practice to enable this kind of communication, but it's just like talking or writing. What I am about to explain to you will be the basis for our future communication. Sophie, you must trust me! This is about you, your origins, and your future!!! I have put together a short guide for you. Follow the guide step by step; if a step doesn't work right away, don't despair, just try it again.
We will meet in one of your dreams.

Did I just read that correctly? We'll meet in a dream

1st Step – Dreamscape
Create a place for yourself where you feel secure and comfortable, and above all where you can be undisturbed. Think of something beautiful, something you would like to experience. Then create your own dreamscape, the place you want to meet me. Dream something you've already dreamt of before. The only limit is your mind; anything is possible, but let's start with something simple.

2nd Step – Invitation
To make contact with you, I need an invitation. You can only appear in a dream with an invitation; that's an important rule. You decide who is part of your dream. You saw me in the video, so you have an image of me in your memory. I do look older now than I did in the video, but overall it will still work. An invitation means: you wish that I were in your dreamscape. I become a part of your dream, here an example. If someone loves books, then a library is his ideal dreamscape. He imagines himself in a library,

and in a corner he meets the person he wants to contact. You bring an environment and a person together.

3rd Step – Dreams
Dream your dreamscape from step 1, and send an invitation as described in step 2. Close your eyes and imagine your environment, like you're meditating. Don't go to sleep – that's important – just think about your dreamscape and begin to invite me, bringing me into your dream, this way we'll meet one another and can talk undisturbed.

Step 4
The fourth step is important at the beginning. You need to let me know before you start. Just send me an email with the subject "dream" and I'll know that you want to contact me. What's important, Sophie! Only you can invite me; I can't invite myself into your dream. You will learn why. Let me know when you're ready; I'll wait for your answer. Be strong.
- dreamer89 -

The bus driver shook my backpack, scaring me half to death, "Excuse me, we're here." I frantically grabbed my things and left the bus. I had been daydreaming on the bus, thinking about the dreamscape invitation.

Maybe it's all just happening in my head? If that's not Kay-Ky, then what is?
While I questioned myself, another bus appeared driving back towards Heaven.

This is no coincidence; this is perfect!
On the bus, I sent Claire a text and asked her to make an excuse for me when she got to school after her doctor's appointment.
Is this how it feels when a person starts to lose it? Starts to go crazy?
I read the email with the guide again, with a plan in mind to construct a dreamscape and invite dreamer89. He would help me to get answers to all my questions.

SWEET DREAMS

I stepped off the bus in front of Heaven, wanted to get back as quickly as possible to try constructing a dream path to communicate with dreamer89.

My destination was the workout room upstairs under the roof. It was a great place to relax; I spent time here whenever I needed some time out or a little peace. No classes, the room was free. As I ran up the stairs, I started typing an email to dreamer89.

From: Sophie
To: dreamer89,
Hello dreamer89,
I have some time now, and I'm going to dream.
Hope so much to see you.
Sophie

The message was already sent when I climbed the last steps to the top floor. In the moment I opened the door to the workout room, my phone piped up, telling me I had a response. There were some comfortable cushions at the end of the room. I picked one up and put it in a corner. Eyes on my phone, I realized how tense I was, and hoped dreamer89 had time now.

From: dreamer89
To: Sophie
Give me 10 minutes; follow the instructions!

My heartbeat practically increased from excitement, kind of like a date. I got comfortable on the cushion. "Ten minutes" dreamer89 had written; that gave me time to concentrate on my dream and the instructions. I closed my eyes, and the dark room helped me to concentrate on what was important. I went through the steps of dreamer89's guide in my mind. I started to imagine my dreamscape and felt a certain sense of unease and tension. One last time, I looked at my phone. It had already been five minutes. I closed my eyes and entered the dream.

A white wooden house, a little ways away from a dune with a view of the ocean, it was a warm summer day. The wind blew through my hair, and I sensed wafting warm summer air and the smell of the ocean. Waves that ran out over the beach covered my feet with warm salt water and sand. I turned around and ran towards a large sand dune that climbed away from the ocean, separating the interior and the sea. A rough path passed through the dune towards the beach house. The wind created ever-changing textures on the sand, and as I ran up the dune barefoot, I saw the wooden house with a veranda turned towards the ocean. There must be a lovely view of the ocean from the veranda. Everything felt so light, and I felt my body relax further; a warm, pleasant feeling flowed into my legs. A person can rest here; it's gorgeous. I ran up the sand dune, just a few more steps to the stairs on the veranda, and my heart began to beat more quickly. It was definitely not physical exertion since I worked out four or five times a week. It was stress, caused by the absurd attempt at meeting someone in my own dream. I noticed my dreamscape start to waver, but I repressed the thought, concentrated again, and walked up the stairs to the veranda. Not yet at the top of the stairs, I could already see someone sitting, relaxed, in the swing. When he saw me, he smiled. I couldn't believe it. Dreamer89 had followed my invitation. Sitting on a swing on a white veranda in front of a white house by the ocean, smiling at me.

"Great to meet you, Sophie! You did that perfectly. There aren't many people who can do it so perfectly the first time."

"Thanks for the compliment."

"You've chosen a beautiful place. It's beautiful – Straight from my office and into a vacation; what could be better?"

I stood there, stiffly, and didn't say a word. There were so many questions. With great effort, I forced myself to speak.
"Yes, it's very beautiful here. To be totally honest, I still can't believe all of this, so I might seem like I'm a little short. How did you get here?" Dreamer89 looked at me, surprised, and I realized how dumb the question sounded.
"I took a taxi!"

He smirked and tried to repress his smile, but couldn't stand it anymore and laughed out loud. I stood there, feeling a little dumb, but was infected by his hearty laugh and had to laugh with him.

"In reality, I'm sitting in my office chair and dreaming about a beautiful beach house and relaxing in a porch swing. Nothing is real; it's all just a dream. That means we're both in this dream, and we can exchange information – without anyone listening in."
He looked significantly older than in the video, which was already several years old. Can anyone eavesdrop on us here?"

He smiled, and I noticed that his laugh created interesting little dimples at the corners of his mouth. He sat there, relaxed. He'd put his hair back in a ponytail again, which I liked very much – much better than his long hair. A sporty pair of sunglasses protected his eyes. Dreamer89 looked attractive, and totally Kay-Ky too, which actually doesn't happen all that often.
"Sophie, we're in your dream and we're absolutely safe. Besides us, there's no one here. No one can hear what we say. Unless you dream the person here."
"Can I ask you something, dreamer89?"
"Yes, just ask."
"Are you really the boy from the video?"
 "Yes, I'm him. Why do you doubt it?"
"Do you see the cross on my forehead?"
Dreamer89 looked in my direction. I couldn't see his eyes through the sunglasses, but I could tell he was looking at me. At my face – my forehead, to be exact.
"Yes, I can see your cross. You know, it isn't really a cross. It has a name – it's called an aphmal. An ancient Celtic name for a special symbol with special characteristics. You only call it a cross because it looks like a cross at the beginning. This is the first thing I want to explain to you today. The aphmal identifies you and your ancestry. It is the symbol of the Arverni, a thousand-year-old Celtic tribe. The aphmal helps you recognize who belongs to the community."
Dreamer stood up and walked towards me. He came closer and closer, threateningly close, and remained standing right in front of me.

"Can I look at it more closely?" he asked, standing directly in front of me. He was over a head taller than I was and looked down at me from above. I felt unsure and ashamed, as though I was naked, but I nodded in agreement. He bent down a little so he could look at my aphmal, as he called it, close up. He came so close that I felt uneasy. I breathed shallowly, but I could still smell his aftershave. Was this just another fantasy in my addled brain? Can you smell in a dream? I stood there, stiff as a board, holding my breath, while dreamer89 casually inspected my forehead. Seconds turned into minutes and just wouldn't end. He adjusted his glasses several times, as though it would help him see a little better.

"Crazy – this is crazy," he said.

He took a step back and sat down again in the porch swing. For a moment, it looked as though what he had seen on my forehead hadn't met his expectations. "Is everything okay?" I asked shyly.

"Umm, yeah, everything's okay! Sorry, I was just fascinated by your aphmal. It's so beautiful! Sit down by me and enjoy the view. Unfortunately my time today is limited. I have to be at a very important meeting in 15 minutes. I don't want to be impolite, and I want to give you the chance to ask me a few questions and get some answers

"I assume your parents didn't tell you anything about your Arverni heritage. No one explained to you who or what the Arverni are. What kind of traditions they have, what rules they have, and so on."

I sat beside dreamer on a rocking chair, and we both looked at the ocean. The waves whooshed in the same rhythm as the rockers on my seat.

"Yes, you're right. When you put it that way, I don't know much at all."

"What did you see when you looked at my aphmal? What was it that surprised you so much?" Dreamer89 stared at me like I was from another planet.

"What do you mean?"

"Oh, well, you were just so surprised when you looked at my, umm, aphmal … right?"

He laughed at me.

"Aphmal is correct – yes, I was. You're one of us, Sophie! You're an Arverni and your Aphmal is beautiful."

Dreamer89 looked into my eyes, and I didn't know if that was a good thing or a bad thing.

"A what?"

He answered with a slightly forced smile.

"An Arverni. This is what you don't know about your heritage. Normally, children in Arverni families are told about their origins before their sixteenth birthdays. They learn that they are part of the Arverni community. I'll tell you more about it the next time we meet."

"Hang on, I don't understand you're tossing a few crumbs at me and then you tell me you don't have any time and you have to go."

Head sunk, I cried quietly. I felt him take hold of my right hand.

"Believe me, I know exactly what's happening to you. This is just the beginning. Just let it out ... it helps to get things out in the open. The first things you have to do, Sophie, accept what's happening to you, accept your aphmal! Accept that your life is going to change completely from this point forward. You're in the process of becoming a different Sophie, and I'll tell you more about that as well. All in due time. You don't need to be afraid that it deforms your face; quite the opposite – it looks great on you."

"You say so, but it's not that easy!"

"I know, Sophie, it's anything but easy – remember my video. I had no one to explain the Arverni heritage to me. I'm an orphan, just like you, and my parents died in a plane crash. There was no one to lead me through my aphormation."

"Lead you through what? You're talking in riddles! What's an aphormation?"

"The aphormation starts 21 days before the sixteenth birthday when the aphmal appears. All Arverni going through the aphormation are called aspirants, just in case you hear the term some time."

"Can I ask something else – something more personal?"

"Yes, of course, don't be shy."

"Who are you? What's your real name?"

I looked dreamer89 in the eyes. Saw a sign of uncertainty. My question had taken him off guard.

"Amar – my real name is Amar. It's an Arverni name. Amar Wellberg, to be exact, and I'm a dream specialist and hotel director by trade."

"Amar – sounds interesting. What does it mean?"

Amar looked at his watch nervously.

"That's another question I'll answer for you next time, I promise. We both share a similar fate."

"Amar – sounds better than dreamer89."

"Thanks. Sophie also sounds very nice. Do you have a middle name?"

I proudly told Amar that my mother had given me my middle name.

"My middle name is Xama, although it's not officially recorded anywhere. Dad said that's what my mother wanted – so, my name is really Sophie Xama. But no one knows my middle name. Dad explained it's too dangerous for me to use it. I had to promise not to tell anyone. Since then, I've been Sophie."

"Sophie sounds good, but I do like Xama better. Xama is a traditional Arverni name, and a lovely one at that. Do you know what Xama means?"

"Yes, father told me before he died. He said Xama meant chief."

Amar nodded.

"That's exactly right. Your father was correct; it's dangerous to use this name publicly since it indicates an Arverni background. Can I use the name? I would like to call you Xama."

"Sophie Xama."

"No – just Xama."

I looked at Amar, surprised. I didn't really understand, but I nodded anyway.

"Very well, Xama. Let me tell you one more thing about your aphmal, so that you'll be prepared for the changes that are going to take place in the next few days and weeks. An aphmal is a very special sign that isn't visible to anyone but Arverni, and even we can only see the aphmal in our reflections. There's lots more to know about our organization, but I'll tell you more about that later. Your aphmal is still in the very early stages of its development, which I can tell for two reasons. It's not yet fully distinct, and it's still in an intermediary stage, the cross stage, which is why you call it a cross. It also doesn't yet fully stand out from its surroundings."

He kept looking at his watch as he spoke. Everything he said made sense, but I still hesitated, asking myself whether he really was who he claimed to be. I kept looking up at his forehead, part-

ly covered by his sunglasses. I couldn't see anything on his forehead – no cross, and no aphmal.

"I know you have to go, but I want to learn more about you."

"Of course, what is it?"

"How could you see my aphmal, if it's only visible in a mirror?"

"You can only see the reflection of an aphmal, and only Arverni
can see it at all. I assume that you don't have any Arverni friends,
at least not yet. So you don't need to be afraid of anyone seeing
you as disfigured or different. It just won't happen."

"I understand, but why is that?"

"A good question, which has unfortunately not yet been answered by science. Let's just say it's a type of natural protection
the aphmal has."

"But how can you look at my aphmal so intensely – directly, and
not in a reflection? Does it have something to do with your sunglasses?"

"You surprise me, Xama. Right, that's the trick. These sunglasses
are more than just sunglasses; in reality, they're aphmal glasses.
Their purpose is just that – making aphmals visible. We just cam-
ouflaged them as sunglasses so people don't see right away what
they really are."

Amar looked at his watch again, taking his sunglasses off and
handing them to me.

"Try them out yourself. Put them on and look at my forehead."

I took the sunglasses and looked at them for a moment. They
were much heavier than normal glasses. There were teeny tiny
buttons hidden on the sides. While I put them on, Amar stood up,
reached into his pants pocket, and took out a packet of tissues
and a little container that looked like it contained foundation. He
put the container on the table behind us, sat down again, and
showed me his forehead.

"What can you see on my forehead?"

He bent his face in my direction, expectantly, and I put on the
sunglasses. But I didn't see anything – his forehead was still flawless.

"Nothing, I see nothing – no aphmal."

"Very well, the camouflage blocks it. He spat on the tissue and
wiped it across his forehead. I could see something right away.

There it was – hidden under the foundation – becoming more and more visible with every second.

He's like me! He has an aphmal on his forehead. Amar is the boy; I can trust him.
After he rubbed the cream off his forehead, I saw it in full size. He was right it looked different from my aphmal. It wasn't a cross – instead, it had two more lines to the right and the left that came together above it like a sort of roof. I was transfixed. I felt a warm, pleasant feeling. I removed the glasses, and the aphmal had disappeared. I put them on, and I could see it again. I repeated the procedure a couple of times…. If that's not Kay-Ky, then I don't know what is. Amar recognized I had seen everything I wanted to.
"Now, you know that we're both Arverni, and that you can trust me completely. I still have five minutes, and then I'll disappear from the dream. Before I do, I want to tell you one more very important thing. You need to listen very carefully and follow my instructions. You are in grave danger. There is a dark side of the Arverni, a splinter group from our community who are also Arverni who follow other goals – not good goals. This group is always looking for aspirants. They track them and kidnap them, and they don't have good intentions, Xama. That's why you can't talk to anyone about this, not even your friends – NO ONE – Xama. Do you understand?"
"Yes, I understand – but what happens if these others find me, the evil Arverni?"
"I'll be totally honest with you, Xama. They will probably kill you."
Shocked and perplexed, I looked at Amar, who was already standing up and looking at his watch.
"That was a mistake. I shouldn't have told you that now, – damn. I'll explain to you next time we meet. Xama, you can't tell anyone about this. Don't write any blog posts about it, nothing on Facebook or Twitter, and no texts either."
He lifted my chin slightly with his finger and looked deep into my eyes.
"Promise?"

I looked at him and squeaked out a "Yes, I promise." I saw he was relieved. He took the cream from the table, dropped a thick glob of it on a clean tissue and blotted it onto his forehead.
"Can you please check if you can still see anything?"
I put on the aphmal glasses and looked at his forehead. The aphmal had disappeared.
"It's gone – invisible." "Very good – now you."
"Me too?" "Yes, you too!"

He repeated the same procedure on me.

"Very well, now we're both invisible. When you wake up from the dream, you'll see the camouflage has disappeared. What happens in a dream stays in a dream – all you can take with you are your memories! I'll send some bottles to your address. Don't go out of your house undisguised. Anyone who's wearing these sunglasses could be one of the evil Arverni, looking for your aphmal. I know, I've created more questions for you today than I've answered. We'll meet again soon. What's important is that you accept your heritage; you're an Arverni. In the coming weeks and months, you will discover yourself as if for the first time. Don't fight it, Xama – accept it. Before I go, I have to commend you. You are an extremely strong Arverni. I've never had a first dream visit before in such a beautiful dreamscape, considering the emotional strain you're under. Dream communication can only work if you're not too tense; that's the only way to maintain the dream, Xama. You are an especially strong girl."

Although it was supposed to be a compliment, his statement hurt me. He didn't see me as a woman, just a girl.

"Before you go, Amar, will you tell me something?"
He looked at his watch again.
"I just have one more minute; time for one more question." "All of this is too much for me. I just want to be a normal girl, nothing more. All of this is a mistake, a nightmare. When I wake up from this dream in a moment, everything will be normal again. No cross, and no aphmal on my forehead. Everything will be like it always was, like before."

"I understand your fear and your worry. But you aren't a normal girl; you're an Arverni. The quicker you come to terms with that, the easier it will be for you to deal with it. Don't make the same mistake I made; don't resist it, it's your purpose. You'll see; it isn't all bad."

Amar walked to the railing of the veranda and looked out at the ocean.

"I must leave now but do look at your aphmal as often as you can. It will give you positive energy and strength. The more time you invest in getting to know it, the better you'll feel."

While Amar was still speaking, his surroundings abruptly started to change. He became paler and then, all at once, he disappeared. I closed my eyes for a second reflecting on what just happened, when I suddenly felt someone grab my shoulder and shake me. When I opened my eyes, the beautiful beach had disappeared, and I saw a woman with a bucket and a broom instead.

"Everything OK, angel?"

I realized I was in the workout room. The cleaning lady standing in front of me. She must have woken me up; she had torn me from my dream.

I still felt a little shaken and decided to go straight to my room. Amar had scared me – I had more questions than he gave me answers. I started to feel tired. All I wanted to do was lay down in my bed and relax, and try to digest everything. I tried to remember everything Amar had just told me, surprised at how clear all the information still was in my thoughts. It was a special kind of dream. Amar was someone special, not just because he was so attractive and athletic. No he wanted to help me and he had a special gift. He could appear in dreams – if that isn't Kay-Ky, then I don't know what is.

THE COMMUNITY

Amar ran along a hallway in the Aphobia hotel. He was running late. The dream with Xama lasted much longer than he planned, and he still didn't feel good about leaving her alone with so many open questions. He had no choice. The meeting he was about to go to was very important for Xama, likely even essential to her survival. Amar knew that punctuality was both valued and expected of Arverni. A glance at his wristwatch revealed that the council had just started; he was too late. Amar knew today's was no normal council meeting. Today, he could complete a part of the task he had taken on. He had sworn that no more aspirants would have to die just because the community refused to act. He was part of the council and felt responsible, so he wanted to remind everyone that aspirants were the future of the Arverni. His goal was to place Xama Dupre under the protection of the community as a new aspirant. No more, and no less.

The council met every four weeks. It was called the council of elders. But since most members weren't older than 45, this did sound a little strange. Amar, who was also a member of the council, was only in his late 20s – the youngest member.

Amar wanted to ask the council for special approval to represent Xama Dupre before the group. A formal matter, since he believed all members would agree to it. It is the job of a parent or next of kin to represent their son or daughter in the meetings. Amar knew the rules. But from his own experience, he also knew how difficult it was not having parents, and unable to find anyone willing to help you to be accepted in the community. Without the community, you were always on the run, in a fight for survival. The only way to win the fight was to go into hiding until the end of the aphormation. Amar knew that Xama would never make it; even he hadn't made it without help, and he was ready to take every step he could for her.

21 months is a damn long time.

Amar knew that Eric Dupre had hidden his daughter Xama, and he also knew that Eric Dupre had left the Arverni community at his own request shortly before his death. With this decision, Eric

Dupre had also permanently forfeited his children's' right to be accepted into the community. Amar needed to come up with something that gave Xama back that right.

What could have caused Eric to leave the Arverni? Amar had tried to research the reasons and discovered something strange. All information and all protocols on his case, even the council's own decisions, were no longer accessible. Amar's status had not been high enough to view the documents. This gave him more motivation to find out why Erich Dupre voluntarily left. It might even explain his premature death. Amar knew he was stirring things up with his research. He had to concentrate on Xama and her safety, especially since her camouflage wouldn't work as her aphormation progressed. That's why he was trying to find her. Amar knew from his own experience that when the aphmal showed itself, fear of the unknown would increase. What was better than the internet to look for answers – That's why he reactivated his pseudonyms in various forums, waiting patiently for questions. It didn't take long before Xama contacted him. When he discovered her cry for help, he immediately knew she was a new aspirant. He had gotten his case on the agenda, and now it was important to represent the facts in such a way that all the members would follow his recommendations. As he ran along the last hallway, he was forced to remember that even he had only survived through luck. When he needed the community's help, there was no one there. He had been closer to death than life back then.

The community has to accept Xama.

From his own experience, Amar knew Xama didn't have a chance without the community's protection. The hunt would certainly begin. Merciless, just like with all the other aspirants, she wouldn't survive this hunt. As long as her powers remained untrained, she was only prey. Amar could still remember the horrible pictures from a year ago, when a 16 year-old girl was found, disfigured and drained of blood. The press invented the most awful stories and wrote that she'd been imprisoned and tortured and that the killers had allowed her to slowly bleed out in an unimaginably gruesome way during a ritual murder. Most people believed the press was just exaggerating, as usual. Except that only a few people and himself knew it was actually true and even worse than reported. He knew who did it, and why. What kept him up at night was that he had come too late to save Céline – that was the girl's name. Céline was an aspirant, and she didn't even know it. But she had to die because she possessed something others desperately wanted – her blood. Céline was an orphaned and alone, same as Xama. Nobody there to explain to Céline what will happen and help her to survive. Amar didn't sleep after Céline death – guilt kept him awake. Amar swore to himself that this would never happen again.

When he finally arrived at the conference room, he opened the big entryway door and slowly walked in. Amar glanced left and right, trying to get an overview of all the members present. It looked as though they were all there, which surprised him, since there was only one item on the agenda for today's meeting.

Amar surveyed the room and greeted each of the attendees in the unique Averni way by brushing the left ear over the left cheek of the person he greeted. The other members then repeated the same gesture. From a distance, it almost looks like a brief kiss on the cheek.

The council only had twelve members, so everyone knew one another personally. The Arverni community was small and had shrunk even further in the recent years. Most Arverni had their own businesses or managed companies that belonged to the community. No one outside the community, however, knew how powerful and wealthy the Arverni actually were. They didn't just own countless businesses, but also an unbelievable number of patents and rights. They had invested in banks and owned multiple international hotels and restaurant chains, as well as franchise businesses. Despite all these riches, no one knew about the Arverni organization, a community controlling each and everything.

Amar was almost done making the rounds and was now greeting the head of the table, the directorate, which consisted of five members. He excused himself for his lateness, although he knew that he had to take responsibility for this and bear the consequences. He went to a table at the side on which various objects were arranged. Some looked like medical instruments, others like tools of torture, but all of them had the same purpose. They were used to cause pain to any person who broke a rule. Amar picked up a bracelet and slipped it on, went back to his table, and pressed a symbol that stood out on the side of the bracelet. At lightning speed, the bracelet closed on Amar's arm. His face betrayed the pain he was feeling. He looked down at the bracelet – the trigger Amar had pushed didn't just close the bracelet, it also activated razor sharp blades that bored into his arm. Any normal human would have expected the wound to start to bleed. But that wasn't the case with Amar; he kept himself under control. He looked up at the Arverni chief, who had taken his place in the middle of the five. He nodded at Amar briefly in response. The Arverni community had guarded and practiced the traditions of their culture since the dawn of time. Amar knew exactly what was waiting for him, and he was prepared and ready for it.

The Meta, the council chief, was in his late 50s, and very lean. His cheekbones stood out, adding distinction to his face, and he gave the overall impression of not being in the best health. He greeted Amar heartily and hugged him several times. He took Amar's arm, on which the bracelet was activated and pressed the symbol again. Amar stood there quietly, lowering his head in a clearly subordinate manner. The Meta removed the bracelet, held his arm high, and placed his right thumb in the middle of Amar's forehead. In the moment, his thumb touched Amar's face; his whole body shook as though struck by a bolt of lightning. The Meta removed his thumb, but continued to hold up Amar's arm. Amar didn't move. Slowly and carefully, the Meta touched Amar's chin, lifting his head so he could see his arm. A stark quiet fell over the hall. Everyone stared at the Meta and at Amar's uplifted arm. The wounds from the blades of the bracelet were clear to see. Except that, not a drop of blood escaped from the cuts. Amar noticed this and a satisfied, smile spread over his face. Suddenly Amar's arm began to glow with a strange red light, and everyone could see his wounds changing. As unbelievable as it was, an enormously rapid healing process was taking place right in front of all. It took only a few seconds for his wounds to disappear. His arm's red glow faded, and the Meta slowly lowered Amar's arm and let it go. Amar stood there, not saying a word, but his moist eyes blinked in thanks to the Meta. The Meta answered with a silent yet meaningful nod.

The Meta then went to his place and blew into a small whistle lying on the table in front of him. A bright note spread over the room, and the members stared, tense and focused, in his direction. The Meta sat face contorted in pain. That was the sign for everyone to follow, so they all sat down, expecting the Meta to open the meeting.

"Dear members of the council, thank you all for being here. As you can see from our agenda, there is only one matter on the docket. This matter is, however, of special urgency."

His eyes scanned the circle; someone sitting at his right wanted to help him, but the Meta indicated with a motion of his hand that he didn't need any. Slowly, he stood up. It was visibly difficult for him, although he tried not to betray this fact. Everyone knew that the Meta was seriously ill. Perhaps this was what made him so special. He walked slowly towards Amar and placed the whistle in front of him on the table.

"May I ask you Amar, to present on today's urgent matter of Mrs. Dupre?"

Amar nodded. He took up the whistle, briefly blew into it, and then placed it back on the table. He stood up and walked towards a computer, picked up a remote control pressed a few buttons and a huge screen came down. An image appeared on the screen as if by magic. Once the image was bright and clear, Amar began to speak:
"Honored Meta, colleagues. All of us knew Eric Dupre, and some of us were even friends with him. His wife Adele Dupre died while giving birth to their daughter Xama. Eric took care of his daughter from that day forth. Eric and Adele were members of our community. Eric was a respected member of the greater council, and for a time he was responsible for important duties. He was tasked with protecting one of our most vital business divisions at the headquarters. During his Finitum, Eric Dupre made a request that his daughter Xama be received and placed under the protection of the community. Since, according to our statues, this kind of request may only be made at the beginning of the aphormation, he was denied. Eric made the decision to

leave the community on his own accord to protect his daughter himself. Eric Dupre is no longer able to make his request for protection now as his daughter Xama started the Aphormation. He died shortly after he left the community from an immune disorder as a result of his Finitum."

A murmur passed through the hall; each member of the council knew what this meant for Xama Dupre. But what was even worse, was the fact that the Arverni Codex, passed down for hundreds of years. This Codex Eric Dupre had followed to the end, was what had cheated him out of the most important thing in his life – his own daughter's safety. Amar knew the council understood this. He knew he was on the right path; He continued with his presentation.

"Since Xama Dupre is an aspirant without parents, and without any other relatives, I hereby request to be recognized as her guardian."

Hands shot up; the majority agreed. There were side conversations among the conservative block, and they were becoming more intense. It seemed as if the council members were against Amar's suggestion.

A hand signal from the corner indicated someone wanted to speak. Amar recognized Wagner; he was one of the extreme conservatives, and lived and acted in strict accordance with the ancient rules. He opposed modernizing the community and tried to stop it in any way he could. Amar picked up the whistle and carried it to Wagner's table, then laid it down before him as the Codex provided, even though he knew that Wagner would try to do anything he could to keep Xama from being accepted.

Wagner blew the whistle, put it down, and began to present his argument.

"If a person like Eric Dupre voluntarily leaves the Arverni community, he knows his family will lose all future claim of help from the community. In accordance with the law, we cannot accept Xama Dupre into our community."

A loud noise rose in the room, seeming as though Wagner's argument had found some followers.

"I ask for quiet – Amar Wellberg has the floor," the Meta intoned towards the conservative block. Silence fell. "Before we come to Wagner's point, I would like to conclude the first question. May I please ask again for a signal from all who support my application as Xama Dupre's guardian."

All hands were up, except for those of the conservative block.

"This means that the council authorizes me, Amar Wellberg, to act as guardian for Xama Dupre and to represent her rights before the council. Thank you for your trust. Now to our laws. By withdrawing from the community, Eric Dupre has forfeited all of his family's rights. Wagner is correct in saying that Xama Dupre no longer has a claim as the daughter of Eric Dupre."

Another murmur passed through the room, and everyone looked at Amar, wondering at his statement. Wasn't he the one demanding Xama Dupre's inclusion?

"I hereby place a request that Xama Dupre, who is under my guardianship and who enjoys all the rights of my family, be accepted into the community of the Arverni as though she were my own child."

Now everyone knew what a brilliant chess move Amar Wellberg had made. His guardianship had given him a new way to integrate Xama Dupre as a member of the community.

The members all stared at the screen, where a picture of Eric Dupre and a small child reflected.

"I have assembled some important facts in order to present this request before the council."

A hand shot into the air, one of the five directors signaled for attention. Amar picked up the whistle and carried it to the director. He laid the whistle in front of him on the table. The small, heavyset man grabbed it, blew it, and placed it back on the table in front of him again.

"Amar, thank you for adopting Xama Dupre. We all knew Eric. We all miss him very much, and we also know that the situation for him and his daughter Xama was very difficult, even more so when we did not accept her. However, her acceptance into the community requires that we check some important characteristics to make sure she is an aspirant. Decision must take place during the aphormation; only during this period is it clear and apparent whether a person is of Arverni heritage. This, dear Amar, means we need proof."

The room became loud once again. Voices for and against the request filtered out. Amar knew the conservative members of the council were against including an aspirant without family. In their view, orphans lost their right to be part of the community forever upon the death of their parents.
The director stood up and picked up the whistle, then carried to Amar, who blew into it again briefly. Amar knew it was his turn to deliver facts and proofs, and that Xama's future depended on his speech.

"You are correct, Karel, and I can assure you I have proven her heritage to myself, which is my duty as the applicant."

As Amar spoke, he plugged his glasses into the system. A picture of Xama appeared, her forehead clearly visible in high resolution with the aphmal in the middle of it. The murmuring grew louder. No one thought Amar would provide such clear proof. Amar was relieved; his aphmal glasses were taking good pictures, even better than he'd hoped. His last remnant of uncertainty had disappeared. He was about to win.

"Meta, colleagues! As you can see in the picture, Xama Dupre has an aphmal that is not yet fully developed. She will celebrate her sixteenth birthday in 14 days, and her aphmal will continue to develop until that point."

Another large picture appeared, showing the aphmal in more detail.

"As we can all see, this is a not yet fully pronounced aphmal, since the side arms are missing."

Amar positioned a laser pointer at both ends of the cross. Darker colored skin could be seen very clearly. The members were satisfied up to this point, and Amar knew he had reached another goal. But he also saw something on the image he'd also noticed in the dream. There was another mark on the picture. When he changed to the next image, a rumble and murmur went through the hall. He could hear different interjections:
"That can't be," "That's not possible," "This is a fake."

Amar remained relaxed despite the unrest and continued speaking.

"Dear Meta, members of the council, I ask you to please examine this section here more closely." Amar positioned the laser pointer and encircled one area of the aphmal, but his hint wasn't necessary. Everyone in the room had already discovered what Amar wanted to show them. Amar practically gloated over his triumph, moving the laser pointer again in a circular motion around the aphmal. It was clear that the color of the skin in this area was different from the rest, like a round shadow around the aphmal.
The first members didn't believe what they saw, stood up from their chairs, and moved closer to the screen to reassure themselves their eyes did not deceive them. The first discussions started, and Amar was certain that the time had come. He had to act. He took the whistle and blew into it powerfully. Silence returned, and everyone looked at Amar.
"Based on the facts that there is a visible aphmal on the forehead of Xama Dupre which is still in an early phase. I Guardian Amar Wellberg, known to the members of the council, request to accept Xama Dupre as a full member of the circle of the Arverni. I will support her as a guardian and guide her through her aphormation."

Amar hardly finished his speech when the first hands went up. It took only a few seconds before all hands were clearly and emphatically signaled in agreement. Amar had achieved his goal.
"I am pleased to see that you are following my suggestion. Xama Dupre is hereby accepted into the circle of the Arverni, and enjoys all rights and privileges of the community."

Amar was pleased with the result – he had succeeded in saving Xama. He had failed once before and had promised himself it would never happen again. The council members hands slowly sunk – all but one hand at the lower end of the table that signaled someone was requesting permission to speak. Amar followed protocol and carried the pipe to Kantar, a burly critical man, one of the conservatives, entirely against the acceptance of aspirants without parents. Amar was unsure which direction the discussion would take; he was however sure it wasn't going to be good. Kanaar picked up the pipe, stood up, and blew into it.

"Thank you, Amar, without your help and prudence, the Arverni community would likely have lost one of its most important members."

Kanaar paused – all eyes fixed on him.

"Honored council, what we have witnessed is truly a incredible, short of a miracle." Kanaar paused for effect.

"We all know what this means and what our duty is."

The hall fell quiet, thick with suspense, everyone's attention directed at him. Kanaar relished the moment.

"It is our duty to accompany Xama, to protect and develop her skills. We all know that the aphmal she possesses is special. She is the chosen one. I therefore, request that Xama Dupre receive the protection of one or perhaps two Achilleans. The best Achilleans should be assigned immediately to guard her safety with their lives."

Kanaar raised his hand symbolically. He knew that the person who placed the request could not vote, but he also knew others would follow his signal. Amar radiated inside and outside – he had won Kanaar over to his side, a person who was normally nothing but critical and negative. The hands went up again, first a few, and then all of them. Kanaar's application received unanimous approval, and Amar nodded, thrilled at the outcome. Kanaar thanked everyone, picked up the whistle, and carried it back to Amar, patting him on the shoulder:

"Very well done, Amar."

Amar didn't know yet that Kanaar had discovered something else besides the circle around the aphmal – something, which drew

Kanaar's full attention and that, caused him to support fully Amar's application.

"First: Xama Dupre is from this point forward an Arverni, with all the rights and duties thereof.

Second: I will personally represent Xama Dupre as her guardian, educate, and provide her with the information she needs to know about our community. I will accompany her when she completes her apheid here before the council.

Third: Xama will be assigned two of the best Achilleans, ensuring her with the highest level of protection."

Amar passed the whistle to Meta – he blew three notes then began to speak.
"Dear members, today's meeting is closed, the results have been entered in accordance with protocol. As in every meeting, I will invite the members to dinner and share a celebratory glass of beer or wine.
Amar remained sitting, breathed deeply, and enjoyed watching the meeting room empty, every person who walked by congratulating him personally. But it wasn't the meeting or the result that touched him so deeply. What moved him most was being a part in determining the future of the Arverni. And not only that: he had remained true to himself and to his values. He also kept the promise of ensuring that aspirants without families would be accepted into the Arverni community, lessening the shame he carried.

He had done it. He, Amar Wellberg, had ensured the future of the Arverni and as promised, protected Xama Dupre.

Just as he was ready to stand, he felt a hand clap him on the shoulder. Amar turned and recognized Kanaar, his biggest supporter.
"Amar, I want to personally thank you for ensuring the future of the Arverni. We both know today's meeting was about much more than protecting Xama Dupre."

Amar was taken aback. He looked up at Kanaar and wondered what his true motives were.

"Please give me your personal assurance that nothing will happen to Xama until her development is completed, and she can follow her destiny. It is crucial she does not fall into the hands of the Brotherhood; under no circumstance."

"Yes, yes, but I would also very much like to meet Xama Dupre."

Amar stood up and looked directly into Kanaar's eyes. He had a feeling Kanaar had some strange things on his mind.

He wondered why Kanaar wanted to meet Xama. The busy defense guru – suddenly interested and willing to stoop just to get to know an aspirant? Very strange indeed.

"Yes, that's right Amar, you've offered your services for the education of Xama Dupre, and you have been named as her guardian, in itself a big responsibility.

As head of security, should it emerge that Xama Dupre develops certain characteristics – if she is an Identidem – then I will deal with her personally. You know what that means. Should she fall into the hands of our enemies, then you must guarantee with your own life that the Arverni will not be endangered. You will kill Xama Dupre before our enemies realize what she is."

A LETTER FOR SOPHIE

The next few days weren't easy. I felt like crap. I kept thinking of the cross, leading me to the same questions:

Why me? Why does everything have to be so hard?
Since I didn't have any answers – everything was just Kay-Ky. Yes, that's it, everything's just Kay-Ky.

As promised Amar had sent me a package containing a round silver make-up case with my name engraved on it. Actually, I didn't really like silver jewelry that much – the make-up case was a little too flashy for my taste, but seeing my name on it and knowing it was a gift from a friend I had only met in my dreams, well, that was something special and extremely Kay-Ky.
When I opened it, I found a note inside:
"Look at your aphmal as often as you can in the mirror; it will help you to accept your new self, and it will also give you positive energy. You'll see after a few weeks, you'll love it. As I told you in your dream, it's important that you tell no one about your origins or about your aphmal, and please don't forget to always camouflage it when you're around other people."
I read the letter a second time right away, and it gave me some hope. I started to like the make-up case better and better it's the most beautiful gift anyone has given me in the last weeks, or in the last months even. How much I wanted to thank Amar.
Well, why not?
I pulled my phone out of my pocket and sent him an email:

Hello Amar,
Was so happy to get your gift. I'm desperate to see you again.
Sophie Xama

I had written Sophie Xama at the end of the email instead of just Sophie. Following Amar's instructions, I looked in the little mirror and stared at my aphmal. At first, I felt like I had some kind of contagious disease that prevented me from coming into contact with other people. But then I felt the aphmal fighting the negative feelings and felt my insecurity slowly turning into waves of happiness. It felt amazing, and I enjoyed the positive emotions; I couldn't get enough of them. Feelings of pure joy like electric charges streaming upwards through my legs, seizing my whole body, setting each hair on end. It was simply double Kay-Ky – there's no better way to describe it.

I began to cover the aphmal with powder, but despite not being able to see it, I still felt a little anxious. Amar's reference to my impending danger hadn't helped; in fact he had frightened me. I felt like crying. I felt so alone. I stared at the email, but there was nothing there. Amar seemed to be away; a shame, I had so wanted to thank him, and I needed someone to talk to.

Why is life so unfair?
"Hello Sophie – how are your birthday preparations going?"
"Hi Karen – well, to be honest, Claire and I are a little behind schedule."
I made a mistake and asked Karen how she was doing. She stood there, motionless, staring at me with big eyes. She could no longer repress a quiet sob, and began to cry inconsolably. Fat tears ran down her beautiful face and thought: well, I've done it again.

What should I do?
Without hesitation, I hugged her tightly letting her know she wasn't alone.
"It's okay, cry it out. I know what you're feeling– everything hurts."
I knew how she felt only too well. As I held Karen, I stroked her forehead. Suddenly strange and unsettling visions came into my mind's view. I tried to comfort Karen, resting my hand on her head. All at once I saw a person open a medicine cabinet removing several pill bottles. Then began to dissolve huge amount of pills in a glass of water, the individual then proceeding to drink the entire glass. As they slowing turned around to face me – I immediately recognized the beautiful face belonging to Karen. Shocked, I released Karen, and the images disappeared in an instant. Confused at my sudden reaction Karen asked me:
"Everything okay, Sophie?"
"Karen – no, nothing's okay."
"What do you mean? What's up?"

"I just had a vision, in it you were swallowing a glass of murky water, into which you had dissolved a huge amount of pills. You intended to kill yourself. Tell me that what I saw isn't true."
Karen looked at me and started to cry again.

So it was all real, what I just saw – but how can that be?
"Karen – why would you want to end your life? Why?"
"How do you know that, Sophie? That's my secret."
I held Karen tight, pressing her close to me.
"Let me explain it to you this way: we've both gone through the same thing, and I know exactly how you feel, almost like a big sister would. I feel the same thing, but that's not important. What's important is that I'm here to help you. I too ask myself why life's been so unfair."
" … and, have you found any answers?" Karen sobbed.
Super – the exact same question I've been asking myself every day for the last few months.

I couldn't answer that.
"Yes – I've decided I don't want to throw away my life, although I 've thought about doing it lots of times, just like you."

Was that it? Was that the best answer, he reason why life was better than death?
"One reason I decided to keep living and keep fighting is for you. You, and lots of others like you who I want to help."

Kay-Ky, how did I come up with that? That's really pretty good.
"Karen, instead of throwing away your life, try to help others. That will help you feel fulfilled, and you'll give others hope."
"That sounds good, Sophie. But it's not that easy. Everyone I loved is gone, lost forever."
Karen was crying again.
"That's how you feel right now. In fact you have a purpose. There's someone out there who needs you."
Karen looked at me with teary eyes.
"You're a special person, Sophie, I knew that the first time I met you."
"What do you mean by that?"

"I can't say, exactly, everything just feels better when I'm near you. All negative emotions are easier to handle in your presence, I feel much better."

I placed my arm on Karen's head again and she was right – the horrifying images were gone – simply disappeared.

"I'm here for you Karen; whenever you're down, call me or come by my room and we'll talk."

Karen pressed herself against me, a warm "Thanks, Sophie" escaping her lips. But there was something more – there was a spark of hope spreading through her, I could sense she had a desire to live. As she made her way towards the door, I felt a warm sensation enveloping my entire being. Then as fast at had materialized, it vanished in an instant.

Something strange is happening to me!

I no longer needed to talk to someone; I was only occupied with the thought of what had just happened.

How is it possible that I could immediately know what Karen was planning? How could I bring Karen out of her emotional state so quickly?

More question, I needed to meet with Amar urgently.

Something strange is happening to me. I could feel a change within me. Back in my room, I made a beeline for the bathroom. I washed the foundation from my face and looked into the mirror. The girl looking back at me was a different person, a stable and happy one. For the first time in months, I felt fulfilled and confident.

It was crazy Kay-Ky. It wasn't Sophie I saw – it was Xama.

From the time I met Amar, I looked at my aphmal regularly. Looking at it every morning would bring an immediate sensation of having a new lease on life. I was on a natural high, as if I had swallowed a magic potion.

Claire as well as my schoolmates noticed a change in my attitude. The moment I felt down I would grab my little mirror and gaze at the aphmal and without fault it would perk me right up. Amar was right – I remember when he said that I would learn to love it. Even though at the time I had my doubts.

Exhausted, I laid down on my bed. My phone showed the time was only 7:58 p.m.; it didn't take long for my eyelids to droop. As I fell asleep, my subconscious began to churn up the caustic nightmare. It was the same every time:

I was in a bed, with a group of men moving around me in a circle, mumbling something I couldn't understand. They all had their left arms around each other, and their right hands touching the face of the man next to them. It was exactly the same dream, over and over, and it seemed to be happening more frequently. I woke up, terrified and dripping with sweat. But this time was different; it seemed even more real, even more tangible, and for a moment I almost believed I recognized one of the faces. I reached for my phone and looked at the time. I was surprised to see it read 8:01. That was impossible. If the time was correct, then the whole dream just took three minutes. But it felt like hours – hours filled with fear and uncertainty - impossible!

What's happening to me?
There it was again – a fear threatening to close off my throat. Soaked in sweat, I dragged myself to the bathroom and looked in the mirror. I took only a few seconds for the aphmal to work its magic - I could feel my spirits lifting, and it was like the nightmare was just blown away. My exhaustion, the fear, everything was gone, and I felt fantastic again.

Thanks, aphmal.
The hardest rule I had to obey was that of not being allowed to tell anyone about it. No one besides Amar, and he only appeared in my dreams. Every day I would write him an e-mail, but got no reply. I started to formulate excuses: "surely he has to work" – "maybe his email isn't working," anything to put my mind at rest.

I was alone again. I considered using the cross to discard the sadness I felt, but decided against it. My pain only increased when Claire told me she was head over heels in love with Alex. At times I envied her. Right now she's telling everybody within earshot about her newfound happiness. She's told Mike they just don't belong together. Sometimes life can be so simple, so pleasant. Unfortunately, I'm not like Claire. I worry way too much about how other people feel. That's just how I am.

Preparations for the joint birthday party were way behind schedule. As we discovered, the theme "Crypt of the Undead" wasn't exactly easy when it came to decorations. But since we'd already handed out the invitations, we didn't have any other choice but to find ways to turn the party room into a realistic catacomb. Alex knew of a store that sold cheap Halloween decorations and costumes for hire. Claire and Alex headed to the store while I made up an excuse and went to buy Claire's birthday present.

We all met again later in Heaven at around 6 that night. Claire was excited she had the perfect place to buy our party decorations.

"We absolutely have to go together; I already went ahead and got a few things."

Claire opened a sealed tube.

"This is a wall decoration – I've never even seen one of these before. Just wait, you're going to go nuts."

She handed Alex the end of the tube and unrolled the wall decoration a little ways. Kay-Ky, it really did look unbelievably real. There was an ancient-looking wall printed on the foil, and when you looked closer you could see it was all made of gravestones. It couldn't have been more perfect – exactly what you would think a catacomb would look like.

"This wall decoration is going to turn the whole party room into a crypt. What do you think?

"Crazy, Claire – that really looks Kay-Ky, and absolutely realistic."

"You'll have to thank Alex, it was his idea."

I wanted to shake his hand. Instead he pointed to his face signaling he would prefer a kiss. Feeling pressured not to spoil everybody's fun, I kissed him on the cheek, whispering my thanks.

We started setting up the party room with the rest of the decorations. The hall looked amazing, I wanted to buy more stuff - so we decided that we would go back the following day to get more stuff.

"Do you want to get an ice cream? Alex and I are taking a side trip to the coffee shop – do you want to come with?"

"Thanks for the invitation, but I'm tired, I need to lie down. Enjoy the evening and have fun."

I left them and went upstairs towards my room. As I walked by the reception desk, I saw Maria, the receptionist, talking with a mail carrier. I was trying to sneak by when Maria noticed me.

"Sophie, here's a coincidence. This man from the post office was just looking for you. He has something you need to sign for."

"Glad I caught you – I already tried twice to deliver this package, but I couldn't reach you. Didn't you get a message?"

I looked at Maria, and we both shrugged our shoulders.

"What is it? I didn't order anything."

The friendly courier held a slip out towards me.

"Sign here please."

Curious, I wrote my name on the slip and he promptly handed the package over to me. He handed me a receipt and pushed the package, which was sitting on the counter, in my direction. Maria looked on and said: "Sophie, it's probably a gift for your birthday." I thought about this for a second – it would be nice, wouldn't it? But then harsh reality hit me.

Who would be sending me a package? I didn't have anyone.

My friends don't send packages. Maria was wrong, but I didn't want to tell her that. The package was large. I had to satisfy my curiosity. But when I tried to read the sender, I realized the box was upside down. I tried to turn it over. My first attempts only lifted the heavy box slightly, and only by employing all my strength was I finally able to flip it over so I could read the address label. Maria was just as curious as I was. When I finally located and read the address, I was startled.

Maria looked at me in surprise.

"Is everything alright, Sophie? What's going on?"

I stood there, tears welling up in my eyes. It took several seconds for me to be able to look at Maria:

"Who would play this sick joke on me? Sending me a package with my dead father's name as the sender".

"What – the sender is your dead father?"

"Yes, well, his name is on there. Someone is probably playing a mean joke on me."

There was no other explanation.

Maria pushed her glasses up the bridge of her nose, not knowing what to say to me.

"Let me take this up to my room, there I'll be able to figure out who really sent it."

"You do that, Sophie – what nerve. Some people don't have any respect."

"Do you need help to carry it, should I call Karl?"

"Let me try it – if it's too heavy, I'll let you know."

Since I knew now how heavy the package was, I prepared myself accordingly and – I don't know how – Somehow I found the strength to lift it from the counter....

Maria looked at me in disbelief. "Are you sure you want to carry that heavy thing?"

I told her not to worry, and walked off with the package. When I arrived in my room, I placed the box on my desk and studied the label. It very clearly stated my father as the sender, but I discovered more information underneath the name in smaller letters.

"Kessler notary office."

So that was it? It was a package from the notary. I grabbed a pair of scissors and started removing the twine wrapped around the paper. Done and ready to open.

Am I really ready for what awaits me inside?

I started to unfold the flaps. The package was filled to the brim with crumpled paper. I noticed a white envelope with a red heart. It was obvious that the letter was for me, as I picked up with my trembling hand I recognized the writing on the front. It was Dad's; there was no mistaking it. He had the most beautiful handwriting, the way the curvy letters spelled out my name, brought tears to my eyes.

The words read "For my beloved Xama, from your Dad I simply couldn't hold the tears back.

But why, Dad? Why did you have to go?

I miss you terribly dad!

LEGACY

Memories and images of Dad flitted through my mind. Crying, I saw my compact mirror lying on the night-stand.

That's it the aphmal will help me!
Again, it only took a few seconds to collect myself. I could rely on the aphmal; it felt like a roller coaster ride – one minute I was down the next I was right back up again.

I went back to looking inside the box when a metal box revealed itself.

So, that was what made the package so heavy!
I took out the last wads of paper, smoothed them like all the others, and placed the papers on the stack. Now the metal chest stood alone in the middle of the package. A little tense stared at the hunk of metal; there was nothing unusual about it, just a block of metal. I breathed in deeply and gave myself a little push, then tried to grab the chest with my hands flat against the sides. I picked it up slightly, feeling its weight, then gripped even tighter to lift it out. Carefully, I placed the chest in front of the box on my desk. My eyes ran across the outside of the chest in the search for something uneven, something to indicate a way to open the box. But I didn't see anything: no hinges, no edge of a lid, nothing that gave any clue of how to open the metal chest. I looked at it again from the top, then from the side, but there was nothing there to help me to open the box.
Maybe it's backward?
With a little effort, I turned the metal chest 180 degrees. But it looked the same: nothing new. Nothing to show me how I was going to open this hunk of metal.

Maybe there isn't a way to open it?
The only thing I haven't examined yet is the bottom.
With another effort, I picked up the chest and tipped it backward along one side. I let it down carefully onto the desk in front of me. In the moment I set the chest down, I recognized the bottom did

look different from the rest. It didn't have the same metallic shine, and when I looked closer, I could see myself – the bottom of the chest was a mirror! I started to feel the edges of the mirror with my fingers – as if I could see more with my fingers than I could with my eyes. The mirror seemed to be a part of the metal chest; there were no edges that stood out, nothing to indicate that it was glued on or attached in some other way. The mirror just felt like part of the box. I vaguely remembered Chemistry class and the unit we had had on metals that could act as mirrors. The teacher had explained that these metals were treated with fine sandpaper and then polished to a high gloss with diamond paste. These metal plates were metallic on one side and looked like they had been ground smooth on the other, so they reflected all the light that struck them – like a mirror. Someone had done that to the bottom – or was it the lid?

But why? Why a mirror?
While I was asking myself why, I started to formulate a guess. When you set the box at the right angle, you could use one side as a mirror to look at yourself. I sat up a little so I could see myself in the mirror. I saw my body slowly come into view. First, my neck, and then a part of my face became visible. I changed positions, kneeled down in front of my desk and looked into the metal mirror once more. Now I saw my whole face, and my gaze was directed at one particular area of the mirror. I felt energy begin to flow through my body, and suddenly my mirror image transformed. I didn't believe my eyes; it looked as though my reflection was starting to glow – or rather, my aphmal was. A bright red light radiated from my aphmal, surrounding it in the mirror, making it appear much larger than it was. Shocked by what I saw, I moved in a flash, turning my head to the side. I tried to see if there was still a light shining in the reflection out of the corner of my eye, but there was nothing there. All I saw was a normal mirror. Very slowly, I turned my head back around, stretching it upwards so I couldn't see my aphmal in the mirror anymore. Expecting something to happen, I remained in this stretched position in front of the metal box. I slowly felt my head become heavier and my neck muscles begin to cramp, but nothing happened. The reflection showed part of my face, but no glowing, and no changes.

Did I just imagine everything?
Very slowly, I sank my head down. My neck muscles thanked me. My eyes were fixed on the upper edge of the mirror. There it was – the edge of my aphmal started to sink slowly down into the reflection from above. I held my breath and my position and looked at the part of the aphmal I could see in the mirror – but there was nothing there. Nothing special, nor could I feel any of the emotional relief that usually set in immediately when I saw it in a mirror. Surprised, I sank my head down even lower, and when the aphmal was almost fully visible in the mirror, I held my position again. I looked at the reflection, but everything was normal. I closed my eyes for a second and tried to notice any emotional changes in my body – but I felt nothing at all.

All right then, let's see what happens when the whole aphmal becomes visible.

I lowered my head down even more until the whole aphmal was visible in the mirror. In the same instant, I felt something happen. Without having to concentrate on it, the magical, emotional transformation began all on its own. But this time there was something else that held my full attention. Would the aphmal start glowing again? I could see the answer in the mirror. The aphmal did glow – first very slightly, then ever more intensely until the glow became a glare. I didn't move this time, trying to keep the position of the aphmal constant in the mirror. The glow became so intense I had to shut my eyes to protect from the glare, and was just about to turn my head away when I heard a loud metallic cracking sound. Immediately, I knew that something had happened to the metal chest. I opened my eyes and was surprised to see inside the box. The mirror had folded down in front of me, revealing the chest's secret. The box was open – my aphmal had allowed me to unlock it. Unable to avert my eyes from the inside of the metal chest, I still could not believe what had just happened. It wasn't a coincidence that my aphmal had helped me. Dad had planned all this carefully. I felt my pulse slowly returning to normal.

What is the chest hiding? What secrets does it hold?
Both curious and cautious, I took hold of the open side where the mirror had been. I was able to move it without much effort, although it seemed to remain fastened to the chest on one side. It looked like I would just be able to lock the chest up again whenever I wanted. I held the lid open with my right hand, reaching for a white envelope that looked like a letter with my left. I slowly pulled out my hand with the envelope and placed it in front of me on the floor. Now I could see notebooks, a stack of notebooks like the kind we use in school. I reached into the box again and counted each notebook as I lifted it out: one, two, three, four, five, six. There were six notebooks altogether; although I immediately noticed they weren't all the same size. Five notebooks were a normal paper size, but the bottom one was smaller, somewhat thicker, and looked like a bound diary with a strange lock affixed to the side. I carefully placed the notebooks on the floor, looking at the topmost one. It was labeled with almost perfect handwriting – obviously Dad's handiwork: "Book 1 – Ancestry and Succession." Curious, I read the titles of the other notebooks as well:

"Book 2 – Aphormation, Aphmal, Aphora, and Apheid"
"Book 3 – The Law of the Arverni"
"Book 4 – The Arverni Council"
"Book 5 – Enemies of the Arverni"

When I picked up the smaller notebook, I was surprised to see that it didn't have a descriptive title like the others. In place of a title, there was a warning message written in red, in capital letters:
"THIS BOOK MAY ONLY BE OPENED BY THE META! UNAUTHORIZED ACCESS IS DANGEROUS AND WILL DESTROY CONTENTS!!"

What does the warning mean?
Who, or what, is a Meta?
One thing was clear: the book contained different information than the other five, and it wasn't meant for me. I carefully laid it on the stack. Then I looked into the metal chest again and discovered another letter, packaged separately in a plastic sheath. The letter felt heavier, and when I took it out of the plastic and looked closer, I realized why: it had a kind of heavy seal on the back side

to keep the contents of the letter secret. It looked like a safety that would destroy the contents of the letter if someone attempted to open it by force. This letter didn't give any clues as to whom it was addressed to, but its seal made it look somehow very interesting. Suddenly, I was distracted by a thought.

What if Claire stormed into the room right now?

To save myself from having to explain the box, and to avoid awakening Claire's curiosity, I cleaned out the drawer in my bedside table and placed all the notebooks carefully inside. I wasn't totally satisfied with the result, but the hiding place would have to do as a first try. I grabbed the open side of the metal chest and closed it slowly. The moment the mirror touched the rest of the box, the side welded shut to form a smooth surface – it was impossible to tell the metal chest had ever been open. I picked the chest up, placed it in my closet, and threw some clothes on top of it.

All right, now it's almost invisible.
I couldn't believe Dad had written all of this for me in the last few months before he died.

But why do everything like this? Why didn't he just talk to me about it?
I needed to know so I picked up the letter and sat down on the sofa. I asked myself:
What does all this mean?
I knew this was going to be very difficult for me. My emotional skills were very limited. What did Dad always say? I had a sensitive soul. As I turned my eyes back to the letter with a red heart drawn on the front by Dad, my thoughts whirled wildly. I carefully opened the envelope, and a piece of pink stationery slipped out.

"My dear Xama, my sunshine!"
Why is he calling me Xama and not Sophie? He was the one always preaching caution, after all
"If you are reading this letter, it means that certain events have come to pass. Probably the most unfortunate thing is that I can-

not be with you. I realize that by sending you this package and the information it contains I am putting you under a great deal of stress and danger. But it's time for you to know the truth about your origins and the legacy of the Arverni. You have a right to discover who you really are and what your future holds. Things will happen Xama; and if you've found the letter, that means you've succeeded in opening the lock with the reflection of your aphmal. Congratulations; this was an important first step that will allow you to discover your origins and allow me to explain the "Arverni legacy". Before I give you any more details, let me unlock one initial secret. As you remember, I always told you never to use your middle name, "Xama," and to always call yourself Sophie. Xama is your mothers name and I chose it for you. Sophie is only a contrivance, meant to protect you. Others might have discovered a connection to your origins through your real name, Xama. Your mother and I wanted to avoid this, which is why we only called you Sophie Xama, and then later just Sophie. I know this all sounds very strange now, and changing your name when you're sixteen years old isn't easy. No matter what you decide – Xama is your Arverni name. It has a special meaning, but I'll tell you more about that later. From now on, I'll always call you Xama in my writings. Sophie is history, from the day of your aphormation, and Xama represents your new self. Xama is a beautiful Arverni name. You soon understand what I mean by your aphormation – your transformation."

Kay-Ky, Kay-Ky, I get a letter from my dead father, and the first thing he tells me is that the name I've been using ever since I could remember isn't my real name. Actually I didn't think Sophie was all that bad – okay, maybe just old fashioned. Xama sounds a little strange; it's a unique name, not exactly a common one. Xama, Xama, Xama Dupre. Saying it out loud.

"Much of what you will read in the notebooks will seem unbelievable at first, and hard to understand. All of this is normal and to be expected during this transformative process – your aphormation. The more you accept who you are, the easier your transformation will be. But what is the Arverni legacy? The "Arverni legacy" is what we call when both parents, and one parent, explains all the information about our origins, our rules, and the duties connected to them as well as the changes which will happen to their children, bringing them into the community of the

Arverni. If you are asking yourself why I didn't do all this personally instead of writing it down, I can only excuse myself by telling
you that there are strict rules on the subject. The Arverni legacy
may only be transmitted within a time frame of at most ten days
before the 16th birthday. The reason is that something very special happens on the 16th birthday. That day is the first day of
your aphormation – a word that basically means a process of
change. I often thought about how I should transmit your legacy
to you, but in the end it seemed only one option remained open
to me. I love you very much, your Dad."
I tried to use the soggy tissue to stop my crying, but I couldn't. I
just sat there, sniffing. It took several minutes for me to compose
myself again.

So that's it?
I guess I am different!
At the end of my emotional rope, I forced myself to keep reading.

"The next few weeks are very important for you, Xama, and your
life will change. The change is something very special – we
Arverni call it an aphormation. It is one of several terms in our
culture which has survived for thousands of years, and which we
still use today. Aphormation just means change, a very significant
one. Xama it's crucial you don't tell anyone about the notebooks
and be sure you keep them in a safe place. All information is
strictly for you, except for the specially marked book, which
should only be opened by the Meta. The reason is simple – the
contents of these notebooks place you in very great danger.
There are many who are burdened heavily by this information,
and would do anything to destroy the notebooks, as well as anyone who knows about them. Your aphormation will come and
with it many questions. This is why I have decided to explain
everything to you in writing.
I knew dad was always concerned with anything connected to
safety and security. He was, after all, a security officer in a large
company. Curious and bewildered, I shook my head and turned
the page.
"Xama, you are a person with a unique lineage; you are an Arverni. Your genetic heritage has placed something within you that is
becoming active now on your sixteenth birthday. Your mother

and I are both Arverni, which means you are a full-blooded Arverni as well. We were both carriers of the Arverni gene and have passed it on to you. Everyone with the gene descends from a peaceful Celtic tribe, the Arverni. They were first mentioned in history 6 centuries before the birth of Christ. The Arverni developed special powers and abilities thousands of years ago in order to survive. These are still transmitted from parent to child today. In this way, our special powers have survived through the millennia of the history of human development, all saved in just one gene. But it is this gene, and these abilities, which are making life ever more difficult for the Arverni today. Because we are different, over the course of history, we have been persecuted again and again, hunted, and killed. People didn't understand why some have special powers. They were afraid and reacted instinctively by pursuing us and fighting us. You'll find lots of information in the notebooks that describe the reasons for this in detail. Peoples' fear of our abilities has forced us to go into hiding from society and to practice our culture and assemble our community in secret – which we continue to do at present. The community, however, is shrinking. There are just over 1000 members left today; it would seem the Arverni are threatened with extinction. The reason for this is simple, more and more Arverni are trying to give their children normal lives, discouraging them from marrying within the community. Since the legacy is only passed down when both parents carry the gene, fewer and fewer children are been born with the gene. You, dear Xama, carry the gene. Your mother and I were both Arverni; we believed in the good of the community, lived within it, and fought for it until our dying days. A parent's most important duty is to prepare their children for the aphormation, the process of transformation you are about to undergo, and accompany them through it. Neither your mother nor I can be with you during this phase of your life, and we cannot help you through your aphormation. That's why I've written down everything important, which is forbidden according to the law of the Arverni. For your own protection, once you have read everything in these documents, you must destroy them. You must be very strong now, Xama. Promise me you will read the information carefully, over and over again until you have understood its meaning. Share this information with no one. Unless you have a son or daughter one day who also carries the gene, and then it will be your duty as well to transmit the Arverni legacy to your child. Xama, it is very important that you learn as much as possible about your origins and the Arverni culture; it pains me not to be able to talk about all of this personally with you. Please don't be sad now, this is your fate"

Sunk back to an emotional low point, I turned the letter over. I couldn't believe what I had just read. This was impossible – my parents were Arverni, and I was one too. If I didn't already have the aphmal on my forehead, I wouldn't believe any part of the Arverni story or the aphormation either – it's just too much – much too much. I wiped the tears from my eyes with a tissue, only to make room for new ones.

I miss you so much Dad, you just don't know how much!
Now, when I need you the most, you're not here with me anymore –
it's not fair – first Mom leaves me, and then you!
Why? Why???

My thoughts swirled without a clear goal. Endlessly deep sadness. A deep sorrow grabbed hold of me once again. I walked over to the bathroom and looked at my tear-stained face in the mirror. I saw the aphmal. This was the symbol of my legacy, and of my transformation. The mark of the Arverni. As I looked at it more closely, I realized that it was glowing.

I recognized something new. It practically radiated at me, and for the first time I didn't see it as a disfigurement – quite the opposite, it almost shined. It's tough to describe – the aphmal just looked it was crazy Kay-Ky.

The aphmals power was indescribable; I felt it refresh my whole body with positive energy, and a feeling of happiness overcame me, repressing my sadness. But there was more, and I waited for the tingling feeling. It slowly crept up my legs – even more intense this time than before. Staring at my aphmal, I held tight to the sink and enjoyed the emotional recharge. When it became too intense, I closed my eyes to slow the process. Two minutes later, I felt like a different person.

Crazy what the aphmal does to me. Was it really the aphmal? How does it work, anyway?

I washed the last traces of my emotions from my face with cold water. One last look in the mirror, and I was ready to take leave of someone I'd known for almost 16 years. It was like a farewell and a greeting at the same time. While I dried my face and looked at my reflection, I knew that the person I saw in the mirror wasn't Sophie anymore. There was a process underway, a process that was revealing my true self and my purpose. I left the bathroom and returned to the sofa where I continued reading my father's writings.

"I always hoped to be able to tell you everything, and not to have to keep any secrets from you. How often I imagined us sitting together on the sofa, me holding you in my arms and telling you the history of the Arverni step by step. That was my greatest wish. It was not to be; fate decreed I would not see your sixteenth birthday. No matter, my angel, you will grow up into an Arverni, and of that I am especially proud."

Dad's words weren't easy to read. But my aphmal helped me control my emotions.

"Xama, the changes will not be painful, at least not physically. When the aphmal, symbol of the Arverni, appears, your aphormation has begun. The aphmal will become visible on your forehead, exactly 21 days before your sixteenth birthday, and will develop further until the end of the aphormation. But the aphmals development doesn't just affect what you can see on the outside; it will also give you powers and open up possibilities for you to use them in a positive way for yourself. If my package has arrived on time, your aphmal should have appeared yesterday. I couldn't safely send you the information any earlier, since the aphmal box doesn't open without the aphmal. As you've discovered, the box stores its contents securely. It will only open with the correct aphmal. Please store the documents back in the box when you're not reading them and lock it. After you've read everything, you can also use the box to destroy the documents. More on this, at the end of the last notebook."

But I digress — back to the aphmal. It will appear in the middle of your forehead and you will perceive it first, as most aspirants do, as a very negative physical change. Believe me, it won't stay that way, and your emotional state will improve step by step until you see your aphmal as the most important symbol of your change and your new personality.

Crazy – Dad's describing exactly what I've been through in the last few days. Why am I so unlucky? Couldn't the package have arrived as planned? Dad was probably talking about an exterior and an interior transformation – is that what I'm experiencing now?

"The visual development of the aphmal will happen in steps. First, a vertical line will appear in the middle of your forehead, followed by a horizontal one crossing the vertical line in the up-per third so that the aphmal has a cross shape."
Dad made a sketch of it.

He continued to describe the cross and added another sketch to show what the completed aphmal would look like
"Xama, when you discover the aphmal for the first time, you may want to remove it, but no matter what you try, it is a part of you, and it cannot be removed. Many young Arverni feel disfigured at the beginning, but it will all get better in time. Please don't do anything to try and remove your aphmal. Believe me, you will come to treasure it, and there will come a time when you love and need it."

Breathing deeply, I realized my left leg was starting to fall asleep. I was tense. I sat on my bed and reflected on what I'd just read. It clicked with the information I'd gotten from Amar, with the little addendum that new technology had made it possible to look at the aphmal with glasses, which meant extra protection was nec-essary above and beyond the natural protection of the aphmal. I ignored my leg and started to read on again, curious.
"When the aphmal appears in the mirror 21 days before your sixteenth birthday, your real aphormation begins. The first thing you will realize is that your aphmal can help you in different sit-uations. There's no rule on how this works, since the aphmal is a part of your being. What's true for everyone, however, is that your aphmal will give you strength, invigorate you, and help keep you healthy. If you feel weak, if you're sad or unsure, or if you just don't feel good, then find a mirror and take a few minutes to look at your aphmal. I promise you, the results will be over-

whelming every time, and your emotional state will be positively influenced."

I already know that – the change in my emotional state is unbelievable, and it works in seconds.
"The aphmal is the first step of the aphormation. You will learn to use a special power. Something very unique, and something only you can do. A skill you will need order to fulfill your task but more on that later. Your new powers will far exceed human capabilities, extending beyond the boundaries of human thought and action. This is also one reason people are afraid of us. First, they are unable to explain these powers, and second, there are some Arverni who forsake their tasks, break the Codex. They used their abilities in an uncontrolled way, not to help others, but to shore up their own power. Just as with humans, there are some Arverni who have turned away. They can think of only one thing – demonstrating their power and using it as they please. They are still around today, and they are a great danger to our community.

Well, you are probably asking yourself why you need these new powers. It is because of your task – you will most likely hear a calling, task, or a purpose in the Codex and the documents. No matter what you call it, it all means the same thing. Apply your powers to do good and to meet the task you receive during your aphormation. Your purpose is very simple. My father explained it to me this way: help others, do good, fight evil, and try to fulfill your task. This is the foundation of the Arverni; this is our Codex, the reason we exist and the basis for our actions. Help others, do good, fulfill your task. There is so much I still have to tell you, that's why you'll find a table of contents with this letter as well. Make sure you read everything – everything about us, about you and the Arverni. I may repeat myself sometimes in the notebooks, but only because I believe the information is important, and you need to know it."
I realized how difficult it had become to read Dad's handwriting – it looked more and more shaky and was almost illegible. Something had happened.
Now I have to rest; my hand is shaking, and I can't write anymore. The Arverni legacy is my last gift to you, my dear Xama. My

early birthday present. Happy birthday! Stay strong, Xama – promise me that!

– Your loving Dad. –

I lay back, resting the letter on my chest and held it tenderly in both my hands.

So, I'm an Arverni, and the cross is an aphmal, which will keep developing. Besides puberty, hormones, and zits, now I have to go through an aphormation – why did the package only arrive today – after the aphormation had already started? Why didn't he talk to me about it before?

I stood up to look at the address label once more. Then I remembered the mail carrier saying he had already tried to deliver the package a couple of times.

Could that be the reason it was late? When I looked at the stamp, I saw the notary sent the package 10 days ago to me. I asked myself whether someone else knew about this package, or had maybe even opened it? On the bottom, I noticed that someone had tampered with the package by replacing its tape.

Or maybe Dad had to go get a new roll of packing tape, which is why it looks like it's two different colors. There's got to be a good explanation.

My thoughts kept returning to Amar, and I asked myself whether he already knew everything Dad was telling me. Wondering how he learned about his heritage. I couldn't stop thinking about Amar – he was the only connection between my new self and me. I stuck the letter back in the envelope and placed it in the top of the aphmal box. Slowly, I lifted the open mirror of the aphmal box, and when it was about to click into place, a resistance stopped the lid. I closed it with a slight pressure, and it seemed as if the mirror melted into one unit with the rest of the box when it touched. There was no visible edge, and no remaining hint that the box had been open in that spot. With a feeling of security, I placed the box underneath my bed, laid down on it, and, wondering what Amar might be doing right then, I went to sleep.

AMAR DREAMS

It feels as though I'm having an out of body experience seeing, myself walk along an unfamiliar street. I walk purposefully onward, following the throngs of people – my inner voice guides me in a particular direction, without knowing where I'm going. I notice how much wider the streets are here, and how much bigger the cars look. I also notice a large number of yellow cars – crossing the streets like a swarm of ants.

Left at the next crossing.
My instincts are telling me to go left, as though I were being pulled by a magnet. How can my subconscious follow a path when I don't know where I am and where I am going?

This is weird.
At the next crossing, I force myself to stand still and allow the throngs of people to pass by.
What now?
My eyes scan the surroundings. Where am I? Maybe looking for a street sign might help.
5th Avenue and W53th Street, where am I?
Before I knew it, it hit me like a slap in the face.
New York City, in the middle of Manhattan.

5th Avenue was the most famous shopping area in Manhattan – I'd read a lot about it and always wanted to visit. Carry on, Xama, keep going – left – not the next cross street, but the one after, on 55th street. That's where you need to go.

Driven by an inner restlessness, I walked faster, eyes forward. All at once, I seemed to recognize my surroundings, the display windows I walked past, the signs and the neon lights – everything looked familiar like I'd seen it all before, but where? I walked even quicker as though pulled by a magnet. *You're almost there, Xama, you're almost at your destination – there's the entrance.* As I walked by a row of garbage cans, I realized I had seen this place before - in one of my dreams
What's happening?

A neon sign displayed the name Aphobia Hotel.

The hotel is aptly named. I walk in, and go straight to the reception desk.
As the friendly, smiling young man looks at me without saying a word – I start to feel a little awkward. A spark of uncertainty rises. Suddenly he breaks into a big grin and says the hotel is honored that I am staying for the night. He is especially happy I am visiting during his shift, and he has a request for me and asks me whether I wouldn't mind him taking a selfie of the two of us. He intends to show it off to his friends, which will no doubt be very impressed as well as super jealous. He mentioned his friends would never believe what has happened. Dumbfounded at this simple request, so I can. 'T say no. Without wasting any minute, in case I might change my mind he comes over and puts his arm on my shoulder sticks his arm out and starts to click away. With glistening eyes and a shy thank you, he hands over an envelope with the instructions on it:
"Your suite is on the 24th floor, with access to the rooftop patio and a view of Times Square. I wish you a pleasant stay, and thank you again for the picture."

He must have mistaken me for someone else.

What am I doing here?

Once I get to the floor as per the instructions, I start looking out for room numbers.
Right – that sign says 2400 - 2449
Following the sign, I walked to room 2409, and stood in front checking it was the right number. Once inside I noticed how big it was but had the standard layout equipped with TV, coffee table and so on. As I was about to place my things on the floor a door suddenly opened taking me by complete surprise. It was Amar - his striking, flawless tanned face and dark hair tied back in a ponytail. He was as handsome as I remembered. He looked elegant and sleek wearing a white business shirt. Even the sun shining through the windows was smiling down on him admiring his good looks

"Hello, Xama, lovely to see you again – I've been expecting you."

Mouth open, I stared at Amar. I couldn't believe it.

It was him, I couldn't believe it, was I dreaming again?

"Amar, you're here, how…?"
Amar placed his finger on his lips, before speaking.
The reason we are both here is because you've followed an invitation to appear in my dream. This means you are able to communicate via dreams. Just like me. I felt it and this test proved it that I am correct! There are only a few Arverni who have this power, but yours is particularly advanced since you are still in the early stages of the Aphormation. "You are truly special, Xama."

"I don't understand, I was just lying on my sofa, and now I'm in Manhattan in a four-star hotel, with you. Why"

"Well, because I dreamt about you and want you to come here and you followed. As complicated as it sounds as easy it is. This is where I live and work. You're in my dream but we are still in different locations, except the dream is taking place in the Aphobia in Manhattan."

"What are you doing here?"

"Well, let's just say I'm the one who makes sure everything's on the up and up in the hotel. At least, that's one of my tasks"
"Wow, you're in charge of security for the entire hotel?"
"Yes and I do a couple of more things."
"I don't believe it you're not joking?"
"No joke, Xama."
"What else do you do?"
"I told you, didn't I, that every Arverni is given a task during the aphormation."
"Yes, you did, I remember – I've been wondering what my task will be."
"You'll find out when it is time. Your powers will guide you; that's how it's been for everyone, and was for me.

"Don't torture me any longer – what is your Arverni task?"
"Let's just say I'm responsible for communication among the Arverni. Since we're spread out over the whole world, it's not that easy to meet. We avoid meeting in person whenever we can, for safety reasons. Occasionally a few of us do meet from time to time, usually in a hotel."
"Don't you get problems when you use the hotel for an Arverni meeting?"
"Problems?"
"Yeah, well, you must have a boss – if he finds out you're holding Arverni meetings instead of taking care of the guests, you could get into trouble."
Amar laughed.

There they are again, those interesting little lines at the corners of his mouth. He looks amazing. Most of the better-looking guys I've met all turned into assholes. Granted, Amar is much older, so maybe he's past all that. But what is he really like? Could this be just a facade?

Amar walked towards the sofa and opened the minibar.
"Xama, sit down, please. What do you want to drink? We have ice tea, Coca Cola, and Diet Coke."
"A Diet Coke, please."
He poured the contents of the cans into the glasses and set them down on the table.
"To answer your question: this and hundreds of other hotels, all belong to the Arverni. The Arverni are filthy rich, and these riches belong to all members of the community." "You're kidding me, right?"
"No, the Arverni own all of this and much, much more. I'm in charge of a small part – the Aphobia hotels – and other members are responsible for other areas of the business. Do you have any other questions? There are surely some other things we should talk about."
"You're right – no further questions, your honor."
"Could I see your aphmal again?"
I looked at him, surprised. Amar must have noticed:
"I want to see how it's developed since the last time."

Relieved by his explanation, I nodded, still a little unsure. Amar reached into his shirt pocket, pulled out his aphmal glasses, and looked at me through them. He came closer – I felt self conscious, and blushed like a schoolgirl.

I couldn't help it. I was so embarrassed.

Amar pulled back – did he sense my awkwardness?

"Sorry, I cornered you their Xama; but I just want to be sure."

I sat there, shocked. Everything felt so heavy all of a sudden.

"Making sure I'm not a counterfeit? Sorry, Amar, I still haven't dealt with everything I've been through in the past few days.

There's a lot I still don't understand, but you don't seriously think I would do this to myself voluntarily, do you?

"I think you've misunderstood me. For now, just try to understand that we Arverni have enemies, and they would do anything to infiltrate us, expose us, and kill us. Let's just leave it at that for the moment.

Can I just take one more look at your aphmal?"

Amar came a step closer as I nodded and looked at my forehead again.

"What is it?"

"What do you mean?"

"Is the aphmal still there? Did it change?

Amar continued to stare at my forehead.

"Everything's fine, nothing new, and no reason to be worried."

Amar gave me a weary look. Something had changed. I had the feeling he was hiding something from me.

THE APHMAL

I tried to find an escape from the tense situation by asking the first question that came into my mind. "The aphmal glasses you have – they're much more than just sunglasses, right?"

Before I finished the question, I realized how stupid it sounded. Amar nodded, took hold of the glasses, and handed them to me.

"Absolutely right. What you are holding now required several years of development and cost a small fortune. One can't tell they are any different from normal sunglasses. Aphmal glasses are designed to allow an Averni to view an aphmal through a mirror. What's more, the glasses also reveal various chemical substances that attempt to reproduce the effect created by an aphmal."

While Amar went into more detail about the basics of the glasses, I was trying them out when Amar's' aphmal came into view. It was incredibly beautiful - I took a closer look at one area of his aphmal – the lower right corner.

"What do you see? Describe it to me."

"I see a clear and distinct aphmal. It looks much bigger than mine, and makes a good-looking face even better-looking."

Amar smiled. I focused in the lower right corner.

"What are you examining Xama?"

"I wanted to see if your experiment had left a scar or a, blemish but its perfectly smooth as if you'd never burned your forehead."

"Yes. Isn't it astounding? But there's much more you need to know. The aphmal has other characteristics – you've probably already discovered some of them yourself." Amar picked up the ice tea and the Diet Coke, handing me the Coke.

"To you, to your future, and to the Arverni."

As I drank, he set down his glass and kept talking.

I was still playing with the glasses, first looking at Amar's aphmal and without him noticing – at his eyes. He had beautiful eyes. Any girl would have loved to have his long eyelashes and dark contours. *Like a painting.*

"Let's look at the aphmal a little closer today, and talk about its most important characteristics." I set down my glass and allowed him to continue talking

"When was the last time you looked at your aphmal?"

"This morning, just like every other morning."

"Good. And what did you notice?

"Might be insignificant but the A is becoming more noticeable."

"And how did you feel when you saw it?

BINGO – he was right; how could I forget?

"You're right. Every time I look at it, my emotional state changes, and I feel much better""

"Yes, exactly. The aphmal ensures that both your body and emotions are in a good state.

Your aphmal generates happy hormones

"Did it make a difference the longer you looked at it?"

"Yes, after a while it did – my legs start to tingle and then the feeling spreads throughout my body, it's an astonishing beautiful sensation."

"Exactly, then you've already discovered what is called aphmalisation – it's the point when the aphmal reaches its full power The aphmalisation is different from Arverni to Arverni and can change how you feel it. Sometimes it only takes two minutes, sometimes five or more until it starts, this unbelievable feeling. Your body receives new energy, more than you need and enough to perform superhuman feats. I can guarantee, Xama, you will learn to love your aphmalisation. You should try it out!"

"How often can I do it? I mean are there any side effects?"

Amar smiled, "You're cute, Xama. There are no side effects, and there is no limit. The aphmal will regulate itself, however, which means you can't start an aphmalisation right after another one. Try it out yourself, test it and explore the power. As I said, the aphmal will always protect you – you can't hurt yourself with an aphmalisation. There's no aphmal overdose if that's what you mean?"

"Yes, that's what I meant." "Did you notice anything else? Maybe you were getting a cold some morning, or starting to feel sick?" "Not that I remember."

"Not since you've had your aphmal correct? You'll be happy to know that you'll never be sick again. Not as long as you look at your aphmal regularly. I haven't been sick since my 16th birthday – no colds, no coughs, no allergies, no headaches, nothing at all. But there is more. If and when you hurt yourself, your aphmal will speedily heal the wound. Do you remember my video? Well, that was just the beginning of all the powers of the aphmal I have researched."

"Does that mean that you did more experiments on yourself?" I asked, knowing I knew the answer already.

"Back then, no one was there to tell me what was happening to me, so I had to experience it for myself. I had to unlock the secrets of the aphmal in my own way."

"What did you find out?"

"Well, it heals wounds such as burns, cuts, stabs, etc." But it can also reattach severed limbs."

I could tell he was been serious by the way his face muscles were contracting.

"Tell me you didn't do that to yourself."

He lowered his gaze, then looked up at me and showed me his pinky.

"Everything just like new again, as if it never happened."

Just the thought made me nauseous. I had to concentrate hard to fight the feeling.

"I was starved for information and tried different experiments. I wanted to find out what its limits were, and I was willing to take any means necessary to do that. Any means – no limits."

"But you didn't?"

Amar looked me in the eyes, and lowered his head, after a long pause he nodded looking ashamed of himself. I swallowed several times, but I couldn't shake the feeling.

"Have you ever heard the terms 'hara-kiri' or 'seppuku?'"

I shook my head.

"It's an act that Japanese samurais do once they have lost their honor. They kill themselves by inserting a long sword into their stomachs and cutting the aorta. A fast, deadly act. I find it most fascinating, and studied various methods and techniques in detail." As Amar continued speaking, I picked up my Coke and tried to get rid of the lump caught in my throat, without success.

"Fascinated by my aphmal, I finally got myself a sword so I could carry out a hara-kiri. I placed the tip of the sword against my body, I then pressed the handle against the wall, all that stood between life and death.

All I had to do was push my whole body weight against the sword – nothing more an easy act.

Time stood still waiting for me to move."

That was too much for me. I stood up and felt an urgent need to find a bathroom. I just felt sick – like I wanted to throw up. Without looking at Amar, I stood up and .ran. I came back a few minutes later. Thanks to my aphmal, I felt super again

"Sorry, Amar, but that was just too much for me."

"I'm sorry – I got caught up by the memory of it. I can see that your aphmal did a wonderful job! Anyway, I collapsed, crying. I didn't have the courage to carry out the final step." Eyes open wide, I looked at Amar.

"You didn't do it? I smiled at him. That's true courage, not all that samurai shit and killing yourself, but appreciating life – that's true greatness, Amar. You can be proud of yourself for not throwing your life away."

I didn't believe what I heard me saying, something happened to me for sure.

"You're right - even the aphmal wouldn't have protected me with that type of injury – I would certainly have died. What the aphmal triggers hasn't been fully medically researched. One of our top doctors has analyzed the processes that take place in the body and determined based on some series of tests that it makes all bodily functions work differently. Blood values responsible for regeneration and healing are 1,000 times higher, as well as hormones and chemical messengers. Cell division and regeneration are accelerated, but even all this has its limits. I'm also a firm believer that it protects people from ending their own lives. It is your bodyguard."

I looked him in the eyes and ask myself.

How lonely and helpless must he have felt to go that far?

"Thank you, Amar, for the enlightenment, even if the thought still freaks me out. You said that it keeps us healthy; can you explain something to me?

"I'll try."

THE FINITUM

"One year ago, my father died. He became so ill no one could help him. The doctors didn't even know exactly what was making him sick; they were just clueless. Back then I asked myself how this could happen, but now I understand it even less. He was an Arverni, and his aphmal had the power to protect him from illness, so why did he get sick and die from it?

Amar thought a long time before answering.

"Can I ask you how old your father was when he got sick?"
"46," I whispered to him.

"I would've preferred giving you this information later, but your question is associated with it. Just as your aphmal appears shortly before your sixteenth birthday, it will disappear again on your thirtieth birthday. And not just the aphmal – your powers will also dissolve into nothing. This happens to every Arverni, and it happened to your father as well. From his 30th birthday onward, he no longer had any protection. His body couldn't heal any more."

"Does that mean that everything I'm going through now is only temporary? Everything will be just as it should be after my 30th birthday – no aphmal, and no powers, just like a normal person?"

"Well, not exactly. There is one other thing that differentiates us from normal people. We do lose the aphmal and our powers, but pay a high price for having had it."

"I don't understand."
"Let me explain – the 30th year of life begins the Finitum. This is what we call the final years for an Arverni."
"What? The final years begin at 30? What is that about?"
"Calm down and let me finish. On the day your aphmal disappears, your body will age quicker, faster than a normal person. Arverni have studied this phenomenon since we have been in existence. We have attempted to analyze what causes it and how

we can stop the aging process, but our doctors and specialists haven't found a cure for it – and some of the best doctors in the world are Arverni. If you compare our aging process to that of a normal human, you can use the following formula to get a good comparison: Arverni years between 30 and 40 count double, the years from 40 to 50 count triple, and after that quadruple."

My mathematical brain was already dividing my father's age into the various stages – his 46 years, then, corresponded to an age of 68 human years.

"You have probably already calculated that your father died at the age of 68. Massive immune reactions and disorders aren't uncommon among the Arverni and part of the Finitum. I'm sorry you had to go through it like this."

You couldn't do anything about it, Amar – the doctors called it an immune reaction, you're right."

Suddenly, I realized I wasn't as strong as I thought. Tears welled up in my eyes and ran down my cheeks. It was less the idea that my life would end at 30 but the reason why Dad went so soon.

Then Amar isn't that far away from it either. God dammit – I'm only now realizing what all this means.

"Amar?"

I looked at him and felt something else that was tough to explain. Was it pity?

"Yes, Xama."

"How old are you?"

As soon as the question was out, I felt annoyed at my own directness.

"I thought you might ask that question. I'm in the middle of my 26th year. So I still have lots of time – I can still make myself useful for four more years, and then I'll go into retirement."

He laughed so heartily that I had to laugh with him – despite the tears in my eyes. I can't remember a time where I laughed and cried at the same time.

Amar succeeded – He's simply wonderful.

"I'd like to know more about you."

"Yes, of course, Xama, what do you want to know?"

"How did you receive the legacy? If I understand correctly, it's parents job to pass on the legacy."

"Yes, you're right, it's the job of the parents or of a guardian appointed by them to transmit the legacy to their children before their 16th birthdays, 21 days before, to be exact. You're probably asking yourself why 21 days. This is when the aphormation begins. I had a similar experience like yours. All I know is that my parents died in a plane crash in South Africa. All those on board died except for one - a three-year-old boy."

Amar looked at me, and a syllable forced its way through my lips.

"You were the survivor?"

"That's right."

After child services had taken me in, I was fostered by a wealthy couple. They couldn't have children of their own, but they still wanted a family. Unfortunately, it turned out they didn't have any time for me, and only thought about their business. After a while, their marriage broke down, and they separated. Neither one wanted or could take care of me. I didn't fit into their lifestyle. They wanted to return me to child services, like unwanted goods – an adoption with a money back guarantee."

"I didn't even know that was possible?"

"It wasn't really possible – or simple, in the end I had no choice but to go back to the orphanage. After that, I was tough to place, which I definitely had a part in. From that day forward I didn't want a family anymore. As I became older, I got more information from the administration about my parents and my origins. There was a letter my parents had written to me when I was born. A so-called "First Letter," in case I was to become an orphan they had appointed someone who would take me in. They thought of every worst-case scenario. It just didn't work."

"Why? Did you have a contact person?"

"I did, but it turned out that this contact, as well as all their other friends and acquaintances, had been on the same plane. Eventually, I found out that the 25 passengers all had one thing in common. They were members of an organization that controlled a network of different companies; they were all Arverni. When I found out that all of them had received the same invitation, I did some digging. Since my parents, their closest friends, and acquaintances all died at the same time on this day, there was no one left to tell me about my legacy. No one even knew I was still alive."

Amar stood up and walked through the room; I could tell the story still weighed on him.
"To be honest, I never received the Arverni legacy. Everything I know, I taught myself over the years. That, Xama, was the short version of my story. I constantly thought about leaving this life."
Amar lowered his head and looked at the floor;
I didn't know whether it was shame or self-contempt that forced him to break off eye contact. He struggled to talk found it difficult to keep talking, and I wondered how I could help him.
"Let it out, Amar, you can tell me the truth. I know how you feel."
In a subdued voice, he continued talking.
"Xama?"
He grabbed his glass and tried to control the pressure that affected him and his voice.
"I'm sorry."
"It's alright."
I felt bad for Amar, so I put my hand on his. Amar's hand was warm and pleasant soft; I felt the hair on the back of his hand and his long slim fingers. A tingling seemed to radiate from them, followed by a weak electrical pulse. He looked at me, and for the first time I saw the blue tint of his eyes; a dark blue brilliance, intensified by his smile. It was a beautiful feeling; I pulled my hand back slowly.

"Thank you, Xama; I found life incredibly hard back then, and when this cross appeared on my forehead, I was devastated! I wanted to die, that's how bad it was – I was broken, beyond repair."

Amar looked at me, I could see he was struggling to hold back the tears. I stood up and pulled several tissues out of the dispenser on the shelf, then sat next to him and passed them to him, wordlessly.

"Thank you!"

"Now you know my story, and you know how I received the Arverni legacy – in my own way."

"I am so happy you didn't go through with the final step."

"Every time I remember it, I feel sick that I was ready to throw away my life. That's why I help other people who are in a similar situation. This is my way of giving back a little of what the Arverni legacy did for me – this is my Aphora."

I looked into his eyes and saw that this confession wasn't easy for him. During Amar's explanation I thought I sensed a sweet taste in my mouth as if I had eaten a spoonful of pure honey. It wasn't the first time my sense of taste seemed to be playing tricks on me, but I had never tasted it as intensely as I did now.

Surely, this has something to do with my aphormation.

Baffled by the unexplained sweet taste of which I had no idea where it came from, I had almost forgotten to tell Amar about the package from my father.

"Oh yes - Amar, before my father died, he sent me a package containing the Arverni legacy."

Amar jerked up and looked at me, his eyes wide open.
"What did you just say – that can't be!"

WHO WAS DAD?

A mar looked at me in surprise, as if I'd just said something totally absurd. At the moment his eyes met mine, I realized they had lost their blue shine.

"Your father sent you what? Did I understand you correctly? He sent a package of information about the Arverni legacy?" There was a hint of curiosity, as well as something that I found unsettling.

"Yes, that's right, I haven't read it all as yet — it will probably take me a few days, or weeks maybe."

Amar became nervous and tense. At the same time, the sweet honey taste in my mouth disappeared all at once and my tongue started to burn like fire. Something wasn't right. Did it have something to do with how Amar was feeling? My taste buds were changing without me drinking or eating anything.
.Something scared me, and I couldn't tell whether it was my change, or Amar's, or both.

Amar tried to control his excitement.

"You're lucky. Your father wrote you something about the Arverni community. The only problem with that is that all Arverni have sworn an oath — it seems your Dad decided to break this oath to give your legacy to you in writing."

His statement confused me. Dad did something against the rules of the Arverni? I couldn't believe it — not my Dad.

"What kind of an oath is it?"

"All Arverni take a vow during aphormation. The vow includes diverting every possible danger from the community and documenting absolutely nothing about our origins. It seems your father found no other way out than to break his oath to give your legacy to you. You should tell me everything new you've learned next time we meet. You know I'm looking for any information I can find on the Arverni — I'm still learning too, and I need to know what kind of danger these documents pose for all of us — and especially for you."

Damn you, you dumb cow, why did you have to bring it up? Why didn't you just keep the secret to yourself? Didn't Dad say to tell absolutely no one about it!

But what danger was there, really? Amar was in charge of communication. The letters and the content my father left behind for me weren't anything new to him. Why all the fuss?

Calm down, Xama, Amar is honest and he wants to help you.

"What's up, Xama?"
"Oh, nothing, I was just thinking."
"About the written legacy?
Don't worry your head about it. I'm just shocked since it's not normally allowed. I overreacted. It's understandable that your father wanted to transmit the legacy to you. Even if it isn't exactly protocol. Your father must have been in a terrible personal turmoil. That must mean a lot to you, right?"
Amar was right – I hadn't thought of it like that. Dad, who was so faithful, who did everything possible to follow his convictions, had set aside his principles to help me through my change. He had broken Arverni rules to protect me.
"Your father is a well-known, highly respected Arverni. In the Arverni community, however, he has another name."
"What do you mean another name? "
"Andru Resnak. Andru – that's how we always addressed him. I can only explain his name change as a way to protect you. Your father knew how important security was. I can imagine he didn't want to connect you to himself or to the Arverni. There are some things I can tell you about how the Arverni saw your father. I assume that you will also find all of this in his writings. Let me tell you more about the Arverni and about me."

The Aphobia is one of many hotels in a hotel chain called Awood LLC. There are twelve Aphobia hotels in all, and each one has a different theme and different decor, but they are all in selected metropolises all over the world. One, in fact, is in Frankfurt, not very far away from you. It's an important hotel, since we meet there often in the middle of Europe. It's a central airline hub."

I looked at Amar somewhat obtusely. "We?" "I mean: we Arverni. Now, I told you before that I'm in charge of the hotel. To be exact, I'm actually responsible for all the Aphobia hotels. There's a General Manager in each hotel, and they all report to me. Now, that you're one of us, part of this hotel also belongs to you. We Arverni own a total of over 350 companies, some of which we manage ourselves, and some of which are managed by others working for us."

"Amar – what does this have to do with my dad, and with his name?"
"Give me a couple of minutes; it will all become clear when you have a little more background. Remember when I said that every Arverni receives an Aphora during their aphormation, a kind of life's task?
My Aphora is communication – I'm in charge of making sure that we Arverni are able to communicate securely. Your father's Aphora was security. Security is a very large branch subdivided into different sectors. Kanaar is the top Senior Security Officer and a member of the council, and your father reported directly to him. He was well known to the council, which is why I knew him as well. Your father had a very special task, and it made him popular. He and his team guaranteed security for all the activities, events, and meetings of the council. Everything he did was done conscientiously and with conviction."

"You've described that very well; yes, that's what Dad was like – security was his thing, and he was conscientious in everything he did."

His eyes fell on Dad's picture.
"Your father discovered not too long ago that there was an external danger posed by former Arverni who had been shut out by the community, and who wanted revenge. He considered the threat very serious, so he informed the council about it. The council tasked your father with collecting all the necessary information to inform the council about the status of security at the next meeting. They wanted to know what the risks were, and his mitigations. Unfortunately, I wasn't there, but I later found out that the threat level was deemed an A, the highest possible. This

had apparently never happened before. Your father was ordered to do anything necessary to eliminate this threat – he was given a carte blanche. This is very rare and actually difficult to reconcile with the peaceful communal structure of the Arverni."

"What is a carte blanche?
"A carte blanche is an absolution from the council; it gave your father the right to do anything necessary to avert the danger. There were no laws and no regulations. Absolutely nothing to reign in his methods."

"I don't understand how a carte blanche could help him avert danger."
"Well, let's say he decided to eliminate simply the group threatening the Arverni. The carte blanche would mean nothing would happen to him. He would be justified in doing it."
"You mean, he could have just killed the people? Never – Dad would never have done that. He wasn't like that. Not my dad?"

"Calm down, Xama, it was just an example. I don't know what your father actually did, but the danger was averted, and the group disappeared. All of them, except for the leader, were put out of action. The leader, a Dr. Sherman, went underground and wasn't seen again for some time. Shortly thereafter, your father became gravely ill, and the number of others suffering from immune deficiencies began to increase rapidly. It seemed as though the spread of the autoimmune deficiency had something to do with your father's action against Dr. Sherman. Your father withdrew because of his health. He resigned his office and asked the council to relieve him from his role and allow him to leave the Arverni community honorably. Everyone was surprised and wanted to understand what pushed your father to make this decision; no one believed it was just his health. The council had no other choice, so they agreed to your father's demands, releasing him honorably from the Arverni community. After that, he disappeared, and as we now know, he went to Germany with you so you could have a new future under a different name. You know the rest better than I do."
All at once, the doorbell rang, and someone called from outside: "Room Service." Amar stood up and opened the door. A waiter

who looked like a penguin stood in the doorway and whispered something to Amar.

What's such a big secret that I can't hear it?
Amar nodded and shoved a tip towards the waiter.
The waiter handed over a box. He looked so much like a penguin, I couldn't help but smirk. He purposefully closed the door, and just as quick as he had come, he disappeared again. My curiosity was insatiable; I tried to think of just the right question to ask.

A DREAMY EVENING

Amar was quicker, satisfying my curiosity and surprising me once again.

"I've just learned that dinner is served. Our hotel is known for its first-class restaurant, and I've asked the head chef to whip something up for us. I'm excited to see what awaits us myself. Has anyone ever invited you to dinner in a dream before?"

A smile flitted across my face; I had completely forgotten we were both just dreaming.

"To be honest, I can't remember."

Shaking my head, I waited to find out what would happen next.

"Let's go up I promise you, you won't be disappointed."

He took me by the hand and pointed towards the door.

"Just a second," I said.

"I need to get my purse."

Can I really trust him 100%?
What's really behind the door?

Before I knew it, we were walking upstairs towards a door with an exit sign above it – as he opened it, I was hit the night sky – we were on a rooftop patio. Now I remembered what the porter said to me at the reception desk:

Your suite is on the 24th floor, with access to the rooftop patio and a view of Times Square.

What stood before me was mesmerizing. The sheer size of the rooftop was impressive enough. There was so much I had to take in. On one side of the rooftop stood a massive water feature, surrounded by palm trees. A sparkling pool was encircled by expensive outdoor furniture. The patio exuded an air of pure luxury. The pool was surrounded by a huge number of sofas; chairs and loungers arranged into little lounges. It seemed as if each area had its own pavilion, roofed in palm leaves. Amar could see I was in awe.

"He went ahead and gave an introduction to the place and its purpose.

"This is called the Palm Garden. It's a good place to relax after a stressful day and wind down from the chaos of the city."

He walked towards the pool and I followed him, astounded.

"Here, you'll see one of more than 25 pavilions; each has its own theme. Every one of them has something in common. Can you spot it?"

Looking at the pavilions, I noticed how beautiful and elegant they all were. The chairs were all made of rattan and covered with white leather cushions, arranged around a large round table with a glass top. There were lounges to the right and left, and in the corner was a covered swing inviting you to linger.

It was all simply perfect.
"It's all simply perfect, Amar."

What's he getting at?
"You see each pavilion has its own private sphere. It's impossible to see inside the pavilions from the outside, although you can look out from within."

At first, I didn't understand what he was getting, but when he pointed at the nearest pavilion; I understood what he meant by private sphere.

"Plants and palm trees border the pavilions, and they have a glass border that is only transparent in one direction. But that's just more technical stuff you probably aren't interested in. Look here."

On the right, I could see boulders and a wide waterfall splashing into the pool with a refreshing sound. It was so inviting I had a strong urge to dive in and enjoy the refreshing water. Amar pointed to a lounge, where beach towels, flip-flops, and robes were neatly arranged.

"I've reserved this one for us; you'll find a few different swim-suits there. Since I didn't know your size, I had the staff bring up several of them.

After dinner, we can use the pool too."

The thought was thrilling and enticing, and so much more – There was no one here, but Amar and I. We were alone.

"Amar, why aren't there any guests here?"

"Well, it's simple, I reserved the whole pool for us. Have you forgotten we're in my dream? I thought it would be best for us to remain undisturbed.

I had completely forgotten. It's all just a dream.

"Sorry, of course it's just a dream, I had totally forgotten we're just dreaming. Everything it's just that it all feels so real."

"I know, Xama Enjoy it while you can."

Amar walked on, and I followed him, wondering whether I had offended him.

At the end of the patio was the restaurant with an unbelievable, once-in-a-lifetime view down onto Times Square. People streamed in every direction, like ants alarmed and fleeing their nest. Lit signs constantly changed as though animated, bathing the square in a play of lights. Directly below, I could see the new Samsung phone on a massive display. I kept following him, trying to process everything I was seeing. In passing, I saw what looked like a screen used to project videos on. Amar saw me looking at it, and explained what the pavilion was used for.

"That's a video wall – we often play sporting events here, but to be honest, the wall is mainly used by the Arverni."

"Do you talk over Skype or something?"

"Something likes that, except that we use our own technology which is much safer than Skype. It's the same principle, except that we can link up to 20 locations all over the world simultaneously. It's called a multichannel video system. The technology is so advanced it allows us meet in a virtual space like sitting all in the same room. Although the technology is great, it still doesn't beat a dream. We use the video when we can't generate the right conditions for a dream."

Once we reached the restaurant I was taken back by it's familiar architecture it resembled the buildings I had seen a few years before on a vacation to Greece with Dad. The entrance was a white arch. The roof tiles over the entryway made from terracotta giving it a warm, Mediterranean flair.

Amar stood in the entryway, inviting me in, and saying: "A most cordial welcome to the Palm Garden." When I passed through the gateway, I saw a restaurant like none I had ever seen before. There were lots of tables but what made it even more special was that each table was on its own island. Waterways and bridges criss-crossed the whole restaurant. We followed the waiter, who led us right to a table in the middle, pulled a chair back, and offered first me and then Amar a seat. After taking our seats, the waiter introduced himself except for the fact that I wasn't paying attention to what he was saying. I was overwhelmed by the sheer beauty and effort that had gone into creating such a spectacular setting. The tables were adorned with fine China and silverware, pastel colored flowers matched the linen and soft lighting was achieved by way of elegant candles burning into the balmy starry sky, creating a magical ambiance.

I heard someone call my name. I sat up, shocked, and realized the waiter was talking to me. Amar noticed I hadn't heard the question, so he repeated it.

"Do you want an aperitif? We also have an excellent non-alcoholic fruit cocktail I highly recommend it."

"Very good, that sounds splendid."

After Amar had ordered two cocktails, the waiter left. Amar looked at me.

"How do you like it here? Isn't it gorgeous?"

"Yes, it is gorgeous; I've never seen anything like it – thank you so much."

"Then I've achieved what I had hoped for."

"So, what did you hope for?"

"Oh, well, I wanted to give you a treat since you've been through a lot; I know what it's like."

His eyes sparkled. He was amazing, one of a kind.

"Thank you, and by the way?"

"Yes Xama, what is it?"

"Can you make a few other guests appear?"

I had hardly finished my sentence when four musicians came in and placed themselves on a raised platform in the middle of the restaurant.

"Thank you, Amar."

"Is there anything in particular, you don't eat, Xama?"

I hated that question. It was why I hadn't liked going to restaurants ever since I was a child. Well, now the moment had arrived: "Yes, I'm a vegetarian. So no meat or fish, please! I assume you also serve salads and vegetables here."

Amar started to laugh, and I was surprised by his reaction.

Was he laughing at me?

"I like you more and more by the minute, Xama, never in my life would I have believed you were a vegetarian; that makes two of us, means we have something else in common."

I thought I hadn't heard him right.

"Can you say that again, Amar – did I hear you correctly?" "You heard correctly, Xama, I've been a vegetarian for 16 years; I stopped eating fish and meat because of my convictions."

His eyes practically beamed, and I felt drawn to him as if by a magnet. What a coincidence – I meet this handsome man who's been through similar circumstances as mine, and he's a vegetarian too. Is all this really a coincidence? "You said you were a vegetarian because of your convictions; tell me more about them."

"It's actually very simple. When I was about 10 years old, I realized that the only reason we raise animals was to slaughter them and then eat them. I didn't want to be part of that, so I decided not to eat any more meat or fish."

"I don't believe it, that's impossible."

"Why not?"

"Because that's also how I became a vegetarian. When I was six years old, I saw a farmer kill a little piglet on a farm just so we could eat it. It was so cruel, I can still see the piglet twisting in agony."

"Well, this does make it very easy for me to order. If it's all right with you, I'll order a selection from my special menu. Everything vegetarian, healthy, and super delicious. Let me surprise you."

"You're unbelievable, Amar."

"What do you mean?"

"Just … yeah."

"I'm happy we're getting to know one another, and I'm happy you're starting to trust me. My Aphora is to help others, and you're someone I can help."

As the waiter took down our order, I gazed at Amar, admiring his confidence and his strong presence. Lost in conversation with Amar and totally enchanted by his eyes and gestures, I didn't notice the waiter had already served us the cocktails and was waiting patiently on our order. Amar explained our special vegetarian requests to him. Most of the time, all I hear in restaurants is "we don't have that," or "that's not on the menu." But everything seemed so easy with Amar, totally relaxed. I realized I was beginning to like him in a special way.

Amar lifted his cocktail glass towards me.

"To us, to the Arverni, and to fate."

As our glasses clinked, I wondered exactly what he meant by fate. I discarded the thought, and enjoyed the fruity cocktail. It swirled around my mouth numbing my tongue little. I hoped the dream would last; I felt safe for the first time in years. The last time I felt like this was when Dad was still alive. If only I had the courage to get Amar to take this a step further.

"So Xama, what kinds of questions do you have?"

I tried to sort out my thoughts.

"In future, how can I reach you? Do you have a phone?"

"Yes, I do, but you'll have to memorize the number since you can't take anything with you from a dream. Amar handed me his business card. You can call me anytime, day or night

How long have you had your phone?"

"Maybe a year."

"Get a new one; with a new number."

"Okay, but I'm not sure I can afford one right now."

"Don't worry about that; I'll handle it."

"One more thing, Xama, when will you turn sixteen? We're friends now – I want to know when your birthday is."

Without thinking, the information spilled out of me.

"This coming Saturday, and I'm having a party, I' love it if you would come – the theme is "crypts", so make sure you dress up like a zombie, a vampire, or some other undead thing."

He smiled. .

"Thanks – What if I came as an Arverni? They're strange enough, aren't they?"

I started to laugh, then realized he was being serious.

"It doesn't matter what you come as; surely you look different from how I see you in my dreams."

"Probably; if you're using an image from the video in your imagination, then yes. Thanks again for the invitation; I don't think I'll make it since I'll be in Hong Kong for the weekend. But I'll be in touch."

"Promise?"

"I swear."

"I'll look forward to it, there's something else that's bothering me."

"Well, out with it – now or never."
"Why all these security measures, and who is this Dr. Sherman, the one my father couldn't catch?
Who or what are the Arverni afraid of?"
The question hit him like a punch in the face. He raised his eyebrows, and his right nostril started to twitch uncontrollably. He looked down, the question took him by surprise, he was thinking of a quick response. .
"If you don't want to answer, it's okay."
After he had looked up, his face had lost its shine; he looked, tense.

What did I say now?

"Xama, it's more about whether you're ready – ready to hear the whole story." I wasn't expecting this answer.
"I don't understand all of this at all. What do you mean ready for the whole story?"
"Xama, to understand why the Arverni rank security as their most important asset, you need to find out about their history. Let's discuss it in our next dream. Once you've gone through all the information your father sent, you'll understand what we are afraid of and if there are open question left, I try my best to answer them".

"With a nod, I signaled my agreement. I could have slapped myself for killing the positive setting.
Why did I have to ask that question? Man, I am an idiot
Out of nowhere two waiters stood beside us holding a tray with 2 bowls of soup on it, I was pleased dinner was being served.
The soup was delicious but as per usual I managed to wolf it down, a bad habit I acquired from living in an orphanage, a place where if you ate too slowly, you didn't get any more. In order to rectify my action I slowed down to such an extent that it looked like I was moving in slow motion. Amar noticed, and asked:
"If you don't like the soup, just leave it. No problem."
"No, just the opposite – it tastes very good; I'm just eating too quickly – bad habit from the youth home."
I could see my reply made him uncomfortable – I tried to break the tension and asked, "Do you have a pen?"

He nodded and reached inside the pocket of his blazer, then handed me a stylish pen. I took it and wrote the phone number from his business card on the palm of my hand. He gave a little snort.

"That won't work; you have to learn it by heart."

"Why not?"

"As I told you earlier; you can't take anything with you out of a dream; we've tested it in various dreams, and it's never worked. Write your address on the back of my business card, in case I do have time on Saturday."

Excited by the idea of that possibility I wrote the address of Heaven on the back of his business card and gave it back to him along with the pen. As he read it, I looked bashfully at the numbers on my palm and repeated them to burn them into my memory. Amar did the same thing with my address, and it was quiet for a few seconds. While I tried to memorize the numbers, I noticed how the dreamscape around me began to change; all at once, everything seemed blurry. I blinked then closed my eyes briefly, but it didn't work. Quite the opposite – everything got blurrier - even Amar. He realized something was wrong with me, so he asked:

"Everything going alright?"

"Yes, It's just that things are getting a little blurry."

"Someone is trying to wake you from your dream, Xama. Those are the first signs. Your subconscious wants to remain in the dream, but your consciousness is waking up. You can't do anything about it. Memorize the phone number, and we'll stay in contact.

I've really enjoyed this dream – thank you."

I wanted to thank him too, but I couldn't. When I opened my eyes, Claire was looking down at me, holding my shoulders with both hands and shaking me like crazy.

"Sophie, is everything alright? Thank God! I thought you were in a coma. I've been trying to wake you up for the last 5 minutes! Sorry for shaking you so hard, but I didn't know what else to do. Man, Sophie, that was nuts, I was really getting scared!"

I looked at Claire surprised. I had every reason to be mad at her, but of course, she didn't know I was dreaming.

"It's okay, everything's alright Claire, I'm fine – except that ..."

"Except what?"

"It's alright, I was just dreaming."

"You were dreaming? Well, it was a crazy deep dream."

"Let's say it was a very realistic dream, an escape from reality. The beginning of a story."

"What kind of a story? I don't get it."

"It's not important, it's really not important."

I looked at my left palm. Amar was right, the numbers I had written so big and clear on my hand had disappeared. But I still had the digits in my head. I quickly went to my desk, picked up my phone and opened the address book. Claire looked at me, surprised, but I ignored her comments and tried to save Amar's number in my phone. Done.

Is he still dreaming?

The answer was right under my left thumb – with a click on the number, my phone started to dial.

Thoughts shot through my mind light lightning.
Can I just call him now?
What am I going to say to him?
Will he even pick up my call?

I was tense and insecure. I considered just hanging up again, but Amar's voice interrupted the thought.

"Amar Wellberg, hello?"

Should I answer, or hang up?

"Hello, Amar, it's me, Sophie – uh, Xama. I didn't get to say thank you for the beautiful dream."

"Xama, good to hear your voice. That was a very beautiful dream; you're welcome but please do me a favor and buy yourself a new telephone. You know it's not safe to talk on the phone"

"I'll do that I promise."

"Xama, I've sent you something. Let me know when you get it."

"What did you send me?"

"You'll see. Let's end now, before you're located.
I'll contact you – until then, Xama."

"Bye, Amar."

I hung up, feeling like I was in seventh heaven. It felt wonderful to know Amar was helping me.

How much I wanted to know what Amar felt for me. How does he truly see me? Am I a helpless little girl, or does he see me as a woman?

Claire looked at me, questioning.

"Sophie, can you explain to me what just happened? First I can't get you to wake up, then you immediately pick up the phone for no reason, and now you're sitting there floating on cloud nine. What's up with you? I'm really worried about you; you're different, somehow."

"You don't need to be worried, Claire, but you are right, I feel different – a lot is going on, but I can't quite put it into words, except that I'm feeling great, simply amazing".

"You're in love, am I right?"

AN OPEN SECRET

I needed to come up with a story about Amar and how we met. I fabricated a little tale of when I was 13, and how my father and Amar had been friends and colleagues. I had seen him once or twice over the years. Then I saw him at father's funeral, and since then we've e-mailed and, Skyped each other and just recently we met for dinner."

"You never told me about him. I'm totally flabbergasted, as you would say."

"Kay-Ky."

We both laughed, and I was sure Claire was going to buy my story.

"It all makes sense, I have been worried sick now, I know a man is to blame for your strange behavior."

"Stop it, Claire, that's not funny."

"Okay, you're right, no jokes at somebody else's expense. Nevertheless, it seems this Amar has really caught your eye if you're already having these intense dreams about him."

"What do you mean intense dreams?"

"Oh, well, when I was trying to wake you up just now you said something like:

'We'll see each other again, Amar.'

Now I get it. How old is he, anyway? If you've already known him for years, and he's your dad's friend, then he must be ..."

I knew exactly what Claire was thinking.

"Amar is twenty-six, a taller than me, maybe six feet. He has a nice chocolate cultured skin and is very athletic, his hair is black tied into a ponytail – all in all – kayky handsome. On top of that he is very funny, has an infectious laugh. Oh I forgot, he's also very kind; he's happiest when he can help other people. I have to commit – he's hotter than Channing Tatum."

Claire was visualizing every bit of my description. She was surprised at my boldness.

"It's okay – I see. I thought he would be a little older. You said he was a friend of your father, so I thought he might be of similar age. I'm glad he's not. Did I hear you right? He looks better than Channing Tatum?

I knew it, Sophie, you're in love

Invite him to Heaven – I want to meet him, why not at our birth-day party?"

"That won't work."

"Why not?"

"He works in New York. He's hotel manager and he's only in Frankfurt now and then, usually on business."

"Did you even invite him? Who knows – maybe his next business meeting is in Frankfurt and can be arranged on the same date."

Claire was right, I hadn't invited him, but I also didn't dare to hope he would come.

"You didn't invite him, right? You're just scared he'll say no. Noth-ing ventured, nothing gained. If you don't invite him, he can't know that you're celebrating your birthday party. If I were in your shoes, I'd send him a special invitation. If he looks as good as you said – I mean, hello."

"You're right, I'll invite him. But there's no way he'll be in Germa-ny and have time to come."

"That's good. That's the Sophie I know. Tell me more about him. Everything you know."

It's not easy to dismiss Claire; she will nag you until she gets it out of you.

Well, now I have to reveal enough about Amar, so Claire is satis-fied, but nothing that hints at our connection – the Arverni.

It was just before midnight when Claire finally left me alone and quit bombarding me with questions. Now she knew what she should know; I'd told her just enough that I could leave her to put two and two together.

"So you're caught too?"

I looked at Claire.

"What do you mean, caught?"

"Sorry, but the way you talk about him, there's no doubt – you're in love with him."

"Do you think, really?"

"One hundred percent but only you can answer that question."

" ... and how am I supposed to know I'm in love with him?"

Claire laughed. "You just know. Everything changes when you're in love. I'm really in love with Alex this time; we're not just, like, fooling around or sneaking off in the bushes or anything. If he's not with me then I miss him and think about him, and when he is there, I feel so good and safe. When I think of him, I get a swarm of butterflies in my stomach, and when I touch him, it feels like all the butterflies taking off at once. I know I'm getting senti-mental; everyone's different."

Claire was right – it was just like she said.

"Claire?"

"Yeah, Sophie?"

"Thanks."

"For what?"

"For being my best friend and always here when I need you."

"You're here for me too, and that's what friends are for. You don't need to thank me, Sophie."

Claire came over to my bed and hugged me, then whispered in my ear. "We only have each other, and our friendship means so much to me. I'll always be here for you."

For a moment, I wondered whether I shouldn't tell her the truth about the aphormation, but then a voice inside told me not to.

"Claire, I'm here for you too."

"Thanks, Sophie, I'm going to take a shower and then I need to turn in. I'm dog-tired. You should do the same, and I hope you dream about Amar. I'll be dreaming about Alex, anyway, and our last date. It was mega Kay-Ky, but I'll tell you about it another time."

Claire disappeared into the bathroom. I considered reading more of Dad's notebooks, but I couldn't stop thinking about Amar. Was Claire right when she said I was in love with him? I didn't know what it was, but there was something my mind couldn't let go of. My mind was racing, there's no way I could sleep.

Claire went right to bed from the shower.

"When you're done in the bathroom turn out the light. I have to get my beauty sleep."

"I will, soon. Sleep well Claire."

I switched on my bedside lamp and went into the bathroom. Sleeping was impossible; I was much too hyper and had to know what came next in Dad's notebooks. I couldn't stop thinking about Amar. I disappeared into the bathroom, switching off the room light. Claire was right about one thing – dreaming was a good idea. It was my way to be with Amar – and if there was one thing? I wished, it were to be with him. Maybe I could impress Amar with what I learned in dad's notebooks?

That's a great idea – he has been studying everything that came into his hands about the Arverni in the last few years, anyway.

After I'd taken off my makeup and washed my face, I looked at my aphmal in the mirror. It had changed again a little, I thought it looked darker, and stood out even more from my otherwise pale skin.

Was it my imagination? – What's that?

There was a shadow on the edge of the cross. I leaned in and looked at the area around the aphmal. It looked as if a circle had become slightly darker around the aphmal, but it was barely noticeable.

I'm probably just imagining it.

I remained standing in front of the mirror for a moment, enjoying the energy aphmalisation created. Simply just Kay-Ky. I quietly left the bathroom, hoping Claire was already asleep. On the way to my bed, I looked over at Claire and heard her breath peacefully and evenly. Carefully and quietly, my hands searched for the chest under my bed in the weak light of my bedside lamp. My fingers felt around, but they found – nothing. I frantically searched left and right, and slowly a frightening thought formulated in my mind.

It couldn't be that someone found the box under my bed ... and stole it?

I grabbed the lamp from my bedside table and held it under the bed. I had only pushed it towards the head of the bed. Now I remembered; I just wanted to hide it.

What was that? I jolted up and turned to face Claire. For a moment, I had the feeling someone was watching me. Stiff as a board, I looked over at Claire. Monotone sounds reached my ear, but my mind calmed me. It was just Claire's rhythmic breathing. Relieved, I breathed in deeply, but then heard a sound I recognized. It was the door creaking. Our door makes a creaking noise every time someone opens or closes it. I looked towards the hallway, motionless. Fear turned my whole body to stone.

Was it sister Hilde, making her last rounds? If she saw light in the room, she came in for a moment to turn it out.

121

Should I scream, and wake Claire?

I sounded like a scared, helpless 16-year-old. But I wasn't that same 16-year-old anymore; I was an Arverni. I stood up and walked towards the light switch. It was only three steps, three little steps. I would switch on the light and check whether there would be anyone in the hall. Fighting my fear, I walked forwards slowly and silently, step by step. When I reached my arm out to turn it on, I felt a stabbing pain in the middle of my forehead. "Own."

I realized it was coming from the aphmal, and before I could ask myself what it meant, my whole body was hit with an energy wave and set on high alert. I was charged to the max with energy like I'd been hit by an electric shock. I groped for the light switch, turned on the light and looked out. In a flash, I was blinded by a bright light and thought I saw a shadow disappearing down the hallway. Then the room door opened and closed; the sound was unmistakable. Whoever it was didn't even try to be quiet this time. The sound woke Claire up, who looked at me sleepily.

"What's up, Sophie? Can't you sleep?"

"I think someone was just in our room, Claire."

"Lie back down and turn off the light – it was just sister Hilde; she always makes the last rounds."

"I thought so too at first, but I don't think it was her."

"Maybe it was one of the boys, sometimes they dare each other to do stuff like that."

"Sophie, close the room door and go back to sleep. I need my beauty sleep – otherwise I'll get zits, and I hate zits."

"Good idea, after I'd closed the door and turned off the light, I heard Claire say:

"Good night, sleep well."

Still wondering who would want to come into our room and why, I went back and sat on my bed. My curiosity got the better of me; I grabbed the aphmal box under the bed and looked at it once again. Was this the reason someone was trying to get into our room? Did someone know Dad had written down the Arverni legacy for me?

My secret – was it not a secret anymore?

ANCESTRY & SUCCESSION

Tense, I wondered what had just happened. *Why did my aphmal react like that? Was it warning me, maybe?* Amar did tell me that it would protect me.

And that's exactly what it did – it warned me about the intruder. My aphmal knew someone was in the room.

To distract myself, I looked at my aphmal in the mirror on the aphmal box. It started to glow, and the mirrored side opened up. I reached in and took out the labeled notebooks. Dad was so disciplined; everything had its place, and he always knew where to look for things. The opposite of me. How often had we fought because I hadn't cleaned my room? Dad didn't understand how a person could live in such a pigsty. Thinking about Dad made me feel sad again.

Why did you leave me? Why?
I tried to repress these thoughts and looked at the notebooks on my bed.

Book 1 – Ancestry and Succession
Book 2 – Aphormation, Aphmal, Aphora, and Apheid
Book 3 – The Law of the Arverni
Book 4 – The Arverni Council
Book 5 – Enemies of the Arverni
.

As my eyes scanned the notebooks, I wondered which book to start reading first.

Should I start with book 2 – Aphormation, Aphmal, Aphora, and Apheid? or with Book 1 – Ancestry and Succession?

Dad had put that one first. I packed the other notebooks back in the aphmal box and closed the mirror. I opened the notebook and started to read.

– Book 1: Ancestry and Succession –

"My dear Xama,
I can't tell you how greatly it pains me that I can't give you the history of the Arverni and your origins in person. I would have given anything to explain your legacy to you personally, but it could not be."
There it was again, fate, I was sick of hearing about it! Dad always explained everything as fate. What in the hell is fate, and why did I have to lose Mom and Dad over it? Why both of them? Why?
I read on.

"Here, in this book, I have attempted to describe our ancestry and succession so that you understand who the Arverni are and where they come from. Even if it's a little boring, study this note-book carefully. It describes your heritage and your roots.

Over the millennia, we have succeeded in protecting something very special, handing it down to our children as an inheritance. Something that makes us different than normal humans, which gives us power and positive energy, and which helps us to develop unbelievable abilities – but more on that later. Let me begin at the beginning.

The history of the Arverni is documented back into the second century before Christ. Luernius ruled our people; he was the first king of the Arverni. When he died, his son Bituitus became the next Arverni king. Then followed Contoniatus, Celitilus, and Vercingetorix, who was conquered 52 years before Christ by Julius Caesar. From that point on, we lived as prisoners and were oppressed. To free ourselves from imprisonment, a group of Arverni unified their powers. They formed a circle to transmit their abilities – today, we know it as a ring, and a ring requires at least four Arverni. Back then everything was probably different. It was the first time, after all, that a ring had been created. Our lore does not tell us who first had the idea for a ring, but we do know that each Arverni placed his right thumb on the forehead of the Arverni to his right. They placed their left arms over each other's shoulders to form a ring. They began to rotate: first slowly, then quicker and quicker, and the Arverni started to sing. If we are to believe traditional lore, all of the Arverni were part of the ring, creating a ring hundreds of Arverni strong. The whole power of the ring was transmitted to each individual in it. Additionally, each Arverni in the ring developed another special power. Each one was unique. Through these newly won powers, the Arverni became almost unconquerable, and it was easy for them to overpower the guards and free themselves from prison. They were superior to their enemies in every way, yet despite this superiority they were never interested in exercising their power. With the exception of a small group of rebels, who only had one thing in mind: to use their new power and might to destroy the Romans, exercising vengeance and retribution. That was the beginning, the splitting off of a group who despised the beliefs and community of the Arverni. This group still exists today, following the same goals as they did back then, and seeking to extend their power. They pose a great danger to all of us, but more on that later. However, the ring created even more than enormous power and new abilities; the places where the Arverni had put their thumbs changed, and an A with a cross appeared. The Arverni could only see it when they looked at their reflections in still water. This symbol still identifies every Arverni today, and is called the aphmal. After the Arverni people were free and the survivors had been rescued, they fled and hid from the Romans. Times today have changed, but one thing remains the same: since this day, the Arverni have been living in hiding, concealing their extraordinary powers and abilities. Again and again, individual Arverni have been unable to control and have displayed their abilities publicly. They were usually seen as a danger and often pursued and killed. The council came down on hard on those who did not control their abilities, banning them. According to tradition, the first ring allowed us to pass down these new abilities and powers, and this is where our modern concept of a council comes from. Every child with pure Arverni blood develops extraordinary abilities at the age of 16. Today, we know that this is caused by a genetic change in our DNA, and that it's only inherited if both parents carry the genetic change. Over time, there have been fewer and fewer children passing through an aphormation and developing special abilities, and since Arverni don't always marry their own, we are threatened with extinction.

Today, there are only a few Arverni left, and it is foreseeable that one day the last Arverni will be born, and the Arverni legacy will disappear forever. When I met your mother 17 years ago, I knew the first time I saw her that we were made for one another. And so it happened – we fell in love, were married, and you are the result of our love. You, Xama. Since we both carried the legacy within ourselves, you have the Arverni gene too. Now, you're facing your own change – your aphormation."

Dad wrote more about the history of the Arverni – in contrast to his assumptions, I found them all very exciting.

– End of Book 1: Ancestry and Succession –

I don't know how any of you would react if you discovered the truth about your ancestry at 16. I, in any case, had mixed feelings on the one hand, I was disappointed Dad hadn't come out with the truth sooner, but on the other, I felt proud. It all seemed uncanny, as though my life had changed completely from one day to the next. Only time would tell whether the change would be a positive one.

A brief glance at my alarm clock brought me back to the present. Dark red glowing digital numbers showed 2:46. Crazy – had I really just read for more than 3 hours? The time was flying by, and the history of the Arverni had drawn me in completely. It read like a historical novel; the only difference was that in this story I was the main character, and it wasn't fiction either. It was about my origins, and my future. It was my story. 2:52. Should I go to sleep, or keep reading? I suppressed a shallow yawn and decided to get out Book 2. I pushed my pillow into the corner and leaned against it, looking at the title.

Book 2 – Aphormation, Aphmal Aphora, and Apheid

Unbelievable how these four words sound:
For someone who didn't know them, they would look like the be-
ginning of a Latin dictionary – dry and boring. For someone direct-
ly affected by them – they're fascinating and incredibly exciting.

APHORMATION, APHMAL, APHORA, AND APHEID

Book 2 - Aphormation, Aphmal, Aphora, and Apheid. "Xama, now that you've learned a little about the history of the Arverni, I'm going to explain four important terms in this book:

The Aphormation – 'The Transformation,'
The Aphmal – 'The Mark of the Arverni,'
The Apheid – 'Your Promise,'
The Aphora – 'The Task.'

The information in this book is probably the most important part of your legacy – read it through carefully.
In Love forever – Dad."

Dad's introduction made me weepy again.

No tears this time, Xama – you can do it.

"The aphormation is a young person's transformation into an adult Arverni man or woman. If you hear the expression aspirant, it is another term for someone who is going through the aphormation. You, Xama, are in the aphormation phase – your transformation. You're going through lots of changes, and not just physical ones. We Arverni understand the aphormation as a total transformation – physical and emotional, conscious and unconscious. It's difficult to describe this transformation in words, but it's a lot like a caterpillar's metamorphosis into a butterfly. The caterpillar has new, different characteristics after it's become a butterfly. It develops into a higher stage. Of course, its metamorphosis is only an exterior transformation. The aphormation is much more. No one will see you transform; you control how much you tell others about it. Your aphormation will remain your secret.
You're probably asking yourself how you can recognize the aphormation has begun. You will notice a symbol on your forehead, what's called an aphmal. It didn't used to be immediately

recognizable, but today, when everybody has hot water and bathrooms with mirrors, aspirants immediately recognize the appearance of the aphmal and the beginning of the aphormation. The first time you look in the mirror, it will shine in the middle of your forehead. This is usually a major shock. Most aspirants try to wash it off, thinking it's just drawn on, but then realize it won't work. The aphmal looks like a cross at the beginning. It cannot be removed, not even with cleaning agents or solvents. It is a change in the pigment of your skin, which stays even if the skin renews itself. You will soon accept that the aphmal is a part of you – a very important part – but more on that later. Most aspirants are shocked when they realize they're marked by the aphmal. They are afraid they're permanently disfigured. Depression and attempts to maim the forehead are common, especially when parents don't explain the aphormation before the aphmal appears. This explanation is called 'The Arverni Legacy,' and it's when parents introduce their children to the process of transformation, helping them and removing their fears. Since I did not want to let you go through your aphormation alone and unprepared, I have decided to take this step of transmitting a documented record of the Arverni legacy."

I felt goose bumps crawling up my neck, like a net spreading over my back and my arms. OK, so I don't look like a supermodel, and just like most girls my age I don't think I look perfect, but my appearance is still extremely important to me. Even if I don't spend hours in the bathroom like Claire, I still don't leave Heaven without make-up. A dark brown cross in the middle of your forehead, even if it's a symbol, disfigures you. I remember how I felt like someone had pulled the rug out from under my feet when I realized it wasn't a dream, and it wasn't painted on. Like in a nightmare, I started to fall into a deep hole, deeper and deeper without stopping. The wildest thoughts shot through my head – of a tattoo someone had painted on my forehead as I slept – of some kind of magic that had marked me. It's like you slump down, desperate, with no answers and no hope, the last bit of self-confidence running through your fingers like fine sand. That was exactly how it was, and even after I recognized the aphmal was only visible to me and only in the mirror, I still felt disfigured and confused. When the aphmal appeared, it was like I fell into a deep hole; I feel like I'm still stuck inside, slowly crawling my way out. Tired and yawning, I turned the page.

"The aphmal symbolizes the aphormation, the transformation of a young person who carries the Arverni legacy within him- or herself. Exactly 21 days before the sixteenth birthday, the aphormation begins with the appearance of the aphmal in the middle of the forehead. It has been so for every one of us, and it will also be so for you! The length of the aphormation is also always the same – 21 months. Many things happen during this time, much that you will not understand at first and which you cannot explain. It is, unfortunately, impossible to describe all of this in detail, since some of what will happen is unique. There are some changes only you will experience. My own aphormation was several decades ago, and I don't remember all the details. The two significant changes I noticed were the development of my personality and the Aphora. Aphora essentially means a purpose or task; you will receive a task to do during your aphormation. The Aphora is your life's work. Every Arverni has an Aphora, or task.

The appearance of the aphmal occurs without any pain, and, aside from its visual effects, does not cause any other negative changes or even discomfort – quite the opposite. The aphmal on your forehead is shaped like a cross. The vertical part of the cross is about 5 to 6 centimeters long, and the horizontal part about 3 to 4 centimeters. In the first phase, the aphmal is often confused with a religious symbol. In the following days and sometimes months of the aphormation, the cross will slowly become complete until it appears as a full aphmal, the symbol of the Arverni, a crossed A. Xama, this must all sound very strange, but I can assure you. Aphmal, aphormation, and Aphora are all ancient terms among the Arverni, and in just a few days or weeks these names won't sound unusual to you anymore. Step by step, you will become used to the language and the changes. It will become very important in your life, something to be proud of, something you will love above all else, something that will help you, protect you, and always provide you with new motivation – physically and mentally, giving you new, unknown powers."

Again and again I read through this paragraph. There are some things Dad was telling me about the aphmal that I couldn't confirm – maybe just not yet?

"Let me explain the aphormation now; the aphormation occurs in three phases. What is important in the first phase is for you to know exactly what will happen to you and to your body. You will discover many new things about yourself, but all of this is part of the normal Arverni legacy. The earlier you accept that you are an Arverni, the easier your aphormation will be.

What does dad mean, that it would be something special? If I looked back at my emotional state over the last few days, it was special – especially awful and shocking – was that what he meant?

"The aphmal has multiple special characteristics; one important one, as I have already mentioned, is as a symbol of your transformation – the aphormation. It indicates you are in the process of becoming an Arverni. We Arverni have invested much in researching our origins and analyzing the Arverni gene, many open questions remain. Likely the most important is this one: why is the aphmal invisible to humans, and why is only its reflection visible to Arverni? There are many theories on this question. Some believe that it lets us recognize each other; others say it is a protection so we may remain undiscovered. We still don't know the truth. What we do know is that the fear of looking marked and disfigured is unfounded. You don't need to worry – none of your friends will be able to see it.

I read the paragraph again – did I understand it correctly? The Averno's enemies are also Arverni? What does he mean by that, and what about "the changes in your personality will take some time?"

Are there even more changes coming? I couldn't get the thought out of my mind. A fleeting glance at my alarm clock told me it was already 3:56, which is I kept nodding off. I briefly considered whether I should go to sleep or read on. I developed a three-step plan... I would read on, then start to feel bad, and third pretend to be sick and not go to school. I shook off my sleepiness and turned another page.

"Besides the visual transformation, the aphmal has other inter-esting and powerful secrets. The aphmal is your personal body-guard, your fitness coach, your doctor, and the source of your energy – all in one. Your aphmal will tell you when you are in danger. If you are asleep, it will wake you. If you are distracted, it will alert you. If someone has you cornered, it will show you a way out. What's important is for you to trust your aphmal; when you need it, it will be there for you."

That was it, of course! That was the reason the aphmal alerted me when someone came into the room. Now I understood – the aphmal recognized the threat and guided me to turn on the light. It prevented me from hiding under the covers, which would have been more like me. I read on, excited.

"But there's more. It is a source of inner peace and energy, and it's easy to use. The only thing you need is a mirror and a couple of minutes. When you look at your aphmal in the mirror, the source is activated. This makes your aphmal extremely valuable. Your emotional state changes the longer you look at it. Sadness turns to happiness, exhaustion to power, weakness to strength, and fear to curiosity. It converts all negative energy into positive energy, and ensures you feel well, balanced, and happy. It is probably the most impressive part of the aphormation, and it's how you know you're something special now – an Arverni. With its help, you will learn to use your strength to complete your task – your Aphora.

The aphmal protects you from illness, it ensures your body is fit and your emotions are positive, it also controls your immune system and protect you from pathogens of all kinds. It's actually better than any doctor and any medicine. It is a vaccine against everything, and it's extremely effective."

When I read this sentence a second time I felt weak, as though all my blood was rushing to my legs. If I understood correctly, the aphmal could help me feel less exhausted. That was what Dad said. Well, the proof is in the pudding, as they say, so I slowly opened my bedside table drawer, looking over at Claire to reas-sure myself she was asleep. I reached in, took out a compact, opened it carefully, and looked at my face I turned a little to-wards the lamp on my bedside table and looked at my aphmal. I noticed the power Dad described beginning to take effect immediately. It was the first time I had looked into this small mirror so intensely, and after a few minutes I folded the compact back up, leaned back on my pillows against the wall, closed my eyes, and enjoyed the tingling feeling spreading throughout my whole body. It felt much longer than it actually was. After just a few seconds, the feeling had passed. my exhaustion and all negative thoughts had gone, I felt invigorated and read on.

"Ah – I almost forgot the most important thing; the aphmal has one more special power – but has side effects."
The powers Dad had already listed were already so overwhelming that I couldn't imagine that there was anything to top them.

"Your aphmal can enhance your performance and your ability to concentrate to a superhuman level, like a superpower. We know from experiments that this superpower creates physical and mental dependency, similar to a drug. This leads to overstimulation and severe consequences. Since I know you have a strong will power, I won't go into the negative effects any further. But please be careful no matter how tempting, it can be dangerous to use the superpower too often. Now that I've told you about the risks, you should know how to activate the power. You must place your right thumb in the middle of the aphmal. You will notice immediately that when you even bring your right thumb near it, the aphmal will pull it in like a magnet all on its own. Once the two touches, pure energy will begin to flow, preparing your body for the physical and mental increase in performance. The only thing you need to know is: it's the right thumb that releases the highest form of aphmalisation. You're probably wondering what the difference is between looking at your aphmal in the mirror and activating it with your right thumb. Activating it with your thumb is something completely different; it's difficult to explain, but it's at least twenty times more intense than when you look at your aphmal in the mirror. Your other senses are expanded; it is the ultimate form of aphmalisation. It's like it gives you superpowers for a while. As soon as your right thumb and the aphmal connect, your power and concentration are immediately boosted. It's best to try to start your first aphmalisation when you're alone. You can stimulate your aphmal, as many times as you want, but the intensity of the superpower will depend on how soon one aphmalisation follows the next. You cannot forget that this will push your body to limits it has never experienced before. Your body needs a break to regenerate between stimulations. You'll find out on your own how quickly you'll be ready to use the power again. Some famous Arverni became famous by using the power. They're in the history books for their intelligence or artistic abilities. What people don't know is that all of them paid a price for fame, and endangered the Arverni community by using aphmalisation for personal gain. Sometimes, their superpowers drew the attention of researchers and scientists, who wanted to study them. When this happens, the Arverni community has to act. The council has passed a law that regulates use of aphmalisation. Offenses are not tolerated, and abuses are punished with immediate effect. Please don't underestimate the directorate I've summarized the most important laws in notebook four. It's important that you know that you have rights and duties as a member of the community and that you're subject to Arverni law. The law helps the community survive in the modern world. The Arverni do not value being famous – quite the opposite – we try to live in secret, and you should do the same. You have to complete several steps to be accepted into the community; I have made preparations so you can take them, even after I am gone. Someone from the council will take care of you and ensure you are accepted."

My acceptance into the community – someone will take care of it – was this someone Amar?

"In the next notebook, I collected some information for you about the council. There is a simple, clear organizational structure that guides the Arverni community. At the head are the council members, the directorate, and the leader of the council, who we call the Meta. All decisions are made confidentially. We try to integrate into society. There are, however, many Arverni who have made important discoveries and completed research for the good of humanity. Some of them have become well known for their work. These include some of the biggest names in history, like Leonardo Da Vinci, Van Gogh, Mozart, Einstein... they were all Arverni, and they all owe their fame to aphmalisation.

Some have even exceeded the boundaries of what is allowed, and were punished for it. A group of these rebels has gone underground. They're the biggest danger we face today. Their main goal is to destroy the community. Others have gone beyond the margins, and have suffered the consequences of the addiction created by too frequent aphmalisation. There are some very famous Arverni who have become famous due to their Aphora and powers. The information in these notebooks has the potential to change world history. Everything I've written is only meant for you; after you've read everything, you must destroy it. The aphmal box will help you do so, but I'll write more on that later."

I couldn't believe that – Da Vinci and all the others were Arverni? If anyone found that out – Dad was right; it would create chaos. I glanced at the clock to discover it was already after 4:00 in the morning. I couldn't imagine sleeping – I was much too excited and curious. My conscience reminded me that I was supposed to go to school, but I could deal with that later. I had to learn more. I turned another page.

"You've probably already triggered aphmalisation by looking at your aphmal in the mirror. When I was your age and my father gave the legacy to me, I couldn't wait to try out my aphmal right away."

I briefly faltered while reading, pausing. Dad was right – I should try out the maximum aphmalisation. I visualized myself placing my right thumb on my aphmal, but I was scared. What if I reacted so strongly that I woke Claire up? I didn't want to create a scene, so I put the idea aside and read on.

"Now it's time to explain another important part of the aphormation – the Aphora. The expression Aphora describes a task you receive during the aphormation. You might think someone will assign you this task, but that's not the case. Your Aphora will develop on its own; a special power will develop to complete this task; it will help you handle the challenges that come with your Aphora. The power depends strongly on your personality – think of it as a surprise. But how do you receive the Aphora, your life's work? Here's the answer: fate determines your Aphora. I know exactly what you're thinking now. You always said you don't believe in fate. You always thought I was using fate when I didn't have an answer for your questions. But that wasn't true – unfortunately, I couldn't explain everything to you back then. You weren't old enough, and as a faithful Arverni, I was forbidden from talking to you about it before your aphormation. How often I thought about breaking the rules and telling you the secrets of the Arverni before your aphormation. But I decided against it. I kept my honor. Now I know I made the wrong decision. I wish I'd explained everything to you personally.

For Arverni, fate influences all aspects of our lives. Humans believe in different gods; we Arverni believe in fate. Fate will determine what your Aphora will be, and equip you with the powers you need to accomplish it. Fate directs you, as it does all of us, whether we accept it or not.

Let me tell you about the last of the four concepts – the apheid. The apheid is a ritual that will occur in the Temple in front of the council and invited guests. The family determines the list of invited guests, and the council invites them. The aspirant appears before the council for the first time to take the apheid. The apheid is nothing more than a promise to the community. The aspirant promises to use his powers and abilities to fulfill his abilities. The apheid ends when the Meta instructs the aspirant to make an oath that requires him to always use his powers and abilities only for others and in accordance with the law, never against them. The aspirant's nose will bleed while he utters this ancient saying. The Meta will seal the apheid by using the aspirant's blood to place a thumbprint in a special book. The aspirant is then officially part of the Arverni community. All of this might scare you, but it sounds worse than it is. Your mother and I went through this ritual; you will too, in order to join the Arverni community."

Dad's words made my heart sink, and the positive feeling I had just a few minutes before disappeared again. Searching for a tissue, I set the notebook to the side and stood up. I tried to sneak to the bathroom; I absolutely did not want Claire to hear me and wake up, not now. I closed the bathroom door behind me and was overcome by the tears I'd been holding back. Dad – why didn't you tell me all this before? Why didn't you break your vow? I looked in the sink and watched the tears drip into the bowl. I felt progressively worse then I had an idea. I wiped the tears from my eyes. Breathing calmly, I looked at my aphmal and searched for changes. The dark skin around it was sharply outlined, as though drawn on with a marker. I already felt my sadness subsiding. With my right hand, I started to touch the aphmal with my fingers gliding carefully across it as though it were a foreign object. There was no difference between it and the rest of my forehead. Then I suddenly felt a small electrical pulse spreading from the middle of my aphmal over my face, then over my whole body. What happened? As soon as I asked myself the question, I knew the answer. When the fingers of my right hand stroked the aphmal, my thumb happened to touch it, triggering this intense, unfamiliar feeling. I looked at the aphmal again and felt more content and happy. I slowly and purposefully moved my thumb towards my aphmal. Even before they touched, I thought I could feel something. I felt an invisible power moving my thumb, like a magnet. I couldn't hold it back. It was as though all the energy in the room was flowing through my thumb into the aphmal and then spreading out like water over my whole body – a pure energy shower. "Ahh." Wow, shit, that hurts. A slight moan escaped my lips, and it felt like a swarm of electrically charged butterflies were fluttering around me, each brushes of a butterfly's wing releasing an electric shock. I felt happy and energetic. It was like launching a rocket, an explosive force. I tried to remove my thumb from it, but my first attempt failed. I could only lift it with great effort. The flow of energy stopped in a flash, the butterflies disappeared, the rush of feelings faded out just as quickly as it had started, and I floated, feeling weightless like the rocket had entered into space. That was a really freaking intense aphmalisation. Kay-Ky – an energy shower and a drug all at once. There's no way to describe it in words; you will just have to believe me that it is a supercrazyawesome Kay-Ky feeling. As I removed my thumb and the flow of energy stopped, my senses changed. I know this sounds a little crazy. The first thing I noticed was my hearing; suddenly, I could hear things I'd never heard before. I could concentrate on one sound and filter out everything else – totally crazy. I could hear the water running down the pipes. I noticed the same thing with my eyes. If I concentrated on something far away, like the label on my shampoo bottle, it was like my eyes zoomed in until I saw it in front of me, clear and distinct. It was a little bit uncanny – definitely something I couldn't explain, but in the last few days I'd become used to accepting the sudden and the unexplained. When I looked in the mirror I saw a laughing Sophie – or was it Xama? I was changing. It felt like shy, helpless Sophie was being replaced more and more as Xama came into focus.

What's happening to me?

My thoughts raced at lightning speed. Everything I had just read ran through my mind like a movie, I could remember whole sentences, like I was reading the notebook right in front of me. I glanced at the alarm clock in the bathroom and almost jumped. Hard to believe it was already 4:32; in about 90 minutes, my alarm clock would ring – well, let's just say it would try to. I slowly snuck back to my bed to continue reading until I would have to get up. I understood more and more what Dad meant by fate, and I realized there were a lot of things I had misinterpreted. For Dad, fate was something real, not just a cliché like I always called it. Only now did I understand that Dad was just following his beliefs and Arverni law;. Dad, I'm so sorry I made fun of you and your beliefs so often and was so mean to you. I sat in my bed with my back to the wall, covered my legs, and got cozy. I had an hour and a half before the alarm would remind me I had to get ready for school.

"History teaches us that neither humans nor Arverni can deal with the truth. It is the fear of the unknown. Humans who are afraid are capable of anything, even killing us. Little by little, you will understand more about the history of the Arverni, including details I can't leave to you in my writings. I will repeat again: always remember that this information is only for you, and for no one else. On the last page, you'll find instructions for destroying the notebooks so they can't be reconstructed. Please follow these directions as soon as you've read everything. Dear Xama, as a devout Arverni, it wasn't easy for me to break the law knowing the danger I am putting you and the Arverni community in. I did it for you, so you could have the Arverni legacy.
With my eternal love – Dad."
END – Book 2.

Exactly at 5:50, just before my alarm clock was supposed to ring, I got up, switched it off, and went into the bathroom to look at my aphmal again. Charged up like a high power battery and ready for the day, I left the bathroom and greeted Claire, who was walking towards me barely awake.

"How on earth are you awake already? Could you not sleep?"

"Quite the opposite, Claire, I can hardly wait to go to school."

"Seems like you're back to your old self again. Give me fifteen minutes to splash on a little water, powder, eye shadow, mascara, and lipstick – in that order – and we can go to breakfast."

While Claire put on her "I'll make myself 3 years older" make-up, I thought over everything I'd learned that night. It was amazing – I could remember every single detail I'd read. I was proud I'd gotten through Dad's second notebook. Now I knew what to expect during my aphormation. But I certainly wasn't satisfied — quite the opposite. I wanted to know everything Dad had written down. He was right, being an Arverni is something special, and I began to feel something new ... pride. Proud to be an Arverni, although I didn't really know what that meant yet. My plan was clear – the first thing I'd do when I got back from school was keep reading until I'd gotten through all the notebooks. I could hardly wait to learn more about the Arverni. I just had to tell someone about everything I was learning – maybe Amar?

The Arverni Council

School was super Kay-Ky easy because of the aphmalisation, I practiced every morning. I was bored all day, only interested in one thing. What will I learn about the Arverni and myself next? What is the council? What laws are there, and whom do the Arverni fear?

On my way home, I thought of places I could read undisturbed. Should I go to the library? What if someone already knows about the notebooks and is looking for them? Claire eliminated my need to make a decision. A text message informed me she was getting together with Alex right after school. She was on the pill now, after all. All Claire wanted was to get me to pretend she was in the room that, so no one realized she was spending the night with Alex. Not a bad deal. I can read the Arverni legacy all night without interruption, and Claire and Alex can …

As soon as I got back to the youth home, I got comfortable and opened the box, picked up the first notebook, and gazed expectantly at the title "The Arverni Council." I turned the first page and started to read.

"One part of your legacy, Xama, is your introduction to the community and the council. It's important you know what the council is, and what its duties are. I've summarized the information in the following book. There's a lot to say about the council, it has many secrets. No one outside of the council knows when and where it meets. Sometimes, a council meeting may also take place in another form, a form we are not accustomed to. The Arverni community has been around for more than 2,000 years. If you can believe the ancient stories, then the first council was created in a moment of distress. The Romans were persecuting the Arverni community. Driven into a corner and with no way out, the elders formed a ring. They put their right arms around one another while they touched the middle each other's foreheads with their left thumbs. According to the stories, this concentrated the power of the community into each Arverni in the ring. This allowed the Arverni to stop the Romans and survive to the present day. The council was formed, and from then on has remained a part of Arverni culture.

Today, the council consists of twelve members. Eleven members are elected directly by the community. The Meta – the leader of the council – is elected by the council members themselves in a traditional ceremony. The Meta is the most important person in the community, since he determines the direction and the future of the Arverni. Only the council knows the rules for selecting a Meta. The Meta occupies his position until his death. Then the council selects a new Meta, normally from the council itself. Women have no access to the council, and they cannot be admitted to the council –more about this in the next notebook."

Why don't women have access to the council? I always though tradition was something to be proud of. But if women can't be trusted with anything, then there's not much to be proud of. No way I'm sticking to that tradition.

Shaking my head, I read on.

"The council is responsible for issues that concern individual members or the council as a whole. They make financial and strategic decisions to ensure the future of the community."

"The council consists of twelve members; five of them are entrusted with financial tasks, and the rest with very special tasks. In votes, each member gets one vote save for the Meta – his vote counts double. This ensures that the council always comes to a decision."

What are the financial and what are the special tasks, and who handles them?

"The council is responsible for the finances and the capital owned by the Arverni. Leander and his organization keep the books and present them to the council – monthly reports, annual reports, and everything else necessary to manage hundreds of companies and investments. You should know that the Arverni are immensely powerful and influence politics and economics. They're also very wealthy.

Kanaar represents one of the most powerful organizations in the community. He is responsible for the security of each individual Arverni, and the community as a whole. He manages security, the Achilleans, and much more."

Was Kanaar Dad's boss when he worked in security?

"When I was part of the community, I was in Kanaar's organization. He was my direct boss, and I led internal security for him. Everything which had to do with the security of the community and of individual Arverni was my responsibility. Up until the day I voluntarily left."

Why did Dad leave the community? There must be a reason, not just a difference of opinion. There must have been more – maybe I'll learn more about it in another chapter.

Although this notebook didn't unveil any new secrets, it was important to know how the Arverni were organized. I learned of an organization under the leadership of Ardell responsible for educating the community. Schools and even universities were under their control. This meant Arverni had access to education. I already knew Amar was responsible for communication, and that Arverni were capable of dream communication. What did surprise me was that the Arverni had their own medical branch, including hospitals all over the world. Aaron, a professor of medicine, was responsible for this area. And finally technology, a very important area because the community both invests in and uses new technologies. Duncan and his organization were in charge for technology. All in all, the council was just a team of the most responsible individuals from the whole organization; at least, that's how it seemed to me. I didn't get what was so special about them – at least, not yet.

As I locked the notebooks back in the aphmal box, Claire came storming into the room, wailing, threw her purse on the dresser and disappeared into the bathroom without saying a word. It wasn't the first time I'd seen her like this. But this type of emotional eruption hadn't happened since she had been with Alex. Something was wrong and she needed my help. I hid the aphmal box and went to the bathroom door.
"Claire, is everything alright? What happened?"
She wailed, and sighed:
"Everything's fine – give me a couple of minutes and I'll be OK."

Claire came out of the bathroom, her face tear-stained.

"I'm ok, sorry about my crying attack."

I knew she was lying.

"I don't believe you, Claire...
Something's not right with you and Alex – did you fight?"

She looked at me, started sobbing again, and hugged me.

"You're right, that pig lied to me. He told me he broke up with his ex, and today I heard they've been calling each other."

"Did you talk to him about it?"

Claire let go and sat down on her bed.

"Yes, I did, but maybe not in the nicest possible way. He just said that he wasn't interested in her anymore, and she was bothering him, and that I should calm down."

"But you don't believe him – or why are you so angry?"

"I don't know if I can trust him. He claims I'm the only one, and that he loves me. I don't know what's happening to me – I'm so jealous, and I'm so afraid of losing him. Maybe it's because I'm so crazy about him."

"I have an idea!"

Claire looked at me, surprised.

"Okay, what is it?"

"I'll find out the truth for you! Unlike you, I'm a neutral party – I'm objective."

"How are you going to get the truth?"

"Let me handle that – just ask yourself whether you're ready for it. What if he really isn't honest?"

I shouldn't have said that.

Claire started to wail again.

"Then I'll leave him, and he can go to hell – or back to his ex, I don't care."

"That's the Claire I love – it's a plan. Give me his number and I'll call him on my phone."

It rang for a long time, and I thought he wasn't going to pick up. I put him on speaker and got close to the microphone so Alex wouldn't realize Claire was listening in. Just before I was going to hang up, Alex answered.

"Hello?"

"Hello, Alex, this is Sophie Xama."

"Sophie who? Oh – Sophie – yeah. Claire isn't here, she left an hour ago."

My sense of taste told me he was telling the truth.

"Did you guys have a fight?"

"No, where did you get that?"

There was the bitter taste, telling me Alex was lying to me. So, it did work during a phone call.

"You had a fight, and Claire left. Why, Alex?" "What's all this about, Sophie? What do you want to hear from me?" "Only whether you were fighting because of your ex."

"Yeah, we did, but that doesn't have anything to do with you."

"Only if there was nothing to it, Alex. I am Claire's BFF, after all, so it does in fact have something to do with me if somebody's lying to her."

"This is bullshit, I am not interested.

Claire and I are together." "Do you love her, Alex?"

Claire looked at me, even more tense than I was. "Yes, I like her, I do think I love her."

Alex is telling the truth.

"Then what's all this business about your ex?"

"There's nothing – I already told Claire that. Why don't you be-lieve me? All of this is Kay-Ky. She just couldn't handle the fact that I dumped her, and now she's trying to ruin my relationship. If she keeps it up, she'll push Claire away."

I don't believe that, Alex. I believe you, and I'm going to talk to Claire. Thanks for being honest with me."

"I don't know what you all think of me, but I am being honest with everyone."

"Sophie?" "Yes?"

"Tell Claire that I love her really, a lot, and give her a hug from me. Maybe it will help her from being jealous."

"I'll tell her – good night, Alex."

"Good night, Sophie."

I looked at Claire, satisfied with the conversation. "He wasn't lying to you, Claire, and it seems like he's a stand-up guy." Claire just looked at me. "How could you know whether he's telling the truth or not?" "He was telling the truth, trust he wasn't lying." Claire nodded.

"You always were strange, Sophie – if you keep this up, soon I won't know you anymore. Little miss goody two-shoes, always doing everything perfect, and hating to be the center of attention. What happened to shy Sophie? Isn't she around anymore?"

"You're right, Claire. Sophie isn't here anymore. But Xama is, and she's more confidant, smarter, and focused. And she's just starting to discover who she is."

Claire's fight came at just the right time. A few minutes ago, I was still asking myself what my task, my Aphora, could be. Now it was so clear. How could I not have recognized it sooner? – I can taste truth and lies. My power enables me to know 100% whether someone is telling the truth or not. I could tell guilt or innocence without clues or arguments or reason. Everything was just a matter of taste – sweet or sour.

KAYL AND ARUN

I t's not very often that anything special happens right in front of Heaven. But today was definitely special. A police car drove up with its blue lights flashing and parked in front of the entrance just when Claire and I were leaving to buy the last things for our birthday party.

One of the police officers got out and opened the back door, then led the passenger out. Claire and I both stopped. In slow motion, a dark-haired, wide-shouldered, tall boy of about 17 or 18 got out of the police car. The driver escorted another boy who was sitting behind him out the car. We saw the back of the police car was split in two by a grate. It seemed the police had a good reason to separate the passengers.

"I hope you've both calmed down." I heard one of the policemen call out. Grabbing the muscular dark-haired boy's arm, he pulled him in our direction. The second policeman followed. The other boy was blonde and athletic, although he seemed to be a little older – maybe 19 or 20 – and taller too. When the policeman walked around the car with the blonde boy, he called out something unintelligible to the dark-haired one: it sounded something like "Wota – Wota."

It must have been another language; I could hear it, but it didn't make any sense. But his words certainly had an immediate effect. The dark-haired boy tore himself free with all his strength and lunged at the blonde boy, who had freed himself from the police officer and waiting in an attack stance. He called out again "Wota – Wota," sending his opponent into a rage – he went totally berserk.

Mouth open, bewildered, I looked first at Claire and then back at the boys. Both police officers were surprised by how fast their reactions were. They stood paralyzed, more worried about their own safety. The dark-haired boy started pummeling the blonde boy like a wild man. He used a fighting technique I'd never seen before, punching with both his feet at the same time as though they were fists. With unbelievable speed, he pounded the blonde boy again and again, the blonde boy elegantly blocking his

145

punches without fighting back. It was as though he was impossible to hit, always reacting just a hair quicker than his attacker. You could almost believe he knew in advance where the punches would fall, so he could dodge every one. Both were very well trained, but the way the blonde boy moved was almost artistic.

Claire, who had obviously had enough of this display, had already walked on towards the bus stop and was looking back at me.
"Oh, come on, Sophie, these pubescent meat-heads will calm down on their own. Let's go shopping."
When the blonde boy heard Claire call my name, he turned around and looked at me. He completely forgot he was being attacked and stopped making any attempt to defend himself. He just stood there, looking at me. In the same instant, a kick hit him at full speed in the face, followed by another punch. It was strange – it was as though I could feel his pain too. I knew the fight was over. The blonde boy swayed, looking at me, but couldn't stay on his feet any longer and fell to the ground. Lying there, he kept staring at me. Blood ran from his nose, and I thought I could read his lips. He was saying my name: "Sophie?"
The dark-haired boy, sure of his victory, looked first at his opponent and then at me. He had noticed the blonde boy was distracted, and he took the advantage. But then something happened that no one expected. The blonde boy called something out to the dark-haired one. He gave him his hand and pulled him back up on his feet, as if it had all just been a big show. The two hugged each other, then walked towards me. I stood there frozen. I had no idea what had just happened.

What do they want from us? Or me?

The blonde boy spoke first:
"Do you know where we sign in here?"
I looked at him, perplexed, and saw blood running down his nose.
"You're bleeding!"
"I know, but it's not bad."
The dark-haired one piped up, proudly:
"I wouldn't have been able to do that if you hadn't distracted him – I really should thank you for that."

"You should... what? Thank me that you broke his nose? I think you both must be crazy!"

They looked at each other, laughed and nodded.

"You're probably right about that! What's your name?" the darker of the two asked, coming forward.

Claire stepped up beside me, seeing the two of them wanted to strike up a conversation.

"Sophie, we have to go, otherwise we'll miss the bus."

"Sophie, that's a nice name. It's special. Does it mean anything? My name is Kayl, anyway, and this is my brother Arun."

"Hello, Sophie, I'm glad to meet you and ..."

"I'm Claire," she sputtered, stubbornly.

"What? You're brothers? That's even worse; you broke your brother's nose." Claire repeated.

"Forget what you saw. You're right; we're a little strange," Kayl said, attempting to explain.

"But that doesn't mean we don't care about each other. We respect each other. More than most other siblings you know – that's for sure,"

Arun, the darker-haired of the two, interjected in his defense. He put his arm over his brother's shoulder.

"It was more like a workout than a fight. We do that all the time to stay in shape.

Now and then one of us might hurt the other one, but that's rare. It's usually me that gets hurt. It does me good to knock Kayl around a little every now and then."

Arun grinned at Kayl, who nodded at him in agreement, blood still streaming from his nose.

"Normally both of us look out for each other, but I was a little distracted before."

"Normally? None of this looks normal to me. And if you look out for each other, then why is Kayl bleeding from his nose? Doesn't that count as an injury? And what was it that distracted you?" I asked.

"Calm down," Kayl said, "it's not really that bad. This isn't a real injury."

Kayl avoided my question without answering it. Arun could tell I wasn't impressed by what he'd done and nodded in agreement with Kayl. Then he reached into his pocket and pulled out another white handkerchief, passing it to him.

"Sophie's right, Kayl, you're bleeding, and it doesn't look good."

"And what would you call a broken nose that won't stop bleeding? Nothing to worry about!"

"Umm, yeah, I don't think it's broken."

"Okay, then why is it all pushed over to the right instead of in the middle of your face? You look like an alien!" I really hit the bulls eye with that. Kayl clearly didn't like having his appearance insulted.

"Really? Are you joking?"

"No. It's no laughing matter. Your nose is all pushed over. It looks like shit." Kayl turned to his brother Arun. "Arum, is that true? Is my nose out of place?" He tried to feel whether it was in the middle of his face. He looked at Claire, who affirmed my statement with a nod.

"Well, let's just say it isn't exactly where it was before."

"What do you mean not where it was before?"

"Well, not exactly perfectly in the middle – just pushed a little to the left."

Kayl turned towards me.

"Can you help me put it back?" he asked. If I let Arun do it, it'll probably end up looking worse."

Not knowing what to say, I asked another question.

"Maybe I should take a pass? This isn't exactly my specialty, unfortunately." Kayl grabbed his nose between his palms.

"It's pushed over to the right?"

"Yeah, a little."

"Let's go, Sophie, this is just too much," Claire said.

With a jerk, followed by a crack, then a slight moan, Kayl pushed his whole nose to the left. Blood shot out, coloring the handkerchief red and running over his fingers. I held my breath and had to look away. I didn't know what to do next. I felt totally helpless.

He must be in pain, awful pain, doing that to himself.

Kayl breathed in deeply and closed his eyes like he was trying to suppress his pain. He took another handkerchief Arun handed him, pressed it against his nose, and asked me a question. I didn't react, so he repeated it.

"How does my nose look now?

"Is it in the middle again?"

"Can I leave it there? Do I still look like shit?"

I stared at Kayl's nose. Yes, it looked centered, but twice as thick as normal, disfiguring his striking, well-shaped face.

"I think you have it back in the middle again, as far as I can tell. I'm not sure whether you always had such a fat nose, but except for the swelling it's alright."

Excuse us, we have to catch the bus."

"Thanks – the swelling will go down again in a couple of days if I don't let Arun break my nose again. I'll be careful. He won't be able to do it again so easily. I hope I don't look so shitty anymore?"

I could feel myself blush like a tomato. "Sorry, I'll take that back – I didn't mean to insult you."

"So you aren't shocked by my appearance. That's good – to be honest, it was actually your fault Arun broke my nose."

Claire couldn't control herself any longer.

"Just be careful what you're saying – otherwise, you'll have to answer to me, and I've had a black belt for years now." Claire snapped at Kayl.

"Well, then, welcome to the club – both of us are black belts too, and we've also learned a few other martial arts as well," Arun tossed in from the back.

"So the two of you are just a couple of jokers. First you clobber each other, and then the bystanders are to blame." "You asked me why I was distracted. When I saw you, I lost my concentration. That's the worst thing that can happen during a fight. Arun had the tiniest of chances, which he used. Which I do applaud him for."

"Both of you are so totally Kay-Ky. What planet are you from, anyway?"

"We're both extreme martial artists, but if you have time and want to go out for coffee with me, or maybe a pizza, I'll tell you all about our fascinating skills."

"I simply cannot understand it. You're both a little strange. First the two of you are beating each other up in front of an orphanage, accompanied by the police, and then all of a sudden it's all my fault. And then you ask me whether I want to go out with you? Maybe that knock on your head shattered not just your nose, but your whole brain too?"

"Could it be? If you accept my invitation, you can find out for yourself. Like you said, I do have a few things to make up for."
Kayl's eyes began to shine even more intensely, and I suddenly found him quite nice, despite his macho show.

Well, why not? Why shouldn't I go out with him?

"Okay, Kayl, I'll accept your invitation, but only when your nose is back under control. No more fights with your brother – promise?"
"Promise, Sophie, I'll never let Arun hit me on the nose again."
"How do I find you?"
"If you're moving into Heaven, then we'll see each other all the time. Otherwise just write to Sophie in Heaven, I'm sure I'll get it."
"Super, I'll look forward to it."
"Have you fought it out now?" one of the two policemen asked, "It's always the same thing with you two. Although I can't remember the last time you won, Arun."
"I never have before," Arun announced, proudly, "This was the first time."
"We've got to go. Be good and check in with child services – otherwise we'll take you in again."
"No need, Mr. Sergeant, Sir, we'll be good – I promise!"
Kayl and Arun followed the police officer, and I noticed Arun smiling at me on the way into Heaven. It was a warm smile, and made me feel comfortable – almost safe. Although his macho behavior really wasn't my thing, I found him somehow interesting – more interesting than his brother, Kayl. But there was something else. Arun was trying to point at something with his finger. He crossed his two pointer fingers and held them up in the air. Was Arun showing me a cross? The same symbol I had on my forehead? That can't be. I imagine things. But as much as I couldn't understand the thought, I couldn't let go of it either.
What did Arun want to say with this symbol?
Claire stood beside me the whole time with her mouth open and, contrary to her nature, didn't say a thing. She just looked at me with her eyebrows raised.
"Am I getting this right? Those two muscle-bound meatheads are fighting each other, in front of a bunch of people, then one of

them excuses himself by saying you distracted him and that's why he lost the fight and then to make it up to you he asks you to go out with him – and you accept?

What's happened to you, Sophie Dupre? I don't know you at all anymore. You, who were so quick to judge their immature macho display. Then some cutie wants to talk to you who you don't even know, and you just go out with him. That's not the Sophie I know – either your hormones are going nuts, or you're up to something, and you're not letting me in on it.

"If only I knew, Claire. But there is one thing you have to agree with – both of them were cool, and they both looked pretty good. Don't you think?"

"I don't believe it – they might have looked good, and they were certainly friendly. Those are the types of guys women swoon over, but not you – not my Sophie."

"You're right, not me."

"What does that mean? You just said ..."

"Yes, and I will have pizza with him to get to know him. I've got to make up for distracting him. That doesn't mean I'm swooning. Let's just see what happens – although, to be honest, I like Arun better. He's dark, like me, and he's also shy, like me."

Claire shook her head. "What's up with you, Sophie? You're so different, I hardly know you anymore. You're changing a lot right now, can't you see it?"

"You're right, it's time for Sophie Dupre to change from a day-dreaming, shy little girl into a confident woman – what do you think of that?"

Claire just stood there, shaking her head.

"Honest? Super Kay-Ky"

We both laughed, and hugged.

On the way downtown, I couldn't get the incident with Kayl and Arun out of my head. For some reason, I found Arun more interesting than Kayl. There was something mysterious about him. Both of them had a friendly, warm way about them, even though both, as Claire had rightly said, were pubescent meatheads, and most of these macho types don't have too much going on upstairs. Although that did remain to be seen in this case. Claire was probably right. Otherwise the two of them wouldn't have started fighting in front of Heaven. You don't do something like that when you're moving into a new place. Oh, well, I'm sure I'll get to know them in the next few days – Maybe I'll find a way to get to know Arun as well. I still need to ask him what the symbol meant. It probably didn't have anything to do with what I thought. But there was something secretive about Arun, something that had awakened my interest. We'll see if the two of them are really as crazy as they looked today. No matter what, I did feel a positive energy when I was around them, and a sweet taste on my tongue. Something told me I could trust them. Claire was right – I really had changed. But I read in Dad's legacy that the aphormation takes 21 months. 21 months – I'm excited to find out what's going to happen to Sophie Dupre next if things keep up like this.

The Law of the Arverni

Claire stayed in the city a while, but I took the first chance I could get to go back to Heaven. The whole trip, I kept thinking about the two brothers Kayl and Arun. I couldn't get Arun out of my mind. If I wasn't mistaken, none of this was a coincidence. When I returned to my room. I carefully took out the next to last notebook and looked at it. Although they were all the same color, a classic blue, each book was special. I wondered what was left to learn? Curious about "Book 4 – the Law of the Arverni" – I turned the first page and started to read.

"Dear Xama, the book you hold in your hands contains an introduction to Arverni law. Let's start with the basics: the Arverni are a peaceful people who live in accordance with ancient customs, rules, and duties, some of them over a thousand years old. Life stands in the highest, most prominent position. No Arverni has the right to take the life of a human or of another Arverni. There is one exception to this, however, which requires the unanimous decision of the council. If a human or Arverni is killed by the hand of another, the council determines whether it was murder or not. If it was murder, the one who committed the crime is also sentenced to death. His death is then administered in the same way his victim died. It does not matter to the council whether any other laws see the matter differently. If the council determines guilt, it will assign a punishment and carry it out. There is a unit for this purpose within the security division that follows up violations for the council. They also respond to other dangers that affect the council or the community. This unit, which reports directly to the head of security, consists of the so-called Achilleans. Achilleans are specially trained fighters whose Aphora, their task, is to ensure the safety of members of the community. They usually also develop powers which predestine them for this task. Achilleans fear nothing. If necessary, an Achilleans will give his life to protect the community or a member of the community. If an Arverni violates his apheid and uses his powers and abilities in a way that goes against his purpose, he will be subject to punishment and will be banned from the community. Since all Arverni work in companies that belong to the community, banning also means losing a job, losing status, and losing regular income. There are three very important rules everyone must conform to, and these are the values, the foundation upon which the whole community is built: Arverni do not steal, cheat or lie. There are certainly Arverni who do not conform to these basic principles. If there is no proof, they are not judged by the council. Judgments are not made based solely on accusations. There must also be sufficient proof to justify the judgment. Another important law of the Arverni regulates the place of the woman. This is a very ancient law and greatly restricts the role of women. In the last few years, there have been many attempts to change the law but there has never been majority support. The conservatives refuse to assign any rights to women. They are prohibited from becoming members they have no influence on the development of the community, the business. In accordance with Arverni law, a woman is to stand her husband and support him in his role. She is to raise the children. There are many who want to do away with this law, but the two-thirds majority required for this has yet not been reached. It's not just the conservatives – there are also other members who are against women's equality. Many council members reject change because of the secrets they guard. It's time for this law, and for the position of women, to be modernized. I am sure you will live to see it – you will be a part of the change."

School Can Be Fun

The last two days and nights were absolutely crazy. Studying for school, getting ready for the birthday party, and hours of reading about the Arverni legacy to understand who or what I am. There was so much to do that I simply had to work all night. Thanks to my aphmal, I could do it without any side effects. I did notice that I kept running into Arun or Kayl. One or both of them kept popping up no matter where I went.

Was this really a coincidence? Were the two of them trying to cross paths with me? Am I just noticing it because I find the two of them so interesting, or is there something I don't know?

Whatever the case, Arun was anything but pushy – more restrained, really. It was remarkable that he kept showing up wherever I was. Normally, our glances would meet and he would flash me a smile, which I would return, of course. He rarely spoke to me, and when he did it was more small talk than anything else. But there was something that made him interesting, and it wasn't just his appearance. There was something I couldn't define but wanted to find out more about any way I could. That had to wait – there was something more important than Arun. There were just a few days left until our birthday party, and there was still so much to do. It was clear to Claire and I that we had set ourselves a lofty goal when we planned to have the "best party in town." There was nothing for it but to stay up until midnight working on the party room and our decorations. Claire was worn down after a couple of days, even though she was usually the one going to bed long after I did and waking up earlier in the morning. To be honest, she looked awful, exhausted; even her talents in make-up were no longer sufficient to hide the black rings under her eyes. This evening, however, we both realized we just couldn't keep going, and I suggested she knock off early and go to bed. I already knew she wouldn't be able to resist my idea, and when we dragged ourselves out of the party room it didn't take ten minutes for Claire to fall asleep. Her even breathing, – some might have called it snoring – told me she was fast asleep. I had waited for this all day long. Now, I could finally read more. A glance at my alarm clock told me there were still more than 7 hours left until I had to get up – that should be enough. Being an Averni and possessing 24 hours did come in handy. I really need it right now – school, the birthday party, and learning about the Arverni are all important, and I can't put any of them off. What did you think? Would I, one of the top students with the best grades in my school, have skipped out on school and acted sick? Thanks for your confidence, but unfortunately there were three important things I had to do this week, and making up my homework wasn't one of them. There was definitely still a chance I'd get all A's. Be honest – with all of these powers, wouldn't you just download everything you needed for your homework into your memory real fast? What an ability! Who would be satisfied with a B in math, chemistry, or writing when they could have an A? Not me! School was awesome, thanks to my aphmal. Studying had completely changed – I could remember anything I wanted to. I invested time, preparing myself for each assignment and each class, but with a lightning efficiency. I didn't have to repeat anything; I just read everything once and it was already saved. To be honest, it kind of made school fun. During class, I just took in everything the instructor projected on the screen and memorized it. At the same time, I read the next chapter in the physics book and memorized all that information too. It was like I had a digital copy of the whole book, including all the pictures and photos, in my head. This little advantage made it much easier to look for and find something in the book. I just needed to read the question and I already knew the answer. What can I say? Being an Arverni was getting better and better – it's all just simply Kay-Ky. I did the same thing in chemistry and math, although I also noticed in both subjects that my logical understanding had increased dramatically. As we all know, memorizing doesn't get you very far in math. Either you've understood how to do a certain calculation, or you founder and never get the result quite right. Another thing that surprised me was that my aphmal allowed me to recognize logical connections immediately. I read the rules for statistics through and suddenly understood how to use them. Even when I read through complex calculations, I knew how to get the result and could immediately call up all the steps. That was super crazy amazing Kay-Ky. Now maybe you can all understand why I liked to go to school, and why playing sick wasn't an option for me. It is simply too much fun to use my new abilities and see what I can achieve with them – where the limits are. To be honest, my ambition and I might have overdone it a little bit. My teachers noticed, of course, that I was really stepping on the gas, and my perfection almost had negative consequences. It was a little excessive of me to not only calculate all the problems correctly in math but to also deliver a proof for one of the questions, then go ahead and write my "A" grade right on top.

It was arrogant – why did I do that?

I did go a little too far there, especially since it was going exactly the same in all my other subjects. In chemistry, we had to draw a chemical reaction of hydrocarbons and explain the process. I don't know what got into me, but I dissected one of the most famous proofs in all of chemistry, made a substitution to optimize it, and then put the whole thing back together. I optimized the chemical process and was able to achieve a reduction in energy use of 36%. The result made me jump up from my chair – it was a revolutionary discovery. I was lucky my chemistry teacher didn't understand the whole thing – it was a little over his head. He graded my solution as incorrect, so my genius remained hidden. He wrote me a nice commentary under my work that my analysis was slightly paralyzed. I can't imagine what would have happened if he had shown this assignment to a college professor or an industrial researcher. I might have even won the next Nobel Prize, and what would I have told them then? Certainly not that I'm an Arverni and have an aphmal, even though that's the truth. Following father's instructions would have meant even Albert Einstein would have kept his secrets to himself, not letting anyone see he had special abilities. I had to practice restraint; otherwise I ran the risk of giving myself away. I also mastered my German essay. My German teacher had written me a three-page inscription under the essay about how this was the best literary work she had ever read in all her 20 years as a teacher. The dumb thing was that Ms. Weber gave my masterpiece to one of her friends to read, and he was an editor in a publishing house. He was blown away by it too, and my problem got even bigger. Well, in the end Ms. Weber and the editor convinced me to finish writing the story. They probably just wanted to know what happened next, since the story was so gripping. Do something right and all of a sudden you'll get another contract – dammit – of course, I wrote it to be engaging, it's a romance. It's all about heartbreak. That's what the reader wants, after all. But I didn't intend everyone to get all addicted to it. My attempt to get an A in German turned into a major project. They all wanted me to turn 25 pages into a 300-page novel, as quickly as possible. The editor and his publishing house pressured me with money, first a little, and then more and more. I knew that I could do it, and still didn't feel overburdened. So, I finally submitted to all the pressure, letting myself get carried away by the money and praise. It is strange – since I've had the aphmal, everything's been so easy.

So I had another item on my to-do list. It was just good the birthday party was going to be on Saturday, so I could cross it off at least. I also had a great idea for the book project, but the editor wasn't extremely excited about it – he was more of a conservative type. Only when I threatened to turn down the whole project did he agree, reluctantly, that I deliver the first ten chapters to him spoken on a recording instead of written and printed out like normal. He wanted to make it dependent on the quality of my recording as to whether this process would work or whether I should just deliver a written manuscript. I was sure this was the perfect solution for me. Why should I write anything down, when I could record it? I knew I would be able to develop the first ten chapters in my mind and then record the words directly as they came into my head – perfect, and ready to go just like that. So that my perfection in recording my thoughts didn't cause extra attention, I added a few passages and removed others, giving the impression that I was developing the contents step by step. At the end, I recorded everything I had thought of initially, without making it obvious I could have simply dictated the whole novel without a single change – it's great to be an Arverni. The correction passages took me a little extra time, but made everything much more believable. In this case they were necessary; otherwise the editor would have noticed something was fishy, and maybe would have thought I was just reading off the page. Now you know approximately how much stress and fun school was. While my head whirled from school, the birthday party, and the

Arverni, I felt exhaustion creeping up on me mercilessly. My first thought was to correct this with my aphmal, but then I decided against it. I got undressed for a nap, and pushed off showering and brushing my teeth until the next morning. It was a pleasant feeling to relax, and when I snuggled down into my blankets, it took only seconds for me to become immersed in a dream.

I ran down the street, totally out of breath. Someone was running after me and was getting closer. Afraid of slowing down, I didn't dare look back; instead I kept running straight ahead, across an intersection and into a narrow alley. Out of breath, I realized it was a courtyard. I was trapped. There was only one way in and one way out. The stranger started walking towards me, slowly. He reached into his coat pocket and took out something shiny that looked like a long knife. I wanted to cry out when a door opened up behind me and a voice I recognized called my name.
"Sophie, Sophie, here – here."

At first, I didn't dare turn my head. But then I did and saw the man with the knife start to run. No – he was running quicker and quicker, rushing in my direction.
"Sophie, come here!"
I heard the familiar voice and saw Arun holding a door with one hand and waving at me with the other. Something blocked me, and as much as I wanted to move towards Arun, I couldn't. Arun, seeing me stand there petrified, ran towards me, then past me.
"Wait here!" he called to me in a quiet, warm, and yet command-ing tone.

Why didn't he stop beside me? Why did he run past me?

I saw the attacker with the knife threatening us wildly and com-ing closer as Arun ran directly at him.

He's not going to…

But Arun did exactly what I had hoped he wouldn't. He attacked the assailant just as he was, unarmed. The unknown attacker tried to stab Arun. He threw a punch and hit the attacker directly in the face, followed by a knee jab. The attacker dropped the knife and fell to the ground. Arun picked it up, pointing it directly at him. It looked as though he was going to stab him.

No, don't do it Arun – let him live.

Arun looked in my direction, lowered the knife, and walked towards me. I felt as though I would collapse at any moment, which is exactly what happened as soon as Arun stood in front of me. He reacted again in a flash. He took hold of my wrist, and as I slowly collapsed into myself, he turned me around and held me in his strong arms. Then I heard a noise in the background growing ever louder, ever more intense until I opened my eyes and recognized the sound. It was my alarm clock, showing 6:30. Time to get up and go to school. Totally worn-out, I asked myself what kind of a crazy dream that had been.

Why on earth did Arun show up in my dream?
Why him, and why not Amar or Kayl?

ENEMIES OF THE ARVERNI

T oday was the day, I had decided to read the last chapter after school. Although my expectations were low, in light of recent events, I was still interested to learn about who or what the Arverni feared. Once I was home, I set down my school things, took the aphmal box out of my bedside table, and got comfortable on my bed. As I held the last notebook "Enemies of the Arverni" I asked myself what was coming next. What would become of me? I started to read.

"Although the Arverni community is peaceful, members are banned from the community for grave violations of the rules. More and more often, this is creating new enemies whose frustration leads them to try and seek revenge on the community or individuals. Individual cases are handled by security. There are also cases in which the Arverni are attacked directly – mainly because they use their powers in an uncontrolled manner. This causes fear in humans, who then persecute or even kill the Arverni. Especially in the Middle Ages, many were accused of witchcraft and were burnt at the stake. Today enemies of the Arverni come from our own ranks. They are hateful. They are after the blood of aspirants.

Some years ago, the council issued a contract to some Arverni doctors and researchers. The members were all over thirty years old, and already in the Finitum. Because of this, they had a common interest in researching why the Finitum begins at the age of thirty. What causes it? How can it be stopped?

One of our most successful doctors received the research contract. Dr. A. Sherman convinced the council that the Finitum could be traced back to medical and physical causes, which essentially means that there is a chemical process at work in its development. If one was able to describe and understand this process in detail, one could also alter it or even suppress it. It might even be possible to reverse the process. This was exactly what the members of the council wanted to hear: that the Finitum would be researched, all ambiguities cleared up, and the aging process would be altered or even stopped. Sherman promised the council he would present measurable results within 12 months. Money was no object, meaning Sherman could hire excellent specialists, and his research team was making enormous advances. The council provided the resources they needed and influenced Arverni to donate blood for the experiments. If there's one thing that truly functions well in the community, it's the involvement of its members. If the council asks for support, no Arverni refuses to help.

Sherman had enough Arverni blood to conduct decades of research. Coincidentally, one of the donors was still in the aphormation. The aspirant went to donate blood with his father. Sherman's researchers detected something in the aspirant's blood sample that was missing in all the other samples. They researched further, and in contrast to their assumptions, it was not the Finitum, which initiated a change. Quite the opposite: everything was predetermined long before, during the aphormation. Something triggered by the aphormation also eventually caused the Finitum. There was something in the aspirant's blood that was responsible for the aphormation, the aphmal, and the development of special powers. Sherman called it the Arverni gene, and informed the council of his discovery. The council was split: some were so impressed by Sherman's discovery that they saw only the positive side. Others asked themselves whether it was right to use aspirants and their blood for the research, and where the boundaries really were. After Sherman presented all of his results, he told the council members they could live long, possibly eternal lives. There were frantic discussions. The Meta stepped in and posed the question for a vote. The hall became loud again, and when the question was asked who supported continuing the research, we saw hands raised, slowly. The Meta counted, and there were exactly six members who voted in favor. He asked the opposing question, and there were five members who were against. That meant that the Meta's vote would decide – for, or against. Everyone in the room looked at him, tense, awaiting his judgment. He made it short and painless, and informed the council that he was voting against the research. Thus, the judgment was that Dr. A. Sherman's research must be discontinued immediately. The results were secured in the archives, all work was paid, and the research team immediately disbanded. Some members were shocked: all hope of a healthier and longer life and an end to the Finitum was lost.

Sherman voiced his disappointment, cursing the Meta. He packed his things in a rage and before leaving, he said.

'Because of this decision, I and all in agreement with me will leave the community of the Arverni immediately. No one can force me to cease pursuing my cause. I do not accept the decision you have made. It is a result of the Finitum – you are no longer able to make clear and logical decisions. A council of old, senile men without the confidence to dare to be more.'

Sherman left the room; he knew he had to react quickly now. With his phone already at his ear, Sherman instructed the person on the other end to activate immediately Plan B. He made him personally responsible for completing the financial transaction at once. Furthermore, after successfully completing the transaction, he was to inform the team. Everyone on his list was needed; all others had to be deactivated. Then go underground, to the new location.

At the same time, as the Meta was summarizing the decision, the security division was tasked with ensuring the council's decision to halt the research.

The research laboratory Sherman had used exploded, burning to the ground. A few researchers and workers were killed; they also found bodies, which indicated Sherman, and his closest associates had been in the building at the time of the explosion. The police were satisfied with this explanation. The Arverni council knew Sherman had staged the accident so he could disappear. But that wasn't what angered the council, and especially the Meta – it was the fact that Dr. A. Sherman had succeeded in transferring over 460 million Euros out of Arverni bank accounts. This meant Sherman had what he needed to continue with his research. The council convicted Sherman, and from this point forward he became the most wanted Arverni. And not only that: he was also the most dangerous.

The council realized this when a sixteen-year-old aspirant was found dead drained of all his blood which Dr. A. Sherman and his research team were responsible for.

The council met and gave my organization instructions and me on how to deal with Dr. Sherman once and for all. The council resorted to a measure, which hadn't been taken in hundreds of years: **carte blanche**. This meant I was able to deactivate Sherman and his team without fearing any consequences – to kill every last one of them if necessary. It came to a battle – we lost some young Achilleans. Sherman lost some of his researchers and mercenaries, but he was able to escape my trap. From this point forward, Sherman swore his revenge on me personally and on the council. His ability to manipulate other people was faultless. He lost his power like every other Arverni going through the Finitum. But after his research team achieved a breakthrough and was able to extract the Arverni gene, Sherman wasted no time and injected a small amount of it into him. His aphmal was reactivated and so were his powers – stronger than ever before. He brimmed with confidence and energy; he became even more unpredictable and dangerous. He used his powers whenever possible, a man on a mission. Sherman became megalomaniacal and carried out his retaliation campaign against the community with every means necessary. He was blinded by rage. Since he has a personal score to settle with me, you are also in particular danger. Firstly because you're an aspirant, secondly because Sherman swore his revenge against me. He is possessed – possessed by an insane idea."

DR. AGOR SHERMAN

Las Vegas, Nevada, USA

A black Mercedes SUV moved along a driveway towards The Palms hotel in Las Vegas, stopping directly in front of the entrance. The driver, a tall man in a black suit and black sunglasses, got out, shut the door, and stood next to the car as though petrified. It looked as if he would open the back door any moment to allow one of the many celebrities who arrived here every day to step out. But nothing happened. He stood quietly beside the vehicle and looked at his surroundings very carefully – he was scanning the immediate area working out a potential escape route. As he took a step towards the Mercedes, he knocked on the hood, creating a loud, muffled sound. It was a signal. All of the doors accept the driver's door opened at almost the same time, and three men cloned from the driver stepped out. After brief instructions from the driver, all of them spread out in different directions – within seconds, the entrance to The Palms was cleared of people – a situation the hotel had never experienced before. The driver of the Mercedes monitored the area again, and when he had gotten the thumbs up signal from each one of his three colleagues, he pulled a phone out of his suit pocket, typed something into it, and then it vanished again into the suit just as elegantly. Not a minute later, one of the most expensive limousines in the world – a black Maybach 62 – drove up the entrance and stopped behind the SUV. The tinted windows on the Maybach impeded a view of the vehicle's interior. The driver of the Mercedes checked the surroundings once again and got another status update from his colleagues. He nodded, acknowledging everything was in order, and knocked on the door of the limousine. A tall, blonde, suntanned man got out of the passenger side and moved around the vehicle. He, too, had the stature of a bodybuilder.

"Good day, Mr. Booz – I'm happy to see you and your men here."

"Jack, my name is Jack."

"Very well, Jack, my name is Peter Sanders. Would you mind assisting Dr. Sherman out of the car?"

Jack perceived this as an order, opened the back door, and thought to himself that his client would likely appreciate a short security status update.

"Everything is in order, Dr. Sherman. Welcome to Las Vegas."

"I expected nothing less, James."

"Jack, sir, my name is Jack."

Dr. Sherman looked at Jack with a piercing stare.

"There is only one single reason I have commissioned you –Jack."

"Yes, sir."

"And that is? Jack?"

Jack thought about this, nervously shifting his weight from one foot to the other.

"Security, sir. Your security and that of your colleagues and friends."

"Cross off the colleagues and friends part rather concentrate your and your team's efforts on my own security. After all you are being generously compensated for it. Have we understood one another, James?!"

"Was this intentional or was he simply senile?"

Jack considered for a moment whether he should correct Dr. Sherman again. He remembered his Special Forces training in the Marines – even if a commander's answer was wrong, you didn't contradict it!

"Yes, sir! Understood, sir!"

Jack took a step back and thought to himself – *what an asshole!* Sherman gripped a handle on the Maybach with his left hand so he could bring a walking stick into position with his right. Jack noticed a chain leading away from Sherman's right hand. At first it reminded him of a handcuff, but when he looked closer he realized the end was attached to a small silver chest....

Dr. Sherman attempted to pull himself up out of the seat with the help of the handle and the walking stick, straining. The chest on his hand was definitely a hindrance. For a moment, Jack considered whether he should offer his client help, or maybe just hold the chest. But not even his assistant stirred, and when he noticed Jack starting to take a step forward, he grabbed his jacket. Jack's thought of helping Sherman was stifled.

"Don't even think of helping me, James.
I'll manage on my own, understood?"

Sherman was now standing in front of the Maybach, supporting himself on his walking stick with his left hand, and holding the strange little metal chest in his right. His hands shook as he tried to maintain his balance and his composure with all his might.
Jack looked at him more closely; something wasn't right with this Dr. Sherman. He stood before him, a sick old man, his grey, almost shoulder-length hair all combed back, allowing a view of his bony, striking face. Jack asked himself whether Sherman had gelled his hair, or whether the shine was just because the hair was greasy. Whatever the case, his appearance was anything but pleasant. Sherman's deep eye sockets and prominent cheekbones reminded Jack of a marathon runner losing energy and breaking down just before reaching the finish line. A second look showed him a custom terracotta suit that seemed to have no wrinkles at all. A white shirt with a casually open collar. All in all, someone who had plenty of money. Jack asked himself how old Sherman might be? It was tough to tell. The contract, mentioned something about a wealthy businessman, middle aged, needed for a period of four or more weeks, personal protection. Middle aged? He's got to be over 70. He didn't have any further information about his client, only that he demanded the highest level of security, which surprised Jack. If a person requires the highest level of security, he's either in life-threatening circumstances or already half dead. Jack and his team were the best, which was why he had gotten the contract. What annoyed him now, however, was that although he had figured several surcharges into his offer, he had forgotten the 50% asshole surcharge. Jack knew each one of his colleagues personally; he had served with several of them in the army, and would take a bullet for any one of them. Maybe that was why he was so demanding and direct in dealing with his employees. Jack always tried to be decent, and solve problems in a sensible way. But the two sentences he had exchanged with Dr. Sherman offended him. Worse than being stabbed. Sherman had stomped on his values – more than that, he had wiped his dirty shoes on them. Sherman was an asshole, and assholes have to pay the 50% asshole surcharge. If he refused, he and his men would withdraw immediately and have fun in Las Vegas for a couple of days. He hoped that was what would happen – he knew only too well, however, that in the situation Dr. Sherman was in, he would give anything for his security.

Sherman was afraid – deathly afraid – so scared Jack could smell it. Jack turned to the blonde bodyguard and took his arm.

"We'll accompany Dr. Sherman to his room, and after that we refuse to carry out the contract unless you pay a surcharge."

"What kind of surcharge? We have signed a contract."

"Yes we have, but since your Dr. Sherman doesn't respect the people who carry out a service for him then, there is a clause in my contract which applies."

Sherman, still trying to find his balance, realized the two of them had stepped to the side and discussing something. He slowly walked towards the hotel entrance and tossed off another comment to Jack.

"James, everything alright? Don't you have a job to do?"

In that moment, the asshole surcharge went up a tick in Jack's mind.

"Huh? What kind of clause?" the bodyguard asked.

"A very simple one – I call it the asshole clause. It states that should a client treat me like an asshole, I have the right to end the contract at any time, unless ..."

"A what? I don't understand you – you can't just end the contract. What do I need to do, Mr. Booz – how can I make it up to you?"

"Nothing. I'll send you a contract extension today; the whole job has gone up around 100% in price, but as I've said – if you want to save a little money, I can give you the contact details one of my colleagues. If you don't need security level 4, and don't want the best, you could always ..."

"Calm down, Mr. Booz, send me the changes later; just double the price, it's all fine."

Wow, Jack thought to himself, bulls eye.

"Understood, then, we are in agreement."

Jack held his hand out as a sign of the deal and the blonde man shook it.

"I'm happy to be working for Dr. Sherman again, please be assured he is secure."

"And what about me?"

"You'll have to talk to him about that. He did say earlier I should only protect him, not any of his friends or colleagues."

"But that statement certainly must have include me?"

"Are you completely sure about that? Let's talk more later – I have to work, but we'll definitely be able to find a solution to that as well, just add another 10,000 dollars for the 4 weeks. What are 10,000 dollars, when it comes to your security?"

Jack walked to his colleagues on the other side, and Sherman and the blonde bodyguard followed him.

"Bob, thanks."

"Welcome to The Palms Hotel, Mr. Sherman," the General Manager called out, offering him his hand. "My name is Gerald van der Thun, and my team and I will be doing everything possible to make your stay as perfect as we can."

Jack's gaze now slipped to the red-haired beauty who had taken a spot beside the hotel manager. She introduced herself.

"I'd also like to welcome you, Dr. Sherman. My name is Andrea Vincente, and I'm Mr. van der Thun's assistant, our general manager. Please feel free to ask me anything you may require, anytime".

Jack's thoughts wandered at Ms. Vincente's offer, and he had to get control of his imagination. He knew exactly what he would do with her around the clock.

"Many thanks for your hospitality; may I introduce myself: my name is Sanders, Peter Sanders, and I am Dr. Sherman's private secretary."

At least Sanders had manners, Jack thought.

"Very glad to meet you," the general manager answered as Andrea Vincente was still checking Sanders out with her piercing green eyes – she seemed pleased with everything she saw.

"Welcome, Mr. Sanders, we have spoken on the phone, haven't we? I'm certain we will be able to work well together." Pete Sanders gave Andrea Vincent the once over, nodding in agreement. Sherman, who was standing there visibly strained and bored, vented his frustration.

"Would you direct me to my room. In one sentence – I can't stand it when people babble on, stealing my time and breathing up all the oxygen."

Sherman walked on, leaving the others behind.

"Air thieves! Nothing but air thieves!" he grumbled to himself so loudly that they all heard him.

Van der Thun and Vincente stood there, appalled.

"What was that?" Vincente asked.

"An asshole, a real asshole," Jack let slip.

"I believe you are correct," Vincente agreed with him, earning an angry glance from her boss.

Sanders, who found all of this embarrassing, changed the subject. "Please, have the luggage brought up from the Mercedes to Mr. Sherman's suite, and please bring my suitcase to my room."

"Most certainly, and as you've asked, we have reserved you the Skyloft suite and furnished it according to your requirements. Please follow me – access to the Skyloft suite is only possible through one specialized elevator. You are absolutely safe here, guarded from the public. We have executed all of your require-ments 100%, which you will discover to your own satisfaction."

The hotel manager went first, followed by Sanders, Vincente, and Jack a little distance behind.

Jack also instructed one of his employees, who disappeared with a nod. Van der Thun made his way towards the elevator door, engraved with the letters Skyloft VIP brushed aluminum. Only upon closer inspection did it become clear that this was no sign, but rather the extension of a standing secretary on which an iPad had been integrated. With a familiar movement, he activated the iPad and input a four digit code. The noise, as well as the lit num-bers on the iPad, indicated that the elevator was traveling down from the 20th floor. It only took seconds for a gong to sound and the elevator door to open, revealing an elevator lined in marble and mirrors. Mr. Sherman went into the elevator first, followed by Vincente and Sanders. Jack followed van der Thun as the last one in, providing security as van der Thun activated the elevator with a golden key card. Van der Thun explained that the golden room key also entitled the holder to play in the hotel's casino in the high roller area without any limits, which was the first thing to get Dr. Sherman's attention.

"So as not to dampen the gambling fun, both keys have already been loaded with 30,000 US dollars each. If you wish, to play, the casino is open 24 hours a day."

"First I need to freshen up a bit," Sherman burst out, surprisingly. Vincente and Jack both had the same thought:

Somebody really should freshen him up – really.

Andrea Vincente asked herself why this Dr. Sherman had even come to Law Vegas. She even dared to ask the question, bravely:

"You didn't come to gamble, like most of our guests, did you? If you're interested in one of the many shows we have here in Las Vegas, just let me know. I can arrange for tickets – please, just call me."

Sherman's glance silenced Vincente.

"Air thief," he said again, so loud everyone could hear him, and left the elevator.

"We'd be happy to accept your offer, Ms. Vincente, Sanders said to deescalate the situation. Dr. Sherman and I will look through the available shows later on, and I will contact you about getting a couple of good tickets. I assume that you'll also have a way of procuring tickets for us to sold out shows?"

"It would be my pleasure, Mr. Sanders – whatever you and Mr. Sherman are interested in, just let me know and I'll be sure you get the right tickets."

As Sanders smiled at Vincente in agreement, a smile became visible on Sherman's face for the first time as well.

When van der Thun opened the door to the loft, Jack went in first. "You all wait here until I come back."

Jack's directions were simple and explicit, and delivered in a tone that made it clear that they must be followed. To everyone's surprise, he was suddenly holding an automatic weapon in his hands, which certainly underscored the seriousness of his statement. After a couple of minutes, Jack returned to give the green light and everyone went in.

"Welcome to our Sky Loft!" Here, you have the best view of Las Vegas Boulevard. A personal pool with hot tub on the rooftop patio. Your own poker room with a croupier if you wish. In total, you have over 30,000 square feet of space available here, including three bathrooms, six bedrooms, a billiard room, an office, a bar, a cinema, and much more. Sanders looked at Sherman, shocked. When he had freed his wrist from the chest and chain, he lifted his fist and showed them all the way to the door with his thumb. Sherman accentuated his gesture with the words:

"Get lost!"

Sherman's gesture had the desired effect. Everyone left the loft. Everyone except Sanders, who let himself sink into one of the big leather sofas. Sherman made himself a whiskey at the open bar.

"You want one too, Pete?"

"I've lost my appetite for it. How can you?"

"How can I what? Calm down."

"Your arrogance cost us two hundred thousand dollars instead of the agreed eighty thousand. I hope it was worth it to you."

"Okay, I'm not doing so well. I just wanted to get to the room, since I knew my emotional state is so low right now. The pain in my legs is becoming unbearable." Sherman passed Sanders a glass half full of whiskey and sat down beside him with his own glass.

The glasses clinked together.

"Peter, we are about to solve the riddle of Arverni inheritance. You know what that means. I have been looking for the answer for 50 years, and I have dedicated my whole life and the lives of many others to this endeavor."

Sanders looked first into his glass, and then at Sherman.

"If we are, as the researchers assured me yesterday, at a point after so many years of research where the gene can be created chemically, then ..."

Sherman had a light in his eyes; the hand in which he was holding his whiskey glass began to tremble noticeably.

Sanders knew what this meant, and ended the sentence Sherman had begun.

"Then we'll have the answer to the most important of humanity's questions — immortality. Your condition is becoming unstable; you require the Arverni gene."

Sanders stood up and went to the small metal chest Sherman had placed on the glass table. He looked at it for a moment, then picked it up and passed it to Sherman. He placed it on the sofa beside himself and started punching in the security code. With a loud click-click, he opened the small chest and folded the lid back. An injection gun became visible, as well as three small glass ampules filled with a golden, glistening liquid. Sanders took an ampule out of the chest, held it up to the light, and looked at the fluid inside the ampule, which was now glowing a radiant gold — it seemed somehow precious.

"Isn't it beautiful, Peter?"

Sanders walked a few steps in the direction of the rooftop patio and looked outside through the big glass windows; something in Sherman's statement had touched him. His eyes began to water; he was about to cry.

"It's not. It's not beautiful, because a 16 year old had to die, so you could continue living - How many more have to die?"

"Peter, I thought we'd already discussed that. The same thing is happening to you. Your aging process has already begun, and it's only going to get faster until the Finitum will destroy your body - You might still have 10 – maybe 8 years – no more."

Sanders placed the ampule into the injector.

"We did discuss it. But I just can't ignore it like you do. How many have died already? Innocent young people. It kills me inside – I can't sleep anymore. I hope you're right, and that the researchers have discovered a way to bring this goal of ours to an end. I can't go on like this."

"I know – the two of us are very different, but I can understand your position. Tomorrow we'll meet with the researchers and I am sure we will discover we're at the finishing line. Peter, pull yourself together. Everything we had to do – we did it all for a reason."

Sherman stood up and walked towards Sanders with the injector in his hand. He tapped his hand on Sanders' shoulder.

"Get a grip – I need you, now more than ever before, Pete!" Sanders turned around slowly, set down his glass, and hugged Sherman.

"I need you too, father."

Sherman hugged Sanders with the injector in his hand. His tremors intensified, and Sanders noticed the uncontrolled convulsions. Sanders loosened his hug.

"Father, you have to take your medicine; it's getting worse."

Sherman nodded and went into the bathroom, turning around on the way and saying: "I love you, son."

Sanders turned back towards the glass window and looked at the throngs of people below. He couldn't control his emotions any longer, and started crying.

FINAL PREPARATIONS

Our preparations for the birthday party were as good as finished. The first decorations were done and the room was starting to look like a crypt. Then, for some reason, that dummy Alex got the idea of totally knocking over the plan four days before the party. He was convinced we absolutely had to have a castle gate and a fountain. *What a stupid idea!*

Then, he wanted to change the wall decorations at the last minute. No idea what was going on with him – he probably got a brain freeze last time he went to get ice cream with Claire and ended up cryogenically freezing one of his five brain cells. That, at least, would have explained the mental depths he had sunk to. But what really disgusted me was that Alex was totally hitting it off with Claire with his macho attitude – she thought he was just super!

How can she like a pleb like him?

In my opinion, Alex and Claire are like vanilla ice cream and mustard. It just doesn't work. But what fascinated me was that my best friend thought this mating season behavior and overblown masculine idiocy was so super manly. Since it was my birthday party too, I didn't want the whole thing to turn into a flop because of somebody's massive overestimation of their own talent for details. Whilst trying to put up spiderwebs, we heard a loud knock. Claire wasn't far from the entrance, so she called to me.

"I'll go and open." We had locked the door so that our decorations would remain a surprise. Looking at my spider web, I suddenly heard Claire let out a piercing scream. The door was opened a crack, and Claire was holding onto it tightly. Something must have frightened her.

"Sophie, I think there's someone here who would like to talk to you." *Who could it be? Hopefully Arun.*

Suddenly, my aphmal went on alert. It felt like a needle jabbing me in the middle of my forehead. My aphmal was going crazy in a way I'd never experienced it before.

Is it a warning? If so, from whom?

In the moment I got to Claire's side, she pulled the door open. A life-size skeleton was standing in front of me, shaking around, with someone behind it making weird noises to boot. Unfazed I played along and screamed for effect, stepping back a step out of fear. The skeleton stopped moving and Kayl and Arun suddenly appeared from behind it. A little surprised, I looked first at Kayl and then at Arun. Arun was winking at me. Kayl pushed in front of Arun and blurted out:

"Hello, Sophie, how are your – did we scare you?"

I noticed immediately that Kayl's nose was significantly smaller - his face even more striking, and he really was good looking.

"Thanks for asking – a little stressed out, but otherwise I'm doing fine."

I wanted to say something else, but Claire interrupted me.

"Well, then, I'll just leave you guys alone. Alex, can I do anything to help you?"

Alex answered suggestively, as always.

"I could probably think of something, Claire."

"Alex – where is your mind? Maybe later, if you're nice to me."

Claire disappeared, and Kayl passed the skeleton to Arun. Arun just stood there, looking a little like a lost puppy. He looked at me shyly, then looked back at the floor, which I found somehow sweet.

How's your nose, Kayl? It looks a lot better, anyway."

"Everything's back in place, Sophie – doesn't hurt anymore, and is as good as healed."

I looked at Kayl's nose and was surprised that everything had healed up in such a short time. No scratches and no swelling, not to mention no blood was visible, all of which would have been normal for that type of injury.

"Who told the two of you I was down here in the party room?"

Arun looked at me, surprised by my question. "You don't think I'm going to give away my sources?" Kayl said, looking back at Arun.

So, it was Arun – he knew we were down here in the party room. "Okay, that's what I thought, but why did the two of you come down here?"

What a dumb question. What was I thinking?

"We thought we could help you a little," Arun piped up from the background, excitedly rattling the skeleton he'd been holding in his hand the whole time.

"Help decorate your party room. I hope you have a spot for our friend here," Kayl said to substantiate Arun's answer.

"I think we can find something – come on in, and we'll all find a nice place for him. What's his name, anyway?"

Kayl looked at me, questioningly, and Arun answered:

"That's Fred. Fred, may I introduce you to Sophie?"

Together, we all thought over the best place to position Fred so he could be as effective as possible. Arun had the best idea: putting Fred right in the entrance, with his right hand outstretched to greet the guests. He pulled something else out of his pocket and used some tape to attach it to Fred's hipbone. It looked like a little MP3 player. He skillfully placed the wires coming out of the little device along Fred's right arm. Not a minute later, he was asking me to shake Fred's hand.

A little unsure what was going to happen next, I looked at Arun? For some reason I was expecting a shock to hit me when I took Fred's hand, Fred started to talk in a deep, intimidating voice.

"Hello, my name is Fred, and I'd like to welcome you to the best and spookiest birthday party the world has ever seen."

I couldn't help breaking out in laughter.

"Do you like it? I wasn't sure if you'd appreciate the idea."

I answered him, still laughing.

"I like it very much. Super idea for the entryway – really great job, Arun, thanks a lot."

Alex asked Kayl if he could help him with the heavy tables, and they disappeared into the back. While Claire blew up the balloons, Arun helped me with the two fog machines we had rented. It looked as if he'd already done it all a hundred times. He knew exactly what to fill in where and how to set up the whole machine. It only took ten minutes for the two fog machines to start spitting out sweet smelling, thick fog.

"How do you know so much about this?"

"Kayl and I played in a band, and we used the exact same model for our stage shows."

"Kay-Ky."

"What?"

"Kay-Ky, that's just a word, and it stands for everything that's super awesome or interesting – everything I like, really."

"I've never heard it before."

"You won't either – I invented it, and only my best friends know it."

"But now I know it – does that mean I'm one of your best friends?"

Arun looked into my eyes, and his had a charming bluish shine, even more intense than they had been before. At the same time, I noticed a sweet taste, almost as powerful as if I had a whole spoonful of honey in my mouth.

Strange – what's happening to my sense of taste?

"Sorry, Sophie, I didn't mean to pressure you. It's okay if you don't – don't yet count me as one of your close friends. You don't know me yet, anyway, and what you've seen of me up to this point wasn't exactly exemplary – more like macho behavior. You should know, however, that that's not me at all."

"So, what are you like, then?"

"You'll have to find that out for yourself. In any case, I don't think I'm being cocky when I say I think getting to know me better will be worth it."

As Arun said this, his face changed colors markedly enough for me to notice it.

"You're not blushing, are you Arun?"

Arun was blushing, and he knew it.

"I'm Kay-Ky sure that you will see me as one of your good friends, someday."

"So, you're Kay-Ky sure – that sounds a little cocky already, or maybe you're just stuck up? But since you only just learned what Kay-Ky means, I guess I can forgive you this time."

I smiled at Arun and he responded with a sweet smile – so sweet that I felt again like I had a mouth full of honey.

Strange – what's up with my sense of taste?

"You won't regret it in any case, Sophie, I won't disappoint you."

Somehow, it seemed like it was getting easier and easier for me to talk to Arun. All the nervousness I had felt at the beginning had completely evaporated. It just felt good to talk to him. Arun was making progress as well. At the beginning, he only very rarely looked at me, and then looked back to the side or down at the floor, but now his nervousness and shyness had evaporated as well. He did have beautiful eyes, and when he looked at me, they shone a bright blue.

"Is this your way of hitting on me? Is this what you do with all the girls, Arun?"

If seemed as if my direct statement had put him off his stride – he looked away again and blushed. This touch of speechlessness and a little shyness made him even more likable, even more interesting. I can't explain it, but Arun was very attractive to me – somehow, I found his strength combined with his sensitive nature very sexy.

"To be honest, no, I'm not hitting on you. It's not my thing, and I'm not very good at it either, as you've found out for yourself. Kayl tells me so all the time – he says I have more to learn from him, but I am who I am – a little more reserved."

Arun wanted to explain the situation and regain control. What I thought was great was that he was just being honest, not playing a role. No posturing, no macho affectation – I saw Arun as he really was. I thought he was just like the taste in my mouth – sweet as honey.

"And what comes next? What's the next step?" I was tempted to keep flirting with Arun – it was fun.

"What do you mean by that?"

"Oh, well, what are the next steps in your nonexistent or not-yet-successfully-executed hitting on me? What comes next? If I know something about it in advance, then I can go ahead and start considering whether I will like it, and planning how I'll react."

"You mean – then it will be easier to turn me down."

"Maybe just string you along a little, we'll see."

Arun realized he had lost control, and looked visibly unsettled.

"So, what comes next?"

He thought it over briefly, looked at his watch, then beamed at me again and continued to stand there, rigid.

I repeated my question, wanting to challenge him.

"Arun, what's your next step?"

Arun answered very quietly, looking directly at me.

"I'll kiss you!"

The sentence was totally unexpected, and practically smacked me in the head. I suddenly felt myself blushing. With this one sentence, Arun had succeeded in regaining control of our flirting.

"Sophie, you're not blushing now, are you? I see a slight change in the tint of your skin – could it be I imagine things?"

Luckily, Claire, Alex, and Kayl came back with a bottle of champagne attached to a balloon.

"So, both of you, there are just 5 minutes to midnight, and that means it's about to be our dear Sophie's birthday. Will you two please pause your fine conversation and grab a glass?"

Alex was battling with the champagne bottle and had already removed the silver paper and the wire, but couldn't get the cork to come out. Claire, already holding glasses in her hands, waited impatiently, spurring Alex on. "What's going on? You're usually not so reluctant."

"Come on, Alex, let 'er rip!"

Arun looked at me, bashfully, and I nodded to him with a wink, agreeing with his thought.

With a loud pop, the cork shot through the room and hit a wall. Claire tried to follow the bottle with a glass, frantic, but she couldn't catch all the champagne that was spraying out. Alex, a little surprised the cork had gotten away from him, slowly filled the first glass. Claire passed it to me and grabbed for the next one. Once everyone was standing there with a champagne glass, Claire started to count.

"10, 9, 8, 7, 6, 5, 4, 3, 2, 1 – HAPPY BIRTHDAY dear Sophie!"

It really sounded beautiful when all the glasses clinked against one another at once in the middle of the circle. After a drink, Claire took my glass away from me again, passed to Alex, hugged me tight, and gave me a kiss.

"All my very best wishes on your birthday, Sophie – I'm so happy to have you as a best friend."

"Me too, Claire, me too!"

Alex, who had already set the glasses down on the bar, hugged me as well and pressed a kiss onto my cheek.

"Happy Birthday, Sophie – best wishes."

Kayl, standing next to me, figured he was next in line and hugged me too, also kissing my cheek.

"Me too – all the best on your birthday."

Claire passed me an envelope and said I had to open it immediately.

"Open it, and read it out loud!"

I looked at all of them, excited. Slowly and carefully, I opened the envelope to reveal a birthday card. When I had read the print: "There's a surprise waiting for you in here!" I was about to open the card when my aphmal warned me once again. Something wasn't right; I felt a fine pinprick in my forehead again, becoming more intense. Something was up with the card. I saw the excitement, the expectation in Claire and Alex's eyes that something was about to happen. Kayl's eyes, in contrast, looked flat, and Arun's eyes beamed warmly at me. Arun had very beautiful eyes – it was difficult for me to turn away from his gaze.

Slowly and carefully, I opened the card in expectation that something was about to happen. The card started to vibrate, and something inside started whirling like mad and whistling. Prepared for the unexpected, I didn't want to spoil my guests' fun, so I dropped the card and screeched in fear. Arun looked at me, smirked and just shook his head a little. But it was enough so that I noticed it. He knew I wasn't really scared. Claire, Alex, and Kayl seemed happy with their successful surprise, but Arun just smirked at me approvingly, whatever that meant.

"HAPPY BIRTHDAY Sophie, you have to read what the card says out loud. That's the real present," Claire yelled.

I bent over, picked up the card, and expected something to happen, but this time my aphmal didn't react. Unbelievable – my aphmal was feeling better and better.

"Dear Sophie, best wishes on your birthday.

Since you're 16 now, it's about time you go out and meet people – young males to be specific. That's why Alex and I thought we'd arrange a couple of blind dates for you. Wouldn't it be funny if we found Mr. Right? Happy birthday, your BFF, Claire."

I stood there with mouth agape, speechless.

"You're trying to hook me up?"

"We want you to have fun that's all."

"Blind dates are really exciting, Sophie, and who knows? One of them might lead to something." Alex interjected.

"Oh, and what is it going to lead to? A one-night stand! I know you guys only mean well, but it's not my thing – sorry." I found the whole thing really dumb, somehow. A blind date. Claire – how could she? I guarantee it was all that dummy Alex's idea. How am I going to get out of this crappy situation?

Unsure and bashful, I looked at Arun, who was making strange signs. It was like he was pointing at himself, does he mean?

"Let's do the following: we'll turn your invitation to go on a blind date to a pizza party with Claire and Alex as the hosts and Sophie and Arun as invited guests."

It was barely out of my mouth before I was asking myself whether I might have had a little bit too much champagne. How could I pull Arun into all of this?

Claire looked at me, surprised, and tried to find the right words.

"Umm … that's … that's a super idea, Sophie!"

What kind of craziness am I talking? Just be quiet, just smile.
Arun, who had held back a little to let the others speak first, approached me. I felt goosebumps spread over my arms, and with ever step Arun took towards me, the feeling grew more intense and spread even further. He lifted his glass up towards me, slowly, and our glasses met in the middle with a clink. As I took a small sip, I kept my gaze focused on his beautiful eyes and noticed he was still smirking slightly.

"I'd be happy to, Sophie – I'm very glad you want to share your birthday present with me. I promise you I'll behave myself."

Now Kayl was the one standing there like a lost puppy dog. Alex had his mouth agape as well, his amazement visibly etched into his face. I wasn't certain, but somehow it seemed I could see something like rage or hate in Kayl's face. Arun reached into his pocket and pulled out a wrapped present, handing it to me. "I wish you all the best on your birthday, and hope your wishes will come true."

I was about to open the gift when I heard Claire pipe in from the side.

"That's not how you do it – where's the kiss? I want to see at least a kiss on the cheek."

I smiled at Arun, nodded with my eyes, and held my cheek towards him invitingly. I could see radiance in his eyes – it was of an intensity I had never seen before. When he was standing directly in front of me, I noticed for the first time how tall he was. He bent down a little towards me, and in the instant his right hand touched my chin, it was like there was a crackling all over. I felt something similar to when I used my aphmal. Everything started to tingle, and the butterflies in my stomach beat their wings like wild. His mouth came closer, and he turned a little towards my ear.

"You did just ask me what was coming next, and I told you I would kiss you!"

Arun pressed his warm lips on my cheek and, to be honest, I wished he were kissing me just as intensely on the mouth. It was simply a crazy Kay-Ky feeling. Arun took a little step back, and I recognized a sense of triumph in his eyes. He nodded slowly, and his eyes wandered to the gift I was still holding in my hand.

"How about you open it?"

I carefully removed the wrapping and opened the little present, waiting for my aphmal to warn me of an impending surprise, but there was no reaction. Something glittered at me when light hit the box. I folded back the lid and saw something that looked like a crystal, but with a peculiar shape. It was like a blossom – a rose blossom, to be exact. It shone in gorgeous colors, reflecting the light. I reached in and took it out carefully, and in the moment I had placed it in my open palm to show it to everyone, I noticed something unique happening. The reflected light was coming together into a beam of light, and the rose was beginning to glow. It glowed in different colors, like the source of a rainbow. When the colors met in the middle of the rose, it shone with a beaming bright light.

What was that?

I stood there, shocked, not knowing what I should do and looking at Arun uncertainly. But he didn't react at all. They all just looked at the rose blossom on my hand, apparently absorbed in the play of light.

"Isn't it beautiful? I don't know exactly what it is, Sophie, but it's beautiful how it lights up. It's probably battery-operated – but beautiful."

"You're right, Claire, it is beautiful."

Arun looked into my eyes intensely, and for a moment I was un-sure what he meant by the look. He lowered his eyes to the rose and continued talking.

"It's a rose of Akar – at least, that's what it's called. This is a re-production, a battery-operated version made of glass. The real rose isn't too much more beautiful though. But if you believe the stories, it's supposed to give its owner strength and power – at least, that's what ancient sayings describe."

I looked at Arun and saw Kayl take a step in his direction and whisper something tensely in his ear so no one else could hear it.

"In which sayings, Arun?" Claire interrupted him, curious. Then I said:

"I think it's beautiful, Arun. And it's not just that – this rose has something special about it, something attractive – I can't really describe what it Where did you get it?"

Arun hesitated a moment and seemed unsure whom he should answer first. Kayl grabbed Arun's upper arm, his grip practically deforming Arun's skin. Kayl was trying to influence Arun with this grip, I could feel it.

"Excuse me, Claire, let me answer the birthday girl's question first."

Claire nodded to him.

"Sophie – I also got it as a present. In fact, that's the whole point of the rose – to give it to someone you like, someone you wish well. The right moment will come when you too will give it away – that's the purpose of this type of rose. At least, that's how my mother explained it to me."

"You got the rose as a gift from your mother?"

Arun nodded, his eyes visibly saddened, and Kayl turned away his face. He hadn't been able to keep Arun quiet.

"Yes, she gave it to me as a going away present, and told me to give it away myself to someone I liked. You do like it?"

A going away present? I repressed the question that arose in my mind in the moment. It probably wasn't the right time, first of all, and secondly, the words "going away" reminded me of Mom and Dad, which I didn't know quite how to deal with from an emotional standpoint.

"I like it very much, Arun, and I am honored you gave it to me. Give me a hug."

Nothing better occurred to me in the moment than to give Arun a hug. I hoped that I could also free him from his brother's grip at the same time, and hoped Arun's hug could help hold me up. Help me get a grip on my growing emotional tension, which I needed very much. As I went to Arun, Karl withdrew to the side, and Arun's strong arms hugged me very gently, without pressure. I whispered in his ear:

"Please hold me tight, very tight."

I felt his muscles tense, and his arms close even more tightly around me. It was a wonderful feeling of safety and security, and as Arun held me tight, I felt myself slowly getting better.

"Tighter, Arun, please," I whispered, so quietly only he could hear it. I wasn't even sure if I was moving my lips or actually speaking, but Arun reacted to it and held me tighter.

He gently took my head in his hands, placing it against his shoulder, and his arms encircled me even closer. Our bodies melded into one another, and I could clearly feel Arun's chest and arm muscles – and there it was, the feeling I was looking for – what I needed so desperately. Support – someone to hold onto me and give me safety and security.

"Thanks," squeezed past my lips, very quietly, and Arun released the pressure and the secure bond of his arms slowly.

"Well, aren't the two of you a cute couple – both so shy," Claire snickered, looking up at Alex, who was holding her in his arms.

Kayl, who for some unknown reason was suddenly staring at everyone grimly spoke up, annoyed:

"I have to go to bed. Have a nice birthday, Sophie."

He had hardly finished his sentence when he shot a bloodcurdling look at his brother and disappeared like a stubborn child. Claire looked at me, puzzled and I looked at Arun, who shrugged his shoulders at me to signal that he also didn't understand why Kayl had reacted so badly. The only one who didn't notice was Alex – probably because a thing like trust didn't even exist in his personal value system.

"Not bad, bro – that cheap Chinese glass version of a flower got you a hug. Who knows what you'd get if you had invested a little more money. Keep it up, bro, I'm sure there'll be more – lots more!"

Alex laughed in his macho way, and I was ashamed at his words.

"Arun, don't listen to Alex – this is the second best birthday present I've ever gotten in my whole life. The best one was from my Dad and there's no way to top it – which means you nailed it."

"Wow, Arun, did I hear that right?" Alex spat out, a little pissed off.

Claire, obviously finding the situation awkward, rammed her elbow into Alex's side and tried to rein him back in.

"I think it's a really great present too – let's have another toast to it."

Claire picked up the champagne bottle and topped off all the glasses again.

"To you, Sophie, cheers."

"Cheers."

"Aviva!"

"What is Aviva?" Claire asked Arun, curious.

"It means: I hope it tastes great and does you good – or something like that. In any case, that's how Kayl and I learned it. When you drink something, you're supposed to say Aviva as a toast."

"I have one more wish, and I would really be happy if you all could fulfill it for me."

Claire looked at me, very surprised. "I've never seen you so self-confident before. You're always surprise me – somehow, it seems my Sophie is changing."

"Exactly – and that's why I wish for all of you to call me by my middle name!"

"By your middle name?"

"From now on, I'd prefer if you all call me Xama. Sophie's who I was – but from now on, there's only Xama."

"Well, if that's what you want, then that's how it will be. I might still call you Sophie now and then, but I'll get used to Xama, although that is a very strange name."

"Actually, it's not" Arun piped up.

"Xama is a beautiful name, with lots of …" Arun choked off the sentence when he noticed that what he wanted to say wasn't meant for Claire and Alex.

Since I didn't have any desire at the moment to discuss my new name or whether anybody liked it, or what it meant, I looked for a polite way to break up the party.

"Guys, I don't mean to be rude, but it's almost 12:30, and we have to get ready for tomorrow night. After all, it's going to be the best party, Heaven has ever seen. So let's call it a night and go to bed."

Everyone agreed with me, Alex and Claire drank up the last of the champagne, and we all headed for our rooms. Arun left us at the reception desk and wishing us a good night. Then Claire remembered her question from before.

"Arun – you still owe me an answer to my question! Think of something interesting, I'm excited to find out how you'll explain the origins of the rose of Akar. You can tell me all about it tomorrow."

"Love to, Claire – Our mother told us the story of the rose of Akar over and over again. Tomorrow, I'll be happy to initiate you into the secrets of the rose. Good night, Claire – good night, Alex – sleep well, Xama, and thanks for a lovely evening."

As I watched Arun walk down the hallway, a host of thoughts ran through my mind. First the cross on my forehead that turned out to be an aphmal with unbelievable powers. Then the truth about me, and the Arverni, and my aphormation, and now Arun and everything developing between us. All that in just a few days. What's going to happen next?
"Are you coming, Sophie – um, sorry – are you coming, Xama, or do you want to spend the night here?" Claire called out to me.

Now I realized Alex was already at his car in the parking lot, and I couldn't see Arun anymore either. Did I black out for a second? Was I really that lost in thought?
"I can understand why you're staring at Arun – they're both very nice, and look great too. Personally, I think Kayl's just a little bit hotter than Arun, but there's no accounting for taste, as we know. No matter – they're both in bed already, and you're just staring down an empty hallway. That's a little too much of a good thing. So come on, let's go to bed. I'm totally exhausted – otherwise I'm going to fall asleep right here in the hallway."
I followed Claire to our room, but there was something I couldn't get out of my mind. Arun and Kayl come out of nowhere, keep running across my path, and tonight they showed up out of nowhere.
That's not an accident. What's going on here? Who are they both, really? There was one thing I was sure of: Arun felt something for me. My feelings couldn't deceive me.

Ingenious Gene

Las Vegas, Nevada, USA

P ale and visibly weakened, Sherman lay the injector beside the sink and turned on the hot water. He tested the temperature with his finger as he looked at his face in the large wall mirror. His skin was grey like his hair and sallow and lined with wrinkles, making him look significantly older than he actual was.

We're almost there, we are about to unlock the Arverni gene and with it the secret to eternal life, strength, and power.
Immortality !!!

He washed his face with the hand soap and a white washcloth, which lay artfully, folded on the marble countertop. Again and again, he rubbed his forehead, the washcloth slowly taking on a darker color. Sherman dried his face and stared into the mirror, especially at one particular spot on his forehead.
He could see something strange there – it looked like an aphmal, but it wasn't one – at least, not one which was clearly drawn. It had interruptions here and there, as though some parts of the aphmal were invisible. The overall image of the aphmal looked like a puzzle with half of the pieces missing.
Sherman continued to stare at his forehead but didn't feel anything – no change in his emotions – nothing. All at once, his right arm, which he was using to support himself on the marble countertop, started to shake – first a little, and then worse and worse until Sherman grabbed it with his other hand. But not even that stopped the arm from continuing to shake. He sat down on the edge of the bathtub and thought, letting go of his arm, which at once began to shake again in a disordered fashion. He took up the injector in his left hand, then, placed it directly against his carotid artery and squeezed the trigger.
„zissschhh..."
With a brief hissing sound, the device revealed it had fulfilled its task. The ampule with the golden, shimmering fluid was empty.

Sherman pulled air in through his clenched teeth and breathed deeply several times. He enjoyed it, as though he was inhaling the smoke from a cigarette into his lungs, and the nicotine displayed its effects immediately. He laid the injector to the side and looked at his arm, which was completely still. He raised it slightly, made a fist, and stood up. He supported himself again on the sink as before, but this time nothing shook.

His gaze in the mirror showed him exactly what he had hoped for so fondly. The missing parts of his aphmal began to darken, ever darker, and the rest also became more heavily colored and had greater contrast. Seconds passed, and soon a perfect aphmal became visible on Sherman's forehead. His face changed as well; the grey color was gone, and the sallow tinge was replaced by a fresh, colorful look. The wrinkles in his skin were smoothed, and the person looking at him might have been 20 to 30 years younger, his hair changed from gray to dark and it looked stronger and thicker.

All in all, a different Sherman stood in front of the mirror. He looked at his aphmal, smiling, and you could practically see his emotional state change for the better, and watch him transform from a grim, serious old codger into a laughing, dynamic, middle-aged man. Sherman stood up straight, stretching out. His posture was no longer bent, instead, he stood upright and tall. He smiled again into the mirror and looked at his face from the side – first from the right, then the left, then his neck, and it was obvious he was very pleased by what he saw.

Well, now let's just see what this old body can still do.

Sherman moved the thumb on his right hand towards his aphmal, and as it was just about to touch his forehead, pulled there as if by magic, he tried to hold the thumb back. He wanted to stop his thumb from touching his forehead. Suddenly, a bright flash came out of the center of his aphmal. A beam of light, pure energy absorbed by his thumb. It sparked and flashed between his aphmal and his thumb without interruption, lighting up the whole bathroom. Sanders could also see the flash of light from outside, lighting up the edges of bathroom door.

Sherman stood there, his mouth open wide, enjoying the exchange of energy. Moaning, he succumbed to the pressure and placed his thumb on the aphmal. A twitch, followed by a loud moan wracked his body. Sherman closed his eyes and enjoyed the moment of regeneration. Seconds later, when the energy subsided, he removed his thumb, remained standing for a moment in front of the mirror, and looked at himself again, visibly satisfied with the results he saw in the mirror.

That's much better now – inconceivable how I can succeed in making my body another 20 years younger.

Sherman grabbed the injector and left the bathroom. Peter Sanders realized that Sherman had left the bathroom, but continued to stare out of the window. It seemed as if he were afraid of looking directly at Sherman.
"I believe I can dispense with asking you how you feel now? You look fantastic, almost like my brother instead of my father."
Sherman smiled:
"I don't need to explain to you, Peter, the transformation an aphmalisation triggers. You know it yourself. Especially in the Finitum stage, when your powers are fading, it is at least ten times more intense. Aphmalisation rejuvenates simply everything. It feels very good – a sort of fountain of youth. We possess something humanity has attempted to research for thousands of years."
Sherman poured himself another whiskey.
"Do you want one too?"
Sanders waved him off.
With the whiskey in his hand, Sherman walked towards Sanders.
"Pete, can you imagine what this means for humanity? If we succeed in chemically reproducing the isolated Arverni gene and using it in a targeted way, the world will be at our feet. Power, riches, and prosperity as well as eternal life – anything is possible, and even much more than that."
Sherman placed his hand on Sanders' shoulder. Sanders continued to stare out of the window.
"Father, this means that humanity will no longer fight over drugs, gold, money, or oil. No – they will start wars over the Arverni gene. Humans will do anything to avoid aging. For with aging comes death. They will kill to live. Crime, murder – these are all

logical steps they will take to get the Arverni gene. In the end, humanity will exterminate itself to be able to live forever."

Sherman took his hand back.

"Pete, you see things in too negative a light. Yes, humans will do anything, but they won't need to start wars over it. There will be enough so that any person ... "

Sanders interrupted Sherman.

"Can become immortal! What will happen then to the world population?

Who decides about new life? Will there is enough to eat?"

"You're right, Pete but we can't give everything up when we're so close to the end. You know the consequences – without the Arverni gene I will die, and you will follow me soon after since you are also already in the Finitum."

"What is it that you expect from me? Young people just discovering they are Arverni have to die so that you can live on – so that you can complete your research. And what's worse – so that you can satisfy the hate that burns inside of you. Sometimes I think that in reality, you only have one true goal. You want to kill all Arverni. A genocide, so no other Arverni remains alive but you."

"Pete, we've already had this discussion multiple times, and it always ends the same way."

Sherman went to the table where the chest was sitting with the injector in his hand, took out the next to last ampule filled with the golden liquid, and placed it into the injector.

Sanders turned around and Sherman saw he was crying.

Sherman placed his hand on Sanders' cheek and breathed in deeply.

"Pete," he said, his voice changing in intensity, and looked deep into his eyes.

"Pete, you go into the bathroom now, take the injector, We'll continue our discussion and plan the next few days. Days which will ensure our success."

But there was more there than Sherman's spoken message, something he had anchored deep in Sanders' consciousness. Something he had been planning for a long time but never executed – but now the time was ripe. It had to be done if he didn't want to lose his son.

Peter Sanders tried to refuse Sherman's command with all the energy he still had left, but Sherman's influence over him was too great. Since he was still touching his face, as well, his power was too strong, controlling Sanders' consciousness.

Peter Sanders nodded, wordlessly picking up the injector and going directly into the bathroom to follow his father's instructions.

BIRTHDAY PARTY

A ll night long, I thought about Arun and Kayl. It definitely wasn't a coincidence; of that much I was sure. I had to know why they were here. Arun will tell me the truth. With the help of the reception desk, I found out Arun's room number, and since it was the same number on our internal telephone system, it was easy to call him. With the receiver already in my hand, I considered what I wanted to say on the phone. But the more I pondered, the fewer ideas I had. After a few minutes, I placed the receiver back down, frustrated, and pushed my plan off to the evening.

Hopefully something more will occur to me when I see Arun at the party.

Around 4:00, I set off towards the party room to check over everything once again and finish up the final preparations. Claire had wanted to be back already by this time, but I knew that when she was together with Alex, space and time had little meaning anymore. Shortly after 4:30, Alex and Claire arrived at the party room, and we all went through the prep list again together. The room looked perfect, and with Fred standing at the entrance we had the best bouncer you could imagine. Slowly, my emotional state transformed from relaxed to agitated – it felt as though my insides were exposed to high voltage current. When the first guests arrived, something strange happened. Every hug only charged me up further, up to the point where it began to feel painful to hug someone or even shake his or her hand. To distract myself from the feeling, I got a glass of champagne at the bar. Claire, who had already had a little too much champagne, linked arms with me. In that moment, I felt an internal vibration whose cause remained a complete mystery to me.
"All the best on your birthday, Xama – now you're an adult."
Claire held her glass up to me, and we both emptied our goblets like it was nothing but punch. Lost in thought, I turned over her statement: "Now you're an adult," Dad's and Amar's sayings resurfacing in my memories.

"When you are an adult, you will develop an ability in order to fulfill your Aphora." Sunk deep in thought, I tried to set the empty glass down on the bar, but in the moment it touched the surface it burst in my hand. I felt multiple stabs on my palm, multiple shards penetrated deep into my skin. Claire screamed aloud as she watched me practically crush the glass. I opened my hand slowly; glass shards fell to the floor. I looked at my shredded hand blood pooled in the middle of my palm – first a little, and then more and more. I tried to keep my hand still to control the blood, but as it filled up my palm gravity took over and it dripped onto the floor. Claire became hysterical and screamed.

I have to calm her down. I needed to distract her.

"Can you get me a bandage? I'll go to the bathroom and clean out the wound."

Claire stared at my bleeding hand in a state of shock. I shook her a little with my other hand until she looked at me.

"Claire, please listen to me: go and find me some bandages! There's a medicine cabinet there in the front – there must be bandages inside. I'll try to clean the wound. Claire nodded, stared at me helplessly, and ran towards the entrance, frantically searching for bandages. Inside the bathroom, I looked over the drama and asked myself what had just happened. Did the glass already have a crack? Why did it burst like that – like an explosion?

Carefully, I began to pull out the visible glass splinters with my fingernails. Pulling out each splinter without any pain. Suddenly the door was shoved open, and Claire was standing in the bathroom, shaking and holding the first aid. She looked as though a vampire had sucked out all her blood. Once the last splinter was removed, I began to clean the wound with a swab and stop the bleeding. An angry gash across my entire palm revealed raw flesh.

Claire was frantic:

"You need an ambulance Xama, you could bleed to death, you need stitches. You'll get blood poisoning, you'll get an infection and they'll have to amputate your hand. I feel sick, I need to ... "

Claire disappeared into the stall gagging and emptying her stomach out. I tried to close the gaping wound with Band-Aids and bandages, wrapping the rest of the stab wounds with the gauze. Claire was right– the whole thing looked awful, and I was surprised at my own calmness and balance. I barely knew myself – wasn't I the one that always felt nauseous immediately any time I saw a drop of blood?

When she came out of the bathroom, snow white and totally exhausted, I had already finished binding up my wound and taken a look in the mirror to strengthen my emotional equilibrium. Everything was perfect. Thanks to my aphmal I was feeling super again, and it looked like my attempt at bandaging was a complete success as well. Besides an ever-stronger itching sensation, I didn't feel the wound at all, which was highly astounding.

"We are going to the hospital immediately, and I'll inform the youth home administrators. You need help, Xama! We need help! We can't handle all this alone!"

"Claire, I've treated the wound myself, a doctor couldn't do a better job." I showed Claire my hand. "I'm feeling fine. I just took a pain killer; it's just a small cut. It bled like crazy, but that's it. No reason to panic. I don't need to remind you that both of us are celebrating our birthdays today. You don't want the administrators or anybody else to show up here and make us call off the whole thing off, the party we've invested weeks on, do you?"

I placed my other hand on Claire's shoulder and caressed her face with my fingers. The moment my fingertips made contact a sense that I could help her get back to her normal self came over me. Claire's emotional state improved slowly but visibly she looked at me and started smiling. She placed her head on my shoulder.

"I'm so happy I've got you. How do you stay this calm? I don't get it."

"You don't have to, Claire, you just have to trust me. Then you'll see, everything will be all right again. Earlier you asked me what my wish for today was – my wish is to keep on partying, I promise I'll go to the doctor tomorrow."

Claire looked at me wide eyed.

"Ok then, if that's your wish. Let's go have some fun."

Confident, we both left the bathroom arm in arm, aiming to enjoy ourselves. The party room had already filled after the first half hour. It seemed as though everyone we had invited, and even a few we hadn't invited, had shown up. Everyone except Kayl and Arun – I hadn't seen either one of them yet. While making small talk with a classmate, I suddenly spotted Kayl. So, they did come. Ending my conversation, I fought through the crowd toward Kayl, who was standing at the bar and ordering himself a beer.

"Hello, Kayl, nice to see you."

"Hello, Xama, I didn't expect to see you here!"

"Tease."

"How's the party going?

As you can see, pretty awesome." That's the right attitude."

I wanted to know where Arun was even though it felt awkward to ask.

"Where's your brother hiding?" pretending not to care that much

"He still had some homework to do; he might come later. If not, then I'll tell him you said hello."

"That's very nice, Kayl, thanks a lot."

What Kayl had just said really upset me. I was sad, I wanted to see Arun – there was so much to talk about – and infuriated because I simply couldn't believe what Kayl had just told me."

"Did you hurt yourself?"

Kayl was pointing at my hand.

"Yes, although I can't explain how it could have happened."

"Holding a glass."

"Good guess."

"That just exploded, and cut your hand open."

"How do you know that?"

"It's a method used to deactivate a targeted person or, should I say, infect them. Without making a fuss, without exchanging shots – just a prepared glass which transforms into a weapon at the moment the contact person touches it and sets it down again. It explodes and injures the targeted person. If it's been prepared in accordance with K2G, the contact person will be dead in about 60 minutes." I slowly felt beads of sweat collecting on my forehead.

"Is that just a joke, Kayl, or what's all this supposed to mean? What's K2G?"

"K2G is a fast-acting contact poison which is certain to kill, pain-free, within minutes through skin contact or – even better – through penetration into a bloody wound. A weapon primarily used by the secret service."

Kayl was scaring me, and he enjoyed watching my fear increase.

"So, then, what should I do now?"

195

"Have another glass of champagne. I'll get us a couple of glasses, but please don't break another one."

Kayl was already on his way, otherwise he'd have gotten a kick in the ass as payment for screwing around with me. I looked at him but thought about Arun. Suddenly, I saw a shadow fly in from the side and tear Kayl down to the floor. Everything happened at lightening speed; the attacker sat on Kayl, punched him once with a balled fist, and stood back up.

Own, that must have hurt – right on the broken nose, a direct hit.

Now I could see that the shadow was Arun, holding his hand out to his brother and helping him stand up. The guests had already collected around the fight, and I was running towards Arun as well

"Nice to see you at my birthday party – of course, I had hoped you two could get through tonight without beating each other up. But maybe someday I'll be able to see you both without a brawl breaking out."

Arun nodded and looked at me in such a way that I couldn't help but forgive him.

"Sorry, Xama! That was really dumb, but my dear brother did just punch me down and tied me up to the radiator in the bathroom with some shitty rope. Just so, that I couldn't come to your birth-day party."

Arun reached out and showed me his bloody wrists.

"That looks terrible; I'll get the first-aid kit,"

When I arrived at the bathroom with the first aid kit, Kayl had already defaced the whole sink with blood from his nose.

"That doesn't look good, Kayl, let me see."

Kayl raised his head, and I could see that Arun had broken his nose again. This time, it was pushed over to the left side. I took two bandages out of the first aid kit and wrapped them to make them into two little rolls.

"Try to stick that into your nose," Kayl took the two rolls and, one after the other, half of them disappeared into his nose. I t seems like I felt more pain in watching than Kayl in treating his nose. Arun watched everything from a distance; he had sat down on the tub, the faucet between his legs, and was letting cold water run over his wrists. Anyone could see he was jealous.

196

Or maybe that was just wishful thinking on my part?

"This is going to hurt again. I'm going to try and put your nose back in the right place."

"Just leave it there; I'll break it again – for sure!" Arun screamed across the bathroom, enraged.

"How could you beat me down so underhandedly, and tie me up? You knew how much I was looking forward to tonight. Why, Kayl? Fucking why?"

Kayl looked at me. "I didn't want to share Xama with you, not this evening. My plan was to invite Xama to dinner, and I hoped I might succeed without you around. That's the honest answer, brother."

"Brother, I was a pleasure to break your nose – and I will do it again."

"Both of you calm down; if you think I'm honored because you're maiming yourselves on account of me, then you're mistaken. I detest violence."

I grabbed Kayl's nose with my thumbs and pushed it to the right with a crack. A chill ran down my spine when I heard the noise. Kayl's looked at me, but he didn't say a word – not a peep. Both of the bandages inside his nose filled immediately with fresh blood and colored bright red. Kayl pulled them both out and exchanged them for fresh ones.

"Looks pretty good from here – a little swollen again, but straight. Probably better than last time. You did a perfect job, Xama"

Kayl and Arun both laughed.

I went over to Arun.

"Can I see your hands?"

"Well, I'll just go. Thanks for the invitation, Xama have a good party and Arun, I am sorry!" Kayl said.

"How can you hurt yourself like that?" I asked Arun.

He looked deep into my eyes.

"It's when you want something at any price, and when you're ready to accept pain for yourself. We both wanted to come to your party, but then Kayl knocked me out with something and carried me into the bathroom. There, he tied me to the radiator with a rope. When I came back to my senses, I realized I was held prisoner, so I tried to rip the radiator out from the wall, but I couldn't."

"You tried to do what? Rip the radiator out from the wall?"

"Yeah – but when that didn't work, I tried to pull my hands through the cord, but since Kayl didn't slouch on his knots, I first had to soften up the cord to be able to stretch it."

"Let me guess: you rubbed your hands against the cord until it tore open your skin. It started to bleed and the blood softened the cord."

Arun nodded, and I swallowed; my whole body shivered.

"Please stop. You are both completely insane, complete nut cases."

"You're probably right, Xama, crazy for you."

I looked at Arun and the color of his face told me it had been a real challenge for him to say that to me directly.

"Can you please hold my hands again, it felt so good!"

I took his hands into mine. He had long, slender fingers, and his hands were much larger than mine. I felt a tingling energy flowing between us. Arun closed his eyes, and I noticed that my right hand – the one with the cut under the bandage – didn't itch anymore.

"It's a beautiful feeling, Xama, you won't believe it, but the burning stopped the moment you touched my hands. That's very strange – now it tickles. Something is happening to my hands."

When Arun said this, I could see that his right hand had almost completely healed. The wound on the left hand was also starting to heal; it was changing before my eyes. I let go of Arun's hands, and he opened his eyes immediately.

"What's up, Xama? It felt so good."

"Hold on, I want to try something out!"

Like I'd gone crazy, I unwrapped the bandage from my right hand, when I was shocked to see that the deep fleshy cut was now completely healed.

What's going on here?

I took Arun's hands again, this time, the feeling was more intense in my right hand than in my left.

"Xama, look at my right hand – it's as good as new, and the left one is healing too. You possess the power to heal. Unbelievable how quick it's happening; I can see it."

I let go of his hands, looked at him, and gazed into his beautiful eyes. Arun had noticed something was different about me.

What on earth should I do now? Should I tell him who, or what, I am?

Arun bent down to me and kissed me on the mouth. It was a warm, pleasant kiss, and when Arun's soft lips touched mine, hundreds of butterflies took off in my stomach.
"Thank you, Xama
"If that's how you express your gratitude, Arun, I'll be happy to help you again."
"That's a good idea, Xama."
"Arun, there's something else I want to know."
"What is it?"
"Do you have a girlfriend?"
Arun smiled at me. "No, I don't, but I also don't have time for one right now."
"I understand."

Now I've given myself away – saying "I understand" even though I don't understand at all.

"There's something else, Arun."
"Well, out with it."
"Who are you? Why did you and Kayl suddenly show up, and why are you always around me? Is this part of a plan? I'm afraid, Arun!"
All at once, Arun was white as chalk. He knew now was the time to tell the truth. Kayl would be angry with him, but the time had come.

SILENT KILLER

Las Vegas, Nevada, USA

Not five minutes later, a new Peter Sanders came out the bathroom. With a smile on his face, he set the injector back into the chest and locked it as though it contained a precious stone. Double-checking the lock was securely fastened; he poured himself another double whiskey, which could easily called a triple.

"Father, the reserve genes are running low. We've only got one ampule left; we need to think about replenishing it."

That was exactly what Sherman wanted to hear – his son on his side. His ally, in spirit and deed. Sherman knew only too well that this condition was founded in only one fact. He had used his power to influence the consciousness of others on his own son. Sherman was a master of manipulation. Although he had sworn to himself that he would never use it against his own flesh and blood, he had done it again. He had used something given to him to fulfill his Aphora, his task, on his own son without a second thought in order to reach his goal of immortality.

"You're right, Pete. Let's first check whether everything is in order at the laboratory, and where we stand with the current research findings."

Sherman pulled his phone out of his pocket and dialed a number.

"Ola, Miguel, how are you?"

"Everything's in order, Dr. Sherman; as I told you three hours ago, we're on the threshold of a breakthrough. We have almost done it. The last tests were all positive."

"Very good, Miguel, that's fantastic!"

"Dr. Sherman, there is, however, one small problem."

Sherman hated this style of communication.

"Problems, Miguel? You know I can't stand problems, especially not small ones. I want solutions, not problems – comprende? Or do I need to make myself more clear?"

"I understand, Dr. Sherman – only, in this case, I think you should take on the solution yourself. It's more your special area than mine. I can't do much here, and if we don't find a solution immediately then we can't continue our research."

Miguel's voice had changed, and Sherman realized he was serious.

"Out with it – what is it this time? How much more money do I have to cough up? I'm making all of you filthy rich, and it's still not enough. You're all scum! Miserable scum!"

"Dr. Sherman, we need more of the Arverni gene. We still have one ampule; it's only enough for three more tests, and we need to complete at least ten tests to be sure we're on the right path."

"I don't understand, Miguel. Bloody hell, what did you do with all the Arverni gene you already had? There were more than thirty ampules."

"You contracted us to run the series of tests in parallel to accomplishing our goal more quickly – but in order to do so we need more of the Arverni gene."

"How long will the gene samples you still have last?"

"About three days."

"Shit – shit – shit."

Sherman paced up and down the room, deliberately separating himself from Sanders.

"We do have the girl, and you've connected her to the Extractor – she's still producing more blood, and we can extract the gene, so what's the problem?"

"Yes, and that worked well until yesterday, but since yesterday her blood has only been renewing itself very slowly. We cannot take more – otherwise she will die."

Sherman nervously shifted in place.

"Shit! Well, shoot the little pipsqueak up – give her vitamins – anything she needs. Make her healthy again, so you can keep going."

"We tried that, for days, and then we cut back the amount of blood we were taking from her bit by bit, to zero. Currently we are no longer taking any blood from her, which is why we can no longer produce more of the Arverni gene. However, she is also not regenerating – her condition is deteriorating. Hour by hour – she is dying."

Beads of sweat collected on Sherman's forehead.

The same symptoms as the boy – after a few days of drawing blood, blood regeneration stops in aspirants for some reason, and they die, the rest of their blood becoming useless for synthesis of the gene.

Sherman paced back and forth across the room.

"Listen to me very carefully now, Miguel."

Sherman's voice had changed in tone, becoming piercing.

"You will take the rest of the blood from the little girl – down to the last drop – and extract the gene as long as you still can, understood? I will think of a way to replenish the supply. I'll be in touch."

"Dr. Sherman, that means the little girl will die, immediately!"

"She'll do that anyway – save the gene as long as she's still alive. That's an order, Miguel, and if you don't carry it out, I will extract your blood, drop by drop. I think we have an understanding. Do the job, Miguel."

Sherman hung up and shoved his telephone back into his pocket.

"Why now? So close to our goal – bloody hell."

Sanders looked at Sherman with eyebrows raised, pretending he hadn't heard anything that was said.

"Pete, we're really almost there, as Miguel has ensured me, but we do need more of the Arverni gene. We can no longer complete the necessary series of tests."

Sanders looked at Sherman, saying nothing. Sherman walked through the room and remained standing in front of Sanders. It didn't happen often, but this was one of the few moments it did. Sherman was nervous and unsure.

"If we don't have enough Arverni genes, we have to get more. It's as simple as that – hunting season is open again."

Sherman grabbed his son by the shoulders, pulled him in and hugged him.

"That's the Pete I love!"

"We'll do it together!"

"You're right, Pete! The hunt for new aspirants is on."

FRIEND OR FOE?

A run looked at me with eyes open wide. He seemed serious and tense and he had changed. I thought he would say something, but didn't. He was searching for the right words. He couldn't figure out where to start – and then, suddenly – he broke his silence.

"You don't need to be afraid. Kayl and I are here to protect you. Arun grabbed a paper towel hold it under the water and rubbed his forehead. Arun pointed into the mirror and I got hot flashes when I saw the Aphmal on Aruns forehead. The most beautiful aphmal in the world.

Arun is an Arverni – how can that be?

We're both Arverni. Amar sent us; he convinced the council to accept you into the community and to place you under the protection of the Achilleans. You're right, it's a plan. A plan I would give my life for. Xama – I would do anything to make sure nothing happens to you. I have sworn an oath to give my life to protect yours – you don't need to be afraid."

Arun looked at the floor, and it looked as though it pained him or as though he felt guilty. I went to him, lifted his head by his chin, and kissed him and touch the center of his forehead with my thumb – more a symbolic gesture than anything else.

"Thank you for telling me the truth and for protecting me; that's what I would have expected from you anyway. That's what friends do for each other, isn't it?"

Arun smiled at me and his dark skin tone was back.

"Man, am I happy to have that out of me now. You can't believe how relieved I am. Kayl will be damn angry with me, but I'll survive. We have both made a promise. An oath, which restrains us from telling the truth. But no matter what kind of punishment awaits me, I had to tell you the truth."

This time, he bent in my direction. I held on tight with all my strength and embraced him. It wasn't a hug anymore – it was more like an attempt to find stability. Stability in a situation in which I no longer knew who or what could still hold me up. I was on the brink of freefall.

We kissed deeply and it seemed as though neither of us ever planned to end the hug or the kiss ever again. I felt Arun's arm muscles tense up and his right hand grab my butt. With a push, he lifted me into the air – a feeling of weightlessness as though I could fly. Still kissing and embracing, he carried me over to the sink and set me on it gently. His hands stroked my ears and I felt his fingers in my hair, his lips and his tongue feeling warm and thrilling. All at once, he pulled back his head, and we both breathed in deeply.

"I don't know about you, but I could kiss and touch you all night."

Saying nothing, I grabbed Arun's strong shoulder and pulled him back in towards me.

"We have a lot to talk about, and I owe you a lot of answers. But we can't forget that this is your birthday party, and there are surely a few guests waiting on you out there. They want something from you too."

"Maybe, but isn't it what the birthday girl wants that's important?"

Arun smiled and kissed me.

"Yes, it is."

In that moment, Alex stormed into the bathroom.

"That's what I thought – there you are. I don't want to be impolite, but there's a whole bunch of people waiting on the birthday girl. If you can tear yourself away, the party is outside of the bathroom."

Alex disappeared, having delivered his message.

Macho, what an A ...

"You read my mind. That's exactly what I was just thinking."

"Let's go back out there – but there's one thing you still need to know, it's very important to me."

Arun looked very serious again all of a sudden, and focused.

"One more thing — it's very important."

"I've fallen in love with you. You should know that."

Arun blushed, which was his way of saying it did mean a lot to him.

"Can you please get me back down off the sink?"

As Arun hugged me and picked me up, I kissed him again and whispered in his ear.

"I'm in love too – with an Arverni – isn't that Kay-Ky?"

We both left the bathroom, one after the other, and mingled with the birthday guests. I accepted congratulations and presents, while Arun stayed close to me, flashing me his enchanting smile, reinforced every now and then by an air kiss. Strange – I somehow felt much safer now.

After I'd done my duties, I gave Arun a sign and we met on the dance floor. I placed my head against his chest and enjoyed simply letting myself sink into him. We danced until another guest interrupted me with a gift in his hand. Arun disappeared towards the bar and I paid attention to my guests – without taking an eye off of Arun. I couldn't explain it, but he had a magical attraction for me.

THE HUNT BEGINS

Las Vegas, Nevada, USA

Peter Sanders stood before Sherman, his thoughts whirling like mad. "What's going on, Peter, what's bothering you?" "I was just asking myself whether we're doing the right thing being here in Las Vegas. Now, when we're looking again for aspirants. I don't think it makes much sense to be here and taking a break."

Sherman smiled.

"It does make sense to be in Las Vegas. This is where our search for an aspirant will start, and Ocram Steel will help us find one. Use your charm and get us two tickets for his show from that friendly assistant. After the show we'll pay him a visit."

Sanders nodded,

„You can rely on me completely, just consider it done. I'll rely on my charms – be right back."

Full of energy, Sanders left the room and you could hear the door loudly locking behind him.

Sherman paced back and forth, tense and fully lost in thought. Something was running through his mind. Suddenly, he stopped and stood in front of the window, looking down at the people walking along Las Vegas Boulevard. He went for his phone and looked for a contact he hadn't called in a long time. His finger paused a moment above the name before dialing the number. Sherman stared at the display on his telephone for a fraction of a second, he considered breaking off the call, his finger circling above the red button.

"Sherman, is that you? Dammit – why are you calling me? Are you crazy? I told you never to call me again. We're not friends anymore, Sherman, we are enemies – when will you get that?"

Sherman let the caller blow off a little steam and breathed in deeply – this seemed to be an important call for him.

"Alright, alright, I understand you – we're enemies!"

"If the others find out I'm on the phone with you I'm dead – you know the Arverni law."

"Calm down, you're dead anyway. How many years do you still have? Two, three, or maybe four. If I remember correctly, you're at the end of your Finitum. That's why I wanted to know how you were doing – we were friends, after all, good friends."

"That was a very long time ago, before you turned into a criminal, Sherman."

"We're all criminals – each in his own way. Let's forget for a moment that we're all bad people. How are you really doing? I heard you're not doing that well."

Sherman breathed in deeply, hoping that his information had had the planned effect.

"How did you find out you bastard? Who are you still in contact with?"

"Calm down – I'm not going to tell you that."

"Dammit, Sherman, why are you calling me? I know it's not a curtsies call.

"Because I want to help you. Friends help each other."

"You want to help me? Unfortunately I don't believe a word of it. Why would you help me, Sherman? I don't need help."

"You remember, surely, that I'm the older of the two – not by much, but at least five-years. I'm doing splendidly, just like a fifty-year old should be doing. Just had a complete checkup and, amazingly, everything is in tiptop shape – anyway I don't want to bore you with the details. I called you to help you."

"And I've asked how you intend to do that?"

"The same way I did for myself. I will end your Finitum and correct the process of physical decay. Would you like to use your aphmal again? How about an aphmalisation ten times more intense than any you've experienced before? Can you even still remember when you used your aphmal last? Was it ten years ago, or maybe twenty?"

The caller fell silent.

"You're a real asshole, Sherman."

Sherman felt that everything he said had hit the mark with his conversation partner. At the same time, he had just finished writing an email and sent it together with an attachment.

"I don't trust you Sherman, you're a traitor and a bastard and something deep inside of me says I shouldn't trust you and can't believe you – not a single word."

"You don't have to. I wouldn't, in your place. It's true! Whether you believe me or not! As unbelievable as it sounds, I've succeeded in extracting the Arverni gene and unlocking it, eliminating the negative characteristics. Can you still remember how we re-searched the problem together? We were so close – you can't imagine how close.

"So, you've succeeded in unlocking the gene, where's the proof, Sherman?"

"In a bit you should receive an e-mail with a link that will answer any open questions you still have."

Sherman laughed to himself – everything was going according to plan. Not in his wildest dreams would he have believed that he would have kept him on the phone this long.

"Is that really you, Sherman? I can't believe it – you look like a ..."

"Like a fit 55-year-old. OK, I might need to lose five pounds, but otherwise I'm in excellent shape. When I run a 10K with my girl-friend, who by the way is 30 years younger than me, she's the one to run out of breath, not me."

"Very well, Sherman, very well. And what other proof do you have besides the fact that you're fit, physically active and, as it seems, aren't suffering the effects of the Finitum?"

Well, those are all very good proofs, proofs that show results – and that's what we researchers were always interested in re-sults."

"What more proof do you need? What would satisfy you?"

Sherman knew his conversation partner had smelled blood, and that's what he wanted. Everything was going according to plan.

"How would you like a pure dose of the Arverni gene? Something to regenerate your aphmal and make you, let's say, five to eight years younger during the first treatment. Would that convince you?"

Sherman heard his conversation partner breathe deeply.

It had worked – something he hadn't even believed possible seemed to be happening. His biggest enemy – who had been his best friend – was coming back to his senses.

Everyone has a price. For some, it's money; for others, a little more of this miserable life. Everyone has a price.

"That – that would be proof, Sherman. But how do we do it?"

„You tell me where and when we should meet. I'll be there and I'll bring back a few extra years of your life, and then I'll disappear again. No one will know a thing."

Sherman knew he still hadn't removed the last traces of doubt, so he waited for an answer.

"Alright, Sherman, we'll meet, and if you've lied to me, you will learn the true meaning of the word Finitum. If you're in good health, then you'll leave again quickly, but uninjured. Can you be in New York in two days? I'll send you a text message with an address; we'll meet there at 8pm for dinner. I'll reserve a table under the name Kruger."

"We'll do it. See you in two days."

"In two days."

"One more thing – I'm looking forward to seeing you again."

"Not me, Sherman."

Sherman hung up just as Sanders knocked on the door. Sherman glanced at the monitor installed in the wall saw Sanders and opened the door.

"Well, that was fast – did you get the tickets for the show?"

"What do you think, father? It will cost me a dinner with that nice female assistant, and probably more, but otherwise everything's in order. We have tickets for the 8:00 show."

"Well done, Pete, then everything's going according to plan. Also please book us two plane tickets for tomorrow to JFK? We have to interrupt our stay here briefly. I have a very important appointment in New York.

SURPRISE GUEST

B ored, I set off to look for Arun. Once I was at the bar, I joined a group and started a conversation so I could keep watch for him. I was sure he would follow me, but I couldn't find Arun anywhere.

Either he's still dancing, or someone's got him wrapped up in conversation.

Minutes seemed like an eternity, and I couldn't follow the conversation anymore I was thinking about Arun so much, so I went back towards the dance floor to look for him. But once I'd arrived there I still couldn't find him. Uncertain, I looked at everyone and in every corner of the room — it was large, but you couldn't just hide yourself anywhere.
He couldn't have left, not without saying goodbye and a kiss.

Suddenly, the entryway door opened and I saw Arun. He was coming in with Kayl and another guest who did seem a little older – maybe in his early thirties. His ponytail stood out.

Ponytail? It can't be – that's Amar. Those two have Amar trailing behind them. Amar made good on his promise. He came.

They had just seen me. Amar waved at me, and they all walked directly towards me. With every step closer they came, my pulse began beating faster. I couldn't believe it. Amar was at my birthday party. He had interrupted his flight to the states to be here. I was meeting him personally, in reality, and not just in my dream.

Kay-Ky, Kay-Ky, Kay-Ky.

Amar smiled at me –. Damn, just a few more steps, and then they'll be standing right in front of me. What on earth will I say? My tongue is sticking to the roof of my mouth, and I can feel the tension starting to make me crumble, slowly but surely.

"All the best wishes on your birthday, Xama. As you can see, I've done everything in my power to get to your birthday party on time."

I stared at Amar and didn't know what I should say. Claire had also noticed Amar and appeared beside me all at once, wanting to know who the new guest was.

Amar had a dark leather coat on which, in my opinion, was a little too long. It had an elegant cut but looked like a poor imitation of the Matrix. Amar reached into his pocket and pulled out a white envelope. Slowly handing it to me.

"What's a birthday without a present? Once again, all the best, Xama, and thank you very much for inviting me."

Dumbstruck, I took the envelope and held it in my hand staring at Amar. His dark eyes had something mystical about them, almost uncanny. They were even a thousand times more intense than in the dream. Everything about him seemed perfect somehow – his face, his eyes, smile – simply everything about him was perfect.

Everyone was looking at me, and I looked at Amar, who realized I was a little absentminded.

"Don't you want to open your gift, Xama?"

"Of course, sorry, I'm just so surprised you're actually here and this is not a dream!"

Claire and Kayl looked at me, surprised. Arun looked away.

"Dreamed? You didn't tell me anything about that, Xama" Claire interjected. "Open the present – we're all curious what it is."

I carefully attempted to open the envelope, and pulled out a letter written in a perfect cursive.

"Read it aloud, Xama read it!" Claire called out, bouncing, and it seemed as if she might have already had a glass or two too many of wine. I looked at Amar, and he nodded at me.

"The very best wishes on your sixteenth birthday, Xama. A birthday that will change everything. How about a change of scenery? When was the last time you were in an exciting city?"

I shook my head and kept reading the letter. "I'd like to invite you for a long stay at the Aphobia Hotel in New York."

I looked at Amar with eyes wide.

"What a present, Xama – New York, America, USA, Manhattan, the Statue of Liberty. I have to tell Alex right away."
After Claire had disappeared, Amar looked at me more seriously.
"You have to come with us, Xama, you're not safe here anymore. I did tell you things were very dangerous for aspirants."
Totally irritated by Amar's statement, a question ran through my head – I fired it right at him.
"I thought Kayl and Arun were here to protect me – what could happen to me?"
Alex appeared suddenly and joined Claire.
"Go on, Xama, tell Alex what's in your birthday letter. Alex doesn't believe me that you got a week's stay in a hotel in New York in America for your birthday."
"Not only that," Amar said with a clear voice, and reached into his inside pocket to pull out some plane tickets.
"This, Xama, is your ticket. This one here belongs to Arun, and that's Kayl's. We're all flying from Frankfurt to JFK, New York tomorrow evening."
There it was in black and white.

Xama Dupre

FRA - JFK
Boarding 17:30
Gate Z3
Seat A3

Kay-Ky, a plane ticket to New York – what more could you wants for your birthday?
"Let me see it," Claire called to me, and I handed her the ticket, speechless."
"Whoawhoawhoa, Xama, that's not just a ticket to New York – that's a first class ticket. You're flying with all the famous people! I can't believe it – man, that is super Kay-Ky."
"That it is, Claire – super Kay-Ky."
Surprised and unsure at the same time, I looked at Amar, who smiled at me affirmatively.

"What about school? There are still eight days until summer break."

"I cannot believe it – Xama, you're getting a flight and a hotel for free and the first thing you think about is school," Claire interjected.

"Don't worry about it. I've already cleared everything with the school administration, and the three of you have special permission to start your summer break early this year. Can I speak to you in private for a moment, Xama?"

Amar's eyes were hypnotic, and all I could say was "Yes."

"Yes, let's go up to my room. We can talk privately there. I also have something to show you".

In the moment I said this, I noticed Arun shooting me a jealous look. Was it because I wanted to be alone with Amar?

I went ahead, and Amar followed me.

OCRAM STEEL

Las Vegas, Nevada, USA

More and more people were streaming down Las Vegas Boulevard towards the entrance to the Bellagio Hotel. Looking from the other side of Las Vegas Boulevard, the mass of people looked like a large anthill, gaining in size every second and piling up in front of the hotel only to disappear into it very slowly. For weeks, the same spectacle had been taking place every evening at the same time. But, contrary to what you might assume, the people hadn't come to see the famous water shows and impressive fountains inside the Bellagio Hotel.

No, they had all come to see something unusual, something one-of-a-kind. The new magic and illusion show "SURPRISE" by Ocram Steel. All of Las Vegas had been talking only about "SURPRISE" for months now, and the somewhat inconspicuous looking magician smiled from an ad poster on every corner. Las Vegas is known for the extreme, but this kind of phenomenon had never been seen here before. The show "SURPRISE" was sold out for twelve months within just a few days, despite admission prices of 280 dollars or more per person. Depending on the seats, people paid up to thousands of dollars for a ticket – if they could get one at all. This evening, like every evening before, the theater inside the Bellagio was filled to the last seat. Sherman and Sanders had also taken their places in one of the suites when an announcement sounded.

"Ladies and gentlemen, please make certain your partner, friend, or the person who accompanied you this evening is with you. It wouldn't be the first time someone went missing at "SURPRISE." Please take your places, the show begins in just a few minutes."

Another announcement and a gong signaled that it was time to start. Immediately, the doormen shut the large entryway doors and the theater darkened. Violins, accompanied by horns, created extra excitement, which the orchestra slowly and skillfully built to a crescendo.

A yellow spotlight turned on, projecting a gleaming circle in the middle of the stage from the left. Another spot moved in from the right to the middle of the stage as well, directing itself so that both spotlights overlapped to form one circle.

The fans of Ocram Steel know that the magician appears on stage in a different way at every show. Each time, he succeeds in enchanting his audience anew. It has already become one of his many trademarks, and everyone in the room is expectant, wondering what will happen next on stage. All at once, the first spotlight goes out in a crackling accompanied by the orchestra. Shortly after that, the second spot goes out too, and the stage is suddenly dark.

The orchestra falls silent, and a clap of thunder seconds later turns both spotlights back on again, beaming – on the stage, a figure stands in the glossy light. More spotlights illuminate the figure, and the audience recognizes it's a young woman who's appeared on the stage, lost. With another clap of thunder, the spotlights go off again and then right back on – it was only a couple of milliseconds, but that's all Ocram Steel needed to appear as well on the stage behind the woman. The audience applauds and only stops when Ocram Steel raises his voice and speaks to the young woman.

"It seems to me that you've gotten lost in the theater – or did you want to assist me this evening? Might I learn your name?"

"Eva, my name is Eva," the young woman said in a shy voice and looked back and forth excitedly.

"Glad to meet you, Eva, my name is Ocram Steel – but you can call me Ocram."

A laugh went through the audience.

"Ocram, how did I get up here?"

"Well, I can't answer that question for you, but I can show you to your seat. How would that be?"

"Yes, please."

"Do you have your ticket with you? Where are you sitting?"

"My husband has the tickets?"

"No problem, we'll find him. There must be a man here missing his wife."

Ocram Steel had just finished formulating his question when everyone heard a man stand up out of one of the rows in the middle of the hall and wave. A spotlight and a microphone found him, immediately.

"Is that your husband, Eva?" Ocram asked the young woman.

"Yes, that's my husband, Klaus."

"Klaus, are you missing Eva?" Ocram Steel asked in the direction Klaus was standing.

"Yes, I certainly am."

"Klaus, what's Eva's seat number?"

Klaus, who looked a little nervous, searched for the tickets in his jacket pocket, but without success. Ocram Steel saw this and called to Klaus.

"Just read off the seat. The number is there as well."

"417F," Claus called, visibly agitated.

"Klaus, do you mind if I bring Eva by personally?

Eva, just link arms with me. I'll take you to Klaus."

Eva linked arms with Ocram Steel, and in an instant there was a clap of thunder and the light went out again. A flash lit up the stage, and you could see it was already empty. A clap of thunder later, the stage was lit brightly, and Ocram Steel was standing in the middle of it.

"Ladies and gentlemen – if you're looking for Eva, she's already sitting in her seat at 417F and can now enjoy the show, just like all of you. Welcome to "S U R P R I S E" – and I can promise you one thing, you can't believe everything you see, for some of it isn't real."

The audience erupted into applause, and Ocram Steel knew he had everything under control. As usual, he'd succeeded in enchanting his audience. Eva and Klaus were highly sought-after for conversations later in the evening. Everyone wanted to know how the illusion worked asking whether the couple were in on the show and not just accidental participants. Ocram Steel's fame was only increasing – his show was regularly featured in the news and on TV. Surprise had become the most talked about show in America... It wasn't just audience members, but also scientists and his magician colleagues that were intrigued by his magic.

The hype surrounding the greatest magician of all time, as the press had already named Ocram Steel, had only just begun. The recently unknown Ocram Steel was working hard to keep this mysterious aura as image by avoiding the secrets about himself a secret and to keep himself interesting, and he avoided all contact with the public. He gave no interviews.... Just as spectacularly as he appeared on stage, he disappeared again. The presidential suite in the Bellagio Hotel was monitored by security 24 hours a day, and the rumors said that Ocram Steel never left his suite. The newest information rumor making the rounds is that Ocram Steel was 29 years old and was discovered when he did a show at a birthday party. Whatever it was, Ocram Steel embodied the unique and the unknown, and he more than fulfilled his role as a magician – he had something magical. People weren't just fascinated by him as a person – his show "SURPRISE" was different from other shows. Up to now, no one had discovered any explanation for his illusions, and insiders were amazed that two Ocram Steel shows are alike. Scientists and experts argued over how Steel's unbelievable illusions work, but in contrast to Copperfield and others, no one had found an explanation for how Ocram Steel could enchant his audience anew every evening. But what was truly extravagant, truly special about what Ocram Steel did is that he brought his audience with him into a world of magic – nothing is as it was before; the laws of gravity have been displaced. The visible becomes invisible, and the impossible appears to be possible.

But the magician's success had also created questions in the public mind. More and more experts were becoming interested in the Ocram Steel phenomenon and were trying to unlock the secret of Ocram Steel and his show SURPRISE. In the past few months, Ocram Steel's management had cancelled all interviews at his direction and not even one journalist had gotten a chance to speak personally with Ocram Steel. After having declined multitudes of interviews the pressure became too much and so Ocram decided to give an exclusive interview.

Ocram Steel was an exceedingly private person. After his management announced the show SURPRISE would continue through to the 9th of December, and would no longer perform, rumors began to spread. An answer to the question of why Ocram Steel would simply disappeared at the height of his career, just as spectacularly as he had appeared.

There seemed to be a special reason why Ocram Steel had agreed to this interview – requested it, in fact. His management was looking for the perfect opportunity to continue to market the show, but Ocram Steel had something else in mind. He wanted to eliminate the rumors he had read about himself in the newspaper. Everyone – the whole world – should know that he wasn't a charlatan. He wanted to prove to everyone that his powers were real. He wanted to tell the world a secret, even if he placed himself in mortal danger by doing so – he couldn't hold it in any longer. The time was ripe for the truth. They were all about to find out who, or what, Ocram Steel really was.

IN DANGER

Amar sat down on my bed and without wasting any time, he said.
"Xama, You need to listen to me, it's damned important for you to understand everything I'm going to tell you now."

"As much as I hate to say it, you don't have a choice. You have to come to New York with me. The minute you are discovered – which will happen very soon, if it hasn't already – you're lost. Arun and Kayl are the best of the Achilleans, but not even they will be able to protect you. When the attack happened both of them – Kayl and Arun – will do everything possible to protect you. They will fight till the end and die for you!"
Shocked and disgusted by the scenario Amar was painting, I interrupted him. "Absolutely not."
"That's right, Xama, that's what we need to stop."
I looked at Amar sadly.

Now, when Arun and I are just falling in love. Not again – I can't lose someone I love again.

"But why? Why is any of this happening? I don't understand it. It would be best if you all flew home alone and I waited here until they came and got me. Then hopefully everything would be over. I absolutely do not want anything to happen to Arun or Kayl on my account. Where is the danger coming from? Why me? Why now? There must be hundreds of other aspirants out there – why do I always have to be the one who draws the joker? Why me?"
"I think you know the answer to your question – am I right?"
I nodded, but didn't say a word.
"I was very surprised at your dreaming abilities, and how far you had already developed them right from the start. And at a point in time when your aphormation had only just begun. I don't know anyone who aphormed so quickly. It took years for me to create my first dream.
How do I do what? I don't even understand what's happening around me. If only Amar knew – I'm not doing anything.

"Xama, your aphormation is different from anything I've ever experienced, seen or heard of before."
Amar stood up, suddenly, and walked through the room.
"There's something else that makes you unique, Xama."

Once again, I had to think of how much I wished for a normal family. Father, mother, siblings, friend.

"So, what is it that makes me so unique?"
Amar remained standing, looked at me, and said: "Right now, you're the only aspirant there is."
"What do you mean, the only one? There are other Arverni."
"Yes, there are, but right now you're the only aspirant! That's why the other side would do anything – and I mean anything – to get you."
Amar started to cough suddenly. At first, I thought he was choking, but when he coughed into a handkerchief and it colored red, I knew that there was something wrong with him. Immediately, memories of my Dad came to me. It was like deja vu. Dad had exactly the same symptoms – coughing and bloody phlegm. Symptoms which then developed rapidly. Amar was sick – did he have the same incurable disease as Dad did? Was it something only Arverni got?

"Is everything alright, Amar? Are you feeling OK?"
"Excuse me, I swallowed something, I'm fine thank you."
A bitter taste told me Amar wasn't being honest. Should I confront him about it and tell him that I could taste the truth?

"What else did you dream?"
For a moment, I considered whether I should tell him about the dream I had where I was lying shackled to my bed. I decided not to do it, not yet, besides he was withholding stuff from me himself.
"Amar, why are there Arverni who are persecuting and killing other Arverni? What's the reason?"
I could feel how he battled, unsure whether he should tell me the truth.
"You can tell me – I can feel you're unsure. Please, tell me the truth, I need to know. It does have to do with me, after all."

"You're right. It does have to do with you."

Amar breathed in deeply and coughed again into his handkerchief. I felt that it wasn't easy for him to talk about it.

"A so-called Dr. Sherman, also of Arverni heritage, has been researching the symptoms of the aphormation – or, better yet, the Finitum – for years for the community. He was tasked with discovering why the Finitum begins in the thirtieth year of life and, what's more important, why it switches off the power of the aphmal and everything else which makes an Arverni special all at once."

Amar fell silent, thought, and paced back and forth.

"And what did he find out?"

"Not much at first, his series of tests didn't result in any new discoveries. Sherman believed that the answer to the council's question of how to turn off the Finitum could be discovered in the blood of the Arverni. He assumed that a special gene was the cause of the aphormation and the Finitum and that both were triggered even during the initial aging process, beginning in the sixteenth year of life."

"So, Sherman needed aspirants for his research."

"Right – he made his request to the council that each aspirant should give a set amount of blood – donate blood, practically – to make research on the Arverni possible."

"But – that sounds fine – or were there too few aspirants?"

"No, there weren't –Sherman's research team was on the right path and seemed close to unlocking the Arverni gene. But then something truly horrible happened.

Amar remained standing and looked at me, then coughed again.

"Do you have a glass of water? My mouth feels so dry."

I went into the kitchen and came back with a glass of water.

"What happened that was so horrible?"

"Sherman deactivated everyone in his research team – all but two of them." I looked into Amar's eyes and they told me there was more. He was affected, was he one of the two?

"You were one of them – right?"

"Yes, correct, I was one of the survivors! One of the ones who escaped – the other was Sherman's assistant. He had spared his assistant – I, on the other hand, was scheduled for deactivation. I was just incredibly lucky. I was assigned at that point in time to the research team as an aspirant, and was donating blood to support the research."

"Did you see it? Did you see him kill the others?"

Amar took a sip of water.

"Yes, I saw everything – but he didn't kill anyone."

"Sherman has a very rare Arverni ability. He is able to influence people and control their thoughts. He erased the memory of each individual in his research team. None of them could remember anything anymore, not even their own names, their children, or their wives. Only later did we realize Sherman had strengthened his ability through his own research; he had tested out his research results on himself and thus violated another Arverni rule. Since he hadn't killed the Arverni in his research team, the council couldn't sentence him to the death penalty. But he was banned forever from the Arverni community and from the council.

Sherman and his assistant then went underground, continuing their research at different secluded places all over the world. Sherman himself used his ability from that time forward, breaking the Arverni Codex. He missed no opportunity to hurt others, deceived people, and stole from them every chance he got. Sherman is a criminal."

"Okay, and this Dr. Sherman is after me now, right?"

"He's not after you, but after your blood, since it keeps both him and his research alive. Sherman is extremely dangerous. He will die without the gene – without your blood – this is his motivation!"

Amar approached me – he could tell his statement had affected me, and wanted to comfort me. But I didn't feel weak at all. I also didn't feel any fear, or any hatred towards this Dr. Sherman, although I was deeply disgusted by what he was doing. But even without feeling afraid, I enjoyed Amar's embrace – although I did wish Arun was in his place instead.

"If you'd told me this story a couple of days ago, I would have been crying for days."

"Yes, your aphmal is making you stronger. This is only the beginning of your aphormation. Now you realize why it's crucial that you fly tomorrow with us to New York. You're much safer in the Aphobia with a lot of Arverni around you. Sherman won't dare to

show up there. There is, however, another reason you have to fly with us to New York."
"Okay, what else is there?

"You have to offer your apheid before the council, it is an important condition of sealing your acceptance."
"I did read something about the apheid, but don't have any idea what's going to be demanded of me."
"You don't need to either, not yet. I will prepare you for it when the time is right. It's nothing bad – just an oath. You will swear to support the Arverni community until your death, and to live by its values."
"Sounds a little odd, but I trust you Amar. I guess that means I'll be packing my suitcase tomorrow morning. Let's go back downstairs and enjoy the party; I do still have to say goodbye to my only girlfriend, after all."
"Right away, Xama, but there was something else I had hoped to see, if possible?"

What was it that had aroused his interest?
I didn't know, so I asked him.
"Yes, what?"
"Your father's letters – the Arverni legacy. We talked about it in the dream, you remember?"
Could I trust Amar? Father had specifically warned me I should never show it to anyone, no one at all. No one included Amar.
"Just a little look, Xama – I'm so fascinated myself with the history of the Arverni, and I'm always learning new things."
Since I trusted Amar, I switched off Dad's instructions in my mind for just a moment, went to my nightstand, pulled out the metal box, and handed it to Amar.
"Crazy, an aphmal box – your father was the head of security for a reason, I see. And your father's letters are inside? The Arverni legacy? Might I take a look inside?"
"Of course, if you can open the box, then you can also look inside and read them."
Amar looked at me with eyebrows raised, and smiled.

"You know as well as I do that the box only opens its contents to the one who possesses the right aphmal, the key to the box. I can't open it with my aphmal."

"I think we'll still have plenty of time in New York, Amar – there are lots of guests waiting on me downstairs, and tomorrow I'm leaving. I will take the aphmal box with me, and you'll be able to take a look inside. The right time will come, I promise."

Amar was still holding on to the box convulsively, and it was visibly difficult for him to let go of it.

"You're right, Xama, we'll do that. We'll take a little more time once we're at the Aphobia, and you'll show me what's inside, and I'll help you understand it."

Amar passed me the box and I placed it back in its spot in my nightstand, grabbed Amar's hand, and pulled him out of my room and downstairs into the party room. I could feel that Amar was completely distracted by the box and its contents – but what was the real reason?

Sweet As an Apple

Las Vegas, Nevada, USA

I n the same rhythm, similar to a swarm, people left the theater. But there was one little detail that made the difference for each individual visitor. Everyone, down to the last guest, was completely fascinated by Ocram Steel and his magic show. The show made the people feel satisfied and balanced, and it also created something special. Each person who was there beamed with peace. It was the same phenomenon every evening – no one could explain it, no one except for Ocram Steel. But this evening there was one guest who had followed the show attentively and who knew precisely what Ocram Steel's secret was.

Ocram Steel disappeared, back to his hotel like he did every evening, immediately after the show and wasn't available to speak to anyone. There were no exceptions, and it seemed as if the show had exhausted him and he had to recover from it a little.

Sherman and Sanders didn't let the managers' statements deter them, and they set off towards Ocram Steel's suite. As expected, the entrance was secured by an elevator and security personnel who successfully fought off the press and other paparazzi. When the mob dispersed somewhat, Sherman stepped forward and was promptly informed by security that Ocram Steel was not available to speak to anyone.

Sherman grabbed the man by his tattooed arm.

He looked Sherman in the eyes and wanted to loosen himself from the grip, but Sherman began speaking to him in a changed voice.

"Ocram Steel is expecting us, and he has given you the order to bring us directly to him without any detours – now, and immediately."

"Come with me, please! There is another elevator; this one is just a smokescreen. Follow me."

The security officer walked to another elevator not far and spoke to a colleague, who reacted a little perplexed. Sherman didn't want to run any risks, so he placed his hand on his shoulder as well, touched his neck, and spoke to him. Seconds later, they were all in the elevator on the way to Ocram Steel's suite. Once they had arrived there, other security men opened the suite, after Sherman had given them some friendly instructions as well. Sherman and Sanders were astounded at the luxury of the suite, the first impression of which put their own suite to shame. Sherman looked around and discovered what he was looking for – the bar.

"Would you like one too?" he asked Sanders.

Sanders nodded.

"Not bad – cask strength 30 years old. Mr. Steel has good taste."

"Thanks for the compliment," they heard from a corner of the room. Ocram Steel came into the room with wet hair and a bath-robe.

"And thanks, for giving me time to take a quick shower. All I ask is how you succeeded in bribing my security service? Must have cost a fortune – that's why I pay them so extraordinarily well, so something like this doesn't happen."

Steel walked directly to a console.

"I wouldn't do that, if I were you!" Sherman called out in a deep voice. Sanders knew what was going to happen next, so he stood up and grabbed his whiskey.

"Believe him – he's right. He's always right", Sanders said tense.

"What wouldn't you do?" Steel asked him.

"If I were you, I wouldn't activate the alarm under the console in front of you and pull the gun out of the drawer at the same time. Isn't that what you're thinking about right now? If I were you, I would take a little more time and greet my guests."

Sanders held his glass up and signaled his agreement.

Steel remained standing.

"How do you know what I'm thinking?"

"Are you the magician, or am I?" Sherman answered.

"Would you like a whiskey too?"

Steel nodded.

"Alright, who are you and what are you doing in my suite?"

"Here it is," Sanders piped up.

"We've come to help you."

Sherman picked up a cloth that was lying on the bar, dripped some whiskey into it, and rubbed his forehead. Then he threw the cloth to Sanders, who also rubbed off his forehead with the cloth.

"You surely have a pair of aphmal glasses – or should I lend you mine?" Sherman said with his voice raised.

Steel remained frozen to the spot and it seemed as if the question about the aphmal glasses had drained all of the blood out of his head and down to his legs. He went to his closet, opened a drawer, and took out a pair of sunglasses, then put them on and went back to Sherman. He looked first at Sherman's forehead, then Sanders', and then took his glasses off, laid them back in their place, and sat down on the sofa.

"How about a whiskey now?" Sherman passed Steel a glass.

"You're not council members – I know all the Arverni in the council. You are ... you are."

"The others!" Sherman said, in an ice-cold voice.

Steel was visibly afraid, his hands shaking.

As Sanders enjoyed his whiskey, Sherman took the initiative.

"Now just a minute – those are just stories about us being the evil ones. We say we're the balance – the equalization – the other side. Sometimes we are evil, that much is true, but we aren't going to let things go that far today, are we?"

"Not that far," Sanders repeated, and suddenly held a knife in his hand.

"We've seen your show, and I have to say – not bad manipulating hundreds of people all at once. A power only a few of us have, very few."

Sherman went back to the bar and picked up a large, green lime.

"Pete, catch this sweet apple and enjoy it."

Sanders caught the lime, placed his glass down on the table in front of him and started to cut the lime into quarters. The juice ran over his hands.

"Careful – the apple's juicy!" Sherman interjected.

Sanders took a quarter of the lime in his mouth and chewed around on it as though it were an apple, without puckering up his mouth once.

Steel could almost taste the sour juice of the lime, and just this imagination alone was enough to make his mouth water.

"Leave something for our friend, Pete."

Sanders had already put half of the lime, including the rind, into his mouth, and was still chewing on it. He stood up, went to Steel, and gave him the second half of the lime.

"It's a delicious apple, but a little juicy."

"Go ahead and try it, Mr. Steel", Sherman said again, in a more forceful voice.

Although Steel was lost in thought, he took a quarter of the lime and bit into it like an apple. A short time later, he had the whole lime in his mouth and was chewing on it blissfully, without losing even a bit of his control.

"Tastes good, eh? Just a shame it's not an apple, but a lime instead."

The moment Sherman said it, both Sanders and Steel started to gag. Sanders spit the mouthful he was chewing on into his hand and Steel ran into the bathroom with his mouth full of lime. He reappeared a moment later after he had washed out his mouth.

"What do you want? Who are you?"

"The second question isn't important, but we're going to have a thorough discussion about the first one. Sit down, Steel."

Steel sat on the sofa. His thoughts were doing somersaults, looking for different answers.

"I'll try to explain to you as briefly as I can what we can do for you, and what we will expect from you in return."

ARRIVAL

All day long, there was only one thing on my mind: the flight to New York. Not just because flying to New York was exciting and so totally Kay-Ky. No, the real reason for my nervousness was that I had never flown before in my life. This was my first flight.

But I don't have to tell anyone else that.
My excitement increased by the hour, and my aphmal helped me deal with the situation. Just as I was on my way to the bathroom, planning to look at it again, I tasted a honey in my mouth. Seconds later, Arun opened the door to the party room and greeted me kindly with a "Good morning, Xama" and a kiss on the cheek.
"I thought I'd just check in and help you clean up."
"Couldn't you sleep either?" Arun smirked, "Yeah, that's right – I mostly just lay there awake and brooded. Xama – I've fallen in love with you."
The sentence hit me like a hammer. Had I heard him right? Arun blushed, and my honey taste suddenly changed into sweet chocolate – strange.

Did that have something to do with the fact that I loved chocolate more than honey?
Kay-Ky, what on earth should I do?
Led by my feelings, I hugged Arun and kissed him on the mouth. There it was again – the feeling of security when his strong arms embraced me. A beautiful feeling.
I whispered in Arun's ear.
"It's very nice of you to come and help me. I believe I've fallen in love with you too. Sorry if I'm a little awkward, but I've never been in love before. Up to now, I've always lost all the people who ever meant anything to me. That's why I've built such a wall around myself. I'm glad you decided to climb over it." We both laughed and looked at each other, but didn't know what we should say.

"Have you packed already?"

What kind of a question was that? When he knew I had repressed everything up to this point.

"To be honest, I haven't even started. Some people are used to traveling, but it always takes me a little longer, and then I usually forget some things too."

Arun smiled at me and picked up 4 boxes at once, holding two in each hand, and balanced through the door and up the stairs. It seemed as if he had also only recently aphmalized. Arun brought all the boxes upstairs in record time, and as I cleaned up the last of the glasses, he sat down by me at the bar and looked at me. To hide my nervousness, I worked faster.

"You're a little tense, Xama, am I right? I feel something in your presence."

So he had aphmalized, I knew it. But that didn't automatically give him permission to analyze my emotional state.

"That's unfair, Arun."

"What? That I'm interested in how you're doing?"

"Not that – but that you know how I feel. That gives me a feeling as though my insides were pushed out – even worse than being naked."

Arun thought.

"Naked – yes, I can picture you that way very well."

"Soo, that's what I thought. You're one of those guys, huh?"

"Not really; you should know I've only gone out with one girl up to now, and it didn't last very long."

"Okay, and why not, if I might ask?"

Arun looked away, and it looked like he was ashamed.

"You don't have to tell me about it, Arun! Sorry that I asked."

"It's okay. You'd find out sometime anyway. Kayl stole her from me. After she had gotten to know Kayl, I wasn't interesting any-more. Kayl looks better, he's better at sports, and he's also not as shy – he just comes across better."

"She didn't deserve you, Arun, and it's for the best. Otherwise I might not have even gotten to know you."

Arun shook his head.

"You certainly did that well."

"What do you mean?"

"Well, I asked you how you feel. Aphmal or no aphmal, I think I could have noticed even without an aphmalisation that you're very tense. Something is bothering you, and you should know that friends are there for one another when you need them. I'm here for you, Xama. So let it out — what's weighing on you? You can tell me, maybe I can help you — even if all I do is make a good suggestion. Sometimes it helps to share your problems with friends."

Arun was visibly troubled, and if I can't trust him, then starting tomorrow I won't have anybody left anymore anyway, since my best friend is staying here.

Claire, I'm going to miss you. Should I tell him?

"I'm just so worried because of the trip, I keep thinking about the flight."

"That's totally normal, Xama, you're leaving your comfort zone, your best friend – everything important to you."

We both stayed in the party room for hours afterwards, just sitting there, looking at each other, and talking. Arun told me more about himself and Kayl and everything he knew about the Arverni. I shared my story with him, and we both discovered to our surprise that our hands had found each other and connected. Arun had big hands, and I slowly felt his slim fingers and interlocked them with mine. I thought this would be a good opportunity to learn more still about Arun and about the Arverni.

"Arun, what kinds of powers are there, anyway?"

"You mean powers that develop during the aphormation?"

"Yes, exactly, how many are there?"

"No idea how many there are – I only know a couple of them, the most important ones."

"What are the most important ones?" "Oh, well, healing, then dream communication, reading thoughts or manipulating them, telling or seeing the future, and so on. I don't know all of them."

"Well okay, which powers did you develop?"

Arun looked at me oddly.

"Do you really want to know?"

"Of course, I'm interested – why do you ask?"

"Only because it's not really that special of a power. Actually something really pointless – it's not even really worth talking about."

"So now you've made me curious – now I want to know what it is that's not so special."

Arun looked at me, unsure.

"I can paralyze other people, or kind of switch them off – that's what I call it."

"You can what? Switch other people off?"

"Yeah – I said it wasn't anything special. That's why I became an Achillean – the power is perfect for that."

"Can you do it to me?"

Arun looked at me surprised. "You mean I should switch you off, just like that, for no reason? You're crazy."

"How long will I be switched off? Or can you switch me back on again?"

"Switch you on is what I can't do. Depending on how strong it is it could last from a minute to multiple hours."

"That's okay – then just switch me off for 1 minute; that should be enough for me to see how it works and how it feels."

"You're being serious?"

"Yes, I'm being serious. What do I have to do?"

"You don't have to do anything. You're the victim. But it's not like it's exactly painless, and I don't want to hurt you."

"Why didn't you just switch Kayl off?"

"Switch Kayl off – oh, how I wish I could. It doesn't work with him. We can't use our powers on close family members. It's a family protection – a part of the Arverni legacy. Powers don't work on first-order relatives. How nice it would be if I could use my power on Kayl; what I wouldn't give to just switch him off once in my life."

"That means I can't use my powers on my own family."

"Yes, that's how it is."

"Good, then go on, switch me off. Can you do it with a kiss?"

Arun looked at me, visibly tense and surprised.

"I've never done it with a kiss before; I have to touch you to do it, so a kiss should work."

"Go on, then, let's try it out for the first time, Arun."

"I don't know, Xama, I'd rather not. What if I hurt you?"

"That won't happen – and if it does, I'll heal myself!"

Arun's hands touched my face, and it felt good. He held my head and his lips came closer and closer until they touched my own. The feeling was soft and warm, and Arun pressed me closer to himself. All at once, I felt a pulse penetrating my body through Arun's lips, but then dissipate again immediately.

Arun's lips separated from mine. He stood up again, surprised, and looked at me uneasily.

"Did you feel anything?"

"Yes, quite a lot – it was a warm, beautiful, passionate kiss."

"Yes, but that's not what I meant. I tried to switch you off and nothing happened. That's not possible – it always worked before, with everyone. Surely it has something to do with the fact that I can't hurt you. That's it, that's why it didn't work."

"Calm down; that's it Arun, that's why it didn't work."

"How do you do it? What do you do when you want to switch someone off? How does it work?"

"Well, I just think about wanting to switch them off, and then it just happens. There's no one, two, three step instructions, if that's what you mean. I can just do it – it just works when I need it to."

"Do you want to try it again? Maybe it just didn't work right."

"What are you trying to prove, Xama?"

"You're right, Arun – I'm not trying to prove anything to you, I just think that I ... let's just forget it."

"That you what? Xama?"

"That I can learn powers when other people use them. If you try out your power on me, then I can learn it too."

"I've never heard of that before – that doesn't exist, Xama. You're just imagining it."

"Good, then just try it one more time, switch me off."

Arun looked at Xama angrily.

"You don't know what you're saying. I won't hurt you, and I also won't bring any harm to you. It won't happen, Xama. I have sworn a promise, an oath that stops me from trying it out on you. It won't work."

"Please, Arun, just one last tries. If it doesn't work this time, then we'll forget about it. I'll kiss you, and when I press your hand, then you switch me off. Please, Arun."

My lips touched his, and I pressed Arun's hand. In the same instant, I felt a powerful pulse of energy move through his lips and penetrate my body, advance up to my aphmal, and then it was like it was reflected. Then, an enhanced pulse of energy pushed through my lips into Arun, and an invisible force hurled us both apart.

A little later, I opened my eyes and saw that I was lying on the floor. I got up and saw Arun also lying on the floor. He wasn't moving. I called his name, but Arun showed no reaction. I stood up, a little dazed, and went over to him, turned him over, and tested his pulse. Luckily everything was OK.

"Arun! Arun, wake up!"

I shook him and repeated his name.

Suddenly, Arun opened his gorgeous eyes.

"You're really strange, Xama. Didn't anyone ever tell you you're supposed to kiss a prince to wake him up, not shake him?"

Arun laughed, and I laughed with him and pressed a big wet kiss onto his mouth. "You scared me, Arun! Did you know that?"

"Hopefully – you just switched me off, just like that. Didn't we agree I was going to try out my power on you?" Arun stood up, took me by the arm, and held me tight.

"You're something special, Xama – what just happened clearly proved it. You're something special."

"You too, Arun, and I are sorry that just happened to me."

The two of us could have kissed each other all night long, but there was still a lot to do. With the excuse that I still needed to pack my suitcase for the flight tomorrow, our first date ended. The party room was back to its old self, and Arun accompanied me to his room, then took his leave with a kiss. It felt like a whole spoon full of warm chocolate, just super delicious Kay-Ky awesome.

Claire was, as expected, not in our room, and probably wouldn't come back all night. Alex had his own pad, and that meant there was no one there who could bother him. Which was fine with me, since it meant I could concentrate fully on packing my suitcase. It went much better than I thought. I didn't have all that much, anyway, and everything I owned fit into my two large suitcases. I was a little unsure whether I should pack the aphmal box with Dad's legacy in a suitcase or in my carryon luggage. Better safe than sorry, I thought to myself, and decided on my backpack. The box almost filled it up, which meant that I needed another carryon bag. My subconscious kept nagging at me, and I saw strange images before me. Images that came from an earlier dream. I saw myself lying in bed, shackled and suffering. No matter what I tried, they only disappeared briefly and then reappeared in ever more frequent intervals, lasting longer and longer. Something wasn't right – I never had these dreams before when I was awake, and I had to stop them before I went crazy. Good thing I have an aphmal – after a few minutes I felt Kay-Ky ok again.

I've never felt better!
It's always so unbelievable! Having an aphmal really is something very special.
After everything was packed, and I'd checked my tickets and passport several times to make sure I had everything, I retreated to my bed. I couldn't fall asleep right away, however, and had the strange urge to check over the contents of the aphmal box one more time. An unbelievable invention, I thought to myself, after I had opened it. Step by step, I took out all the contents and placed everything to the left and right beside me on my bed. Everything was there – the letter from Dad, all five notebooks, the camouflage cream, and the little locked book with the instructions it must be opened by the Meta. I took the little book in my hands and asked myself what kind of a message Dad could have written to the Meta. My thoughts searched for an answer, but exhaustion overcame me, and I packed everything back into the box, placing the rose of Akar on top as well. In the moment I touched it I thought of Arun and suddenly had that Kay-Ky delicious chocolate taste in my mouth again.

Hopefully the taste doesn't have any calories – otherwise I'll be round as a bowling ball if it keeps up like this.
After I'd shoved the box back in my backpack, exhaustion attacked mercilessly, and I stopped trying to resist it. But before I could fall asleep, thoughts continued to swirl through my mind.

What's going to happen now? With me in New York? With Arun? With the Arverni?
At some point, hours later, I fell asleep.

Everything was right on schedule. Arun knocked on my door and greeted me with a "Good morning, Xama." When I noticed he was hesitating, I took the initiative and kissed him on the mouth. He hadn't bet on that, and I could see he was surprised. Good thing

I'd played this situation through in my mind. It was simpler than I thought.

"Good morning, Arun, did you sleep well?"

"I laid awake for a long time and couldn't sleep – you know."

Raising my eyebrows, I signaled to Arun that I didn't know what he meant.

"Oh, well, I was thinking about you."

"And about what, exactly?"

The color of Arun's face chanced suddenly.

"On you, you know, how you smell, how you feel, just everything. You're just very pretty. Everything about you."

With a smile and another kiss, I rewarded his compliment, but kept it to myself how often I thought about how Arun influenced my sense of taste. For me, Arun was the embodiment of the sweetest chocolate.

Is this how it feels when you're in love?

Arun grabbed both suitcases, and I followed him with my back-pack and a large purse. Just when Arun was lifting the suitcases into the taxi, Alex came speeding up and braked frantically in front of it. Claire jumped out of the car and ran towards me.

"I wanted to see you again and give you one last hug, Xama."

"That's nice of you, Claire. Promise me you'll come visit me soon?"

"There's nothing I'd rather do; I promise you that as soon as I can afford it, I'll come visit you in New York."

I hugged Claire one last time, but was so mentally absent that I didn't even realize Alex was also parting from me with a kiss on the cheek. As we drove off, I looked back once again at Claire and waved goodbye.

Now I was alone again, leaving my best girlfriend. Will we ever see each other again?

During the almost eight hour flight, the airplane shook roughly several times, making me wince every time. Arun explained to me that this was caused by what's called turbulence, variations in air speed, and that it was completely normal. Whatever the reason for it is, turbulence made me feel afraid and break out in a sweat. Images from my dream reappeared in the same intervals as my fear of flying manifested itself, but this time I saw something different, something which completely shocked me. I saw myself lying in bed again, but I wasn't moving. Everything was silent and still. When I concentrated on the images, I saw my face for a brief moment. This moment was enough, and I knew it wasn't me who was tied to this bed. Something was different from yesterday – the body didn't just lie there motionless, the hands, face, and skin were all also pale and sallow.

What did that mean?
.Arun felt that something was wrong with me. He held my hand, intertwined my fingers with his own, and stroked them gently. He smiled at me, but I still had the image of a motionless girl before my eyes, and I had a hard time returning his smile.

"Excuse me for a moment, Arun – I'll be right back." Now it was time to turn my negative emotions around – thank God I didn't have to wait for the bathroom. Surely, Amar and Kayl had also noticed I was disappearing into the bathroom so frequently. Without my aphmal, I never would have survived this flight and these strange dreams. Despite stimulating my emotional state multiple times, I was anything but relaxed and peaceful when we landed in JFK in New York. These daydreams, added to my fear of flying, immediately destroyed all the positive energy. Despite regular aphmalisation, I couldn't get the terrible images of the shackled girl out of my head. Again and again, she appeared in my thoughts, and as I left the plane, I saw the bed before me again – only this time, it was empty. The girl had disappeared.

While Arun and I were waiting on our luggage, Kayl and Amar went off to look for a cart to put all our suitcases on. When they were both a little ways away, I felt Arun's hand in my hair; he was gently rubbing along my neck and very carefully touching my right ear. It was unbelievably Kay-Ky. Honestly, it was better than Kay-Ky. While he touched my neck with his lips, he whispered something.

"It was the same for me – it will get better with every flight, you'll see. Anyway, I think it was totally – Kay-Ki, or whatever you call it that you flew here to New York with me."

I nodded, agreeing with Arun's statement, although the thought of another flight called up the taste of soap in my mouth. Like all the other waiting travelers, we stared at the monitors, installed in endless numbers above the similarly endless seeming baggage carousels. Never in my life had I seen so many TVs in one place before. There was nothing for it for me than to count them. Just on our carousel alone, there were 12 multiplied by 25 carousels, plus a few installed in other places – that came to over 300 TVs. Wow, 300 televisions in one room.

Crazy.

"Arun, how many TVs are here in this room?"

Arun stared at the TV in front of us, looked at me briefly, smiling, and said there were more than 300.

"Can you read thoughts? How did you get that number so quickly?"

He smiled at me.

"I counted them some time ago, when I was standing here and waiting, and since then they probably haven't added any new ones. Sorry, I don't want to be rude, but I'm interested in what's about to come on the news."

I followed Arun's hint, became quiet, and looked into the box in front of us. They were playing a report about a 16 year-old girl found dead near Las Vegas. It was about a murder, people were expressing speculations about a ritual murder, but whatever happened to the girl it must have been grisly – that much was sure. Arun stood there in front of the monitor with his mouth open, and it seemed as if the report had robbed his face of its color

"Xama, wait here a second – I really need to talk to Amar."

"But they're coming right back – do you want to leave me standing here alone?"

"You're right, definitely – certainly not now – I can't believe it! Not again!"

Arun looked in every direction, excited. It seemed as if he was suddenly suspicious someone was watching us.

"What's going on with you Arun?

Arun looked me in the eyes, then looked around again nervously. He was considering what he should say to me.

"It's nothing, Xama – everything's alright. Can I hug you?"

In the same instant Arun enfolded me in his strong arms, I had an extremely bitter taste in my mouth. Bitter and Arun didn't go together – something was different. Arun had lied to me.

"Arun, something's not right – you just lied to me. I tasted – I mean felt – that you weren't telling the truth."

"You did what? Tasted it?"

Arun fell silent for a moment. "You're unbelievable, Xama, and you're right, I wasn't telling the truth just now. I wanted to spare you the truth and wait until Amar was with us. Amar wanted to tell you all about the whole story."

"The whole story? Arun, please help me?"

Arun was visibly unsure of himself and didn't know what to say next.

"The report that was just on the news, the murdered girl. That wasn't a ritual murder. She had to die because someone wanted what belonged to her and they took it from here."

I interrupted Arun, questions and more questions firing through my mind.

"What did her murderer want?

In the moment I asked the question – I knew the answer.

Arun thought it over, trying to find the right words.

"Her blood – right? That was the reason she was totally bled out. Her murderer wanted her blood!"

"Right, they took her blood – That's why she died."

Arun looked around again, tense, searching for Amar and Kayl, and maybe also searching for someone who was watching us.

Arun, in any case, had transformed from totally relaxed to extremely tense, and the report about the dead girls' body was the trig

"I don't understand all this. So it is a ritual murder, like they suspected on the news."

"Not really as I see the whole matter, but I want to wait for Amar's opinion. I think there is just one single reason the girl had to die in such a grisly way."

Arun was talking in riddles, and now he was making me really curious.

"What do you mean by that, exactly, that there can only be one reason for it? If it's so clear, why are the police so in the dark and asking the public for clues?"

"This is all a little more complicated than you think, Xama. The police are in the dark because they don't at all understand what the motive was for this murder. There's no way they can understand it, either, since they're missing some important information."

"For example …?"

All at once, Arun gave a hand signal and I saw Kayl return it. Amar and Kayl were pushing two large luggage carts down the hall.
"Don't you trust me? Do you think I can't keep a secret?"
Arun looked at me, and I recognized something in his eyes, something I was seeing for the first time. It was fear.
Arun was afraid.
"The dead girl was an Arverni."
Arun's statement practically smacked me in the head, coming to terms with what I had just heard.

Dead girl, 16 years old, grisly murdered – an Arverni.
Okay, all of that corresponded exactly to me. I have the same characteristics. Now I knew exactly what father had meant when he said: "You're in mortal danger!" The person who murdered this innocent girl is after me too. That was what Arun wanted to keep from me.
"So, someone is killing 16 year-old Arverni – how nice that I just had my 16th birthday, and that I just found out I'm an Arverni too."

My attempt to bring a little irony into our conversation rolled off of Arun like water from a rain jacket.
Arun looked around again and waved towards Kayl and Amar, who were still about 15 yards away.
All at once, I realized the answer to my question. Yes, that was it – that was the reason, the motive the police didn't know about. What the girl was missing – her blood – was the reason she had to die, not the cause of death. And she was also an aspirant. She had aspirant blood.
"She was killed because someone needed her blood – aspirant blood, am I right Arun?"
Arun nodded and looked at me, took a step towards me, and took me into his arms, pressing me close to him.
"You don't need to be afraid, Xama, I'm here and I will protect you. After Kayl, I'm the best. You've got no reason to be worried."
Arun smiled at me, and I couldn't do anything besides kiss him.
"Look at that – after 8 hours of holding hands, little brother gets rewarded with a kiss. Keep it up, Arun."

Arun shot Kayl a knowing look and shook his head, but I just kept holding on.

"The two of you have probably been cuddling so much you've forgotten to look for our bags, right?" Kayl said in his macho way.

"There's something more important at the moment," Arun said, and pointed his finger at the monitor, where the news was being repeated.

Amar and Kayl watched the report.

"NO – PLEASE, NO!!!" Amar screamed, and fell to his knees, holding his head. Arun and I were shocked by Amar's reaction, and just stood there looking on helplessly. Kayl was the first to react, grabbing Amar underneath his arms and helping him stand up. Amar walked a couple of steps along the baggage carousel, and I am questioning looked at Arun and made him shake his head. Kayl came over to us, also shocked, and raised his eyebrows with the remark:

"He'll probably get ahold of himself again soon – let's just give him a couple of minutes."

Kayl was right. It didn't take a minute for Amar to come back to us.

"Did you tell Xama?" Amar asked Arun in a sad voice.

"Arun didn't have to tell me. I just put all the facts together."

Amar, Kayl, and Arun looked through the big hall as if they were searching for someone. Amar took a step towards me, and I loosened my embrace with Arun.

"I have to talk to you for a second! Arun, Kayl, you watch out and make sure we're safe here." Arun and Kayl both stood in front of us, turned their backs to us, and watched the other travelers.

"Xama, now you know the true reason why you are in mortal danger. It is the Arverni legacy – not the written stories, the information parents give their children. You're not in danger because your father gave you these notebooks. Of course, lots of people surely would be interested in those as well, and the story of the Arverni is a unique one. The aphormation, the Aphora, and everything else, which belong to our culture is so unique that, many people have already tried to unravel the story. Many things are going to be considered in a new light, and some basic concepts, even basic beliefs, are going to be challenged. We want to stop all of this – it represents a danger to the Arverni and to humanity as well."

Amar held my hands and looked into my eyes.

„Your blood is the true Arverni legacy! It is this legacy, which drives the group headed by Dr. Sherman. He and his group need the legacy to stay alive. That's why they're always on the hunt for new aspirants. They kill them to get their inheritance, the legacy, since it extends their own lives. Let's go to the hotel."

"Wait, Amar, there's something else I think you should know."

Amar looked at me curiously. "I have been dreaming of a dead girl for the last few days."

"You did what? Did you see her in a dream?"

"Yes Amar. The past few days, the dreams started – and yesterday I even dreamed of her during the day, just like that?" „Did you see pictures of her?" Amar questioned.

"Yes, she was shackled to a bed, she suffered, and how she ..."

I fell silent, no longer able to finish my sentence.

"Could you see her? Recognize her face?"

I nodded, and Amar reached into his jacket pocket, pulled out a picture, and handed it to me.

"That was Sonja," he said to me with a deeply sad voice.

I recognized her face, and all at once I felt myself become dizzy, my knees buckling. My backpack pulled me down heavily. A frantic attempt to find support with my hand failed. The floor turned away from me, and I no longer had control over my balance. In the moment I expected to hit the floor, someone took hold of my backpack. I was hanging in the air just above the floor, pulled back up by an invisible hand. Two powerful hands were holding me tight.

"Everything alright? You're worrying me."

I looked at the photo in my hand again, saw the face of the dead girl, and in the same instant everything became quiet and dark. Amar's voice echoed into nothingness. Everything around me disappeared, and I felt weightless.

When I opened my eyes again, I was lying on a stretcher and was covered up to my neck with a space blanket. Arun was standing next to me, Kayl wasn't far away, and I could also make out Amar speaking to a man dressed in a uniform.

"What happened?" I asked Arun.

"You fainted, but Amar barely caught you. Was the flight that bad?"

Shaking my head, I tried to remember. The girl – it was the face of the dead girl that had shocked me so.

"How are you, Xama?" Amar asked, visibly concerned.

"I'm better now, sorry I messed up all the plans, but when I saw the dead girl's face it took my feet right out from under me. I saw her yesterday in the dream still alive, and then today during the flight she wasn't moving anymore and was pale as a corpse. Now I know why – she was already dead."

Tears ran down my face. Somehow, I felt embarrassed to cry, but I couldn't help it.

Arun wiped away my tears with a handkerchief.

Amar bent down to me and used a cloth to remove the camouflage from my aphmal. He passed me his compact mirror.

"Take a look. It will help you – it will make everything better again. Don't worry, you're safe. Then please cover up again."

Amar was right, my aphmal worked wonders. Seconds later, I was feeling amazing again, and I felt more secure than I had in a long time on my feet. Arun took my hand and smiled at me.

"Don't be afraid, Xama. I'm here for you." I nodded at him, lost in thought.

"You're up, Xama. I've told you everything I know, and now you have to answer a question for me. Is it true that you have the ability to taste emotions? I've heard that this power exists, but it's supposed to be very rare."

"I'm not sure, but I believe I have this ability, Arun. I don't myself know what I do have and what I don't -- everything is so different, so changed. I'm not normal, shy, reserved Sophie anymore – that's for sure – but I still need to get to know the new Xama."

"How does it taste, anyway, when you're with me?" Arun smiled at me.

"Wouldn't you like to know?" I pointed at a young boy waiting on his luggage with his parents, biting blissfully into a chocolate bar.

THE DEAL

Las Vegas, NV, USA

Dr. Sherman sipped on his whiskey, delighted. The TVs were covering it as an exclusive story, and every poster on Las Vegas Boulevard advertised the Surprise Show. But that by itself didn't surprise anyone. What did create questions was that every poster included a red banner which displayed: Last Surprise Show on December 8th. The answer to the question all Las Vegas was asking didn't correspond to the official version. Ocram Steel wasn't at all leaving the stage to devote himself to something new. That was a lie advanced for his own purposes. "Ocram Steel doesn't have any other choice but to stop on December 8th, since Ocram Steel will lose all his magic and his powers on December 9th. Am I correct, Dr. Steel?"

Dr. Steel looked at the floor, affected.

"And not only that – that is the day the Finitum begins, your downward spiral – it means you must then prepare yourself for death. What a shame to have to prepare for the end already on your thirtieth birthday. At a time when life is just beginning, when you have achieved something, when your career is really starting, fans are lining up, and when money is flowing in in vast quantities."

Sherman watched Steel and noticed how he followed his words, his frustration building up, and how he looked directly at him. Sherman continued:

"But it doesn't have to be that way. There's a solution, a path you can choose. Something, which will halt the Finitum and regenerate your aphmal and your powers. You've seen our aphmals, Steel. What do you think – how old is Sanders, and how old am I?"

Steel became more nervous, poured the last swallow of whiskey into his mouth and swallowed it right down. He looked at Sanders and then Sherman.

"You're over 50, and your colleague there is over 30, perhaps 35."

"Almost right, Steel, I'm 55 and Sanders is 36. We are both, according to definition and normal aging processes, in the Finitum. I have a girlfriend who is 35 years younger than I am who has no reason to complain, and Sanders is still able to continue the martial arts he learned as an Achillean at the highest levels. We're in our primes – as you've experienced yourself, there is still a little magic in the world."

"He's an Achillean, really? Wow, I've read a lot about them, but never seen one. Who is he bonded to? For whom would he give his life?"

"I'll give you one guess, Steel."

"Okay, all of this is going a little too fast for me."

Steel walked through the room nervously. Beads of sweat were building up on his brow.

"What do you want from me? What should I do for you? There must be a reason you're telling me all this and offering me a way out of the Finitum."

"Very well, Steel, now we're speaking the same language. We can help you ensure your Finitum doesn't begin on December 9th, and in return you will do us a favor."

"You're not interested in my powers, are you? As I've just found out, you do have the exact same ones. What can I do that you can't?"

"Bingo – that's something I'll tell you at a later date, but you're correct, one hand washes the other. We need your powers, and if you help us, in return you will receive a cure for your Finitum, meaning you can continue with your show."

"The cure – there is no cure; I've never heard of a cure before."

"You wouldn't have. We've just now succeeded in unlocking the Arverni gene and removing the negative characteristics of the Finitum. We two are the best proof of that."

"What exactly do I have to do?"

"You will interrupt your show for a couple of days or weeks – let's say because of illness – then come with us and help us search for aspirants."

"I knew it – you are the evil ones. Help you search for aspirants? To hunt and kill young people in their aphormation?"

"Who says we kill them, eh? Those are just fairy tales – medicine today allows us to only hold them for a few days in order to take some blood. It's nothing more than a blood donation; no one will die from it."

Steel thought.

"If I help you, then you'll help me so that December 9th doesn't have to be the end of Ocram Steel; have I understood correctly?"
"Arverni honor."
Steel bit his lip.
"Good, I'll do it." "Very good, that's what I want to hear."
Sherman stood up, went over to Steel, and held out his hand.
"Repeat after me."
With a changed voice, Sherman spoke to Steel.
"I will do everything in my power to help find further aspirants. I will not shrink back from any measure – there is now no justice and no mercy."
Steel repeated the words, and Sherman felt an inner sense of triumph. He had succeeded in recruiting another powerful Arverni and winning him over for his plan.
"Pete, let's go. I believe Ocram Steel would like to recover from his exciting show, and he also needs to speak with his management and call off his shows for the next few weeks."
Sanders stood up, replaced the knife he was playing around with, and held out his hand to Steel.
"Welcome to the team."
"Thanks" Steel replied.
"Pack your bags, Mr. Steel, tomorrow evening we're flying to New York. And tell your management where you're going; you don't want to lose all your fans, after all."
Sherman left the room, and Sanders followed at his heels. Ocram Steel went over to his telephone and dialed his manager's number.
"Kevin, is that you?" "I have to go away, for a few days. Please cancel all shows for this week and next. Just tell the press I'm sick. Invent something to keep them guessing."
"I'm worried, Ocram, what's going on? You told me you could keep this up until December, and then your powers would be gone. This unbelievable ability you have, and now you want a couple of days off even though after December you'll have the rest of your life off. Don't do this to me, Ocram."
"Kevin, just do what I told you. I just need a couple of days, and when I come back I'll be better than ever before, and I won't have an expiration date either. We'll be able to produce SURPRISE past the 9th of December, and integrate something we've never had

before into the show. Something the world has never seen before. I can promise you, it will be no holds barred."

"That sounds fantastic; I'll put out a press release right now. I assume you don't want to say anything."

"Correct! And Kevin, book us a flight to JFK for tomorrow evening – I want to see whether New York is ready for Ocram Steel and for my show. Stay calm – we're about to become insanely rich."

DEAD GIRL

The drive from the airport to the Aphobia hotel took longer than I expected. The driver stopped in front of the hotel entrance and Amar's eye contact with Kayl and then Arun was a signal. Before I had fully registered it, both of them were already out of the taxi. I was about to get up as well when Amar spoke to me.

"Wait a moment, Xama. Kayl and Arun are checking to make sure everything really is safe. After the incident with the dead girl, I want to be 100% sure."

"Did you know her?"

"Who – the girl?"

"Yes, the dead girl – she was an Arverni, I mean, an aspirant, just like me."

Amar looked at me, seriously, and then looked at the floor of the limousine, and began to cough.

"Yes, I knew her, and I wanted to help her – but I wasn't able to. It makes me very sad, and extremely angry."

When he looked back up at me, his face looked different. It was full of disappointment, coupled with pure hate, and I could taste his feelings – first it burned a little, and then my whole mouth was on fire. Everything burned; I had never had such a spicy taste in my mouth.

"Oh, that's spicy."

"What did you say?"

"Nothing – just, my mouth is burning. What was her name?"

Amar's thoughts wandered – my statement that my mouth was burning seemed to distract him.

"Her name was Sonja. But as much as it pains me to say it, Sonja isn't important anymore. The only thing that's important is you, Xama. Tell me, has that happened to you before?"

"Has what happened before?"

"That taste in your mouth? That you taste something different all of a sudden, something that isn't there? I mean a change in tastes without you eating anything, it just happens."

Should I tell him the truth? Why not? If I can't trust Arun, then whom can I trust?

"Yes, a couple of times, and it seems like it's been happening more often lately."

"When did you notice it for the first time?"

"I'm not sure anymore, but I think on my birthday. Yes, that was the first time I tasted something sweet."

"What happened? What was the reason you got the sweet taste in your mouth?"

I could feel Amar's question making me blush.

"Hmm, I had a really nice talk with Arun, and then it happened."

"Interesting – Arun was having positive emotions, and you picked up on them. Your sense of taste told you Arun was feeling good; that's why you had the sweet taste in your mouth."

"Honey – it was the taste of honey. I thought you just developed one power during the aphormation. I guess I just have to be different and test out a bunch of powers on my first day. What on earth is happening to me, Amar?"

"Multiple powers, Xama? Were there more than just the two? The power of dream communication, the ability to taste emotions and feelings other people are having, were there other powers you've discovered within yourself?"

"Yes, I think so, but I'm not sure."

"What else did you notice?"

"I think I can heal wounds – well, speed up healing. On the night of the party I cut myself deeply on and bled a lot, so I wrapped it up and imagined it wasn't as bad as it was, and that it stopped bleeding and healed up again. Then the wound started itching like crazy. When I checked it a little later, the wound was as good as healed. The same thing happened with Arun's abrasions he got from rubbing on a rope. I just held his hands, and the wounds healed immediately."

"What do you mean a little later? When you said Arun's wounds healed immediately, how long did it take?"

"Well, my wounds itched immediately after I bound them up. After about 15 minutes, the itching was so bad I looked at it, and the wound was already closed, so I removed the bandage. After about another 30 minutes, there were no signs of a wound ever being there. Arun's injuries healed immediately; we both watched it. I held his hands and wished inside that they would heal, and then it happened. It took one or maybe two minutes max."

Amar became restless.

"Crazy! Xama! Just as I thought - you're an Identidem."

Amar took my hands and looked at me with respect and pride, and this changed my taste again to cold, sweet vanilla ice cream – delicious.

"What's an Identidem? I can now taste vanilla ice cream, and it tastes very good."

"You taste vanilla ice cream – that perfectly matches how I feel right now."

"Tell me how you feel, then I can understand my taste better."

"Very positive, emotionally, and curious to get to know you better. Proud to have found you. Happy to be here in the Aphobia with you. Respectful of you and of what awaits you and all of us. Fear that you're in great danger."

As Amar formulated his thoughts, my vanilla ice cream taste was interrupted by just a hint of spiciness; maybe I was just imagining it, since the taste disappeared again immediately, covered over by the vanilla ice cream.

"What is an Identidem, anyway? I didn't read anything about it in Dad's letters."

"Identidem means or describes the state of having multiple powers. There is no direct translation, but that's the closest explanation. It is something very special, not to mention unique. An Identidem is an Arverni, an aspirant, who develops multiple powers. Ancient sayings tell there is always only one Identidem. It's not just your ability to develop multiple powers that's special; the speed at which you develop them is also amazing. Other Arverni need months to develop a power, and some never reach the state you've already achieved."

"You said there's always only one Identidem. What happens to the last Identidem when a new one develops?"

"Whenever an aspirant develops into an Identidem, the existing Identidem loses his powers. Usually, he is in the final stages of the Finitum, so he loses his powers and abilities even faster."

"So it's a 'he' right now?"

Amar looked at me, surprised, and my vanilla ice cream taste changed into a peppermint taste.

"As far as I know, there has never been a woman Identidem. Throughout the history of the Arverni, it's always only men. It is time to rewrite history and redefine the role of the woman in the Arverni community. It is high time, and you Xama, are the one all women, and many others, have been waiting for."

"Amar, I'm not sure about all this, it's probably not what I think it is. I'm just testing out the different powers, and then I'll settle down on one."

Amar had to laugh, and my vanilla ice cream taste was back.

"Who knows you're an Identidem? Have you told anyone else, or has anyone noticed it?"

"Not directly said it, but Arun has probably gotten it – I did heal him, and he knows, I think, that I can use dream communication, but I'm not sure."

"Good! keep it that way! No Arverni must discover that you're an Identidem. I'll speak with Arun, but don't tell anyone else – not even Kayl, understand?"

"I'll keep it to myself, Amar, I promise."

My promise was sealed with a knock on the car door. Amar let down the window and Kayl and Arun gave the all clear.

"Let's go, the four of us will talk later upstairs in the palm garden."

I nodded.

I got out of the car and followed him. Arun was waiting, and shot me a sweet smile, which I returned. Kayl walked far in front of us into the Aphobia, securing our entrance from the front.

By the way Xama, there are some things your father didn't leave in his legacy. I don't know of any Arverni who learned them from their parents. It might be that you're the exception."

"What exactly do you mean?"

"The truth, Xama, the truth about the Arverni."

I stared at him, but he kept walking totally lost in thought over what the truth might be, I followed him. Kayl was already opening the door to the hotel, and Arun was watching the entrance. Everything seemed familiar to me, as if I'd already been here before. But of course, in the dream, Amar had invited me to dinner in the Aphobia. As I walked past Kayl and into the hotel, I had a feeling of deva vu, as though I'd already been here hundreds of times. To tell you the truth, simply totally Kay-Ky.

"It's an insane hotel – if you ask me, Xama, the best hotel in New York, and we're VIP guests. Amar is the hotel manager, after all, so his closest friends should at least be VIPs, shouldn't we?"

Kayl always had something dumb to say, so I wasn't surprised at his statement this time either. I didn't dignify it with a glance, however, and just kept looking around the hotel entryway. The hotel was gorgeous as grand and luxurious as I had remembered in my dream – warm tones with a modern touch, nothing kitschy, everything stylish. The floor was a beige and brown marble, and there were giant exotic plants imbedded into exquisite ceramic pots resting on shiny marble floors, and water features in the hall. The banana tree with ripe bananas, which hung down, bent over by their weight, was hard to miss, standing right in the middle. Different waterfalls tastefully integrated and surrounding a red carpet, which showed, guests the path to the reception desk.

"Let's check in; Amar has probably reserved themed rooms for us. I love these rooms," Arun said, and went on towards the reception desk.

Still mesmerized by the elegance of the hotel hall, I followed Arun.

"Welcome back. Mr. Wellberg". Everything has been prepared according to your needs and those of your guests as requested". A moment later the attractive receptionist presented us with a small gift as well as an envelope with our names on it. "Please enjoy your stay with us, and if there's anything you need please feel free to contact any of our helpful staff."

My memories came back bit by bit – the luxurious rooftop patio with the pool and corners and lounges. When I think that I only dreamed all of it, and now it's coming true. What a strange feeling.

"Arun, what exactly is a suite?"

"You will find that out in a minute – but it's really nothing more than a very nice large room."

Amar waited on us on the way. As the four of us headed towards the elevators Amar instructed us to meet in 30 minutes on the rooftop patio.

When I consider everything that's happened in the last few days – it's all just much too much. Now I'm in the most famous city in the world, in one of the best – maybe the best – hotels in New York, and I have a suite. There's only one thing I can say to all that.

Super mega Kay-Ky.

THE PLAN

Mandarin Oriental Hotel, Manhattan, NY, USA

Peter Sanders had booked the best suite in one of the best hotels in New York under a fake name. Ocram Steel had joined Sanders and Sherman in the hopes of not losing his powers or his show. Steel also booked a suite in the Mandarin Oriental – a smaller one – so as not to attract attention. All three met for a conference in Sherman's suite to talk through the next steps.

Sanders poured him a glass of whiskey and offered Steel a glass as well. Steel rejected it, shaking his head.

"Where is Sherman? I thought the meeting was so damn important – don't we want to talk through the next steps?" Steel uttered, visibly tense.

"Patience, Steel, Sherman will be here soon, and if there's one thing you can rely on, then it's that he has a plan. I can only recommend that you remain calm, have a drink, and relax. Otherwise Sherman will think of something else, and cut you out."

"Cut me out? What do you mean by that?"

"It's quite simple – if you're not important for us anymore, then you're unimportant, correct? And we tend to free ourselves from dead weight. Is that understood?"

Steel nodded and thought for a moment whether Sanders might be right, and perhaps a whiskey at 11 o'clock in the morning might indeed help him relax. But his thoughts were swept away as Sherman stepped into the room energetically.

"Steel, I hope you're well rested and had some time to recover. Now we can get to work – there's nothing I hate more than bad work; in my view, it's nothing more than dead weight. As soon as you notice it, you have to get rid of it."

Steel swallowed and attempted to remain calm.

Sherman poured another glass of whiskey.

"Want one too, Steel?"

Steel nodded, and Sherman poured another glass and handed it to him. Ocram Steel took a big swallow, surprised by the sharp taste of the whiskey. It took all his concentration not to cough; he didn't want to expose his discomfort.

"Breathe deeply, Steel, anything that doesn't kill you makes you stronger. What's coming next will require all your energy, and much more. Now is the wrong time to show weakness. Now we'll see how good Ocram Steel really is, how powerful his abilities truly are. Your job now isn't to influence or hypnotize hundreds of people. All you have to do is win just one over for us and turn his convictions around. That's all, Steel."

Sherman positioned himself behind Steel, who was sitting on the sofa, placed his hands on Steel's shoulders, and supported all of his weight on them. Steel slowly sank into the couch, attempting to resist the pressure.

Steel pushed forwards against Sherman's pressure and attempted to stand up, but he didn't succeed.

"When do we get started? I don't want to stay any longer in New York than necessary. If that's what you want from me, I just need a name, a picture, and five minutes with the person, and the job's done."

"Pete, would you please pass Mr. Steel the files?"

Sherman was satisfied with the progress of the discussion. Pete Sanders grabbed a folder lying on the table in front of him, went to Steel, and passed it to him with the words:

"It certainly won't be as easy as you think – if you succeed at all in winning the target over to our side. There's something good in it for you, but you'll find that our once you've succeeded."

Steel opened the envelope and took out a photo, looked at it, and asked himself whether he didn't know the man pictured there with the dark, long hair from back when he was still active with the Arverni community. But his memory didn't provide him with any information.

"That is Amar Wellberg. A member of the council, and one of the most powerful Arverni in the council. Amar Wellberg is responsible for communication, which means he knows exactly where new aspirants are staying and at which point in time new aspirants will begin their aphormation. He is our gateway to a huge amount of Arverni blood and genes. Amar Wellberg is the general manager of the Aphobia hotel here in New York; with the right requests, it should be simple to get an appointment with him."

Sherman was interrupted by the ringing of his telephone and was about to deny the call when a glance at the display and the name shown moved him to take it instead.

"Hello, Kanaar. To what do I owe the honor?"

"Sherman – we'll meet at 8 at the Italian place."

"Very good, at 8."

Sherman stuck his phone back into his pocket.

"Gentlemen, the first milestone of our plan here in New York City have just been achieved. Things couldn't be going better. Pete, you help Steel book a suite in the Aphobia, and have an appointment made between him and Amar Wellberg. Steel, you'll manipulate Wellberg then and pull him over to our side. Be careful – he's highly intelligent, and has a feel for danger. Amar Wellberg is no show, no act – and he's certainly not going to be easy to manipulate. Act slowly and purposefully."

There was a thought Steel couldn't shake from his mind.

"May I ask you something personal, Dr. Sherman?"

"You may ask, Steel; I'll decide whether to answer answer."

"You have the same power of manipulation as I do – perhaps even a stronger one. Why is it so important that I help you manipulate Amar Wellberg? Why didn't you do it yourself? Why me?"

"A very good question, Steel, but what do you think would happen if I got near Wellberg? Do you think I'd have a chance of waltzing into the Aphobia without being immediately laid low by an Achillean, and probably immediately executed? Whom do you think the Arverni fear most? Who is their greatest enemy?"

Steel shook his head, unable to grasp the question.

"Excuse me, Dr. Sherman, I wasn't thinking clearly. I'm sorry."

Sherman looked at Steel as though he weren't even there.

"You don't need to be sorry, just don't do it ever again. I allow everyone one mistake; don't make the same one again. In the future, think of the bigger picture. If it ever happens again, I'll free you of your power to think. You're not worthy of having it."

Sherman stood up and left the room through the same door he came in.

"Off with you, Steel, we have a few things to do. Let's get to work and book you out of this hotel and into one full of Arverni. I only hope, for your sake that they don't find you out. Otherwise the same thing will happen to you as the last man who helped us."

"Oh, and what happened to him?"

"Sherman didn't need to punish him for making the same mistake twice. After the Achilleans found out he was one of us, they did his work for him. There were just a few pieces of him left, and they didn't fit together so well anymore. So take care with your camouflage – Otherwise, it'll hurt."

THE SUNROOM

As we left the elevator, each of us was searching for our own room number – until we realized the rooms didn't have numbers at all, just different pictures.

"I don't even have a room number, just a picture of a sun. Where are you guys staying?"

Arun held up his room key, and I could see the moon on it.

"That goes well together, moon and sun. And you, Kayl?"

Kayl had a card with a picture of the Colosseum painted on it.

"I'll be joining the gladiators – good fit for an Achillean. I have to go to the right here; I'll see you upstairs soon."

Arun and I went further down the hall and reached my door. The door itself looked impressive, displaying a rising sun.

"Well, see you soon – I'll come get you in a minute; enjoy the time and freshen up a little."

I looked at Arun questioningly; he recognized that I didn't understand his instruction and pointed his finger at his aphmal.

"Freshening up for Arverni means using this thing. See you soon, Xama."

I waved Arun over to me with my pointer finger.

"I'm not letting you go without a kiss."

Arun bent down to me and kissed me on the lips. Chocolate in its sweetest, subtlest form – what a Kay-Ky taste.

When I opened the room to my door and walked in, I couldn't believe what I saw. Arun was right; it was simply indescribable. I didn't have the words for it. Absolutely super modern Kay-Ky that was obvious at first glance. I felt warm air blowing towards me. The floor moved, and when I looked closer I recognize it wasn't the floor that was moving, it was the images I saw. The whole floor was a gargantuan television; it must be a kind of video wall on the floor. I could see the sun from above, a view from space. When I walked farther into the room, I immediately noticed I had come closer to the sun, and that my position in space had changed. I walked backwards again slowly and returned to the starting point, far off in space.

I enjoyed every step, flying closer to the sun step by step. Now I could see individual eruptions and magma being thrown up out of the floor. All at once, the walls changed as well, showing the magma flying through the room. When I took another step forwards, hot air blew through my hair. Simply indescribable – what I'd seen seemed even realer because of the warm jet of air. The river of lava forked, and I walked along a lava flow into a very large room, watching an ocean of glowing magma open before me, the pathways to other rooms indicated with even more lava streams. I could have stood there looking at it for hours, taking walks on the surface of the sun, but a glance at my watch showed me there were only fifteen minutes until our meeting in the palm garden.

Only now did I notice that the furniture was all made in a unique design; the colors ranged from orange to blood red. In the middle was an oversized bean bag chair glowing in different colors as though made of magma itself. The whole bean bag chair was moving. It was so Kay-Ky realistic that I simply couldn't stop myself from running up to and touching it. A projector mounted on the ceiling projected flickering flames on the bean bag chair. When I sat in the chair, I felt the warmth. Curious to see the other rooms, I stood up and followed the lava river. When I opened the door, I immediately saw the oversized round bed, a sun just for me. I pulled off my shoes and allowed myself to fall into the sun, blissfully, noticing now that it was a waterbed. The water cushioned my bouncing movements.

The bathroom – I have to see the bathroom.
I followed the lava river into the bathroom, and when I opened the door, I couldn't believe what I saw once again. I expected something special, but what I saw exceeded all of my wildest expectations. The whole bathroom was a kind of grotto, and the stream of lava on the floor collected in an overwhelmingly large cave. If my eyes didn't deceive me, the lava was steaming. Even the sinks were all integrated into the grotto; the whole image looked like a Vulcan cave on the sun. A reddish play of light set off the beauty of this bathroom landscape. Then the thing I was searching for arrested my glance. I first though that water was running down one spot in the grotto. When I looked into it, the waterfall became calm, smooth as a mirror, and I could see myself in it. I turned on the water faucet and washed the camouflage from my forehead. It was a refreshing feeling, simply lovely.

When I saw my aphmal in all its beauty in the mirror, everything was Kay-Ky all right again. I told myself everything would be okay, and as the tingling spread throughout my whole body, I began to feel better and better, and stronger as well. The Xama standing in front of the mirror was different than she'd ever been before. Not shy anymore, not unsure of herself, but strong-willed, focused, and curious about the adventure which awaited her. I curiously opened some of the cabinet doors beside the mirror and was positively surprised. Complete product series from popular brands were already in the cabinet. At first, I thought someone had been thinking about me, since I had usually ignored make-up the past few years, and that's why he or she was offering me this whole array. But my mind told me it wasn't about me; someone was trying to put together a selection that would appeal to the tastes of lots of guests. My watch showed 5 minutes until our meeting, which would normally make me nervous. But all that's over now – no more stress about appointments. If someone wants something from me, he can wait. Right now, I'm going to turn myself into the new Xama on the outside as well as on the inside – we'll see what the men have to say about my creation when they see my new style. Sophie is the past, and Xama's the future.

Bye bye, Sophie.

Now, I'll just pull this tight dress over my body, and I'm done. As I left the grotto, I pulled a purse out of the case to match my dress. When Arun rang, I was already done, and opened the door immediately. Arun, who just stared at me until I almost started to feel unsure of myself again, seemed to have lost his powers of speech.

I kissed him on the mouth, and it seemed as if this brought back his voice after all.

"You look unbelievably great. Just beautiful, and somehow more grown up. I'm over the moon about your new look, and I think Kayl and Amar are going to be amazed by you too – wow."

The elevator opened, and Arun and I walked out into a place I'd already decided was completely Kay-Ky in my dreams. But now it felt even more real, even more tangible, and just perfect. An attentive waiter who noticed me spoke to me and showed me the way to our table. Amar and Kayl were already there. Amar had reserved one of the non see-through and also non hear-through pavilions for us. I went over the walkway through the pool and into the pavilion, and when Kayl was the first to see me I was already surprised by his reaction.

"Crazy – is that really you, Xama? I have to say, you look super hot."

"Amar, thanks so much for the sun room, it is so beautiful; I couldn't tear myself away, and so I'm a little late. It is far and away the most beautiful room I have ever seen."

"Glad you like the sun room, Xama; it's a matter of taste, of course, but I find the moon room more beautiful than the sun room. All of our themed rooms are unique, however, which I am proud of. I must add my compliments to Kayl and Arun's. You look very beautiful. Our shy Xama has turned into a confident young woman."

I sat down at the table, the sign for the waiter to take our drink orders. After we'd all ordered drinks, Amar spoke.

"There are two important things I want to tell all of you. One of these concerns you directly, Xama. Arun and Kayl know it already, and learned it as part of their acceptance into the community. We weren't able to do it for you yet, however, so tomorrow we will make it up."

Kayl and Arun looked at Amar, surprised, and I shared their surprise.

What does he mean now?

Kayl interrupted Amar as I wondered what apheid meant; I had read about it.

"It will be painful and bloody," Kayl interjected.

Apheid, now I remembered. The oath when you're accepted into the community. Dad had mentioned it in his notebooks.

"Bloody? Painful? I don't believe you – you're just trying to scare me, Kayl."

I looked at Arun for confirmation, but his facial expression told me Kayl was right.

"So, it's painful? Why should I complete the apheid if it's painful and bloody?"

Amar, who didn't like Kayl's comment at all, took back control of the conversation.

"It's not that bad – Kayl is overdramatizing it. It is incredibly important for you. You absolutely must swear your apheid before the council – that is the only way you can become a sworn member of the Arverni. Tomorrow is the perfect opportunity – the Meta wants to see me tomorrow, and another director is coming with him. That means we'll be four, and according to the rules that're enough to receive your apheid. The Meta wanted to get to know you anyway, so we can wrap everything up together."

Kayl was scaring me, Arun was quiet, and I could tell Amar was trying to convince me to do something. Was the apheid that important? Important for me? What are they going to do to hurt me?

OLD FRIENDS

Sherman had Sanders position himself behind the Italian restaurant and asked him to stay nearby and watch the area. Sherman had no doubts Kanaar would show up to this meeting alone, but there were always reasons to be careful. He went up the stairs to the rear entrance of the restaurant and in the light he could see someone sitting in the corner through the window. It was the table Kanaar and other members of the council had often used back in the old days.

Sherman walked in, briefly looked around, and then went directly to Kanaar.

"Good evening, Kanaar, so nice to see you again after such a long time."

"Good evening, Sherman. Why here? Why did we have to meet here?"

Sherman sat down and looked around.

"It brings up some old memories, and to be honest, this is the place the best decisions were made in the last few years – right here at this table. Not, as people assume, in the council itself. You and I – we both know it. The next big decision can only be made here."

Kanaar couldn't believe what he saw. Sherman, who was born in the same year as he, who had gone through aphmalisation with him, whom he had known since childhood, looked much younger than he did.

"Sit down, Agor. You look good, exactly like you described to me."

"Thanks, Ezra – and not only that, I feel even younger than I look. If I remember correctly, the Finitum is supposed to make you feel your age more intensely. Isn't that true? You feel older than you are?"

"Let's drop it, Sherman."

"Weren't you going to call me Agor?"

"Did you bring me proof of your success, Agor?"

"Have I! You know me – I'll want something from you in return for it."

Sherman reached into the pocket inside his coat and pulled out a loaded injector. You could see the ampule was only filled with a small amount of a golden liquid. He held the injector towards Kanaar. "There it is, the elixir of life. As you can see, only a small test amount. We only need to prove today that it works for you as well as it has worked for me."

Kanaar stared at the injector with glowing eyes, then at Sherman. "So, that's it – that's why aspirants have to die!"

"That is the extracted Arverni gene. That is what humanity and we have been searching for since the dawn of time. A fountain of youth. That aspirants had to die was unfortunately only due to the circumstance that the council persecuted me, putting my research, my researchers, and our test subjects in danger. One or two did die, it's true. Please remember that in the past you and I made a few decisions together. We didn't count individual human lives – we looked at the big picture."

Kanaar smiled.

"The big picture. A big lie Agor, and nothing more. Is this a big lie too?"

"Why don't you test it out, Ezra? That's why we're both here, after all. You look worse than the last time we met. What do you think – how long do you have left?"

"Leave it, Agor. You want to know something from me, am I right?"

"You're right; let's drop this little game, Ezra."

Sherman bent over to Kanaar, placed the injector against his neck, and pressed the trigger.

A soft sound, and the fact that the ampule was empty, indicated Sherman had injected Kanaar with the gene.

"So, my friend, that was it."

Kanaar grabbed his neck.

"And what comes next?"

Sherman stood up and went towards the exit, turned around once again and said to Kanaar:

"I'll go back to my hotel, and you'll go home. Give me a call and tell me how you feel the next few days."

Sherman opened the door, left the restaurant, and went down the street, then got into a car at the next corner and disappeared.

Kanaar sat there and tried to understand what had just happened. It was a strange meeting – as if he and Sherman were still friends. Just like old times, back when they both had the power to lead the Arverni – forget the Meta, it was the two of them who truly held the reins in their hands. Kana pushed himself up to stand on his weak legs. Expecting pain in his joints to stop him from doing so, he supported himself on the table. Strange – nothing there. No pain, and it were much easier to stand up. Was even this a result of the test? Kanaar stood on his feet and for the first time in years felt solid on his feet. He left the restaurant without the use of his cane, he felt exhilarated.

Sherman, you old devil, you really did it. You extracted the Arverni gene.

The next morning, Kanaar woke up energized and strong, better than he'd been in a long time. He looked at his clock and couldn't believe it; it was 7:30. He couldn't remember the last time he had slept this long; normally, he was up at 4, or 4:30 at the latest, his back aching, his bladder painful, and the struggle of surviving another day began. But today was a different day. Was this the beginning of a new life? A look in the mirror and he couldn't believe what he saw there. His reflection looked at least 10, possibly 15 years younger. His whole appearance had changed overnight. He didn't need his walking stick anymore, and could even stand on one leg. He hadn't even thought in his wildest dreams that the gene could have this affect. His expectations were exceeded in every respect. Kanaar jumped right into his day with an energy he hadn't had in years. Finally, there was hope this state could last forever.

When he went home in the evening around 6 o'clock, he had done as much as he usually did in three or four other days. His secretary found it a little odd; she noticed the change immediately. All she asked him was whether he had colored his hair.

Kanaar shook his head since he didn't understand the question. Only later, looking at himself in the mirror again, did he notice that his hair color had returned. His grey hair had disappeared. His physical condition had changed completely; he was at least ten years younger, and he believed he could feel the process continuing. But with all the positive things he had experienced the past few hours with the injected gene, he suddenly began to worry. Kanaar asked himself:

How long will this last? The dose was minimal – he saw as much yesterday evening. What if the process reversed? He had to contact Sherman. He could ask him how long the effect would last, and where he could get more. Just enough so he could keep up this status – and he was ready to do a lot to get it.

THE TRUTH

Amar took a drink from his wine glass, set it back down, thought for a moment, and started to speak. "It began about three years ago, when Agor Sherman, geneticist and researcher by profession and a respected member of the council, extended his research on his own accord. He had gotten a contract from the council to research the Arverni gene and to find answers to open questions. Questions like: what causes aphmalisation, and what is the Finitum? What makes we Arverni so special? Agor Sherman needed blood for his research, which was to be donated by Arverni. He came closer to answering these questions, but he was not able to reliably extract the gene which initializes aphmalisation and later the Finitum. Every time he believed he had extracted the gene in order to analyze it further, it disintegrated. One day, however, he was successful in extracting the gene from a blood sample without it decomposing. Agor Sherman himself was already suffering the effects of the Finitum and had aged considerably; the time remaining to him was very limited. For this reason, he began to experiment on himself, injecting the extracted Arverni gene, and he determined that it not only slowed the progression of his illness, it was even capable of regenerating his aphmal. His aphmal, which he hadn't seen since the beginning of his Finitum, and which he sorely missed. Sherman was the first Arverni, who was ever able to use his aphmal during the Finitum. His reactivated aphmal triggered further reactions, reversing his age-related issues. It seemed as though he had found a solution to the Finitum and the aging processes associated with it. Sherman asked himself why he was able to successfully extract the gene in that one specific blood sample, but not in all the others. He searched for the cause. The blood donors were anonymous, but Sherman succeeded in identifying this single donor since he had a very rare blood type. What he realized then was like an epiphany.

The donor was sixteen years old."

We were all thinking the same thing, but Kayl said it.

"An aspirant! The blood of aspirants allows them to extract stably the Arverni gene. Is that why aspirants are in danger? Why the girl in Las Vegas had to die?"

"Right, Kayl – that's part of the truth."

"Sherman's research confirmed the assumptions that the gene could only be stably extracted from the blood of aspirants who were in the aphormation. Now that Sherman had gained some clarity on the gene, he presented his results before the council. The physical changes Sherman had gone through were obvious to everyone. He couldn't have found a better way to present the results of his research. Agor Sherman looked at least 20 years younger, and no one in the council could believe it.

While most of the council members were staring at Sherman, a lively discussion broke out in the conservative area, and some members were even swearing at Sherman. Some members saw it as abhorrent or even forbidden, to interfere with the natural aging process or change it in any way. The council was unable to agree. There were some members who clung to the results of the rejuvenation, seeing the research as an unbelievable opportunity. Most, however, developed an aversion to the research which even Agor Sherman could recognize."

"What was your opinion?" I asked Amar.

"At that point, I wasn't yet a member of the council. But I did have an opinion."

Amar fell silent, and you could see that the whole story was affecting him even now. I noticed a sour taste, almost like vinegar, but couldn't quite place what it meant, emotionally. It certainly wasn't anything positive.

"Amar, is everything alright?"

"Yes, thanks Xama. I hope I haven't irritated your sense of taste."
Surprised at his answer, I nodded to him silently.

"The story has gotten me a little carried away – it's strange, it's been a few years now, but it still has an emotional affect on me. Now it seems I've lost my place."

"You wanted to tell us your opinion, that's where you stopped," Arun reminded him.

"Ah, yes, well, at that time I was farther away from my own Finitum. After I had taken a deeper look into Dr. Sherman's research and his plans, I understood that he only had good intentions at that point in time. He wanted to give the Arverni more time and wanted them to understand the secret of their power. I was pulled back and forth in the council; but to be honest, I was on his side. That's changed over time, and today Sherman's nothing more than a criminal who sacrifices the lives of innocent children so he can live longer himself. Abominable."

"How did the council react to Sherman's information?" Arun asked.

"The whole thing took a turn when Dr. Sherman explained that only the blood of aspirants could be used to extract the gene. He referred to the test series he had completed – without permission – which clearly demonstrated that only aspirant blood could be used for a stable extraction process. Sherman's request to obligate the aspirants to regularly donate blood was rejected by a majority of the council. There might have been one or two who had a positive view of the situation because of their own ages, and who wanted to try out the results of Sherman's research on themselves right away. The majority, however, rejected the research project. The mood changed, and Sherman had lost. You should know that aspirants are accorded special protection and are seen as a special part of the Arverni community by the council. Sherman was commanded to halt his research immediately, which induced him to take an action, which had never been seen by the council. Sherman threw his chair and his name badge into the middle of the council and left the room with the words 'you are all finished! You don't even have the foresight to see that much! There is no longer any reason for me to be a member in this club of dumb old geezers. When you're gone, I'll still be here to toast to your memory!'"

When our drinks arrived, Amar interrupted the story. But we three were eager to hear what happened next. I asked what the rest of the truth could be if that was only a part of it.

"Sherman was banned from the community, effective immediately, and was on his own."

Amar's voice faltered, and he breathed in deeply, picking up his glass of white wine and holding it towards us, pleadingly. It was clear it was difficult for Amar to tell the story something was bothering him, but what was it?

"Have you all already selected something from the menu? Xama, should I order us another one of the delicious vegetarian specialty plates?"

My thoughts still focused on Sherman and the council, until Amar brought me back to reality by recommending the hotels specialty. He waved the waiter over and placed our order. We all waited expectantly for him to get back to the story and duly continued to tell more.

"Where was I?"

"Sherman had made a racket in the council and got thrown out, or something like that."

"Right, Kayl. Sherman left the council and the community. The council held a trial of Sherman, but was only able to convict him of small offenses; there was no reason to prosecute him at that point in time. But what the council didn't know was that Sherman had also planned for exactly that scenario – and he was better prepared than the council. Sherman was kept under observation. Your father, Xama, was tasked with watching Sherman and giving regular reports to the council. The council then selected a suitable replacement from the community to fill Sherman's chair. After a few council meetings, the chair was offered to me, which was honestly a surprise."

"And you accepted."

"Correct, Xama, and thereby became responsible for communication among the Arverni. My ability made the decision easy; there's nothing more secure than dream communication. No one can eavesdrop on dream communication, and you can't invite yourself to participate. The invitation cannot be counterfeited, and can only be accepted by the person invited – no substitutes allowed."

"So, what happened to Sherman?" Arun asked.

"Well, Sherman went underground, but kept doing research and needed more aspirant blood. He used his ability to influence people in their decisions without them realizing. It didn't take long for your father and the Achilleans to find this out. They reported it to the council, and Sherman was sentenced to lifelong imprisonment. The council's sentence pushed Sherman further into a corner, he became a fugitive - on the run but still needing blood - aspirant blood."

„I could taste how bad Amar felt as he choked out this sentence. In a way, I almost feel pity for Sherman."

"Someone who murders others like a brute for their blood for his own purpose – doesn't deserve any compassion. He deserves only hate, and he must be killed!"

Amar was extremely agitated and personally affected in some way. This was more than just a story. I watched him very carefully as he told the story and my sense of taste kept changing from sweet, to sour, then to a burning sensation, followed by a vinegary taste, I tasted something was wrong with him.

Amar realized what was happening and tried to contain him, which helped me – the taste dissipated somewhat.

"Sherman wasn't always like that; he had good intentions, but became desperate. Dr. Sherman turned into a monster because he needed a continuous resupply of the gene. Without the gene, he would die within days – he had exceeded his Finitum and death was imminent. But Sherman's situation represents a chance for us! If we succeed in successfully removing his resupplies, Sherman problem will solve itself.

"I would do anything to keep my blood for myself."

"Exactly! We will do everything in our power to keep him from taking it from you." That's how we'll solve the problem of Dr. Sherman."

I looked at Amar questioningly. "Why am I going to be the one to solve the Sherman problem? He'll just find himself another ..."

Amar interrupted me.

"According to all the information I have, Xama, you are the only aspirant. All attempts to identify other aspirants in the last few months have proven futile. Sonja was the only other aspirant apart from you, and we know what happened to her."

Amar fell silent, fighting back tears.

"Being the only aspirant makes you even more desirable!" Kayl said in his sophomoric way, without realizing how it made me feel.

"That is absolutely not Kay-Ky."

"That's what?" Kayl asked.

"Well, I mean, it's not nice – it terrifies me."

Arun just sat there, holding my hand, pressing it harder and looking at me. When I concentrated on him I tasted something sweet and sour – like honey and lemon, two opposite, extreme tastes – what did that mean?

"It's almost certain that Sherman knows of Xama's existence, and we therefore need to form a council of our own in order to defend ourselves from him."

Amar stood up and went a little to the side. Kayl stood beside him right away, taking Amar's hand. Arun stood up, took my hand, and pulled me along.

Arun bent down and whispered in my ear.

"Amar wants to create a ring – it will bind us closer together and give each of us the power of the whole group," Arun whispered while we all arranged ourselves in a circle and held hands.

Amar placed his left arm around me and grabbed my left shoulder. Kayl, who was standing to the right of Amar, did the same with Amar. I followed Kayl and Arun as the last, closing the circle between myself and Kayl. I waited expectantly to see what would happen next, and I saw Arun place the thumb of his right hand in the middle of Kayl's forehead. Kayl and Arun did the same thing, and I copied the others as well, the last to place my thumb in the middle of Amar's forehead and close the ring.

"Communitati - vis - nostrum" Amar sang in a monotone voice, slowly beginning to pull in one direction.

"Communitati - vis - nostrum" Kayl joined in, turning as well.

"Communitati - vis - nostrum" we all chanted in unison, moving with the others in a circle. It all seemed familiar to me – yes, of course, it was part of the dream I had before my aphmalisation. On impulse my body started to shake, followed by a twitching caused by a jolt of electricity in both my hands and Arun and Amar broke off contact with me because of the pain and were thrown to the floor. Amar shook himself and slowly got up. Arun, on the other hand, sat down and held his head. Kayl and I were still standing, although Kayl was also holding his head.

"My goodness, what was that? I've never experienced such powerful energy," Amar said and helped Arun to his feet. Arun and Kayl sat down weakened, and I couldn't think of anything better to do than to sit down as well.

"Sorry I did something wrong – I didn't mean to hurt you all."

"It's alright I don't think you did anything wrong. If anyone did something wrong, it was me. It was naive of me to attempt to create a ring."

"It wasn't at all" Arun interjected.

"I already feel it working – it tingles and tickles."

"You're right, brother, it's starting to work – I feel the tingling too."

"You're right – now feel it as well," Amar said.

I, on the other hand, just sat there, looking at them one after the other. I could feel them sitting there, as though they were charged up. But why didn't I feel anything but tired after all the exertion? And why did I have a taste like prickling carbonation in my mouth?

Was something wrong with me?

VIPs in the Aphobia

Ocram Steel had his office in Las Vegas organize the reservation of a VIP suite in the Aphobia hotel for him. To make it appear as inconspicuous as possible, he had his manager and his assistant fly in as well and book rooms in the Aphobia hotel for themselves. His team informed the Aphobia management that the press was not aware of Ocram Steel's trip to New York City and that it was to be a recreational holiday for Mr. Steel. They asked for discretion about Ocram Steel's stay; otherwise they could expect thousands of people to congregate outside the hotel, which no one wanted.

Ocram Steel's telephone rang as he waited on confirmation of his reservation request. He looked at the caller identification and picked up the call.

"Hello, Kevin, how's it going?"

"Hello Ocram – very good, everything is as you asked – reserved and ready. I just spoke with the general manager of the Aphobia hotel again, a Mr. Amar Wellberg, and explained to him the importance of our visit. He is aware neither the press nor your fans know about our visit. He is, unfortunately very busy right now, but he will try to receive us personally."

"Thanks, Kevin, when will you be in New York?"

"I'm already at the airport with Connor, and the plane takes off in 30 minutes. We'll see you in about 5 hours then at the airport."

"Great, I'll pick you up, and then we'll all drive to the hotel."

"Very well, until then."

"Have a good flight, and say hi to Connor for me."

"Thanks, I will."

Six hours later, Ocram, Kevin, and Connor were sitting in a limousine, driving from JFK to Manhattan to the Aphobia hotel. It was already early morning, and even Manhattan had become a little quieter as the three checked into the Aphobia and moved into the VIP suite and their other rooms. The next morning, they all met for breakfast in Ocram's suite.

"I hope you all slept well, and that we can speak a little now about our next steps here in New York."

"Honestly, Ocram, you're always good for a surprise. When you called off everything at the drop of a hat in Las Vegas, I wasn't sure what was up with you. Then you told me you needed some time out, which I respect, and now you want to make plans. You have to admit this is a little strange."

Connor nodded but was just as interested as Kevin to hear Ocram's answer.

"You are right! I just need a couple of days to revive myself – get back to my old self again. But that doesn't mean not thinking about how we're going to fill up Madison Square Garden here in New York City or pull in twenty-thousand fans.

"You want to do what? Rent out Madison Square Garden and do a show in NYC? Are you serious?"

"Yes, that's why I instructed you and Connor to come here. You are going to work on the Ocram Steel in New York project for the next few days. I think it's time to build up a little bit from our one, two, or three thousand guests per show. Don't you agree?"

Kevin looked at Connor, surprised.

"What can I tell you – I love it when you think about expansion, Ocram."

"Very well – I also need to speak the general manager of the hotel to inform him that absolutely no one should know that I'm currently staying here."

"Of course – his name is Wellberg. Amar Wellberg. He's all booked up right now, but his representative is going to meet us at ten o'clock, if that's fine with you."

Ocram Steel stood up and walked through the room – he wasn't happy with the information that Amar Walberg's representative was going to be meeting them.

"Well, alright, if the boss can't or doesn't want to see us, then we'll just speak with his representative. You and Connor, you two please arrange the necessary details for a mega event here in the Garden in New York City."

Kevin and Connor both raised their eyebrows, astonished.

After Amar Wellberg's representative greeted them all, Kevin and Connor set off to visit a local agency to help them with planning an event at Madison Square Garden. Ocram Steel paced back and forth in his suite, wondering how he could get a personal appointment with Amar Wellberg. What he needed was a good reason. When he saw the news on the television, he had an idea and grabbed his telephone. Minutes later, Ocram Steel was drawing himself a warm bath. He was sure he wouldn't have to wait much longer to meet the general manager, Amar Wellberg.

When Kevin and Connor returned to the Aphobia hotel hours later, a huge crowd of people was standing in front of the entrance. All of them shared just one goal – they wanted one of the hundred tickets Ocram Steel was going to be giving away to his fans tonight at 7 o'clock in front of the Aphobia hotel.

"I can't believe it, Connor, one of the hotel employees must have said something – anyway all of New York now knows that Ocram Steel is staying at the Aphobia Hotel. We'll just see what Ocram has to say about that."

Ocram Steel, feeling refreshed by his warm bath, was already awaiting the news Kevin and Connor had to tell him.
"You won't believe what's happening in front of the hotel, Ocram. There must be 500 people out there, waiting for you to give them free tickets."
"I am both surprised and disappointed at once. Surprised that the Aphobia hotel isn't as reliable and discreet as Mr. Wellberg's representative assured us. It disappoints me that there are only 500 Ocram Steel fans in New York – we'll need to change that. Kevin, please call Mr. Wellberg's representative immediately and tell him that I demand to speak to Amar Wellberg about this incident. Tell him I find it anything but professional and expected something else from a brand like the Aphobia Hotels.
"Absolutely, I'm certain he'll make time for you."
"Connor, please get free tickets for every fan who's still standing in front of the hotel."

NOTHING BUT THE TRUTH

By the time the food arrived, I'd lost my appetite. Kayl and Arun however made the most of the generous and excellent meal.

"What should we do first?" I asked Amar.

"First we have to be sure we see each other or speak to each other regularly, every day. That ensures we're all safe and are working on our plan."

When we were done with the meal, Amar had the table cleaned off, and the waiter rolled a cart to our table. Everyone wondered what it was until the moment the waiter placed four packages, all the same size, in front of each of us.

"There are new iPhones in the boxes. Each of these telephones has the same number down to the last. The last digit runs from one to four. You'll see your numbers on the boxes – who has one as the last digit?"

Arun raised his hand.

"Very good, who has two?"

I raised my hand. Kayl had three, and Amar had four.

"Now, we'll all call the same number every day at 12:00 noon. All of the appointments are programmed into the phone, so it will remind you. Then you will all dial the same number, only 0 will be the last digit – that's the conference number. The number is also already entered into the appointments – when the phone reminds you, all you have to do is confirm. Once we're all on the conference, each of us will speak a sentence containing their number. So Arun will say something with one, Xama, you'll say something with two, Kayl with three, and I'll say something with a four in it. That way we'll know everything is all right and the conference will be over for the day. Do you have any questions?"

"Yes – I understand we're going to call, but why don't we just say we're doing well or not doing well? I don't get all this with the numbers."

"It's purely a precaution; if one of us is caught by Sherman's people and doesn't call, the others will know immediately. But if he is forced to call, then our discussion will determine whether everything is alright or not. It's simple to say everything is all right – but we'll know it's not true since the code word wasn't used.

Now we just need a pin code for our conference. It's best if each one of us says a digit. Xama, your digit?"

"I'll take 1."

"Okay, Kayl?"

"0, please."

"I'll take 1, like Xama."

"Arun 1, so that's 1-0-1. Then I'll take 0 like Kayl, and that gives an easy to remember code that isn't that easy to figure out. The conference is limited to only 4 participants in any case, so no one else can join it. Now I'll just activate our pin code quickly – 1-0-1-0, and done.

Let's put it to the test"

Amar picked up his telephone and stepped away from the table. As he walked, he started dialing the numbers.

Not a minute later, we were all sitting at the table again, waiting for Amar to say something.

"Test passed, team, and now we just have to play the same game again every day at exactly 12 o'clock; if we're all together we can skip it, but otherwise we'll call. All phones are equipped with GPS tracking – if one of us doesn't call or doesn't say his word correctly, then the others will locate the telephone and will engage the Arverni security service."

Kayl looked at Arun, and then at me.

"The two best members of the security service are already on your team, just to remind you," Kayl couldn't help but say.

"You're right, Kayl. An Offense is the best defense, and we're all here to protect Xama's life."

The waiter was also waiting for the moment we all sat back down at the table, and he then served us various desserts, all of which tasted heavenly Kay-Ky.

I was curious and wanted to know whether there was any more information we all needed to know besides the fact that my blood was the true Arverni legacy.

Amar searched for the right words but knew that no matter which words he chose, this part of the truth wouldn't be easy to explain. This truth had been kept secret for generations. It was the best-kept secret the council had. There were times in which Arverni had been killed only for telling these facts. Eventually Amar stood up, supported himself with a hand on the table, and began to speak.

"It is time to view one mystery of the Arverni in a new light. It is the place of the woman in the Arverni community. Women are treasured and loved, but never have had the same roles or rights within the community.

"There is not a single woman in the council!
Kayl, Arun, do you know a reason why?"
Both looked at each other and shook their heads.
"How many women are in the security service?

„None!"
„None - right!"

'It's always been this way, and it will be this way in the future. Let's call it a tradition.' I was not satisfied with this answer, and have researched the question, asking some of the older Arverni women. What primarily interested me is that in the whole history of the Arverni, only men have been Identidems. Only men have developed multiple abilities. No one knew of a woman, and even the women in the community I asked about it were silent on this topic."

Arun looked at me nervously – I felt it, and I could taste his tension. He knew I possessed multiple abilities.
"It's not true – there are women with multiple abilities. I think I'm the best proof of that."
I blurted out the truth, but in that moment I didn't know whether it was a smart thing to do or not. Kayl looked at me surprised; he didn't believe me, and thought my statement was a joke.
"Yeah, of course you do, Xama, I've got several myself!"
"For once, will you shut your rude mouth, Kayl? You have no reason to make fun of Xama. You don't even know what she's talking about right now."
"But my dear brother – could it be that you're in love, and that's why you're overreacting, just a bit?"

Amar, who didn't like the two brothers' fighting at all, wanted to intervene, but I was just a hair quicker.

"Maybe you're right, Kayl. Maybe I just imagining some of them? I know I can relieve wounds, and even heal them. I'm very sure I can taste feelings, and what I taste right now is very bitter – a perfect description of the situation. If I'm not mistaken, I have learned the power of dream communication from Amar. I tried to do the same thing with Arun's ability, but ..."

Kayl interrupted me mid-sentence and reached his hand out towards me.

"Very good, Xama! Then why don't you just switch me off? If you've learned Arun's ability, then I don't need to worry about it anyway. Arun's tried it lots of times, but as you know, he's my brother, and you can't use abilities on first-order relatives. Looks like I'm lucky again. Not a thing to fear."

With every word that came out of Kayl's mouth, my frustration grew and grew. Why was he doing this? Why was he insulting Arun and me?

I really should just switch him off.

As I was trying to convince myself to stay calm, I saw my hand-grip Kayl's wrist. Everything went as fast as lightning then – Kayl shook uncontrollably, as though he had been hit with an electrical shock. While I was still holding his hand, he suddenly collapsed. Shocked, I dropped his hand and stood there, completely perplexed.

"What did I do? What happened?"

"You switched him off, Xama," Arun said, totally calm. He bent over to his brother and felt his pulse. "He's fine, just unconscious – he'll wake up again in a second."

"What did I do? I didn't want to do that!"

"It's his own fault – he deserved it. How much I've always wanted to switch him off for once. Thank you, Xama, for fulfilling my wish," Arun said.

Amar, who was also standing next to me completely nonchalantly, placed his hand on my shoulder and said, in a quiet tone.

"You're an Identidem; that was the best proof for it. Four abilities in just a few weeks, – I don't think that's ever happened before in the history of the Arverni."

Kayl moaned and shook. Arun gave him his hand and pulled him up.

"Wow, Xama, how did you do that? That was a K.O. with your little finger!" Kayl looked very pale, and sat down again.

"So, everyone back? Then I can keep talking," Amar interjected.

"Thank you, Xama, for your correction. You are an example that women too can develop multiple abilities. Is there anyone here who still doubts it?"

Amar looked directly down at Kayl, who was holding his head and saying no in slow motion.

"What I ask myself, however, is this:

If this is the case, then why has there never been a single Identidem woman in the history of the Arverni?"

We all looked at Amar – his question had captivated us all.

"Could it be that the history is incomplete? Perhaps people did not want to hear the truth?" I interjected. "You are completely right, Xama. The truth is that there have been women with multiple abilities. Women who surpassed the men. Women like you, Xama. The shocking truth is that these women disappeared shortly after their multiple abilities became apparent. According to my research, there have been at least three of them. They all disappeared without a trace, forever."

No one said a word. They all looked at me, the mood was at a low point.

Was Mom an Identidem? Was that the reason she ...?

I repressed the thought again, and continued listening to Amar.

"At the beginning, I said the truth had two parts – this part is just as great a threat to Xama's life as the first one. It won't be long now before other council members notice Xama Dupre is an Identidem. Council members fear nothing more than a woman who develops multiple abilities. They will act according to old patterns, and task the security service with solving the problem of Xama Dupre."

"I don't see myself as a problem, Amar – your statement is deeply offensive."

"Xama, that's not what I meant – excuse me for being so direct. I just wanted to let you know how some members of the council think about it."

"I understand. And how does Amar Wellberg think about it?"

"Differently, which I'm very open about, and which doesn't always make my life in the council very easy. It's very important to me that you all understand we aren't just fighting Sherman and his thugs. Whether now or in the future – you are in danger from your own community as well – from the council, first of all, and from the security service as well."

"Anyway, the two best members of the security team aren't going to play along. On the contrary, they'll do anything to protect you, Xama," Kayl said, still visibly shocked.

"Exactly, Kayl. We have all sworn an Achillean oath, and that means we will do anything to protect Xama – if necessary, we will give our life for her."

I looked at first Kayl and then Arun, and didn't know how I should react. Both of them had only known me for a couple of days. Nevertheless, they would both give their lives to save mine – why? I tried to repress the feeling of fear growing within me, but I couldn't. I couldn't help but cry. As the first tears ran down, I became unable to control myself – it was simply too much. I wailed bitterly, one tear after another running down my face. I picked up the napkin in front of me and held it in front of my face with the words "I'm sorry!"

"You don't need to feel ashamed – we're your friends. We're here for you."

I tried to get a handle on my emotions. They all placed their hands on my head and my shoulders.

"Thank you all – and I would do anything to make sure no one has to give his life for mine."

THE GOAL

Kanaar couldn't believe his transformation, and tried it out all day by doing activities he could only do before with pain, not at all, or only in a very limited way. But the best thing about his rejuvenation was that he could look at his aphmal again in the mirror. He had been missing the feeling it created for years. It was too beautiful only to look at for a short time. Now Kanaar could understand Sherman much better – he didn't want to give up his new self either, not for all the money in the world. Kanaar was afraid the rejuvenation would disappear again, and that everything would turn back to its old painful, broken-down state.

He had to act – immediately.

He pulled his telephone out of his pocket and searched for a number in his address book, then called it.

At the same time, Sherman and Sanders were sitting at the hotel bar, enjoying an aperitif, when Sherman's phone rang. As he looked at his display, it brought a smile to his face.

"Pete, our plan seems to be working perfectly, without even needing a plan B or plan C."

"Hello, Ezra, I hope you're doing well and the effects are what you had hoped for."

"Thanks for asking, Agor. The results are better than I could have imagined. Since yesterday, I've been a different person. I never would have thought the stuff would be this effective. My aphmal is even visible and active again. It's incredible."

"I know, Ezra, but unfortunately, the effects won't last forever."

Sherman grabbed his glass, raised it and looked at the golden yellow whiskey, twirling inside it. Sherman knew he had won Kanaar over to his side. From now on he was like the whiskey in his glass – he would follow every one of his commands.

"That's what I thought. Umm, how long will the effects last?"

"That's difficult to say, Ezra, you only received a small dose. Don't waste your time with me on the telephone, go find a young woman or some other conquest, and conquer it. Enjoy life for as long as you can."

Sherman took another swallow and toasted Sanders. Now all he had to do was reel in the fish, very slowly, so as not to let his catch off the hook. He really wanted to enjoy his triumph.

"Agor, I wanted to say, I'm more than convinced of the quality of your work. I always believed your research was a pipe dream, something that would never work. Now that I've tried it out for myself, I have to say, I was an idiot. I am sorry I didn't support you before the council. How can I make it up to you? How can I help you?"

That was what Sherman wanted to hear; the fish was caught. Now all he had to do was filet it.

"I'm happy to hear it, Ezra; I knew as soon as you experienced the true results for yourself, you'd stand behind my research. Good to know I can rely on an old friend. Now, to come back to your offer. I need information about further aspirants. Their names, where they are living, any kind of information you have. As the head of security, that will surely be more than enough."

"You're demanding quite a lot from me – that would mean violating the rules of the community - I could be banned."

"Ezra, let's be honest – how much time do you still have? A year? Two, three maximum. You've got nothing to lose. You can only win."

Kanaar fell silent, Sherman's words hitting him like the tips of arrows. Every argument hurt. Sherman was right; he was already on the losing side. He absolutely had to change this.

"Win? What do you mean?" Kanaar asked, interested.

"If you help me continue my research, I will get you enough of the gene to live at least 50 or more years, more than you've already lived, and that in full health and will all of your strength, your aphmal, and your power. Our research is only beginning – what we've learned so far is that the extracted gene achieves enormous effects. This, Kanaar, might mean in the best-case scenario that the gene gives us not only a longer life, but also Eternal regeneration – the aging process switched off, and death no longer has any meaning. That, Ezra, doesn't just mean a few more years – it means hundreds or thousands of years. Eternal life – immortality!"

Sherman breathed deeply and emptied the rest of the whiskey down his throat to feel the burn.

"You're right, Agor, there's just one small problem you unfortunately haven't thought of. A small matter, but an important one."
Sherman thought, falling silent for a moment; he hadn't reckoned
with this kind of a statement from Kanaar. Kanaar had surprised
him – what did he mean by "a small problem?"
"Let it out – this small matter – what did I overlook" Sherman
answered, emphatically and confidently, even as he asked himself what it could be.

"I can still remember well your introduction to the council, and
that there was a scandal when you could only use the blood of
aspirants for your research. As you know, and as the council confirmed for you on that day, aspirants are, however, worthy of
special protection."
Sherman interrupted Kanaar: "I know this part of the story –
what did you want to tell me, Ezra?"
"Aspirants aren't exactly available in large numbers – with the
disappearing Arverni community, there are less and less beginning the aphormation who could function as potential blood donors."
Kanaar was right, but he had to show an interest in what Kanaar
had to say – more was to come, Sherman was sure of it.
"You're right, Ezra, just like any good product, there are two
things which must be brought into harmony: production and
demand. If the two aren't in balance there are problems, which
we, of course, want to avoid. Now we've come to the point with
which I need your help. You know all the aspirants as well as
their families and where they live. As head of security, it is your
duty to offer aspirants special protection; that's why the Achilleans are a part of your organization. Now we've come to the point
where we can lay out our partnership clearly. You'll get the gene
from me, and I'll get the names and addresses of aspirants from
you. That's all, Kanaar – no more and no less. So, what do you
say? Are you ready to redefine your life for the names of a few
aspirants?"
"You haven't changed, Agor, and I'm not sure whether you can be
trusted. I do, however, value your clarity. You're correct – I do
want the gene, and I'm ready to give you what you want for it."
Sherman interrupted Kanaar again.

"Then everything's great – we have a deal, and we're both getting what we want."

"The problem is that there is currently only one aspirant left. Her name is Xama Dupre, and she is the only one currently in the aphormation. Not just that, it gets worse – the next one up is only 14 years old. It will be more than a year before a second aspirant is available."

Sherman took his telephone from his ear.

"Vat Dictu. Vat Dictu. Now, when I'm so close to a breakthrough."

Kanaar heard Sherman curse; he had expected such a reaction. Sherman pulled himself together again and answered Kanaar.

"That makes the matter somewhat more complex, but it doesn't change anything about the goal. I need to know where Xama Dupre is located. If I'm not mistaken, she is an orphan. Where is she staying?"

"Do we have a deal, Agor?"

"Yes,, we have a deal – her location, Ezra."

"Xama Dupre is currently here in New York City, in the Aphobia hotel, and …"

Sherman practically talked over Kanaar.

"Amar, that good-for-nothing, has her already!"

"Yes, and not only that – she is also being protected by the two best Achilleans we have."

Sherman fell silent for a moment.

"When I think about it, that actually fits into my plans exactly. Can you call the two Achilleans off for a some time?"

"Yes, that's doable. I will try and think of something; tell me exactly when, but make sure you give me enough notice."

"I will."

"One more thing, Agor."

"What else?"

"Once you have Xama, don't forget our deal. If you betray me, I'll hunt you down. From then on, all the Achilleans will have only one job – looking for you, and then I'll personally extract the gene until you're completely drained with not one drop of blood left in your miserable body. Don't forget our deal, Agor."

"I won't, Ezra; I too want to enjoy life for a long time to come. We'll meet again in three days at the Italian place; you'll get another injection, and I'll tell you what comes next in my plan."

Sherman hung up without waiting for an answer from Kanaar. He gripped his glass, raised it up, and held it out to Sanders, who clinked glasses with him.

"We have a contact; her name is Xama Dupre, and she is currently in the Aphobia hotel here in New York City. Our search is at an end – now the exciting part begins. Get me Ocram Steel on the telephone – he is the next key to our success."

A Strange Apheid

Accarding to Amar, the apheid was very important for me and for my acceptance into the community, which I only partially understood. Although Amar was a modern thinking person, there were still a few Arverni rules, which were not up for discussion in his mind. His behavior was reminding me more and more of Dad. Amar, Kayl, and Arun all saw the apheid as a duty, but that wasn't what moved me to my decision to swear the apheid. There was something much deeper within me, driving me and encouraging me, and telling me:

Xama, you must swear the apheid – it's important – it's important for your future. For my future?

Amar had prepared me all morning for the coming ceremony. We went through the individual steps again and again, and I now knew basically what awaited me and what the process would be. Amar couldn't, and didn't want to, tell me exactly what would happen. He artfully dodged my questions. The apheid was a formal ceremony that took place in the Templum. Amar explained to me that every Aphobia hotel had a Templum set up in the cellar in which the Arverni could hold ceremonies. He also explained to me that I wouldn't see anything during the whole ceremony, since I would be blindfolded. Then the Meta would take my hand and request that I swear the apheid. He would say some words, which I was then to repeat after him. During the ceremony, my nose would begin to bleed, and I would use the blood to seal my apheid with my thumb in a special book. All clear so far, but why would my nose bleed, and how would it happen? I had to wait until I had a chance to ask Arun – hopefully he could still remember what exactly happened.

Amar had gotten me a tunic made from heavy fabric with the Arverni symbol embroidered on the back, and a smaller symbol on both sleeves. The dress had flecks of blood at the height of the upper thigh, even though it smelled washed. I duly put the dress on whilst the height of my nervousness increased with every moment I approached the apheid.

A wave of stage fright was making itself known in my stomach. The only thing, which could help me, now was my aphmal.
When I left the bathroom I was feeling excellent – everything was great again; I was ready for my apheid, and even my simple dress seemed more modern. Amar went ahead, and Arun held my hand. We followed Amar through the hotel entrance and all at once, I realized I didn't see Kayl. He hadn't been seen all morning.

Shouldn't he, as my second best friend, also be at my apheid?

"Where's Kayl? Didn't he want to be at my apheid?"
"He will, Xama. Kayl has already gone ahead to ensure that we don't have any bad surprises on the way there. But he will be there."
Amar went straight to a freight elevator, and once we were inside, he used a key to press the buttons for the garage and reception at the same time, and the elevator started to move down. It lasted an eternity, but all at once the door opened, and I saw Kayl. "Nice of you to join us, Kayl, I missed you." "Really – you know I wouldn't miss a blood bath."
Kayl grinned at me, and Arun grimaced. Amar raised his eyelids and took back control of the conversation. "How do things look down here?"
"Everything's okay – there were two Achilleans who wanted to ambush us, but I switched them both off – in my way, of course, not Arun's. But you were right, Kanaar is after Xama."
Amar wasn't happy; I could tell from the bitter taste.
"Good, you go out ahead, and we'll follow at distance – Arun, you secure the rear."

Kayl went ahead and we waited in the elevator.
Amar took a step outside, which was my chance to ask Arun a question.
"What exactly happens during the apheid – why do you bleed from it?"
I looked deep into Arun's gorgeous eyes; he had no choice but to give me an answer.
"The Meta asks you about your apheid, and then he enlightens you."
"I understood that, but what causes the nosebleed?"

"You're not afraid, are you? You don't need to be — no one's died from it yet. To be honest, I don't know; I couldn't remember anything afterward. All I know was from the stories and tales similar to what Amar told us."

Amar gave us a sign; Arun pushed me gently out of the elevator, and we followed Amar. It didn't take very long before we saw Kayl waiting in front of a door. Amar typed a combination of numbers into the door safe and opened the heavy iron door. We all walked inside, into another world. Torches were burning on the walls, and the hallway looked like the ruins of an ancient castle. It smelled musty, and a cold draft spread through the air, enfolding all of us.
You wouldn't believe you were in one of the best hotels in the world.
Amar walked down the hall purposefully, remained standing, and turned around to face the others and me.
"You all wait here and be very careful we're not surprised. You, Xama, turn around – from here on, I have to bind your eyes and your aphmal, as the ceremony requires. Are you ready?"

My mind attempted to grapple with the current situation and to show me images of what would happen now. But there was nothing there – everything was empty.

With a loud, clear "Kay-Ky-Yes," I signaled my agreement to Amar. Amar bound a cloth around my eyes and covered my aphmal. Now the rest of my senses took over — everything was pitch black.
"Now just trust me," Amar said, taking my hand and leading me slowly into a room. It was a strange feeling not to be able to see who was waiting on me and what would happen next. Following Amar's hands and words, I waited to see what would happen.
"Stay standing just here," I heard Amar whisper, "and wait until you get further instructions."

I tried to imagine the room and my surroundings, and then something strange happened. The images in my mind became sharper and clearer, and I had a clear picture of how the room looked. Everything was in different shades of grey. Was this my imagination, or my own creativity? It felt as though I could see in grey-scale – Kay-Ky. Whatever the case, I was standing in the middle of a circle built out of tables. There was a raised podium in front of me, a kind of altar or large table. Two of the three chairs behind it were occupied. Amar had sat down at a deeper table to the left of it. The rest of the chairs were all empty. But there was something else – something was laying on the table to the right of me – a book, and something long that looked like a knife. Now I realized that I had forgotten Dad's book. This would have been my chance to hand it over to the Meta like Dad had told me to. Suddenly, I thought I saw one of the men stand up at the podium and move very slowly. Something was wrong with him, I could feel it. He walked towards me – he slowly came closer, and finally remained standing right in front of me. He made wild hand motions, testing whether I could see anything, but the images in my mind didn't startle me, and I remained standing very still. Now I could feel what was wrong with him. He was very weak. His life energy was depleting. With a similarly weak voice, the man asked me: "What is your name, and what are the names of your father and mother?"

Was this the Meta?

I answered his questions and suddenly also realized another man had sat down to the right of the table on which the book and the knife were laying. He was very tall and athletic.
"Now reach out your hands and repeat the apheid after me."
The Meta tried to give his voice more impact, but it didn't make any impression on me. In the moment both my hands moved forwards, I felt something cold and bony grabbing them. The Meta had very cold hands, and they reflected his overall physical condition.
"Now reach out your hands and repeat the apheid after me."
"communitati - vis - nostrum
 communitati - vis - nostrum
 communitati - vis - nostrum"

I repeated what I had heard as well as I could. In the moment I was finished, I felt in both hands how energy from the Meta was trying to push into my body. Something inside me reacted automatically and blocked the flow of energy, an involuntary counter-reaction. The Meta's hands became warmer, and the flow of energy stopped.

"communitati - vis - nostrum
 communitati - vis - nostrum
 communitati - vis - nostrum"

Again, I repeated the Meta's words and again felt something wanting to push through my hands and into my body, this time significantly more intense. I concentrated and a counter-reaction began, stopping the flow of energy a second time. I could feel the Meta becoming weaker, and that the procedure was weakening him even further. He swayed, and his grip on my wrists became looser. He raised his voice again, and this time he sang.

"communitati - vis - nostrum
 communitati - vis - nostrum
 communitati - vis - nostrum"

I repeated after him, and again he tried to push into my body. This time, his grip on my fingers hurt, and I concentrated to block the attack. I slowly felt the energy being pushed back from my lower arms into my hands. The Meta was unsuccessful; my counter-reaction forced him back. Just in the moment I was asking myself how long it would go on like this, I could feel the Meta become much weaker, losing the grip of his left hand. Like lightning, I pulled my hands from his loose grip and grabbed both of his wrists. He was threatening to fall, and I held him up. It still looked like he was holding on to me, since his long cowl covered both our hands. In reality, I was holding him. His life's energy was running out; he was about to die, and he could collapse at any moment. With this situation before my eyes, all I could think about was helping him, and all my energy directed itself towards the Meta. The flow of energy was so intense that his hands shook, so I had to grip him even tighter. The Meta began to moan audibly, and since I didn't want anyone to notice, I copied his moaning. His whole body shook, and as I held him, I shook too.

My attempt was having an effect. I could feel him becoming better very quickly. His singing drowned out his moans, and I sang with him.

"communitati - vis - nostrum
 communitati - vis - nostrum
 communitati - vis - nostrum"

We stood there for several minutes; I held his hands, and we both shook from the energy forcing its way out of my body and into his. All at once, I saw thoughts which were not my own. It seemed as if I had access to his mind. Images appeared before me at a dizzying speed, like a photo album someone was flipping through terrifically quickly. With a sudden push, the Meta broke the connection and pulled back his hands. He put his thumb under his nose, and before I could react, I felt something warm in my face. His thumb rubbed over my upper lip and touched my nose. What was that? Was it his blood or something? Was the Meta bleeding?

What had I done?

He grabbed my hands and led my thumb to his face, rubbing it over his upper lip. It felt warm and wet.

Was that the ceremony they had told me about?

He suddenly hugged me, whispering something in my ear at the same time.
"You're something very special, Xama. Thank you for extending my life, but it's time for me to go. Don't tell anyone what just happened; you led the ceremony perfectly, like a grown-up Meta, and I have attained enlightenment. For that, I want to thank you. Wait here, I'll get the apheid book."
Quiet returned, and I tried again to see my surroundings in my mind, but everything remained dark.
"Show me your right thumb."
I held my thumb out in front and felt the Meta rub something on my thumb. He held my hand tight and pressed my thumb down on an object.

"That, Xama, is your seal. With it, you have sealed your apheid, and you are on the way to becoming an adult Arverni. Please remain standing here until the other council members have also sealed your apheid."

The Meta removed himself a little, and I was able to perceive the room again in my mind. He first went to the council member on the front, then the one on the right side, and finally to Amar, who was sitting at the left. When he had shown all members the seal, he came back and removed the wrap over my eyes. The room was lit only by candlelight, but my eyes still needed a few seconds to get used to the brightness. The Meta held the book with the seal directly in front of my face, and I recognized my fingerprint. My fingerprint in his blood.

Was that it? Was that my apheid?
What did he mean when he said that I had enlightened him?

Amar was already standing beside me, and he took my hand. The Meta closed the book without saying a word, but his eyes revealed he was very satisfied. I was satisfied that he was feeling better, and that I could extend his life.

Wonder how long it will last?
The Meta turned around; Amar held my hand, and we walked back out of the Templum. Kayl and Arun were waiting outside, excited. Kayl couldn't wait, so he burst out:

"You're covered in blood! Did they break your nose?"
Arun just looked at me, and pressed me into his shoulder.
"It's over. You have sworn your apheid, and that's what counts."
"What do you still remember? Come on, tell us" Kayl wanted to know. "Strangely, I can't remember anything but how I went into the room. Everything else is gone."
"It's the same old shit every time. Nobody can remember what really happens in there. You survived it, anyway, and your nose is still in the middle of your face."
Kayl's remark made all of us laughs – everyone but Amar. He didn't get the joke.

THE IDEA

Preoccupied, Sherman walked down the wrong hotel hall-way, noticed it, then turned back around angrily. The conversation with Kanaar and the new situation with Amar Wellberg were occupying him more than he let on. Extracting a new supply of the gene wasn't made easier by this bottleneck in the aspirants. Sherman knew that he had created another problem. The amount of gene available wouldn't last very long now. If he gave the gene he had to Sanders and Kanaar, then it might be enough for two weeks, maximum. He needed a plan B that allowed him to get the greatest possible amount of time from the amount of the gene he still had. His deliberations always yielded the same result. If the Xama Dupre project took more than two weeks – as he expected it would – he would have to react and make a decision.

When he arrived at his suite, he first made tracks to the bar, which was very well stocked. Sherman poured himself a 40-year-old whiskey, took the glass, and walked through the room. It was a ritual that helped him think things over and settle on the details in his plan B. He could drop Sanders or Kanaar and not inject any more of the gene into one of the two of them. Kanaar was threatening him with death, and Sanders was highly unstable. He had a personal relationship with Sanders – he meant something to him. Sanders were his stepsons. Kanaar had been his friend once, but that was a long time ago. Kanaar would help him, that was clear, but he didn't need any more help from Kanaar. Once he had the contact information for the next generations of aspirants, Kanaar was actually useless, only a burden. A gene thief who used up more of the gene without contributing anything. Sanders would stand by his side in everything that was to come, and he was sure of his loyalty. Sherman took a big swallow and wrinkled his face as the whiskey burned down his throat with all the sharpness of its 54% cask strength. That was what he had wanted to feel, and as he enjoyed the pain, he made a decision.

He would take Kanaar off of the gene, but that wouldn't be enough. Kanaar would take revenge on him that meant Kanaar would have to die. Sanders would do the job for him; he was good at these things. The Italian restaurant was also the ideal place to do it. Once Kanaar had built up a little more trust, it wouldn't be very difficult to get rid of him. The Kanaar problem was solved. For a moment, Sherman asked himself what might happen next when no further gene could be extracted – if the Xama Dupre project was to fail. The gene would last for about 3 to 4 weeks for the two of them; for just one about a maximum of 6 to 8 weeks, and with sparing use maybe 10 weeks. Sherman didn't want to think anymore about the situation. He knew that he would rid himself of Sanders in that case, but he would have to deal with Sanders personally, which he would find difficult.

The telephone in Sherman's suite rang and edged out his final thoughts. Surely it was Ocram Steel; Sanders had reached him and instructed him to call. How much of the truth about Amar Wellberg did he want to or need to tell Steel? What did he have to know to achieve the best results in this situation? Sherman thought it over, picking up the receiver at the same time.

"Hello."

"Ocram Steel, you wanted to speak with me right away, Dr. Sherman?"

"Yes, I wanted to know when your meeting with Amar Wellberg will be, and which strategy of manipulation you want to use. Amar Wellberg is the decisive key in our joint plan, and now even more important than ever before."

Sherman's original plan had assumed that Kanaar or Wellberg would help him get contact information for aspirants. Because of Kanaar's information, Amar Wellberg now had a totally different meaning. Amar Wellberg was the key to the only aspirant. To the gene which kept him alive, to Xama Dupre. Sherman considered for a moment whether he might better handle Amar Wellberg himself, but for the same reasons as before, he pushed the thought off to the side. He needed Steel to get to Wellberg; there was no way around it.

"Steel, please tell me how you are planning on manipulating Amar Wellberg. I would like to know if you need my help? As I've just said, Wellberg is very important."

Ocram Steel was curious about Sherman's interest in how he was going to fulfill his task. According to everything he'd learned about him up to this point, the only thing he wanted was results. Something had happened, and Sherman was acting differently than he had in the past.

"Amar Wellberg is very busy; he has already called off his first appointment with me and sent his representative."

When Sherman heard this, his blood began to boil so that he was ready to roar into the phone. He knew that this Steel was a complete moron, but his intellect told him he needed this moron very badly, so he held back his emotions.

"That means you haven't gotten an appointment with him?"

"Not quite, but I then considered how I could get Mr. Wellberg's full attention, and helped things along a little. After a large number of fans of Ocram Steel showed up in front of the Aphobia, I made an official complaint that I have not been able to relax undisturbed in his four star hotel. There is no question that Wellberg will speak with me personally after this incident. I did also make it clear I was expecting a personal apology."

Sherman was positively surprised.

"Not bad, Steel, that's the type of action I like to see. Tell me how you are planning on manipulating him."

"In the classic way. I am planning to focus him on me and have him carry out all the commands I give him without question. What are you interested in? What kind of information do you need right away?"

Sherman knew that the classic method was the most effective. But he also knew that Amar Wellberg wasn't a typical Arverni, but rather a specially educated one. Very special.

"The classic method is the best, but what if it doesn't work?"

"I've never seen anyone who was resistant to my manipulation."

Sherman was, when it came to the power of manipulation, significantly more experienced than Steel, and he knew that there was a way to protect oneself from it.

"Steel, to be completely certain, please do the following: once the manipulation is completed, apply it immediately. Program Wellberg to respond to a code word."

"What do you mean by a code word?"

"It's very simple – you manipulate Wellberg so that he fulfills the commands of any person who says the code word to him. It's important, Steel, that he follows all commands without exception. You must penetrate deeply into Amar Wellberg's sub consciousness."

"Sherman, I've never done anything like this."

"Then it's time. I am fully relying on you. Call me immediately when the appointment with Wellberg is over."

Sherman hung up before Steel could say goodbye, emptied his glass of whiskey, and looked contentedly out of the window of his suite. Steel knew perfectly well that Sherman didn't take him seriously, and was only using him. But that didn't matter to him – he didn't want to make friends with Sherman. The only thing he was interested in was the Arverni gene and the possibility of using it to keep his powers and continue developing the SURPRISE show.

MANIPULATION

As Amar Wellberg set off towards his office, his assistant and representative were already standing in front of it, looking tense and signaling him they had to speak with him immediately. A short time later, Amar had all the information on the Ocram Steel incident, and had made the only, in his mind possible correct decision to preserve excellent customer service. He would apologize personally to Ocram Steel as requested, and attempt to win Mr. Steel as a future guest at the Aphobia Hotel with a very generous VIP gift certificate.

Amar Wellberg was already waiting on a reserved table in the Palm Garden. Customer complaints didn't happen very often, but when he received one he did everything he could to retain the customer and satisfy him. That's why he had made the invitation to the Palm Garden.

Ocram Steel arrived on the rooftop patio punctually, and the service staff brought him directly to Amar Wellberg, who greeted him kindly.

"I'm happy to personally welcome you to the Aphobia, Mr. Steel, Please excuse me for being prevented from meeting you yesterday upon your arrival."

When Amar shook Ocram Steel's hand, he could feel a slight pulse, something he had felt before. He asked himself where he knew the feeling from.

"Thank you very much for taking the time and personally addressing my complaint. I am also pleased to make your acquaintance."

Amar could feel Steel strengthening his handshake in rhythm with his words. He also noticed a slight tingling, which began to spread and become stronger. Searching the memories in his mind to find an explanation for the situation, he offered Ocram Steel a seat.

"May I offer you an aperitif? I can recommend the Palm Garden Magic."

"Wonderful that sounds good – and very appropriate too."

Amar gave a hand signal and ordered two Palm Magics from a young waitress. It was his goal to find out more about Ocram Steel.

"You have a very successful show in Las Vegas, Mr. Steel, what brings you to New York, if I may ask?"

"You may – my team is currently planning to bring my show 'SURPRISE' to New York ... We want to test out how well we can enchant people outside of Las Vegas, and New York offers the perfect opportunity."

"You're right about that, and I have no doubt that you will continue your success here. New York City is unbeatable when it comes to art and culture. I've been to many big cities, but New York really is the heart of the world."

Amar was interrupted by the pretty young woman who set two beautifully decorated cocktails on the table in front of them.

"Let's toast, Mr. Steel, and I would love to learn more about your show and what exactly happened yesterday – it is my aim that you as a VIP guest of the house, are completely satisfied."

When Amar looked into Steel's eyes, he thought he saw them change for just a moment. Like a bolt of lightning, he remembered something from decades ago, something he had repressed to the darkest corners of his memory. His father had a special talent. He could manipulate people by touching or looking at them. That was what he had felt when Steel shook his hand. It was the same feeling his father had when he manipulated him. Exactly the same eyes as Steel, exactly the same behavior. Amar now knew on what Steel's success depended. Steel was an Arverni and had developed the power of manipulation. That's what made him so successful – it's not a show, not a trick. He manipulates his guests and makes them see things that don't exist in reality. He had violated Arverni law, and made a business out of it.

He must appear before the council and answer for what he's done, Amar thought to himself.

"Very well, Mr. Wellberg. It would be best if I showed you one of my little magic tricks; it will give you an idea as to why people are so fascinated by it."

Wellberg knew he was playing with fire, but he had no other choice – it was all or nothing.

"Excuse me for a moment; I'll be right back, and I'm very much looking forward to your private performance."

Amar disappeared to the bathroom. On the way there, he tried to put all the pieces together. It was no coincidence Steel had appeared here at the Aphobia, just one day after Xama arrived. It took Amar's breath away for a moment – Could it be that the others already knew they were here?

Amar remembered exactly how he had succeeded in escaping his father's constant manipulation. He had discovered a trick back then which made it possible for him to resist it. Amar couldn't believe it – Steel had come to manipulate him. Something held him back from even thinking of the name, let alone speaking it out loud. But one thing was clear to Amar – he was Steel's target, and they wanted to get to Xama through him. They're quicker than he thought – never in his life would he have dreamed they would already be in the hotel. He had to warn the others, so he grabbed his telephone and sent a text message to Kayl and Arun, but not to Xama. He didn't want to upset her any further – she was already under an enormous amount of stress.
"They're already in the hotel – magno pericolu."

Amar locked himself into a bathroom, rolled off a little toilet paper, spit on it, and removed the protection from his aphmal.

We'll do everything we can to resist Ocram Steel's manipulation.

Amar looked at his aphmal in a small pocket mirror, enjoying the energy that flowed through his body. But that wasn't enough – he placed his thumb in the middle of his forehead and a shaking all over his body was the signal of the beginning of aphmalisation.
When Amar sat back down in his seat, he was charged up to his last hair follicle, and ready for the game.
"You wanted to give me a private performance?"
"Nothing frightening – just a little suggestion, I thought."
Amar picked up his drink and held his glass up to Steel for a toast. Steel responded in kind.
When Steel set his glass back down on the table, he took the straw out of the glass and held it up in front of Amar.
"Look at this straw very carefully, it's about to transform."

Amar looked into Steel's eyes, and at that moment he could re-member the many times his father had manipulated him. He had scared him very much as a child. He had shown him horrible things by manipulating his thoughts, and he did it without asking. Steel held the straw in one hand and waved the other up and down in front of it. Amar could see images overlapping; he saw the straw, then suddenly a knife – the straw had changed into a knife. The images changed; first, he saw the straw, and a fraction of a second later the knife. He knew that all of this was only hap-pening in his mind and that Steel was controlling all of it. The aphmalisation made it possible for him to see both images at once and recognize the illusion.

"Wow, how did you do that? The straw changed into a knife – unbelievable."

Amar played along with the game, making Steel believe his ma-nipulation had been successful.

Steel was satisfied; he was sure that it would be easy to manipu-late Amar Wellberg. He lowered the straw and placed his left hand flat on the table with outstretched fingers. He held the straw between his pinky and ring fingers and looked at Wellberg.

"You must look very closely – don't be distracted."

Steel knew he had already created a connection to Amar's con-sciousness and could now manipulate it as he wished.

With a push, Steel pressed the straw against his little finger, and the straw bent over.

Amar, however, saw the images of the straw and the knife inter-changeably. He could see how the knife separated Steel's little finger from his hand because of the pressure Steel created. The finger was lying beside his hand on the table. The images changed more quickly. He jumped up, shocked, and expressed his surprise – that was exactly what Steel wanted to see.

"Everything's alright, Mr. Wellberg, it's just a straw, you see?"

Amar played the shocked audience member, came a step closer, and sat back down at the table. Breathing quickly, he picked up the straw and looked it over thoroughly.

"How did you do that?"

"Pure illusion – let's just say I simply made you believe I had cut off my finger. In reality, the whole time I was just playing around with a straw."

"Now I can understand why people are so fascinated by your show; it's simply unbelievable. I can hardly imagine what a person could do with that kind of ability."

Steel looked at Amar, and his eyes had a strange shine once again.

"You are correct, Mr. Wellberg; there is much I can influence. But as you know, there is also a Codex we artists follow, and it tells us we must not use our powers to bring harm to any other person."

"Very well, Mr. Steel, then we're all safe here in the Aphobia – wouldn't want to see the whole hotel burn down right before our eyes."

Amar showed his teeth and attempted to laugh, and Steel laughed as well. When Amar lost his concentration for a moment, he could feel again how Steel attempted to penetrate his subconscious and manipulate him further. Amar concentrated and deflected Steel's attempt without him noticing. Amar remembered the many times his father had attempted to manipulate him, which he had also always misdirected without him noticing.

„Mr. Steele, I would like to apologies for any inconvenience we may have caused – please accept this small gift, to express our sincere apologies."

Amar reached into his inside pocket and pulled out an envelope, handing it to Steel. Steel took it and used the opportunity to touch Amar. Amar waited, expecting Steel to open the envelope, instead Steele thanked him and put the envelope in his pocket.

"Do you know what's inside?" Amar asked.

"Let me guess – a VIP package, five days in an Aphobia hotel of my choice, all inclusive, as a VIP."

"How do you know?"

Amar acted surprised; he knew Steel had pulled the information out of his subconscious. He had allowed him access to it. In the moment he passed him the letter, Steel had touched him. Amar knew it was a test; Steel wanted to know whether he had direct access to Amar's consciousness. Satisfied with the results, Steel let Amar go again.

"Then I hope that with this small gesture, we may retain you as a future customer in our Aphobia hotels. How long are you planning on staying in New York?"

"I can't say exactly; we are trying to work out the contracts with different agencies to be able to do various shows here in Madison Square Garden. If I've understood my agents correctly, it will certainly take a few more days. So, you will be able to keep me around as a guest for a while, Mr. Wellberg."

Amar attempted to end the discussion so he could talk over the situation with Kayl, Arun, and Xama. He knew now that the others already knew where Xama was staying and were in the process of implementing a plan. He looked at his watch in surprise.

"How the time flies – you must excuse me, Mr. Steel; I have another important appointment – once again I apologize for the breach of confidence, and I will ensure that no further information gets out, and will promise you full discretion here in he Aphobia."

Ocram Steel stood up and held out his hand to Amar Wellberg.

"I hereby accept your apology, and I assume you will fulfill my expectations."

At the moment the two hands touched, Steel attempted to penetrate even deeper into Amar's consciousness. He drove deeper and deeper into it, twisting like a corkscrew.

"Metamora."

"What did you say?" Amar could feel now very clearly that Steel was trying to manipulate his consciousness, but this time he was not prepared for it. Amar blinked and attempted to recognize whether something had changed in his surroundings. But there was nothing, nothing had changed, everything looked normal. Steel's handshake became more intense, and Amar resisted him with everything he had. The power of his aphmalisation was at max; he thought of Xama and about how he would do anything to protect her. Anything – even give his life if he had to. They could not get to Xama. Amar closed his eyes and felt Steel's handshake loosen. He heard him say again:

"Metamora."

Amar didn't know what this word meant, but it sounded beautiful and melodious somehow.

"You will forget everything that's just happened after you excused yourself from your memory forever. You will only remember that we had a normal conversation and that you gave me an official apology."

Steel let go and said goodbye with the words:

"Until we meet again, Mr. Wellberg."
He left the Palm Garden without even looking back.
Amar just stood there, thinking to himself:

So they know where Xama is – then it won't be long now before they will try to kidnap her. We have to disappear.

He grabbed his telephone and sent out a text message.
"We are meeting in the sun room immediately.
It's extremely urgent, Amar."

THE TRAP

"So, you say you did it. You manipulated Amar Wellberg – and I'm supposed to believe that, Steel?"

"You are correct, Sherman. Wellberg realized it and skillfully blocked my first attempts to penetrate his consciousness. He withdrew to the bathroom for a moment and aphmalised there. A clever little fellow. It gave him enough mental energy to inhibit my intrusions into his consciousness."

Sherman just stood there, thinking:

You, worm, have no idea who Amar Wellberg really is, yet you talk about him as though you could even hold a candle to him.

"What did I say? Did you program him to a code word?"

"I did. It was a very good idea, and it worked magnificently."

"You're certain he will react to it, Steel?"

"Absolutely certain, Sherman", I tried it out. I commanded him to forget everything that had happened. When I asked him, he could only remember the apology. He won't even be aware I tried to manipulate him. This means he also doesn't know we're after him."

Sherman didn't believe a word of what Steel was saying, but he was obsessed by one thing.

"Very well, Steel, what's the code word?"

"I'd love to tell you, Sherman, but I would like to have something in exchange. You know what I mean."

Sherman held the telephone at his side and looked up, raising his eyebrows. *This bastard. He'll pay for that. He will die a slow and tortured death.*

"You want the gene, Steel, am I correct?"

"Exactly, Sherman. I want to develop my show further, and I need my power for it. I must be able to retain my abilities past the Finitum."

"Who doesn't want that?"

"You will give me enough Arverni gene for 5 years, and Amar Wellberg will belong to you."

Sherman grinned to himself.

I'd kill you without batting an eyelash for a week of the Arverni gene, and you, you dimwit; you want enough Arverni genes for five years.

"Done, Steel. You tell me the code word and I'll give you enough of the gene for ten years, how does that sound?"
"Where will we meet?"
"Let's meet immediately. Then you can deal with your show, and I'll worry about my own business."
After Sherman had ended the call, he dialed Sanders' number.
"Pete, Steel manipulated Amar Wellberg with a code word. Once we have the code word, we'll have Wellberg, and with Wellberg, we'll get Xama Dupre. You have to do anything you can to get the code word out of Steel. But don't kill him, not yet – only when we're certain we have the correct code word. Call me back when you have it.
Sherman opened the small chest with the injector and looked at the last ampule of Arverni gene, already inside it. He slowly lifted the injector out of the box.

All or nothing. It's all down to this.
Sherman placed the injector against his neck and pressed the trigger. A muffled hissing broke the silence. He closed his eyes blissfully, standing there motionless. He slowly pulled air in through his teeth and inhaled deeply, as though sucking smoke from a cigarette into every corner of his lungs.

It feels good, and everyone wants it, just like I predicted. But that council of old men wouldn't believe me. Those idiots.

When Sherman opened his eyes, they had a new, changed shine. He carefully lay the injector into the chest, his gaze focused on the ampules still laying in it.

Three doses left, he thought to himself and locked the chest.

At the same time, in the Aphobia.

Amar had just arrived at the sunroom when he heard noises and voices coming from the room. His thoughts produced a horrifying image, and Amar frantically opened the door with his master code card, storming into the room.

Arun, Kayl, and I sat at the table, shocked and looked at Amar, who had lost his dark skin tone and stood there, pale as a corpse. Unsettled, I asked:

"What's going on, Amar? First your warning text, and then you storm into the room here as if ..."

Amar interrupted me.

"They know that you're here – here in the Aphobia."

Everyone looked at Amar, surprised.

I wanted to ask whom, but bit my lip instead and stayed silent.

Kayl jumped up from the table:

"Well alright – if they already know that we're here, then let's do what they least expect."

"You mean fight them," Arun remarked. He could see by the expression on my face that I hadn't understood Kayl's meaning.

"Right, dear brother – we'll fight. This waiting is making me too tame, anyway."

This was another one of those moments I simply couldn't stand Kayl. Macho Kay-Ky.

"How could they know we're here? We just arrived," I asked, curious.

"There must be some kind of leak; only a very few people know I am taking care of you and that we're in the Aphobia. No matter – you are in even more danger now. If they know where you're staying, they could attack at any moment and kidnap you.

There are two options – either we flee again and they keep pursuing us, or we follow Kayl's suggestion and we fight."

"We fight," Kayl said, energetically.

Amar looked at Arun.

"What did you expect to hear from an Achillean? I like Xama a lot, and her safety means everything to me. Let's solve this problem for good, and fight."

Amar registered this nodding, and looked at me.

"You have the last word, Xama, this is about you after all. Whatever you want, we will respect your decision."

Everyone expected I would need some time to make my decision, to weigh the different positions. I stood up, held Kayl's and

Arun's hands, then asked them both to do the same with Amar to close the circle.

"We will fight, and free the Arverni once and for all from this threat. I only wish that no more aspirants would ever have to fear for their lives. We will fight!"

No one had expected this statement, and everyone looked at me, surprised.

"You obviously didn't expect that," I said.

"As an Arverni woman, I have a duty, and for some reason I just can't think about running away. What will we do first? We need a plan."

I wasn't the only one who noticed I was changing; something was happening to me. Even Arun and Amar could see that.

"You're right, Xama, we need a plan", Amar said, laughing, and sat back down at the table.

At the same time, somewhere in New York City

Hours later, Pete Sanders found what he had been looking for hours. As a former Achillean and a trained fighter, he knew how to get at information. Especially information his victim didn't want to give up. That was his specialty. However, this time, it wasn't exactly easy, and it didn't go as he had planned. Sanders knew Sherman would be furious with him, but he couldn't change that now. After he had removed all traces, he decided not to call Sherman, but rather to drive directly to the hotel and give the information to him personally.

Sherman was already waiting for Sanders, tense. It wasn't often that he felt restless, but that was the case now. Sherman knew that the job he was giving Sanders would decide whether they would experience victory or defeat. When Sanders called him over the intercom system, Sherman opened the door, excited and curious, and let Sanders come inside.

"I assume Pete, that you were successful and got the information we needed out of this bastard Steel."

Sanders went to the bar without saying a word and poured himself a double shot of whiskey.

"Do you want one too? We have reason to celebrate."

"I'd love one. So, this means you have the information?"

"Yes, I kicked the information out of the bastard. Cut it out. Burnt it out. Sooner or later they all talk – no one can stand it forever – no one."

Sanders passed the glass to Sherman, toasted him, and took a big swallow. You could see that what he was saying troubled him very much.

"A piece of me die every time. Every time a little more."

Sherman listened but was only interested in one thing.

"What is it? What is the code word Steel used to manipulate Am-ar Wellberg?"

"Did you even listen to me? Are you interested in what I'm saying? Are you interested in how I'm doing?"

Sherman could tell now that Sanders was desolate. He felt that Sanders was not doing well, and it wasn't the first time. Sherman knew this situation, and he knew it was going to get worse.

"Sorry, Pete, I know that you're suffering, but that's how it has to be this time. It's important for our success. Without the infor-mation from Steel, we won't be able to extract any more of the Arverni gene, and I don't need to explain to you what that means."

"Steel is dead."

Sherman did hear what Sanders said, but didn't react to it.

"The bastard didn't live through it; he died from the pain and shock. I couldn't do anything for him."

"Pete, I specifically said you shouldn't kill him. Fucking hell!"

"I didn't want to – it just happened. I didn't think he would croak right off."

"What is the code word? What did he tell you?"

"Metamora."

"Meta what?" Sherman asked.

"Metamora" Sanders screamed, and it seemed as though he was annoyed.

"Metamora, Metamora, Metamora" he screamed and walked through the room angrily.

"Metamora was the last thing Steel said before he said goodbye for good."

Although Sherman was emotionless and cold, he felt that Pete Sanders was close to going off the deep end again. He had to stop that however he could. Pete was unpredictable in this condition and extremely dangerous.

"Calm down, Pete! Just tell me how you solved the Steel problem."

"You know you can trust me. Right? Did I ever leave you hanging? I haven't, have I?"

"Pete, you haven't. Please calm down."

Sherman walked over to Sanders and laid his hand on his shoulder.

"I removed all traces. They'll find Steel, and it will look like a crazy fan got to him."

"Thank you, Pete, you solved the problem very well."

Peter Sanders looked up at Sherman. Had he actually praised him?

"And what will happen next?"

"Next, I will meet Amar Wellberg and we'll see whether Metamora is the code word to his consciousness. It will be a very special meeting – a coming together such as has never been seen before."

Pete knew what Sherman meant with this statement, and didn't want to ask any more about it.

"Amar Wellberg won't want to meet with you, you know that, right?"

"An old friend will help me meet Amar Wellberg."

Sherman picked up his telephone, looked for a particular contact, and dialed the number. He radiated a kind of satisfaction – everything seemed to be coming together according to his plan.

"Hello, Kanaar."

"Sherman – I was waiting on your call!"

"Yes. It's time for you to have another dose of the Arverni gene. You don't want to lose the physical advancements you've recently made, do you?"

"I believe this is just the beginning. When can we meet?"

"As soon as you've helped me with a small matter."

"Let it out, Sherman."

"I'd like to meet with Amar Wellberg."

Sherman knew that this wish would surprise Kanaar.

"You want what? You actually want to meet with Amar? And you call that a small matter. That will never happen – never in your life. You know it won't work. He would never meet with you under any circumstances. What you expect from me is impossible. How am I supposed to work out this 'small matter'?"

"There's something that will convince him that he does want to meet with me."

"Sherman – you know the situation as well as I do, and you know there is absolutely nothing which will move Amar Wellberg to meet with you."

"Ask him whether he would trade Xama Dupre's life for a meeting with me. If he gives me an hour of his time and meets me at a neutral location of his choice, I'll let the aspirant Xama Dupre live. I'll promise him that."

Kanaar thought this over.

"You are unpredictable, but very clever. That could work. But what if he doesn't agree to it?"

"Then you'll call me back immediately, and we'll think of another way to convince him. Once I've met Amar, we'll both meet at the Italian place and you'll get what you need so badly. A few years of your life back. If that's not a good reason to get to work, then what is?"

"I'll call you back, Sherman."

Sherman hung up and looked at Sanders, nodding. "We're about to win, Pete. Everything's going as planned – we're going to win!"

At the same time, at the Aphobia.

Kayl, Arun, Amar and I had talked through some different ideas about how I could start an attack. Unfortunately, none of the ideas we had seemed like a genius plan. We did, however, all agree on one thing: we had to create a surprise effect by attacking and not running away. The question of how we would find the others remained unanswered until Amar's phone rang.

"This is Kanaar, excuse me for a second," Amar said, standing up and going to the window."

Kayl and Arun knew the name Kanaar – they clued me in that Kanaar was the security chief of the Arverni, and sort of their boss. For some reason I felt skeptical and tried to hear a little more of their discussion.

Amar got louder, and his answers sounded more emotional.

"Absolutely not. You know that he doesn't exist in my mind anymore. And since he doesn't exist, I can't very well meet him. He is dead to me, do you hear me? – Dead, finished, and he's been that way for many years."

Amar was excited, almost screaming, which surprised Arun and Kayl very much, since it wasn't at all like his normal temperament.

"There's nothing to think about, Kanaar, you know that. I will not meet this devil under any circumstances, and if I do meet him, it will be for only one reason – to kill him."

"Make it up to me? Did I hear you right, Kanaar? There is no way to make up what he did to us – to me. You know it, and I know it. Sherman is a murderer – he has brought shame to all the Arverni, and especially to me."

"He suggested what? You don't believe he's going to keep his word, do you? He's never done it before. I can smell how bad that suggestion stinks through the telephone. Please make it clear to him that I won't meet with him. Not tomorrow, and not on any day afterward."

Amar hung up, and you could tell how excited he was. His jugular vein had grown double in size, and I couldn't just let him stand there like that anymore.

"What was that, Amar? I've never seen you like that before."

"Kanaar wanted me to meet with Dr. Sherman – at his request."

We all looked at him, surprised.

"That's perfect," Kayl burst out, once again saying what we were all thinking.

"You meet with him, and you take him out. That's an awesome plan, don't you guys think?"

Then Arun asked a question that was going through my mind as well.

"Why does Kanaar want you to meet this monster?

What possible reason could there be for this Dr. Sherman to want to see you?"

Amar looked at each one of us.

"It's best if you all sit down."

We followed Amar's instruction, tense, and once we were all sitting down, Amar propped himself up on a chair.

"Sherman wants to see me and speak with me, and in exchange, he has promised Kanaar that he will spare Xama."

"What? I don't understand. If he gets to talk to you, he won't be after me anymore? What's his motivation, anyway? I thought he needed my blood."

"He does need it – that's why I don't trust him. But there is one important reason he wants to see me, and why I don't want to see him."

Everyone was anxious to hear Amar's explanation.

"Sherman is my father – that's why he wants to talk to me."

Boom. Amar's explanation hit us all like a hammer hitting a nail.

I thought I had misheard him. Arun and Kayl must have had the same feeling.

"I thought your parents were dead and you were an orphan like me – at least, that's what you told me."

"Yes, that's right, Xama – my father is dead. I mean, he is dead to me – in my mind, he is dead. He practically doesn't exist anymore. What he has done is inconceivable. It's intolerable. That is why he is dead to me. He doesn't exist anymore. That's why I don't want to speak with him anymore."

"That means Dr. Sherman is your biological father. When you found out what he had done, he died in your mind."

"You've hit the nail on the head, Xama."

"Wow – that's what I call coming out. Now I understand why you're so involved in helping aspirants. Your conscience bothers you because of your father's deeds. I am so sorry you had to go through all of this, Amar."

Amar looked away.

"You're probably right, Xama."

"Then there's another reason we must fight!" Kayl interjected again.

"We'll help you to regain your honor. With us, at least you have one chance to remove the shame your father has brought to your family, the burden that you have to bear, forever."

Amar looked at Kayl. He knew exactly what Kayl meant.

"You're right, Kayl, but it won't work."

"What do you mean it won't work?" Arun asked, breaking off smiling at me.

"I already had the chance to stop my father, but I wasn't able to stand up to him back then – to kill him. Shortly thereafter, my father killed another aspirant. It was like I had signed his death warrant. I had failed, and he had to die."

Amar and I both fought back tears. Arun stood up, went to Amar, and placed his arm on Amar's shoulder.

"You tried, Amar, you tried."

"That's why you have us," Kayl added. "We're your friends – what one of us can't do, another of us can. I'll do it!"

We all stared at Kayl, and each of us knew what he meant by this.

"You help me get to your father, and I'll eliminate him. I'm an Achillean, if you remember – I'm trained for this. I can't do much, but I'm very good at one thing. I'll help you, Amar."

Amar wrinkled his forehead, unsure, and tried to get a grip on the situation.

"If I've understood all of you correctly, then we have a plan. I'll try to make contact with my father, and Kayl will help me solve the problem, once and for all."

Kayl gave a thumbs up, signaling that he found the plan super. Arun agreed as well. All of this was a little too fast for me. Did Amar really want to kill his biological father? What I wouldn't give to have my father alive again. Although I couldn't under-stand all of it, I signaled my agreement, even though I felt very bad.

"Okay, this means that my father wanting to meet me is a chance – I'll bring Kayl into play. Together, we'll both solve the problem – once and for all."

At the same time, at an unknown location.

Kanaar wasn't sure what he should tell Sherman, but he had no other choice but to call him. He knew it. Amar would never meet with his father again, after everything that had happened. He had changed his name and destroyed everything – absolutely every-thing – that could place him in relationship with Sherman. Sher-man had already died long ago in Amar's mind, and in reality, the only reason that occurred to Kanaar why Amar would want to meet Sherman was his final wish to not just think of his father as dead, but to actually kill him.

"Kanaar, you want to tell me that Amar doesn't want to speak with me."

"What did you expect, Sherman, he didn't buy your offer of protecting the aspirant, and to be honest, I didn't either. Like I said – Amar doesn't want to see you, and I don't think that's ever going to change."

Sherman burned inside. He had to vent his frustration.

"That's what he wanted, my lost son. You will ensure that I can get the aspirant, Kanaar. Without her, none of us will ever get any more of the Arverni gene, and you know what that means. Use all the power you have, and get me Xama Dupre. The only thing you need to be certain of is that I need her alive."

Kanaar fell silent for a moment.

"And what about Amar?"

"Well, what about him?"

"You always told me to keep my eye on him and make sure he was doing alright. What if he places himself between me and the aspirant?"

"Then you'll kill him!"

Sherman's words hit Kanaar like a punch in the face. He, personally, had ensured for years that nothing would happen to Amar. Even back when he wanted to take his own life, Kanaar used his organization to stop the worst from happening. Sherman's greatest wish had been his son's safety – and now this.

"Kanaar, I have no interest, and no patience to talk about this any longer. We both need Xama Dupre. You make sure I get her, no matter what the cost."

"One more thing, Kanaar; we don't have any time left. I need the aspirant as quickly as possible; otherwise, you'll suffer the effects of Arverni gene withdrawal in a couple of days, and I'll suffer them a couple of weeks later. Have we understood one another, Kanaar?"

"I'll get her for you, Sherman. In the worst case scenario, it will cost your only son."

Sherman hung up and closed his eyes. He felt something he hadn't felt for a long time. He knew the feeling from an earlier life, when he and Amar were still very close – father and son, like normal. It was the same feeling, but it changed second by second, transforming into something that Sherman hated. Weakness and sadness. As he attempted to drown his chaotic feelings in a drink, his telephone rang again. As he was about to deny the call, he happened to see the name on the lit display out of the corner of his eye, and dropped the telephone in horror. It kept ringing on the floor, and Sherman bent down and picked it up, wondering what he should say.

"Hello, Amar, how are you?"

"Drop it! You want to see me, right?"

Sherman still couldn't believe it.

"Yes, that is my dearest wish. I would very much like to see you and speak with you. I have something to tell you, Amar, something very important!"

"Where, and when?"

Sherman thought for a moment what the best location would be.

"We'll meet in my hotel; how about dinner this evening?" Sherman was about to tell Amar which hotel, when he interrupted him.

"Good, this evening in your hotel, let's say 8 o'clock."

Just as Sherman was about to say goodbye, he realized he was only hearing the ring tone. Amar had already hung up. Now he needed a drink more than ever before. He was going to see and speak with his son – for the first time in 9 years and 6 months. He had to tell Kanaar so he wouldn't mess up the meeting with some plan of his own.

THE EXCHANGE

A mar shook. He was still gripping the telephone convulsively. I took his hand. "It's over, Amar. You did very well, and you overcame your fear." Amar looked at me. "Thank you, Xama. Thanks to all of you."

So there we stood, all four holding each other's hands, looking at Amar. All of a sudden, I could feel energy flowing through our hands. A similar feeling to an aphmalisation. I slowly closed my eyes, and I could tell very clearly that what I was seeing were the others' feelings. I concentrated first on Amar and felt his fear – fear of meeting his father. But there was more, much more than just fear. Amar was full of hate and disappointment, and yet behind all these, positive feelings like hope, affection, and respect were still lurking – even something akin to love. But these feelings were masked by a deep hate against his father. Squinting, I tried to concentrate on Kayl, and it worked. I could see his feelings. Kayl was full of strength and was striving for power, but I could tell he had more to offer than what he showed the outside world. Kayl was full of responsibility for Arun, coupled with brotherly love. His mind told me he had a high level of conviction and motivation. Kayl felt responsible for the safety of those entrusted to him, and would give anything to preserve it. Kayl had his fears under control. His expectation of success overpowered his fear of losing. Kayl was full of positive energy. Squinting again, I tried to fathom Arun's feelings. What I saw there was a bright, colorful bouquet of positive emotions – the clearest were affection and love, so great that they made everything else look very small. Just when I wanted to take a closer look at these feelings, our hands separated and the images disappeared. Arun remained a secret, a secret I had yet to figure out.

Amar summarized the steps we would take from there:

"The first milestone in our plan is clear. I'll meet my father at 8 o'clock in the Mandarin Oriental Hotel. Sherman won't be having dinner with me without protection – I've already tried to deactivate him once before. His Achillean Sanders will certainly be nearby. Let's think about how Kayl can get to him without Sherman getting suspicious. His suite is secured; if you want to get in there, you'll have to have an invitation."

Arun had the best idea. His suggestion was to dress Kayl up like a valet, and when the food was served, he'd be allowed into the suite. At the same time, Arun would ask for Dr. Sherman downstairs in the hotel lobby, saying he was a friend of Xama Dupre who urgently needed to give him some information. That would certainly be enough to lure Sanders, his assistant, to come downstairs and distract him. When Kayl entered the suite, he was to deactivate Sherman immediately, and then Amar and Kayl would both disappear again. At the same time, Arun would try to keep Sanders in check without getting captured himself.

All in all, a plan that seemed too simple to me for some reason. If it was so easy, then why didn't my father – the head of security – already deactivate Sherman and his guard? I was afraid our plan wouldn't work, but didn't want to unsettle the group and kept my feelings that something might happen to one of us to myself.

Amar, who I could see was nervous, went through the steps of the plan one more time.

"We'll leave here at 7 o'clock, so that gives us some time. Xama, you'll lock yourself in here in the sunroom and wait until we call you. Until then, you are to speak to no one, let no one in, and don't leave your room either. Kayl, you need a valet disguise – take one of our uniforms from the hotel here."

Kayl shook his head confidently.

"I'll take the uniform along, but it's easy as pie to get clothes once we're there. There will be piles of uniforms running around the hotel – all I have to do is find the right size and make a quick exchange." Kayl smiled, which in this situation gave us all hope that there was still something to smile about. My gaze met Arun's, who had been looking at me the whole time, and who looked away briefly, embarrassed, when I saw him.

"Everything alright, Arun? You're so quiet – what's your opinion?"

"Everything will work, but to be honest, I'm more worried about you than I am about us. Once we're gone, you'll be here without any protection. That means you're in danger, and I don't like that."

"Then you stay with Xama, dear brother. I can make the call in your place and distract Sanders' Achillean while I sneak into the suite. That's no problem."

Amar still wasn't totally convinced, but finally gave in and accepted Kayl's suggestion.

"Then Kayl and I will meet at 7 and leave. You two stay together until we come back."

Amar stood up and walked towards the exit. Kayl followed him, but turned back around one more time.

"You guys wish us luck, and don't do anything stupid."

When the door lock clicked shut, I looked at Arun. We were both thinking the same thing.

Kayl and Amar were on the way to free the Arverni forever from a stain on the community.

Around 7:45, Amar parked a block away to be sure no one was waiting for him. He and Kayl walked into the hotel, and while Kayl took care of his business, Amar went directly to the reception desk to check in.

"Good evening, my name is Wellberg. I have an appointment with Dr. Sherman."

Amar was received by a friendly front desk worker, who called Sherman right away.

"One moment, please, our security officers will accompany you to Dr. Sherman's suite."

Amar had assumed this would happen, thanked the worker, and waited until a young man addressed him and showed him the way towards the VIP suite. Amar's pulse speeded up to match the floor numbers on the elevator's display, quickly ticking upwards. He felt a tension he hadn't felt for a long time. How long has it been? He wondered, and counted the years to distract himself. When the security officer announced him at the suite and opened the door, he felt as though he were standing at the edge of an endlessly deep hole, just waiting to step out into it.

"Good evening, Amar. I am happy to see you again after 9 years and 6 months. Do please come in."

Amar didn't say anything; he just swayed a little, took a step over the endlessly deep hole in front of him, and walked in.

"I could imagine you might need a whiskey as much as I do – am I right?"

Amar nodded.

Sherman poured two whiskeys and kept talking.

"How long have I prepared for this moment – looked forward to it, even, and now, like you, I can't find the words to describe it."
Sherman passed Amar a glass.

"To your health! Of course, I assume you don't want to toast to me, and you know what? I can understand that. In your mind I'm a murderer, which you're probably right about."

Sherman paced back and forth, which was an expression of his nervousness. It helped him to deal with how tense he felt.

"You've changed, Amar. You've grown older, and more mature, but it seems as though the same old hate is still burning inside you. Am I right?"

Amar bit his tongue until it hurt. He didn't want to answer; he didn't want to speak to his father.

"Well, this is a very one-sided discussion, Amar. I thought it might be. Allow me to ask you a question – perhaps that might loosen up our discussion a bit?
When were you last in Metamora?"

Sherman stared at Amar after he had said the sentence, watching his face. He wanted to see whether anything would change.

"Metamora," Amar repeated. "I don't remember ever being in Metamora before."

Sherman smiled – exactly the reaction he had hoped for had set in. Steel had done his work excellently – he really had programmed Amar on the code word "Metamora." He had never thought it would be possible, especially not since Amar was able to resist his manipulation successfully for so many years.

"Amar, you can tell me, can't you, why you came here tonight? I want to know the truth." Sherman wanted to know how far his influence over Amar went. If he really had full access to his consciousness and his subconscious, he would simply be able to give him commands, and Amar would follow them. Sherman sat down, glass in hand, and waited patiently on Amar's answer.

"Sit down, Amar."

Amar sat down.

"Father, I've come to kill you. That's my plan."

Sherman had to laugh out loud. He really did have total control of Amar. The first time since he could remember that he had control of his son.

"Tell me everything about this plan; I'd like to know every little detail of your scheme."

Pete Sanders walked through a door at the end of the room. He had received a signal from Sherman.

"Pete, might I introduce you to Amar, my son. And Amar, this is Pete, my other son.

Pete, Amar was just about to tell me about his plan – the one where he and an Achillean were going to try and kill me. Amar, please go ahead, and as I said, please tell us every detail."

It took less than 15 minutes for Amar to reveal all the details to Sanders and Sherman. When the phone rang, Sherman and Sanders already knew the call was a planned diversion tactic and that Kayl was on the line. Sanders picked up the call.

"Pete, please ensure we get this Kayl alive. We need him for our next steps.

And now to you, Amar. Forget your plan, and that you want to kill me. I'll tell you now what you really want; it's exactly the opposite of what you've wanted up to this point."

Sherman programmed Amar to his own goals, making him his accomplice. He also ordered him always to call him father. Sanders prepared himself to deactivate Kayl – and, as always, he did it in his own special way.

When Kayl came into the room with the serving cart, everything went very quickly. Sanders was already waiting on him, and fired off a targeted shot. Kayl was hit in the neck – he tried to grab at the wound, but could tell immediately that he no longer had his coordination under control. Kayl collapsed like a sack of potatoes and lost consciousness.

Amar, who was sitting at the table with Sherman, saw all of it. He didn't move a muscle.

"Pete, would you be so kind as to serve us? We don't want the food to get cold. Then please deal with our friend; he doesn't seem to be doing well."

After dinner, Sherman gave Amar another command. He couldn't wait to see how all the parts of his plan were going to come together in a glorious whole.

"Call Xama Dupre and tell her the plan didn't work and that I captured Kayl. Tell her you've decided to work for me, and that I've got a suggestion for her. If she ever wants to see Kayl alive again, she'll need to accept it. Then give the telephone to me."

Amar executed Sherman's commands, dialing Xama's number.

"Amar, it's good to hear from you. Arun and I are sitting here on pins and needles. Did everything work? Did you finish the plan?" Amar fell silent for a second.

Amar was silent for a moment. "No, the plan failed. Sherman captured Kayl."

Amar was silent again.

"What? What do you mean he captured you and Kayl? Did I hear you right?"

"He captured Kayl. He didn't capture me, but I'm working for him. I'm on his side – one of them."

I couldn't believe what I was hearing, and I repeated again:

"Amar, I don't understand at all. Kayl was captured, and what happened to you?"

"I'm working for my father now. He wants to speak with you, and he has a suggestion for you. Here he is."

"Good evening, Miss Dupre. You already know me, so I don't need to introduce myself. Let me be brief. Kayl is in mortal danger, and Amar is working for me now, effective immediately. We've made up. Father and son, just as we should be. I'd like to suggest a little business transaction to you, and I think you should accept it. You'll come to my hotel, alone, in a taxi – emphasis on alone – and you'll exchange yourself for this ridiculous Achillean, who's in the middle of bleeding out right now. You'd better hurry – otherwise he won't make it. The only thing I want from you is that you donate a liter of blood. Once you've done that, you can leave again with your friend. I'll keep my son – after all, we are family. If I need any more of the Arverni gene, I'll call you up for an appointment to donate blood. What do you think about that? No one else has to die, just a totally civilized procedure."

"Why would you think I would trust you? Who's going to guarantee me that Kayl isn't already dead and that you won't kill me too as soon as I come over."

"You're probably right. I wouldn't trust me either. But I'm not stupid. I wouldn't kill my only source for the Arverni gene. I don't need the Achillean, but you are highly valuable to me. Stay on the phone a moment, and then you can talk to him yourself. It will help you make your decision."

Sherman gave the telephone to Sanders, who disappeared with it. You could hear muffled screams, then they fell silent again. A few minutes later, Sanders reappeared and handed the telephone back to Sherman.

"Now that you've had a nice chat with your friend, he's surely explained the situation to you. What do you think about my generous suggestion to have you donate blood?"

Something had changed while I was speaking to Sherman. The same feeling I had felt before from Amar was developing within me. I hated it, but couldn't repress it. What I felt for Sherman was hate, profound hate, and this feeling helped me better understand Amar – and why he would want to kill his biological father.

"I'll come, and I'll donate blood for you. We'll both see whether you keep your word. If you don't do it, and if you don't let me leave the hotel with Kayl, your only source will run dry, forever."

I was surprised myself, at my choice of words, and how confidently I made this suggestion. Nothing that was happening right now seemed to have anything to do with the Xama Sophie I'd known for 16 years.

Sherman was surprised and unsettled. Would this Xama Dupre really kill herself?

"What do you think there is to keep me alive? I've already lost both my parents, and you're about to kill my newly found friends. Think whatever you want to about me, but you knew my father, after all, and there is one thing I got from him. When I set a goal in my mind, I achieve it. This time, Dr. Sherman, you should keep your word. Otherwise, we will both die. I'll die first, but you'll die too, and soon!"

Sherman knew it was serious now. This Xama Dupre had a lot of her mother in her, more than she knew, and he respected that. He even feared it.

"Honestly, I'm surprised at you, Xama – at your attitude, and at your intelligence. I like all of it very much. We'll see each other soon, then, and I'll keep my promise. You will be allowed to go with the Achillean after you donate blood. There's something else I have for you as well – the truth about why your mother died when you were born. I assume you'd be interested to hear it."

Sherman hung up and started eating again.

"Do you like it, Amar? The salmon is outstanding; you must try it."

Amar tried it as he was commanded, but for some reason he couldn't taste the salmon.

"A very special aspirant, this Xama Dupre."

"Yes, father, she is. She is an Identidem. She has already developed several abilities, and I'm sure she will develop many more."

"That's what I thought – a female Identidem like her mother – fantastic. This is getting better and better. How many abilities has she developed already?"

"I think four or five, father."

"Then I'm excited to see what kinds of effects the gene we extract from her blood will show."

When Xama set the phone down, pale as a corpse, Arun wanted to know right away what had happened.

"Amar changed sides and now he's working for his father. Kayl has been captured and he's in mortal danger, and the only way out of all this misery is for me to voluntarily go to Dr. Sherman."

Arun didn't let me get away with just this short summary, and I told him all the details. Then Arun jumped up and started going crazy. I had never seen him like this, so impulsive and emotional. It didn't matter what I tried, I couldn't calm him down. Arun only had one thing in mind: driving to the hotel and saving his brother, no matter the cost. All my attempts to calm him down failed; I only had one option left to save Arun from certain death. I grabbed both of his arms, spoke to him, and sat down with him on the sofa. Before Arun could tell what I was doing, it was already too late. An intense kiss. Arun's body jolted briefly, and there was a tingling between our lips looking for a way out. And then Arun collapsed on the sofa. I put up his feet and pushed a pillow under his head. Since I didn't know how long this condition would last, I wrote Arun a note and laid it on his chest.

**Dear Arun, I didn't have any other choice. When you read this, I'll already be with Sherman. I'll donate blood, and then come back with Kayl. This is the only way to save Kayl. I didn't want to lose both him and you. Please forgive me.
I love you. Yours – Xama.**

Ps. Please don't come yourself – notify the council; I think the council will know if there's anything else we can do. I'll kiss you when I come back – Yours, Xama.

I picked up my purse and disappeared towards the elevator. Minutes later, I was sitting in a taxi on the way to the Mandarin Hotel, totally exhausted. Since it took around 30 minutes, I had an idea, and I tried to dream. Despite my tension, I was able to find some inner peace, so I closed my eyes and attempted to dream about Arun. I imagined him lying on the sofa, and what he might be dreaming in that moment. It took a few minutes, but then I didn't hear the noise of the taxi anymore. I saw Arun looking for something in his room. He opened his closet and rifled through his clothes like a mad man. He was holding something in his hands; he had pulled it out from under a stack of T-shirts. Now I could see what it was – it was a gun. Arun was holding a gun and bullets in his hands. I spoke to him, and he jumped and turned around. "Xama, what are you doing here?"
"I just switched you off, and you're lying in the sun room on the sofa and sleeping. I'm on the way to save your brother and Amar. What are you planning to do with that gun?" "I have to save Kayl. Kayl's all I have." "You're right, Arun, but you won't save him with the gun. They will kill both of you."
"Then what should I do? I can't just sit here and wait; that won't work, Xama."
"I understand that. Contact the council and tell them everything you know. Please be sure the council comes to the Mandarin Hotel as well. That is your job Arun, you will find a piece of paper when you wake up. I've written it down for you as well. Please contact the council, and don't try to take matters into your own hands. I don't want to lose you; we hardly know each other, and there is so much I still have to tell you. Please, promise me you will notify the council."

I was torn roughly from the dream by a dark male voice, so I had to leave Arun behind. "That'll be 21 dollars, do you need a receipt?" Hoping Arun would take my message seriously, I left the taxi and went into the Mandarin Hotel. The first thing I did there was locating the bathroom. Something told me now was the right time for an aphmalisation. Charged up to my eyeballs with energy, I checked in at the reception desk.

A six-foot tall man picked me up at the reception desk and showed me the way to Dr. Sherman's suite. Thanks to my aphmal I felt no fear. On the contrary – I felt astoundingly good. Once I arrived at the suite, there was already a tall, slim man with grey hair and a grey beard waiting on me. He looked very clean, and anything but dangerous.

"You are …"

"Dr. Sherman. I'm very happy you could make it, Xama."

Expecting something to happen – for my sense of taste to go crazy or something else to set off an alarm, I just stood there, looking at him.

"Won't you come in? Amar is here as well."

Following his invitation, I still couldn't help but ask myself what was so dangerous about him. His appearance and his manner were nothing but pleasant.

"I don't need to introduce the two of you, of course, you already know one another."

"Hello, Amar, how are you doing?"

"Hello, Xama. What can I say? I've never been better. Father and I have had a talk and understand one another now. Everything that has been burdening me for so many years is gone, all at once. Xama, thank you for donating your blood for us. Father told me how generous you're being."

With a quick reaction, I grabbed Amar's hand and tried to see his emotional state. What I saw confirmed my suspicions. Amar wasn't himself anymore. Someone had hypnotized him or manipulated him in some other way.

"Can I see Kayl, Dr. Sherman?"

"Once we're finished; then you can see him and take him home with you just as I promised you. So, are you ready? I reserved an extra room across the hall; everything is prepared there."

I followed Sherman into the room across the hall. There was a hospital bed inside.

"Make yourself comfortable, the nurse will be here shortly."

Sherman disappeared, and I sat down on the bed. Questions and more questions appeared all at once. Could I trust him? He'll never let Kayl and I go. Was it a mistake to come here? What happens now?

SALVATION

When Arun awoke, he remembered his strange dream. Still a little groggy from being switched off, he sat up and discovered the hand-written note with my message. A little surprised that he was finding exactly the same instructions on the note that he had just dreamed a few minutes before, he started to think about how to notify the council.

He knew he couldn't lose any time. Kayl and I were in danger; that's why he had wanted to intervene immediately and alone. Who did he know in the council? Who could he contact and ask for help? Arun thought, and all at once he saw a name in his mind. Why didn't he think of it sooner? Kanaar, of course! He was his boss, more or less, and he was the one who gave him and Kayl the contract to protect Xama. He had to contact Kanaar immediately. But what would he tell him? How could he get Kanaar to talk to the rest of the council and get them to help Xama? To save Kayl and Amar, and to eliminate Dr. Sherman forever? While he thought all of this over, he looked for Kanaar's number in his telephone book. He had never called him, but knew he had his number saved. There it was – his display clearly showed Kanaar's name, and Arun confirmed the entry. He excitedly listened to the ring tone, hoping he would be able to reach Kanaar and that he wouldn't get his voice mail.

The phone rang until Arun began to get impatient. What should he do next if he couldn't reach Kanaar?

The ring tone was interrupted, abruptly.

"Hello, who's this?"

"Hello, this is Arun, Kayl's brother."

"Hello, Arun, and to what do I owe the honor of your call? Has something happened to the girl you two were supposed to protect?"

"Yes, that's just it. I need the council's help – the others have captured her and Kayl."

Kanaar breathed in deeply.

"Very slowly now, who caught who? And where?"

"Xama, the girl we were supposed to protect – she just drove to the Mandarin Hotel to deliver herself to Dr. Sherman and to save my brother Kayl in return. In my dream – she gave me the job of notifying the council."

"In your dream? So she can appear in other peoples' dreams?"

"Not just that – she can do so much more. If I understand things right, she's an Identidem. She has developed even more abilities, and the ones she has are extremely strong. She learned my power, and now she can do it better than I can."

"Interesting – and where is Amar?"

"He's also on the other side. I mean, he's working with Dr. Sherman, who's supposedly his father. I know this all seems very complicated – but I need the council's help, urgently. We don't have much time."

"Amar has changed sides – never. Not voluntarily. Okay, I will inform the council. We will meet in the Mandarin hotel. Try to get there, you understand, Arun?"

"Yes, we'll meet in the Mandarin Hotel."

Kanaar couldn't believe it. Not only was Xama Dupre the only aspirant, she was an Identidem as well. This information changed everything, Kanaar thought. If Sherman didn't kill Xama Dupre, he would have to do it himself. A female Identidem – unimaginable. She would be entitled to become leader of the Arverni. That meant Kanaar had two good reasons he had to get rid of Xama Dupre. He was the next Meta. He had a right to it, and had waited a long time for it. He would stop her from rewriting Arverni history. No woman had ever been a Meta before. They had stopped it for centuries. He, Kanaar, was responsible for security, and he knew that this kind of occurrence was part of his job description. He had to be sure Xama Dupre didn't stay alive. He had to do his job and protect the Arverni from being led by a female Meta. Obsessed with this goal, Kanaar started off towards the Mandarin Hotel.

Arun got to the Mandarin before Kanaar, so he waited on him in the splendid entryway.

At the same time, 92 floors up

I hardly felt the needle itself, but my veins burned as my blood flowed out into a bag. The nurse who was taking my blood seemed to have no idea about why it was being done. Sherman had only hired her for this job – at least, that's how it seemed, anyway. Just when I thought of him, the door opened and Sherman came in.

"And how is my favorite patient?" he asked, ironically.

"Very good, especially when you consider that I'm not sick."

Sherman grinned and came closer. What was he planning? Something wasn't right, and a bitter taste confirmed my hunch.

Sherman came so close that I almost felt threatened. He sat down on my bed and began to speak:

"I have something to tell you – something very important."

His eyes had a changed shine to them, and his voice seemed significantly deeper. Something inside me warned me.

"You will now follow my commands very carefully, and you will do as I ask you – do you understand, Xama Dupre?"

I nodded.

"Lay down and stretch out your arms and legs."

I followed his commands, not knowing whether I was capable of resisting them. I could feel Sherman placing cuffs around my wrists and ankles.

"What is this? We have an agreement. You'll let me go if I donate blood for you."

"That's right. But you also said you didn't trust me, and you were right not to.

Look at me." he said then, in a bloodcurdling voice.

"When I stop speaking, you will no longer be able to remember anything – not a single moment of your life – nothing – everything will be gone. You will be very tired. You won't be able to resist the exhaustion any longer, and you will fall asleep."

Sherman was right; I could no longer resist my exhaustion, and I closed my eyes. For some reason, I was forced to think of Amar. Had he manipulated Amar in the same way? Sherman had an enormously well-developed power when it came to manipulating other people. My thoughts were interrupted by a deep yawn, and I noticed everything around me begin to disappear as if receding into a vast distance. One single thought remained active: How were Kayl, Amar, and Arun?

No longer able to perceive my surroundings, Kayl appeared in my mind. He was tied to a chair, and his head was hanging bent down over his chest. His T-shirt was covered in blood, and it was obvious he had been beaten. I called his name in a soft voice: "Kayl, Kayl, wake up!"

Kayl slowly lifted his head. His eyes were swollen shut, and he had gaping wounds on both sides of his head by his eyebrows. His nose was pushed over to the side, just like before. Kayl was in a very bad state and needed immediate medical help.

"Xama, is that you? Are you here with me?"

"Yes, Kayl, I am with you. Try to stay very calm; I'm here to free you."

"Don't make jokes, Xama, they've tied me up. My feet are tied to this shitty chair with a bunch of cable ties. My right arm is broken, a couple of fingers and toes too, and my face is all screwed up. My back is killing me sitting here. I promise I'll stay nice and still for you if you promise to hurry up."

"I will, Kayl, I promise. I have to go again, but I'll be right back!"

Kayl was alive, which was very good. But he needed help, and fast.

I concentrated on Amar and tried to make contact with him, but no matter what I tried, I couldn't reach Amar. As a final attempt, I sent him a thought command, hoping he would get it.

The last one I tried to contact was Arun; I could see his thoughts immediately. Arun was sitting in the lobby and waiting on someone. He must have been thinking about me in that moment. Otherwise I wouldn't have been able to exchange thoughts with him so immediately. Arun didn't know what to do with my questioning thoughts, and was surprised at this new kind of communication.

"Arun, just think about how you want to answer me."

"Xama, I notified the council for you like you wanted. They will be here any moment."

"How did you do it?"

"I was asking myself that too – how could I notify the council? Finally, I thought of Kanaar. He's the chief of security, so I told him what's going on. He told me he would alarm the council."

"Very good, Arun, you did that very well."

"Where are you, Xama, where can we find you?"

"I'm in a room in the same hallway as Dr. Sherman's VIP suite. I'm very tired and have to stop; I need to sleep."

"Are you alright, Xama? Did they do anything to you?" Arun was torn from his thoughts by a slap on the back. He turned around and saw Kanaar, who was over six feet tall, a full head taller than Arun. Arun stood up and was surprised he didn't see anyone else. "Where is the council?" he asked Kanaar.

"They're all very busy. I didn't want to lose any time, so I came alone. Where is the girl?"

Arun didn't completely trust the situation. He responded carefully.

"I think Dr. Sherman has captured her, but I'm not totally sure."

"Then we'll both have to go and find out," Kanaar said, and walked towards the reception desk.

All of this fit very well into Kanaar's plans, since he had been planning anyway to pay a visit to Sherman to freshen up his dosage of the Arverni gene. Kanaar was very sure that he couldn't trust Sherman, and having Arun as a reinforcement was better than trying to do the job alone.

While Kanaar and Arun were checking in at the reception desk, Amar was having a discussion with his father. "What are you planning? You promised that after Xama donated blood you would let Kayl and her go free again."

"Don't be naive, Amar. Do you really believe she would ever come back? I just added a few extra touches – let's just say I influenced her opinion a little bit."

"You did what? Don't tell me you manipulated her."

"How else was I going to get control of her?"

Amar left the room in a rage and went into the bathroom to wash his face off with cold water. He removed the camouflage over his aphmal, looked at it in the mirror, and thought of me. The council appeared in his mind, and then images of Arverni dancing in a circle. Amar asked himself what these thoughts meant and then realized all at once that I had sent them to him. It was a message, but what was it telling him?

Amar began to place his thumb on his aphmal in order to trigger a full aphmalisation. He also tried to create contact with me. I was too weak; I kept falling asleep no matter how hard I tried to keep myself awake. I had already lost too much blood, and if I didn't get help soon, I wasn't going to survive. Just when I was nodding off again, my eyes closing, I realized that Amar was standing in front of me. He had gotten my message. Amar shook all over his body. The energy rushing through his body increased until it was almost immeasurable, but he didn't let up. He kept pressing his thumb to his forehead. He saw me traumatized, lying in the bed, shackled, weak, and waiting on death.

"Xama!" Amar yelled, as loud as he could.

"Xaaammmaaaa!"

"Amar, I'm here. I can't move. I won't make it, Amar. I knew I wasn't a good Arverni. Good to see you again – at least I can say goodbye. Where is Arun?"

"You can do it, Xama. Don't give up. I will help you. I am in the process of releasing myself from the manipulation; I've almost done it. Use your healing power – you have to heal yourself. Please, Xama, don't give up. You have to be strong, do you hear me? You have to be strong!"

Amar cried out from the pain created by his continuing aphmalisation, but he didn't remove the thumb from his forehead. The skin between his thumb and his forehead burned from all the energy that was being created, and smoke appeared. It hurt him terribly, but Amar didn't let up. He kept pressing his thumb against his forehead, and he wanted to cry out to be able to bear the pain, but didn't want Sherman to hear him. With the other hand, he grabbed a towel and stuck it in his mouth. More and more, and deeper and deeper, and all at once he screamed as loud as he could into the towel. Again, and again, and yet again. He tried to lift his thumb from his forehead and the skin from his forehead came with it. He could see raw flesh. Amar was sweating and couldn't stand up anymore. He had lost all his strength. He sat down on the edge of the bathtub and tried again to think of Xama. He saw her – she was lying there, motionless.

"Xama, I'm back! I'm with you again!

I will help you – I believe I can conquer my father's manipulation. I'm not sure, but I've tried everything, and I've fought it.

You have to fight too, Xama – hold on; I'll save you."

Amar left the bathroom and saw his father packing up different things.

"What's all this?" Amar asked.

"Pack your things. We have to disappear, immediately."

"Where is Sanders?" Amar asked.

"He's taking care of our guests, and then we'll meet him downstairs in the car in 10 minutes."

Amar picked up the chest with the injector and ran to the door, then opened it and jumped out into the hallway.

He saw Sanders disappearing into a room at one end of the hall. Amar ran after him as quick as he could in his condition – quicker and quicker. He had to stop him, before he …

Where he crossed another hallway, he saw Kanaar and Arun coming towards him. "Nice to see you, Arun. Now, you come with me – we'll handle these Sanders; that pig wants to kill Xama. If you're looking for Sherman, you'll find him at the end of this hallway in the suite. But I don't think he'll wait on her. You should catch him before he disappears with the Arverni gene."

Arun followed Amar, and both of them ran to the door through which Sanders had disappeared. Before Amar could talk through a plan with Arun, Arun kicked in the door and stormed into the room. Sanders were standing in front of a chair, and he saw Arun flying at him. He tried to reach out his hands to protect himself, but Arun was quicker. He grabbed Sanders around the neck with both hands. A flash lit up the room, and Arun and Sanders both fell to the floor. They both lay there, motionless. Arun moved, and then stood up again, slowly. Sanders were unconscious. Kayl was sitting in the chair. He looked horribly mauled, and he was gagged. Arun removed the gag, and Kayl started talking immediately.

"Thanks, little brother, what was that? Not bad how you did that – K.O. on the first punch, eh?"

"I'll tell you another time. Are you okay?"

Kayl lifted his head and moved it from left to right. Arun could clearly hear the vertebrae clicking back into place.

"That asshole broke my nose, not to mention my arm and a couple of ribs. But otherwise, as far as I can tell everything's alright."

"To be honest, it doesn't look that way. You look pretty messed up. Your nose is totally bent. How could you let him beat you up like that?"

"Let me go; I'm ready to take revenge on that punk."

Arun cut the ties and reminded Kayl of Achillean policy – "if somebody's lying on the floor, or if they give up, you can't keep fighting them."

"Okay, then I'll wait until the asshole wakes up to give him a couple more licks."

"We don't have time for that. We have to save Xama.

Do you know where they hid Xama?" Amar asked.

"She must be here on the same floor; I heard the ass say something to a woman outside the door. Why don't you yell for her?" In the moment Amar stepped back out of the room into the hallway, he saw four more council members coming out of the elevator. The Meta was in front, supported by two other members.

"There they are," Arun yelled, "Kanaar did sound the alarm!"

The Meta was breathing heavily. You could see he was gravely ill.

"We need to find room 1073 – that's where Xama is. She is dying, and we must save her."

Amar looked at the Meta, surprised.

"She called you, not Kanaar, am I right?"

They all nodded and went towards the room.

"She is something special, Amar. You kept that from us. Xama Dupre is an Identidem. And not only that – she is able to further develop abilities she learns. That's something which has never yet happened before in the history of the Arverni."

"Yes, Meta, you're right, but I had a good reason to keep it quiet."

"I know; you wanted to protect her."

When they had arrived at room number 1073, Amar tried to open the door, but it was locked. Amar called my name loudly.

"Xama? Xama? Are you in there?"

It was all taking too long for Arun. He signaled for everyone to clear the doorway and get out to the side. Then he started running. With a skillful kick, he hit the door and it splintered at the lock. Another kick and the door was open. Arun went in first and saw me lying tied to the bed.

Amar and Arun bent over me. Amar felt my pulse, and Arun removed my blindfold. Something stung my eyes – it was the bright light of day. I heard a voice calling my name, and I knew the voice. In a flash, everything was knocked out of focus again, as if someone had turned the lens on a camera hard to the side as far as it would go. The voices, still calling my name, faded away and seemed to recede. I wanted to say something else, but my body was no longer reacting to my mind. My eyelids became so heavy I could no longer hold them open.

Tired. I'm so tired. Everyone just leave me alone. When I wake up, everything will be over. It will all be over. Just let me sleep. Darkness spread, and I could feel the last bit of strength slowly leaving my body. It seemed as though all of my life energy – everything I had left – was spreading out over the bed and into the room. Even my thoughts began to fade away, and a feeling of inner calmness came over me. No more pain, nothing to hold me back from simply falling asleep and resting, forevermore. Everything seemed so light and so easy.

The Meta was the first one to recognize what was happening, and he called to all of them to build a ring. They pushed the bed into the middle of the room and arranged themselves around it. Kayl joined in, despite his broken ribs and all his pain, closing the circle. The Meta began to sing, and they all sang with him.

"Communitati - vis - nostrum
 communitati - vis - nostrum
 communitati - vis - nostrum"

The singing became more intense, and the Meta guided the energy of the ring into the middle of the bed – directly into me. The voices faded into the background, and I felt how they gave me new energy, shaking off the exhaustion, which covered me like a heavy blanket.

Xama, wake up, you cannot go to sleep!"

Someone was speaking directly to me – I could still hear the monotone singing in the background. The voice speaking to me was clear and vibrant and breathed new energy into every cell in my body. I knew the voice.

"Wake up, Xama."

I cannot go to sleep now, **do not** go to sleep, Xama!
The fingers of my right hand slipped over the linen sheet, slowly balling up into a fist. My way of steeling myself against exhaustion.
Would the pain come back?

Again, I strained to lift my arm. All of a sudden, it began to move upwards without the resistance I had expected. A warm, soothing feeling was radiating through my whole body, a feeling of new energy – life energy.

This thought made it impossible for me to stay still, so I moved my left arm. Then both legs at almost the same time. With a barely visible smile, I confirmed the results. I was free – no longer in chains!

The voices became clear and distinct. I opened my eyes again and was startled once again. A large number of faces were looking at me, singing:

»Communitati – vis – nostrum«

As they sang, they moved in a circle, turning around me. They covered parts of their faces with their hands, and I realized that each man had his left arm around the next man's back, linking their circle together. But there was something else. Each man was pressing his right thumb into the middle of the forehead of the man standing to his right – they had built an Arverni ring.

Am I safe now?

Once again, a deep male voice interrupted my racing thoughts.

"Xama, close your eyes."

It was kind of like a command, but it felt more like a protective reflex – so I wouldn't have to see what happened next. Memories from my childhood came into my mind.

Back then, I had also always kept my eyes closed when I felt afraid, with the belief that if I couldn't see anyone else, it also meant they couldn't see me. Why couldn't it just be that easy now? Please, just let it happen.

Fractions of a second, which lasted an eternity. My right arm suddenly felt as though it had fallen asleep and the numbness was just beginning to dissipate. As though it wasn't part of my body anymore. A tingling sensation in my fingers, creeping towards my elbows, confirmed my arm had fallen asleep. Hadn't I just moved it a couple of seconds ago, balling my fingers into a fist?

Silence. Where have the voices gone?

Feeling both curious and anxious, I slowly and carefully opened my eyes and saw known and unknown faces. They were all holding on to each other's shoulders and turning in a circle.

Now I recognized Amar, and Arun, and there was Kayl too – it looked like he had been in another fight. Arun smiled at me and held my hand.

"Man, am I glad you opened your eyes again. I thought I had lost you."

The ring stood still, and one of the elders foundered. He caught himself again, and kneeled down in front of my bed. He held his hand out to me, and I placed my hand in his. He pressed it, kissed it, and whispered something to me.

"I am glad you're doing better again, Xama. You will become fully healed. Your time is beginning, and my time is ending. I am happy to have gotten to know you, Xama Dupre."

The older man stood up and went out of the room, followed by four others.

"Was that the Meta?" I asked Arun, who was looking at me happily.

"Yes, that was the Meta, and it was with his help that we were able to save your life."

"The Meta visited my sick bed, and I didn't even recognize him. What's wrong with me?"

"You all stay here and watch out; I have to go back to the suite for a minute. There's something I have to take care of, something very personal. Let's call it a family matter," Amar said.

Amar disappeared into the hallway and ran along it. When he got to the suite, the door was standing wide open. He walked in and saw Kanaar lying on the floor and bleeding from a laceration on his head. He felt his pulse and was reassured – Kanaar was only unconscious.

Amar looked all through the room, but as he expected, his father had already disappeared. Simply vanished. He must have taken the chest with the injector along with him, since it wasn't there anymore either. Amar ran back into the room where Sanders was tied up, but he had vanished as well. Both of them had disappeared into thin air. Not even surprised by this, Amar went back to the others and told them Sherman and Sanders had vanished.

I remembered that the nurse who took my blood had stored it in a refrigerator in the kitchen.

Arun checked, but the refrigerator was empty.

We all knew what that meant, but no one said it out loud. Thanks to the Meta's and the council's help, I was feeling much better, so I put on my clothes, hugged Amar, and thanked Arun with an intense kiss – to be honest with you, it tasted insanely chocolate, and much more too.

"Just as I thought – I'm going away empty handed again," Kayl called out in his macho tone.

I hugged Kayl and grabbed his broken arm with both hands. It only took seconds until we both felt the bones growing back together. I slowly let go of his arm and asked him if he could lift up his T-shirt for me.

Kayl laughed. "But of course – if you have a little time, I could unbutton my pants too."

I would have liked to slap him for that, but I was getting used to him, after all. I placed both hands on the back of his ribcage, slowly moving them forwards. I have no idea why I moved from back to front, but in any case it worked, and his ribs were just like new again in seconds.

"Anybody else have a boo?"

Amar and Arun both spoke up at the same time, then they both laughed.

In the same moment, Kanaar appeared in the doorway. He was still bleeding from his forehead, and seemed to have suffered greatly from the blow, since he was still wobbling.

"Sherman, that pig, he knocked me down and ran off. We will follow him, if need be, to the end of the world. This time, we're going to turn his little game around. He's not going to be chasing Arverni; no, we'll be chasing him."

I stood up and waved to Kanaar, telling him to bend down.

Kanaar bent over a little, and I placed my hands on his head wound.

"That should help! Let's go now; I always knew the Mandarin wouldn't be able to hold a candle to the Aphobia."

Everyone laughed, and followed me back home – to the Aphobia.

A SPECIAL COUNCIL MEETING

The next day I felt unbelievably weak. It seemed as if the torture Dr. Sherman had subjected me to wasn't quite as easy to get over as I'd thought. A look at my planet-themed alarm clock told me it was already 11 o'clock. Was that possible? Had I slept so long? What was strange was that I still felt tired. I picked up my iPhone and had to squint several times to be able to read my text messages clearly. Searching for one message in particular, my eyes scanned through my inbox. There it was. When I read the text message, it brought a smile to my face:

"GM Xama, I hope you've slept well and recovered a little bit. I was thinking about you all night long, and I'm just happy every-thing turned out well. I love you, Xama, I miss you – Arun."

I read the message a second time, then a third, and typed in a short answer.

"I miss you too. Why don't you just come by? You know where to find me. Xama."

I was still standing in the bathroom, brushing my teeth, when someone knocked on the door. I hastily dried off my face and ran down the long hallway, then opened the door and practically jumped at Arun. His powerful arms caught me, but he had to take a step backwards to keep his balance. I could see Arun was sur-prised.

"Good morning, Xama."

"Good morning, Arun, I missed you too!"

His eyes beamed at me, and even before our lips could touch, I whispered to him:

"I believe I've fallen in love with you."

Arun didn't answer; he just walked forward slowly, carrying me over the hearth and into the sunroom. He placed me down gently on the sofa and lay on top of me.

"Well, if you just 'believe' it then I'll have to work a little harder, to make sure you know it."

We kissed deeply, and it was wonderful to feel his body. Then the doorbell rang, and we both looked at each other, thinking the same thing. Arun wanted to open it, but I pulled him back down towards me. But the ringing didn't stop. The visitor didn't give up and kept on ringing the bell. Suddenly, my iPhone started to ring as well, and we both realized it was probably something important. Arun sat on the sofa, and I opened the door, after recognizing Amar through the peephole.

Amar walked right in and noticed Arun on the sofa. "Sorry if I disturbed you too, but I just got a call from the Meta. He wants us all to meet at 1 o'clock in the big hall for a real council meeting." Amar walked around nervously, went into the kitchen, and then came back out with a glass of water.

"Something's wrong with you – why are you so tense? Is it because of the council?"

Amar took another swallow and sat down on the sofa across from Arun.

"The Meta is dying. He has been sick for a very long time, and the events yesterday took the rest of his life energy from him."

Arun jumped up, disgusted. "That can't be true – not the Meta, not after we succeeded. What's going to happen?"

"That is why the Meta asked me to call the council together, and he wants us to be there as well."

"Why?"

"The first topic he wants to talk about is the danger posed by Dr. Sherman. He has not followed our laws, and he must be judged. The second point on the agenda, to which we are not invited, is that he is going to name his successor."

I knew that this weighed heavily on Amar. He had built up a special relationship with the Meta, and it made him sad to know he would not be with us very much longer.

"It makes you sad that the Meta is dying – am I right?"

"Yes – he was someone who gave me a lot of support, for many years. But I always knew this moment would come. Nevertheless, it still makes me deeply sad."

I sat on the sofa as well beside Arun, who placed his arm around me.

"What does it mean if we're all invited to the council?" Arun asked.

"I'm not sure – the Meta probably wants to make a decision about how to proceed. Xama is still in danger, and my father – umm, Sherman – is a criminal who must be caught and sentenced."

"Do we need to do anything to prepare?"

"You don't, but the Meta asked me to get you to bring the rose of Akar along with you. So don't forget it. The two of you still have a little time; I'll pick you up along with Kayl shortly before one o'clock, and then we'll all go together."

Amar stood up, went to the door without turning around, and disappeared just as quickly as he had come in.

Arun looked at me in surprise.

"That was Kay-Ky, don't you think?" I asked Arun.

"Very Kay-Ky. I think he wanted to say something else to you, but couldn't say it because I'm here."

"Do you really think so?"

"At least that would be an explanation for his strange behavior."

"Then there's nothing I can do about it. I'm curious to know what the Meta has to say to us in the council meeting. Did I understand Amar correctly? He is dying because he saved me yesterday?"

Arun tried to make the facts sound a little better than they were to free me of my rapidly worsening conscience. Maybe there was some way I could help him? Maybe I could heal him? The situation had wiped away all thoughts of cuddling with Arun.

"I'll go take a shower and get dressed; if you want, you can wait for me."

"Too bad, I thought maybe I could join you for a shower?"

"That might be a little too fast – how long have we known each other?"

"Kay-Ky, oh well, another time. It was worth a try."

"It was a nice try. And anyway, Kay-Ky is my expression."

"But I like it – it will be both of our expressions now. I'll go tell Kayl and get ready too. Be right back."

Arun hugged me again, kissed me, and asked me earnestly why I couldn't invite him to take a shower. But before I could get together the words for an answer, he was already at the door, blowing me an air kiss, and then he disappeared.

In my mind I asked myself what would happen during the council meeting. I walked into the bedroom and looked for something to wear. It needed to live up to the occasion of a council meeting, but still needed to follow tradition. I found lots of dresses in the closet, and all in my size. There were jeans there as well, but what was the right thing for this situation? On one side I saw a dress that was black and looked very elegant. It wasn't too flashy, but it did show off my curves – maybe a little too much?

I picked up the dress confidently. I wanted to show this council that Xama Dupre had a personality. When I left the shower, I heard my iPhone ringing. Clothed only in a towel, I went into the living room and picked up the telephone, assuming it was Amar or Arun. The words "unknown number" appeared on the display, and when I hesitated for a moment, they disappeared, and my phone fell silent.

Who could that have been?
This thought was still running through my mind when the phone rang again. This time, I picked up the call.
"Hello?"
"Hello, Xama! I just wanted to ask how you're doing."
The voice immediately created a queasy feeling in my stomach, and I suddenly felt much worse.
For a brief moment, I considered whether I should just hang up again, but decided not to make things quite so easy for Dr. Sherman.
"I'm doing very well now, although if it were up to you I probably wouldn't still be alive."
"Dear Xama – who said anything about that? I have taken very precise care of you for the last few days. That was what was important to me – making sure you stayed alive. You remember, of course, that you are the only aspirant; that's what makes you so interesting to me."
"Why are you calling me?"
"First, I really did want to know how you are doing. I am astounded at how quickly you regenerated. That, dear Xama, was what kept you alive and allowed me access to enough blood for quite some time. I was surprised how quickly you compensated for your loss of blood. You are a phenomenon – or perhaps I should say – an Identidem. You know what an Identidem is, don't you? You certainly didn't inherit this characteristic from your father."
"What do you know about my mother?"
"I know quite a bit, Xama, I knew her very well – likely better than most in the community."
"You're just trying to entice me. I don't believe it."
"Your mother, Xama, was an Identidem like you. She was enormously strong, and she could learn abilities like you can. She

lived with this secret, alone and withdrawn – until she met your father. He noticed, of course, that she had multiple abilities and that she was a very special Arverni woman. Your father made one big mistake, however, in telling the secret to a council member in order to get advice. That was your mother's death sentence. The council decided that your mother represented a danger to the Arverni, and that she had to die. Your father tried everything to save her, but he was helpless. That's why he left the community and hid your mother. When she became pregnant with you, flight wasn't quite so easy anymore, and the Arverni used the delivery to get information about where your mother was staying. You know the rest of the story."

With tears in my eyes, I tried to repress everything he was saying.

"That's a lie. It's not true that the Arverni killed her. She died during my birth. She lost too much blood. It's a lie."

"Just think about it, Xama, she died because she lost too much blood – that's true. But like you, she possessed the power of healing. Your mother's powers were significantly more developed than your own, so do you really believe she wasn't able to heal herself? Do you want to know what happened? Just search; you'll find the answer.

If you recall, I promised you that you and Kayl could go if you followed my instructions – and didn't it happen as I said it would? No matter – you draw your own conclusions about the Arverni. They are a pack of liars who repress their wives and won't stop at anything. Your mother isn't the first woman who was killed only because she became too powerful. And you, a strong woman, want to join this club? I would think it over carefully if I were you – you are putting yourself in mortal danger. Let me know what you decide. As you know, you're welcome to join me at any time. The two of us could achieve great things together."

Sherman hung up and I let my telephone fall to the ground, breaking down in tears.

Was it really possible that the community killed my mother? If that was true, I would find out who it was that murdered my mother, and he would receive the punishment he deserved for it.

Arun knocked on the door and I wondered whether I should let him see me like this. And why not? I couldn't always be in a good mood, after all. I opened the door, bawling, to see Arun standing in front of me with a bouquet of roses, shocked to see me so exhausted and teary. He hadn't expected this, and he totally forgot he wanted to hand the flowers over to me.

"Xama, what happened?"

Still crying, I told him the story while I was getting a vase and some fresh water for the beautiful roses.

"I can't believe it, Xama, that can't be true – it's got to be a lie. The community doesn't do things like that, does it? Sherman is just trying to influence you."

"Whatever the truth is, I'm going to figure it out. I will find a way to bring the truth to light. Excuse me for a second; I'm going to finish getting dressed. I'll be right back." Back in the bathroom, I couldn't help but think about my mother. It made me very sad to think I had never gotten to know her. Tears fell from my eyes once again and collected in the sink.

I have to put an end to all these chaotic feelings. Otherwise I'll never be ready to find out the truth.

Following my own advice, I stared into the mirror until it started to tingle. This time it was more than just something I wanted to do; it was something I needed to do to take the next steps. My thumb landed in the middle of my aphmal, and a chill ran through my whole body, alternating cold and warm. It became stronger and stronger, but I kept pressing my thumb against my forehead and didn't let up, even though everything inside me told me I had had enough.

Keep going, Xama, just a little more. You need all your strength.

The color of my eyes changed, alternating between blue, green, and brown, but I kept pressing my thumb against my forehead, pressing and pressing, until a powerful beam of light suddenly came out of my forehead underneath my thumb and swept through the room. Everything around me was knocked down all at once. The noise alarmed Arun, who was standing at the door and asking me whether everything was all right. I opened the door and stood before him in my black dress.

"Everything's alright now. I'm ready to make sure the truth comes to light."

Arun stood before me dumbly.

"How do I look in my little black dress?" I asked him, teasing.

"Xama – you look simply Kay-Ky amazing."

The doorbell rang again at that moment.

"Probably Amar and Kayl. Open the door for them, so I can put on some makeup."

As I left the bathroom and showed myself to everyone, I could see and hear that my choice of outfit had been the right decision.

"You're always good for a surprise, Xama. Do you have the rose of Akar with you? The Meta asked for it specifically; it's important."

I went back to my bedroom and got the rose of Akar. Then I remembered that there was a sealed book in father's legacy for the Meta. I opened the aphmal box and looked for the little book. There it was, locked; it wasn't going to give up its secrets. I picked it up and could hear Amar yelling: "We have to go now – otherwise we'll be late!" Not a minute later, we were all on the way to the council chambers. I noticed that Kayl and Arun had also dressed well for the occasion. Amar was the only one wearing normal khakis and a sweater, which I was surprised to see. On the way to the chamber, Amar explained the rules to us for the meeting. Only the one who has the whistle can speak, and the Meta can remove someone's right to speak or grant that right. These rules were very simple. Arun asked me whether I was as Kay-Ky nervous as he was. It was my second council meeting, after the apheid. Now I could tell what a miracle the aphmalisation had worked on me. I didn't feel even a touch of nervousness, even when our group entered the large meeting chamber, which looked totally different from what I had imagined.

Everything looked old fashioned yet intriguing. All of the tables were set up in a big circle. When I looked closer, I could tell that the tables were also rounded to reinforce the effect. But the tables weren't connected to each other so that there were openings through which you could step into the middle of the circle, similar to the four cardinal directions. Now I could also see that the tables at the upper end were significantly larger and taller and stuck out above the others. The seats across from it were the smallest ones, and lower than the ones to the right and left. There was clearly some kind of hierarchy here. Amar accompanied us to our seats and, as expected, we sat at the shortest table, looking at the large raised table at the end of the circle. The first council members were entering the chamber and sitting at their seats. At first there were five members there, and I asked myself whether all the rest were coming. Arun poked me in the ribs and told me happily that Kanaar was coming in. He is the chief of security, and supposedly he helped activate the council and save me.

So that was Kanaar – was he the one who murdered my mother?

He sat down at one of the bigger tables on the edges. I placed the book and the rose of Akar in front of me on the table, and tried to control the feelings that rose up within me like lava inside a volcano as soon as I saw Kanaar. I watched what was happening to divert myself. What I noticed was that every time I even touched the rose of Akar, it started to light up.

Arun whispered to me: "The directorate is coming, and then the Meta will come in last." I saw three older men come into the chamber and all sit down at the big tables. The Meta was last. At my apheid, I had already noticed how frail he was, but this time I could clearly see he was not doing well at all. He moved very slowly and had to support himself now and again on a cane. When he tried to climb the steps to the raised podium, he had to stop and swayed for a moment. He wasn't going to be able to do it without help. The two directors helped him to his seat in the middle of the table. The Meta stood there, and we could see he was shaking. All of the seats were filled. Amar, who was sitting to the left of the directorate, showed me thumbs up. Whatever he meant by that, I was glad to see it.

The Meta blew into a small whistle, getting the full attention of the room.

"Dear colleagues, honored guests. I hereby open today's council meeting. To take the wind out of all the rumors floating around, I will begin today's meeting with an announcement." The Meta paused, not to give his words more import, but because his strength was fading, and speaking made him tired. I kept having the impression that he was looking at me, directly at me. Was he watching me? Was it just my imagination, or was there more there? The Meta cleared his throat, and everyone fell silent.

"This will be my final council meeting. This means I will relinquish the position of Meta at the end of this meeting, and we will choose a new Meta. As the law prescribes, this person will then have 24 hours to either accept or reject the position."

A murmur went through the room, and I could see that some of the members were surprised at the Meta's announcement. Especially in the conservative section, sitting to the right of the directorate, the voices and whispers were getting louder. I could hear names from different individual tables. The name called out most often and most loudly made me feel nauseous. Kanaar seemed to be the clear favorite of the conservative section of the Arverni. In comparison to the right side, the left side was fairly reserved. I heard various names I didn't recognize. I even though I heard Amar's name, but there was no clear favorite on the left side. The Meta cleared his throat again, louder, thereby giving the signal to stop the discussions, which functioned astonishingly well. He took another pause to catch his breath, drank a swallow of the water they had set out for him, and concentrated again.

"Thus, we come to the first point on the agenda. Would you, Amar, do me the favor of introducing it for us? I must save my strength for later."

One of the directorates took the whistle lying in front of the Meta and carried it over to Amar, setting it down before him. Amar picked up the whistle and blew into it, then placed it back down in front of himself and started to present the first agenda point.

"The council members are requested to denounce the crime Dr. Agor Sherman has committed against Xama Dupre, one of our members, in accordance with our laws."

Amar read on, explaining the incident, although there was some very important information left out, and in my opinion the whole thing seemed like a very superficial summary. That certainly seemed unfair to me – I was a part of what had happened, although the person who had assembled all the facts obviously was not.

The Meta gave a hand signal, and it seemed as if everyone else in the room but me knew what it meant. Someone carried the whistle back over to the Meta and he blew into it, which I could see required some effort.

"As you have all learned, we have invited guests to bring the truth about this matter to light. Thy will help us to understand the crime Dr. Agor Sherman committed, and to issue a just punishment. May I ask you, Xama Dupre, to answer our questions?"

I felt Arun grab my hand under the table and press it in order to give me some courage. What he couldn't know was that I already had more than enough of it because of my crazy aphmalisation. I stood up, since I believed this would underscore my answer, and said loudly and clearly: "Yes, I will help you to find out the truth." Everyone looked at me disgustedly as I spoke. I recognized immediately that I must have done something wrong; some members were wrinkling up their faces, including Amar, who signaled me with his pointer finger not to talk anymore. Arun, who recognized the violation immediately, whispered to me: "You can only speak when you've got the whistle."

So that was it; I forgot the whistle – Oh well, that happens.

Expecting someone to place the whistle in front of me, I was surprised to see it move back to Amar. He blew into it, left his chair, and placed the whistle in front of me on my table. Everyone looked at me, and I noticed that the Meta was looking at me in a somehow peculiar way. Unsure whether I should say anything, I waited. Amar explained to me that he had a list of questions to which the Arverni would like to have answers. He was going to read them aloud, one after the other, and I was requested to give a brief, concise answer to them.

So far everything was Kay-Ky – except I wasn't so sure what he meant by concise?

Amar started to ask, and I waited patiently until he was done, then took some time to think, and answered as concisely as I could. After more than 20 questions, the interview was finished, and Amar took the whistle from our table and carried it back to the Meta. The first hand signals appeared, and Amar carried the whistle to each of the members in the order they had signaled. More questions were asked, and I was unsure whether I should say anything in response, since I didn't have the whistle sitting in front of me anymore. I hesitantly signaled Amar that I had an answer, and he placed the whistle in front of me. I blew into it, and thought to myself that although this process did create a very disciplined conversation, it was a little bit laborious. I gave all the answers I had, again, and the whistle went back to the Meta.

"Honored council members – as you have just heard, Dr. Agor Sherman is guilty. Guilty of stealing aspirant blood in huge amounts, which is forbidden by our laws. For this reason, we are obligated to judge him and to pronounce an appropriate punishment." The Meta wasn't finished yet, but Amar's hand shot up. The Meta nodded, and Amar grabbed the whistle and placed it back down on is table. "I know that my statement cannot be accepted because of the manipulation I was subjected to. But I believe I remember that Dr. Sherman took more than just a small amount of blood from Xama Dupre. As I remember, he took enough blood to extract the gene for a whole army. The refrigerators he had ready were all full of reserve blood before he and Sanders disappeared; I remember that."

The volume level in the hall increased again, and even Arun was surprised, quietly asking, "How is that supposed to work? You would have bled out if he'd taken all your blood, wouldn't you?"

All at once I could darkly remember the nurse handing multiple bags of blood to Dr. Sherman – there seemed to be more and more of them – but how could that be?

Amar had given the whistle to another member in the meantime. He asked the exact same question.

"How could it be that such a large amount of blood was extracted without killing Xama Dupre? As long as this question remains unanswered, we cannot judge Sherman according to the amount removed. The law is the law."

The Meta raised his hand, and Amar carried the whistle back to him. As always in these situations, it was the role of the Meta to find a solution, and he had a plan.

"Only one member knows the answer. Only Xama Dupre can tell us what really happened, and whether Amar's hypothesis is correct – whether Dr. Agor Sherman must be sentenced to death or not."

Then I started to feel a little uncomfortable. I didn't really know what was happening the whole time – I was out of it mostly, after all. The Meta looked at me again, seemed somehow strict and penetrating – Things started to seem more and more uncanny to me.

"There is only one way to learn the truth!"

The Meta stood up and walked slowly down the stairs, carefully supporting himself on his cane. Slowly but purposefully, he moved into the center of the circle, visibly swaying. Everyone could feel how afraid the room was that he would no longer be able to stay on his feet and would fall. But the Meta fought onward to reach my table, then paused there and breathed in and out heavily.

"The answer, dear Xama, lies in your subconscious. Since you yourself were not conscious, you cannot tell us what you did experience, consciously experienced. Everything else is hidden in your subconscious. The truth about what really happened, and about how much blood Dr. Agor Sherman took from you, is hidden there. I can make this information available using hypnosis, but only if you allow it and agree to the hypnosis, opening up your subconscious." Astounded at his statement, I looked into the Meta's eyes. They weren't clear, and I could tell his life energy was fading. Since I wasn't sure whether I was allowed to speak then or not, I just nodded to him.

He placed the whistle in front of me on the table and asked me to state my agreement or disagreement to undergo hypnosis before the council. I took the whistle and blew into it.

"Honored members of the council – if it will serve the truth, and I believe it will in this case, I am ready to support discovery of the truth through hypnosis."

Was this really I? Did I just say that? Without even thinking it over? What is happening to me – I hardly know myself.

The Meta thanked me and asked me to stand up, so I followed his command. I noticed that he was only a little taller than me. He asked me to bring my chair with me and place it in the middle of the circle. As I followed his instructions, he grabbed both of my arms. I heard his heavy breathing. Unsure whether he was directing me or holding himself up, I didn't move. He looked directly into my eyes and said a sentence.

"Xama, everything I ask you now will be answered by your subconscious. You will allow me access to your innermost self, and you will answer all of my questions honestly. You will follow and execute the instructions and commands I give to you. Do you understand?"

I nodded.

"Please sit down on your chair."

I followed his instructions, but felt as though I were floating. It was difficult to describe – I was present, but somehow standing outside of myself, watching myself.

The Meta began to ask me questions, supporting himself on his cane and beginning to tremble again.

"What happened after he took blood from you? Tell us very specifically what you experienced, and what happened."

I didn't even have to think, and answered as though the answer was already prepared for me.

"The nurse waited until there was half a liter of blood in the left bag and half a liter in the right bag. She kept checking my blood pressure, which dipped all of a sudden. She told Dr. Sherman about it, who came in immediately and held a mirror in front of my face. I saw my aphmal and I could feel him putting my thumb on my aphmal against my will – but I was too weak and couldn't resist it. First, I noticed the tingling, and then I felt better. My blood pressure normalized in a few minutes, and I could think clearly again. Everything was different again, normal again. I could see normally, but felt a burning in my arm and was conscious again."

It was like I was far away; only aware in a muffled way that the room was growing louder, and the members were talking amongst one another. I heard the expression "forced aphmalisation" multiple times.

The Meta cleared his throat, and it became silent again; the side conversations stopped.

"Please tell us exactly what happened next. Especially how long you rested until they took more blood from you."

"Dr. Sherman told the nurse to take more blood, but she explained to him that it would kill me. Sherman explained to her that it wasn't true, and that I had already compensated for the lost blood.

The nurse told Sherman that that would take days.

Then Sherman screamed at her: 'do you want me to take your blood? Right here and right now? Do you want to see how long it takes you to bleed out?'"

The Meta interrupted my story.

"Just a moment, Xama, this is very important. Sherman told the nurse you were already compensating for the loss of blood – is that correct?"

"Yes, he did say that to the nurse; he had found out I had the power to heal myself and other people. He used it, and the aphmalisation meant I healed myself. Sherman was right, I had already made up for the lost blood."

It became louder in the room once again, but the Meta didn't let the conversations develop. He cleared his throat more loudly.

"So, you are able to heal others?"

"Yes, I am."

"A very rare ability, which only few Arverni possess. And you are also able to heal yourself, is that correct?"

"Yes, that's correct!"

"Continue, please. What happened next, after Sherman told the nurse to take more blood from you?"

"She cried and trembled and whispered to me that she was sorry, and then she reopened the valves. Not all the way, just a little. I think she wanted to see what would happen to my blood pressure. But Sherman noticed it and manipulated her, and then when he told her to she opened up both the valves all the way. I could see my blood flowing into the two bags again, filling them, and both of my arms started to burn inside."

"Xama, how long did it take for the bags to fill up, roughly?"

"About 30 minutes."

"So, 30 minutes for a liter of blood. How long were you captured?"

"No idea."

"Let me help you – it was more than 20 hours until we freed you. If we assume that Sherman took blood for the whole 20 hours, then he has more than 20 liters of blood, or 40 bags. This supports Amar's hypothesis. Sherman is now able to extract enough of the gene to provide himself and his followers with it for quite a long time." The Meta paused again and supported himself on his cane.

"I still have one more question, Xama. Do you have any other abilities, or is healing the only one?"

As expected, his question created a large number of questions and a tumult in the room. The Meta put a stop to it immediately with a loud "I asked Xama Dupre!"

"Yes, I have other abilities."

"Please tell us which other abilities you possess and how you discovered them."

The Meta walked around me, slowly and looked directly at each council member.

"It started with dream communication. I believe I learned it from Amar. I'm not completely sure, but after he showed me how it worked and invited me into a dream, I could do it too all of a sudden. Then I discovered my ability to heal other people – I just discovered that one by accident really. Arun had hurt himself, and I healed him. And then it worked on me, too, when I hurt myself, and the wound was healed again in just a few minutes. Then I discovered I could taste feelings like truth, lies, affection, happiness, and fear. I don't know how it happens, but if someone in my direct surroundings is having one of those feelings, I can taste it. And finally I copied Arun's ability – or learned it, I guess."

As I finished, curses began to fly from all corners of the room. Some members didn't believe me and cursed me directly. I heard statements like: "She's lying," and "That's impossible." The Meta had to speak up to regain order in the room. I heard someone behind me yell: "She is an Identidem – she has to go! She is a danger to us!" These words reminded me of Mom again, and a feeling of helplessness and rage spread over me. I could feel my aphmalisation wearing off, and feel myself becoming weaker again.

The Meta asked for silence once again, and everyone followed his command. "You mentioned that you could taste the truth and that you copied Arun's ability. Tell me how you did that."

"I don't exactly know how myself – I asked Arun to try his power out on me. Arun can switch people off – that's what he calls it – and I asked him to do it to me. That was it."

"So, Arun switched you off, and from then on you could do the same thing?"

"Well, Arun's attempt to switch me off didn't really work right. He was probably being too careful since he is an Achillean and is supposed to protect me, not harm me. Whatever the case, nothing happened. He supposedly tried out his ability on me, but it didn't have any effect. Then Kayl told me to try out Arun's ability on him. He was bothering me and making fun of his brother and me. So all I did was wish to switch him off, and then I just did it."

"But Kayl could feel it, unlike you?"

"Well, I don't know exactly what he felt – he was immediately unconscious, collapsed, and was just lying there not moving anymore. We were all shocked, and Arun checked his pulse right away and said he was okay. All I had done was switch him off."

"Quiet, please" the Meta interjected again in order to stem the conversations in the room.

"Do you know the term Identidem?" the Meta asked me.

"Yes, I believe this term describes when a person has multiple abilities, but I'm not totally sure."

"That's right," the Meta, answered, "It also describes something more, but we'll get to that in a moment."

The Meta took my hand and pulled me up; I could feel how poorly he was doing. I had the feeling I had to help him, and tried to heal his condition. I could feel the energy flowing out of me and into him. As I stood next to him, I heard him whisper.

"Thank you, Xama, but you should reserve your strength for others. My condition can no longer be healed."

He took a step back.

"Xama Dupre, thank you for the truth. You may sit back down at your place."

The Meta went back to his seat slowly, rejecting all offers of assistance. Everything around me became real again, and I could see and hear everything clearly and distinctly. I went back to my chair, sat down, and all of a sudden felt like everyone in the room was staring at me. The feeling wasn't an illusion.

"I've forgotten something else, Xama; would you please bring me the rose of Akar I saw on your table?"

I stood up, somewhat unsure, carefully picked up the rose, and held it in my hand, covering it with the other hand so no one could see it was already starting to glow. After I had taken a few steps towards the Meta, the rose began to glow more brightly, and they could see the light through my hands. I came to the Meta, gave him the rose, and he spoke to me again.

"This is a very beautiful specimen. In contrast to the many replicas there are, this is a genuine rose, and there are only three of those in the world. You should count yourself as more than lucky to own a real rose of Akar."

I looked at Arun right away, and saw him shrug his shoulders and smile at me.

So he knew that this …

The Meta interrupted the thought with another instruction, spoken like an order.

"Please open your hands and hold them so that your palms are flat and facing upwards. I would like to place the rose of Akar in your hands."

I followed his instructions and thought he wanted to show everyone that the rose would glow. Slowly and carefully, he placed the rose in the middle of my two open hands, and in the moment the rose touched both of them, it glowed again. But there was something else.

The rose glowed, and began to open the petals of its blossom. Just like a real rose being struck by the light of day, this glass rose opened its petals, revealing the interior. All at once, it emitted a beam of light, like a flash of lightning, sweeping through the room and looking for somewhere to discharge itself. The beam of light changed directions and came straight at me. Like a punch in the face, the bolt entered directly through my aphmal. Hit by pure energy, I remained standing and heard some of the council members yelling at me: "The eye!" "She has the eye!" I wanted to move, but I suddenly saw strange images. The whole room had changed, somehow. The roles were reversed. I saw myself as the Meta, which was completely Kay-Ky. I tried to repress the images, concentrating. Was it coincidence, or an ability? The beam of light suddenly disappeared, and the rose closed its petals, concealing the interior. I heard the Meta asking me:

"What did you see?"

Unclear about what he meant, I stood there. He repeated the question.

"Just tell us what you saw."

It was unbelievably quiet; everyone was tensely awaiting my answer. I briefly considered the best way to formulate my answer, and just said:

"I saw myself."

The Meta wasn't satisfied with this.

"What exactly did you see?"

"There, where you're standing now, I saw myself in your place."

"You saw yourself in my place?"

Despite the side conversations going on in the room, I answered confidently.

"Yes, I saw myself in your place."

The Meta had achieved what he had wanted to achieve with this demonstration. The volume of the conversations in the room seemed to be getting out of control; all the members were talking about the eye. Suddenly, a loud whistle interrupted the discussions, and the room fell silent.

"What you have seen, dear Xama, was the future. The rose of Akar has connected with a very special ability you possess. We call this ability 'the eye.' As we have all just seen, you caused the rose to blossom and looked into the future. What you saw there was yourself, as Meta!

Quiet, quiet!" the Meta yelled, interrupting the discussions with a burst of energy no one had expected.

Speechless and confused, I sat down again slowly at my place.

What just happened? Somehow all of this is going way too fast for me

Arun and Kayl looked at me. Kayl called out: "Super cool, you're out of the closet! But I do think you have probably put yourself in danger. It seems Amar's hypothesis was right."

Arun, who was looking into my eyes and beaming, just said: "Kay-Ky – that was really Xama Kay-Ky. You are something special. Don't be afraid; we're here for you. Everything will be alright."

The Meta supported himself on the pulpit and summarized his discoveries:

"Dr. Agor Sherman has violated our laws created to protect the Arverni. He has taken blood in an illegal manner and has knowingly endangered the life of Xama Dupre. The amount he removed forces me to demand the death sentence for Dr. Agor Sherman. I request a vote."

It was the first time the Meta had demanded a death sentence, and the bitter taste confirmed to me that he did not feel good about it, especially not since the Meta had known Agor Sherman for many years. It was also the first time the death sentence had been declared for a respected member of the community, a council member. But none of that mattered as much as that it was the first time a council member had been requested to vote on his own father's death sentence. The vote would not be over in seconds, as they usually were. Hands were only raised slowly and haltingly. When the Meta asked for the final time: "To vote yes, please raise your hands," five hands were up. One of them was Amar Wellberg's.

I looked at him, and believed I could taste his feelings as though they were my own.

Satisfaction, hate, sadness, and love.

The Meta remarked: "Five members vote yes. Please, everyone who is voting no, raise your hands."

Four hands went up, and the Meta didn't need to ask for abstentions. The votes of the three missing members weren't counted, which meant the results were close, but clear. 5:4 votes for the death penalty.

"The council hereby sentences Dr. Agor Sherman to death. The Achilleans are tasked with executing this sentence. Proof of Dr. Agor Sherman's death is to be presented before the council. The first point on our agenda is hereby concluded. All guests are requested to leave the room. I request, however, that Xama Dupre please remain as a guest for the next point on the agenda, and I request discipline and silence from all council members."

Everyone could feel that the Meta had more energy and was feeling better, and I knew why that was. But I asked myself why I should stay for the next item on the agenda. I had said everything I knew, and even what I didn't know and what was hidden in my subconscious. Arun left with the words:

"I love you; whatever happens, I'll be with you."

Kayl signaled me his support with thumbs up.

When Kayl and Arun left the room, I felt alone. Looking at Amar helped a little, since he was giving me two thumbs up now. But what I kept asking myself was what my role could be in this second part of the agenda. How could I help find the right Meta? Did it have something to do with my abilities? Did the Meta want to use them to find out the truth?

Why does he want to have me here?

An Unexpected Question

The Meta stood up and the room fell silent.

"Members of the council, as I already announced at the beginning of our meeting, I am going to relinquish my position. In accordance with the rules of the Arverni, this means that we must choose a new Meta. I have known many of you for years, and you all know that it has always been important to me to make the right decisions for our community. The right decision is important now, as well, since the new Meta will be charged with the task of leading the Arverni into the future. It is time for a renewal. We Arverni aren't exempt from the necessity to adjust to society. I'm not just speaking about the digital age, but about some of our laws, practices, and rules, which seem to no longer be appropriate in today's time. However, none of this will be my task. It will be the task of the next Meta. My last action, therefore, is to ensure that we find the right Meta in accordance with our rules and laws, and secure the future of the Arverni. You are all asking yourselves now why I have asked Xama Dupre to be here for this meeting. In a moment, I am going to read something to you from the ancient texts, and then we will all understand which role Xama Dupre has to play in this assembly."

The Meta pushed a book that always lay at the side of his pulpit into the middle of it. Each person present knew what this book contained. It was an ancient text, which held a comprehensive copy of all their laws, which had been handed down through the ages. Each person in the room was absolutely convinced, without a doubt, that the laws contained in it were valid Arverni regulations, and they would act in accordance with them.

The Meta opened the book to a spot marked with a piece of white paper. It seemed as if he had prepared himself for this moment. Slowly, and with a clear voice, he read aloud:

"It is the task of the Meta to search for a replacement in due time. If he determines that his time has come and that his powers are leaving him, it is time to convene the council and make a determination on succession. The following rules are to be followed during succession.

Each member present at the council meeting in which the decision is made can apply for the position of Meta.

Applicants for the position of Meta must be free of guilt. The Meta asks who feels called to the task, and would submit to a free vote.

Then, the council members vote. The applicant who receives the most votes will become the new Meta.

If there is a member present at the meeting who is an Identidem, this member will be asked first whether he wishes to accept the position of Meta. The reason for this exceptional rule is that it is the job of the council to find the best-qualified member. An Identidem is the ideal choice because of his abilities."

When the Meta read this paragraph aloud, the voices in the room became louder once again.

"Quiet!" the Meta screamed, and everyone was surprised he still had the strength to lift his voice. He continued to read aloud.

"The candidate selected has the following options:

First: he can accept the vote immediately, becoming the new Meta upon acceptance.

Second: he can accept the vote with conditions; this means that he defines parameters, which must be fulfilled before he accepts the position.

Third: he can turn down the calling of Meta.

In any case, the candidate will have 24 hours to decide on one of the options."

The Meta placed the piece of white paper into the book and closed it again.

Now, the noise level in the room became so loud no one could hear anything but the side discussions. The Meta, however, was able to gain a hearing by standing up and ringing a bell.

Everyone waited to hear his words, although they all already had some idea of what would happen next. "Since we, as we all know, have an Identidem among us, and since it is necessary for the community of the Arverni to make a new beginning, I ask Xama Dupre, in accordance with our laws:

Will you accept the position of Meta – and, if you will, please name the conditions of your acceptance within 24 hours."

The room was turned on its head. The conservative wing hurled rude insults into the room. People were talking about a fraud.

Kanaar himself blamed the Meta, saying he was already suffering the mental effects of the Finitum and his decisions were no longer applicable.

It took minutes for the room to quieten down again and for the Meta to regain the floor.

"This meeting is adjourned!" He looked at the clock. "We will meet at exactly 2:30 tomorrow to receive Xama Dupre's decision. I wish you all a pleasant evening."

What had just happened? I had understood everything, but I didn't know how to handle it.

Was I going to be the Meta?

Amar stormed right up to me and took my hand. He looked at me in a very serious way, and before saying anything, he pulled me through the hall and outside. We left the meeting in a hurry, even before any of the members could come up to me. Kayl and Arun were already waiting outside, eager to know what had happened in the meeting. They said it sounded from outside like a war had broken out.

Amar kept holding tight to my arm, ignoring Kayl and Arun's questions. All he said was:

"We have to get Xama to safety immediately; just follow me; I'll explain everything later."

"I thought we were safe here in the Aphobia?" Arun asked.

"After what's just happened here, we're not anymore" Amar called out, hurrying down the hallway.

"But what happened anyway, to put Xama's safety in the Aphobia in question?"

Amar didn't want to answer; he just walked quicker. I decided to answer myself:

"The Meta asked me whether I wanted to take over his position." Arun looked at me, and Kayl shook his head. "I don't understand," Arun said, and Kayl asked "what on earth?" Amar stopped, looked around him, and said to all three of us:

"Xama is going to be our new Meta! Now we just need to make sure nothing happens to her until she has accepted the position. That will be tomorrow at the same time – before then, there will be others who will try to take Xama out of the running in advance, to get a better position for their own candidates."

"Me no understand," Kayl said. What do you mean Xama's going to be our new Meta? How is that possible?"

"I'll explain everything once we're in safety."

Amar's telephone alerted him to an incoming text message. "We have a VIP suite on the top floor; access is secured by the hotel security force. There's just one elevator, as well, and it's in the lobby. Let's go directly to the suite before Kanaar alarms all his Achilleans and starts the hunt for Xama. I'll explain everything to you in the suite."

Kayl, glancing at the incoming message on his iPhone, confirmed Amar's assumption.

"It's happened already. Kanaar activated the highest alarm level, and commanded all the Achilleans to dial in to a phone conference to get instructions about how to avert the impending danger facing the Arverni community."

Arun's telephone gave off a signal as well.

"Now it's serious; I got the message too."

"If that means Kanaar wants to deactivate Xama to become Meta himself, then you're right, we're all in danger."

Kayl hadn't yet finished his sentence before someone yelled something at us down the hall.

"Give us the Identidem and everything will return to normal. If not, you will bear the consequences."

Arun was the first to recognize them. "David and Gabriel – two Achilleans from Kanaar's inner circle. You three go on to the suite; I'll take care of these two. We'll meet there later."

"No, Arun, please come with us" I begged him.

"We'll see each other soon, Xama, I promise." Arun ran back down the hall like a wild man towards the two Achilleans. Kayl called out to him.

"Now you can show off what I taught you. It's not going to end up well for those two." Kayl's statement scared me. What if Arun was injured, or even killed? Now, when we'd only just fallen in love.

"Let's walk quicker," Amar called out, turning right down the hallway towards the lobby. Kayl and I followed him, although all I could think about was Arun.

I hope nothing happens to him. All of this because of me and this Meta thing.

Amar was already running into the large hall towards the elevator, which allowed access to the suites. The security staff, which monitored the elevator 24 hours, weren't there anymore, and Amar assumed this wasn't a coincidence. He stopped for a moment.

"What's up?" I asked him in a muffled voice.

"There's something wrong. The elevator over there is always watched by two security officers. I don't see anyone there now, and it's not a coincidence."

"Should I check whether the air is clear?" Kayl asked, and Arun shook his head.

"We're changing the plan. I believe Kanaar already knows what we were planning. It seems he's gotten to Rave, my assistant. We'll check."

Amar picked up his telephone and called his assistant, who picked up immediately.

"Rave – I have to change my plan; we won't make it to the suite. Can you order me a limousine to wait in front of the upper entrance so we can get right in, drive to the Mirage Hotel, and go underground? I think we're not safe anymore in the Aphobia."

When Amar got confirmation from his assistant, he hung up and looked at the lobby tensely. The news spread like a virus through the Achilleans' phones via text message. Amar's idea seemed to be working. Multiple Achilleans hiding among the guests in the lobby now all went in the direction of the exit that was at the other end of the lobby.

"Now, Kayl, you can check the elevator; I assume there's something still waiting for us around the corner, and that it's still being watched."

Kayl nodded and set off.

I don't know why, but alone with Amar, without Arun and Kayl, I didn't feel safe anymore all of a sudden. My thoughts straying to Arun, I saw a figure running down the hallway in our direction, coming closer fast. I pushed Amar in the side with my elbow and pointed in its direction so he would recognize the situation. We were in a trap now, and could only hope that Kayl would be able to secure the elevator quickly. I could feel my heartbeat speeding up to match to the distance between us and the onrushing stranger. Looking back and forth between the elevator and Kayl, and the hallway, I wished for a sign from Kayl like I'd never wished for anything before. Suddenly, I realized that the stranger was waving at me. He was about as tall as Arun; please, let it be

Arun. When I looked closer, it was like a load lifted off of my shoulders – it was Arun. Arun was running towards us. I smiled at Amar, who'd also recognized him. I jumped towards Arun without any inhibition, allowing myself to fall into his arms. Arun held me tightly, picked me up a little, and turned me around in a circle. I kissed him, but noticed immediately that he was bleeding heavily from a wound on his eyebrow.

"Everything's okay; I took a hit, but the two of them weren't good for too much more. Today was the first time I got to use my ability to its full potential. I didn't hold back; I just grabbed David's arm and switched him off just like that. I used a new technique to shut off Gabe, and in the moment his fist was hitting my head, I started a controlled lightning bolt to shock his nervous system. Gabe collapsed, trembled, and was unconscious." I could tell this victory did Arun a lot of good, so I held him tighter and kissed him again, but this time with a clear intention. The kiss lasted for an eternity; neither of us noticed that Kayl was already giving us a sign and activating the elevator. Amar tapped me on the shoulder and interrupted our kiss. When I looked at Arun's laceration it was already almost healed; the kiss had had an effect. Amar pulled Arun and me towards the elevator, and all four of us disappeared into it just seconds later.

Amar activated the elevator with a key, and the last ten floors lit up. But unlike we had planned, Amar hit number 64, and the elevator set off.

"Why 64?" I asked Amar.

"No idea. Just chance, I guess."

In the elevator, I realized that in all the panic I had forgotten the sealed book and the rose of Akar on the table in the meeting hall.

"We have to go back; I forgot my book and the rose of Akar."

All of them looked at me for a moment as though I'd just said something totally unbelievable.

"Okay, we'll be back there tomorrow – tomorrow you can get them back."

When the door opened on the 64th floor, Kayl and Arun jumped out and secured the two hallways to the right and left. Arun thought for a moment, and said:

"To the right, keep going, all the way to the back."

As we ran faster, Arun kept securing the front and Kayl the rear.

Suddenly, a room door opened up 10 yards in front of two men and us came out. As I was still wondering whether they were hotel guests, Arun had already switched both of them off. They both lay unconscious on the floor. Arun looked into the room.

"I guess I was a little too quick; they were definitely just hotel guests."

Arun pulled one of the men into the room, and Kayl came by and helped him with the second one. They lay both of them on the bed and closed the room door. Amar, who had already run on, stopped in front of a door with the number 6439. He pulled a keycard out of his pocket and opened the door. Then he turned around and opened 6440 across the hall.

"Xama, you pick one. Kayl and I will take the other room."

Had I understood him correctly? Arun and I were going to share a room? Surprised, I looked at him and saw a wink.

"Yes, you heard right. Kayl and I will take one room, and you and Arun will take the other. But now everybody get into one room, and I'll explain what just happened."

The room wasn't especially large; it had two large beds and a desk, as well as a small seating area in the corner.

As everyone was trying to get comfortable, Amar started to talk.

"You all know how sick the Meta is. He has been concerned for quite some time now with creating a successful succession plan. He found the rule in the law book that an Identidem is the preferred candidate. When he met you at your apheid and looked inside you, he knew you were the chosen one. His decision was clear from that moment on. Xama Dupre will lead the Arverni into a new future. He prepared everything for this one goal. He proved to the council that you are an Identidem, in order to open up the question of whether you would accept the position of Meta."

"Kay-Ky, Kay-Ky," Arun said, and walked across the room nervously.

Amar asked:

"What?"

"Nothing, just expressing my surprise."

"Super, so Xama's going to be our new Meta. Then all I wonder is …" Kayl fell silent, and I finished his sentence.

"Whether she can really do it."

Everyone looked at me, and the room became totally silent.

Amar spoke first: "Whether a person can do something or not – you'll only know if you try! And you're not alone, anyway; there are four of us, and many other very loyal members who will help you. You have the right to the position, Xama. The position of Meta is a great one, with great responsibility over a whole community. I am certain, Xama, that you are the chosen one. The right one. You recently asked me how you would know what your Aphora was, and why it wasn't showing itself to you. Today, Xama, your Aphora became clear. It is your Aphora to lead the Arverni into a new future. The rejuvenation of the community – that's your Aphora."

My Aphora is to become the Meta. I never thought of it before. Is that why I haven't yet developed an Aphora?

"But you're all saying you'll help me, and I don't even know if I want to be Meta."

We all looked at Amar, expecting an answer.

"What you want does play a very important role. But what you cannot forget when making your decision is to evaluate what is best for the community, for we Arverni. There is much more at stake here than just your own self. You heard what the Meta said; it is time for a change. I say it is time for a renewal. I don't want to influence you; if you don't accept the position, Kanaar will become the new Meta. At least, there is a very high probability of it."

"Your name, Amar, has also been mentioned. There are members who are in your favor."

"Yes, but I won't have a chance against Kanaar; he'll win the vote, and he'll lead the community into the future – into a future without hope."

"Everything is going so Kay-Ky quickly – a few days ago I didn't even know what an Arverni was, and now I'm supposed to lead them into a new future? I am completely inexperienced and don't even know the rules – isn't that enough of a reason to say no?"

Arun took my hand. "From your point of view it is, absolutely. But it's also an enormous chance that we'll never have again. Look at it this way: with you, the Arverni have a chance at renewal. Isn't that wonderful? There's so much hope in it, Xama. You should think about that."

"What do you think?" I asked Kayl.

"Well, your doubts are good ones to think about, but you don't really need to worry. With us at your side, you'll be able to handle the job; we're your friends. We're here for you, and we'll help you no matter what happens. Amar is right – you, with our help, will do 1000 times better than Kanaar."

I went to Kayl, hugged him, and pressed a kiss on his cheek. "Thank you, Kayl, that was very sweet, and very well said."

We continued our discussion for a few hours, and Amar explained to us what a Meta's job entailed. More and more, I understood how the renewal of the community was connected to the change in Meats. The Meta is much more than the leader of the council; the Meta is the wellspring of the Arverni community – powerful – influential – wise. As my eyes started to droop with tiredness, Amar stood up, took Kayl by the arm, and wished Arun and me a good night. They both disappeared quietly and carefully into the room across the hallway. Arun was still talking, not noticing at all that I'd already fallen asleep in his arms, dreaming about the most important decision of my life.

MY DECISION

The sealed book from my father lay before me, with the rose of Akar beside it. I looked around – a glance right and a glance left ensured me I was in the meeting room – there was no one there. Was I too early? Where were Amar, Kayl, and Arun? Still lost in thought, I didn't even notice one of the entryway doors opening slowly and someone coming into the meeting room.

"Have you already made your decision, Xama?"

I was startled to hear the voice and turned my head in the direction I perceived it coming from. Shocked at what I saw and speechless from fear, I sat there as though lame, unable to answer let alone scream – scream for help. He came closer to me, slowly, and I could feel my fear consuming my self-confidence. Just a couple of steps away, Dr. Sherman continued to walk forward, grinning, until he was standing directly in front of me.

"You don't need to be afraid of me, Xama. There really is no reason to be. I did tell you I needed you. Didn't I promise I wouldn't kill you? My promise is still good. Especially now, when we two are so closely connected – we're practically one!"

He grinned, and I could feel myself slowly regaining control over my fear. I cleared my throat, wanting to test whether I could make a sound. I was relieved to hear myself.

What is he talking about? Where am I? What is happening?

"I'm not afraid."

"Ah, well, if I trust my new sense of taste, then your fear is waning a bit now – but it still tastes pretty damn intense. Save yourself the trouble of lying to me; I can taste it, just like you can. Since I invited you here to speak with you, I think it's sensible that we both be honest with one another. It tastes much better. What do you think?"

Surprised at Sherman's answer, I asked myself what had just happened.

This is all just a dream. I'm dreaming about him, and about this room. That's the only explanation I can think of – that has to be it.

"Let me make this easier for you, Xama. I invited you into my dream. This new ability truly is astounding; it's so simple to overcome long distances, and the best thing is that you can have a discussion in pleasant surroundings, completely undisturbed."

Sense of taste, dream communication – those are all my abilities. How is it possible ... the Arverni gene in my blood? Sherman took over my abilities through the gene. Shay-Ky - Shay-Ky - Shay-Ky.

"It was actually easy to invite you here. You were already dreaming of this room yourself. Did you know that this room means you and I have one more thing in common? Tomorrow, you'll have to make a decision here. Years ago, I made a decision here myself. I decided to leave this club of sinners and hypocrites. Since we are so very similar – much more than you realize – I am, of course, deeply concerned with advising you on your choice. Just think of me as a father figure."

As I heard Sherman's words, I noticed a burning taste in my mouth like bile; I was about to vomit.

"Besides the fact that you stole my blood, we don't have anything in common. I'm not going to keep dreaming this dream. Never visit me ..."

Sherman interrupted me, his voice changed. "The Arverni killed your mother and your father!"

His words struck me like pointed spears. They bored deep into my already gravely injured self.

"Before you make your decision, Xama, I would like to tell you my truth. You should know that the Arverni alone are responsible for you losing both your mother and your father. And as unbelievable as it sounds, there are even more secrets you should know before you decide."

The emotional pain became unbearable; Sherman was drilling more and more spears into me – I can't take it anymore. I have to end the dream – I have to get out of here – I have to save myself!

With a loud cry, consequence of a stabbing pain on the tip of my tongue, I opened my eyes wide. Arun, sleeping beside me, jumped and woke up as well.

"Xama, what happened? Were you dreaming? You scared me. Is everything alright?"

"Yes – I just had a nightmare and almost amputated my tongue in my sleep." Blood was collecting in my mouth, but even as I was swallowing it, the wound on the tip of my tongue had already started to heal.

Arun fell back asleep, after I had assured him everything was all right. I couldn't stop thinking. I asked myself what really happened to Mom and Dad. It took all night, but I finally made a decision for myself – a decision that would help me to find out the whole truth.

– End of Part 1 – The Mark of the Arverni –

AT THE END SOME IMPORTANT WORDS...

THIS IS MY FIRST NOVEL AND I HOPE YOU ENJOYED READING "THE MARK OF THE ARVERNI". IF SO PLEASE TAKE A MINUTE AND RATE THE BOOK @ YOUR PREFERRED BOOKSTORE AND TELL YOUR FRIENDS ABOUT IT.

YOU WILL FIND IT AT AMAZON AND SHORTLY IN ALL OTHER BOOKSTORES. EVERY FEEDBACK IS WELCOMED AND EVERY REVIEW HELPS ME TO FIND NEW MOTIVATIONS AND IMPROVE AS A WRITER.

YOU WANT TO KNOW HOW THE STORY OF XAMA, HER FRIENDS AND THE ARVERNI CONTINUES?

VISIT ME ON MY HOMEPAGE WWW.IGANMICH.ME AND CHECKOUT THE ARVERNI BLOG. IF YOU HAVE A WISH OR A GREAT IDEA, FEEL FREE TO POST YOUR IDEA.

ARE THE ARVERNI LISTED IN SOCIAL NETWORKS?
YES AND THEIR FANS ARE GROWING.

WWW.FACEBOOK.COM/MARKOFTHEARVERNI
WWW.YOUTUBE.COM/WATCH?V=Z1HWKZIV-20

THANK YOU FOR PURCHASING MY BOOK – I HAVE ONLY ONE WORD LEFT – WHICH EXPRESS MY FEELINGS.

– KAY-KY –

SEE YOU SOON.

www.ingramcontent.com/pod-product-compliance
Lightning Source LLC
Chambersburg PA
CBHW031424240626

47154CB00001B/188